WOLF SPRINGS CHRONICLES
HOT BLOODED

WOLF SPRINGS CHRONICLES

HOT BLOODED

Nancy Holder & Debbie Viguié

DOUBLEDAY

WOLF SPRINGS CHRONICLES: HOT BLOODED
A DOUBLEDAY BOOK 978 0 857 53072 1

Published in Great Britain by Doubleday,
an imprint of Random House Children's Publishers UK
A Random House Group Company

This edition published 2012

3 5 7 9 10 8 6 4 2

The Random House Group Limited supports the Forest Stewardship Council (FSC®),
the leading international forest certification organization. Our books carrying the FSC label
are printed on FSC®-certified paper. FSC is the only forest certification scheme endorsed
by the leading environmental organizations, including Greenpeace. Our paper
procurement policy can be found at www.randomhouse.co.uk/environment.

Set in Carré Noir by Falcon Oast Graphic Art Ltd.

RANDOM HOUSE CHILDREN'S PUBLISHERS UK
61–63 Uxbridge Road, London W5 5SA

www.randomhousechildrens.co.uk
www.totallyrandombooks.co.uk
www.randomhouse.co.uk

Addresses for companies within The Random House Group Limited can be found at:
www.randomhouse.co.uk/offices.htm

THE RANDOM HOUSE GROUP Limited Reg. No. 954009

A CIP catalogue record for this book is available from the British Library.

Printed and bound in the UK by Clays Ltd, St Ives plc

What do you run from?

"Meantime we shall express our darker purpose."
KING LEAR, 1.1.36

This book is for Charlotte Fullerton McDuffie, who has run with the wolves.

—Nancy

To my two grandfathers, Harold Trent and Ted Reynolds. I miss you both every day and see your quiet strength in the character of Mordecai.

—Debbie

The Werewolves of Wolf Springs
Our Laws

We are the descendants of Fenris, Wolf-God. He gave us this creed to keep our pack strong and free. Follow it, or die for the good of the pack.

Loyalty is the highest virtue.
Stay in your place until you have another.
Obey the Four Commandments:
> Never hunt humans.
> Never hunt alone.
> Never tell anyone about the existence of werewolves; it is a secret that must be kept.
> Always obey your alpha, and be submissive to higher-ranking wolves, male and female, within your pack.

And if you misbehave, beware . . . the Hellhound will hunt you down!

1

I *outran them.*

Katelyn McBride soared into the spotlight on the Mexican cloud swing. The swing was a thick rope of braided fibers connected by either end to the sky-high rigging of the circus tent. To the audience far, far below, the swing looked wispy as mist, but it was as strong as Katelyn herself. Nearly unbreakable. She was seventeen, and she was at the top of her game: a beautifully trained gymnast, limber, made of solid muscle. Her blonde hair was pulled back in a bun and her light blue eyes were edged with kohl.

I outfought them.

Music pulsed like a heartbeat as she sat on her swing and pumped her legs, rocking in and out of the spotlight—

— the moonlight —

— and she gazed down at the werewolves of Wolf Springs. They prowled in their magnificent wolf forms on the floor of the arena, which also seemed to be the forest, in a swelling river of tension. Their glowing eyes narrowed with intense purpose.

You thought you could hurt me, but you can't even touch me, she sneered as she executed a backward roll on the swing, then shifted her weight onto her hip bones as she came back around. This was the Cirque du Soleil, the world of greasepaint and gymnasts and death-defying feats of daring. Here she was in charge. Wolf Springs was nothing but a fraud, a lie designed to frighten little children. All you had to do was stop believing in ghosts and monsters and Hellhounds, and Wolf Springs lost its hold on you.

I'm free.

But another voice seemed to whisper, *Never free from me.*

Applause and cheers rose, buoying her up. In the audience were her mother and father, Giselle Chevalier the ballerina and Sean McBride the assistant district attorney, their arms around each other, loving her. Proud, happy. Alive. She swung back and forth, waving. They waved back.

Then a voice whispered urgently, *Run.*

A sharp, icy fear washed over her; everything shifted. The cloud swing picked up momentum on its own, propelling her back and forth like a pendulum. The frantic to-and-fro rhythm was out of control, like her heartbeat, and she collapsed from her balanced pose, grabbing the two sides just in time to stop her fall.

Run.

As she looked down into the audience, huge tongues of fire shot up between the seats. They rose so high they nearly singed Katelyn's eyelashes as she pulled herself upward, holding on for dear life. Spectators were screaming, igniting like kindling. Her cloud swing was gone. She was holding onto twin ropes of Spanish moss. Through the sudden haze of smoke, all she could see were the howling werewolves of Wolf Springs, racing around the trees, trying to find a way out.

"Jump, my darling!" Katelyn's mother screamed. Then her mother tumbled into the center of the wolf pack and the closest werewolves leaped on her. In seconds, she was buried underneath them.

"Mom!" Katelyn screamed.

Some of the werewolves fixed their glowing blue eyes on Katelyn, snapping their blood-drenched jaws. Their eager howls were like the shrieks of demons.

Then a figure streaked with blood and ash rose from the center of the pack. Fists balled over his head, Justin Fenner roared with fury. He stood broad-shouldered in a shredded white T-shirt and ripped black jeans that molded his body. Howling like a werewolf prince, he slashed at all-comers.

Wheeling out of his reach, the werewolves scattered into the smoke and began to catch fire. They screamed and tried to retreat from the inferno, racing back toward Justin. But as he lunged at them, they cowered and cringed, preferring to burn rather than to take him on.

Panting, he looked straight up at Katelyn with his deep blue eyes. He held out his arms to catch her.

Capture her.

"Kat. You are my secret weapon," he whispered, yet she could hear his voice above all the chaos. "Jump. I'll keep you close."

"No!" she shouted, flailing in the rigging. "Don't touch me!"

Then she was falling.

Falling.

Falling.

Frantic, she clawed at the smoke-choked air. She landed hard in Justin's embrace, against his chest. She struggled to get out of his arms but he enclosed her, enfolded her. "I'll keep you forever," he said, gouging his nails into her arms. The pain was an icy shock.

And Katelyn McBride woke up in her bed.

⊷ ⊱⊰ ⊶

Moonlight poured down from her skylight and illumin-ated the bust of her mother that Trick had made for her as a birthday present, presenting it to her earlier that day after Justin had dropped her home. Katelyn stared at her mother's features, frozen forever and yet so lifelike. If her mom had really been there, what would she say to any of it?

What would I say to her?

Mom, I've become a werewolf wouldn't have been at the top of her list.

Then again, if her mother were still alive, Katelyn would still be with her out in California, pursuing her dreams of becoming a performer, a Cirque star, instead of being trapped in a remote cabin in the Ozarks with a grandfather she barely knew. She'd never have been attacked by a werewolf, being transformed into one herself. She would never have seen Cordelia Fenner, her new best friend, driven from her home by her father Lee Fenner, the leader of the werewolf pack — its *alpha* — for failing to tell him that she was worried Katelyn might have been bitten.

As she stood up and touched the bust of her mother, warm skin against cold stone, she also conceded that if she had still been in California, she never would have met Trick. Wonderful, crazy, frustrating, secretive Trick — Vladimir Sokolov, to give him his full name — who cared enough about her to shape this tribute, and had talked her grandfather into buying her a computer and a microcell for her birthday so she could use her cell phone in his cabin situated miles and miles outside the town of Wolf Springs.

When Justin — Cordelia's cousin — had dropped her home, the place had been full of chaos. There had been a break-in while she had been with the wolf pack, and the thieves had stolen her grandmother's silver and some paintings off the wall in the stairwell. Sergeant Lewis, one of Wolf Springs' two police officers, had been taking her grandfather's statement.

Trick had been there, too, planning to give her the bust, and after Sergeant Lewis left, her grandfather had surprised Katelyn with the computer. What she wouldn't have given to have had it when she first arrived in Wolf Springs weeks before.

As she stretched out her tense body, she remembered her nightmare. Before the werewolves had invaded it had been a happy dream, with her performing in Cirque du Soleil just as she had always hoped. *I'm not that girl*, she thought. But she was. She still was. She whirled in a circle, slowly, feeling the joy in movement that had been the constant in her life. Back home, dance and gymnastics had both filled nearly all her waking hours — and kept the nightmares at bay. Sean McBride, her father, had been shot down over four years ago in cold blood. Her mother was dead, killed in the fire that had destroyed their home, and she, Katelyn, had been forced to come to Wolf Springs to live with her grandfather, Mordecai McBride, whom she barely knew.

And then . . . the bite. A monstrous gray wolf with blue eyes, a rogue werewolf no one seemed to know.

All those things had happened to change her. But what they had not changed was what it felt like to be graceful and strong. Stretching, bending in ways that had taken years of practice and sacrifice, she held on tightly to the feeling. She was reclaiming something — what it was that made her Katelyn McBride. The core of her identity.

Now, as she moved in the room in the cabin, she felt life surging through her muscles. She slid slowly and effortlessly to the floor in the splits and arched her back until the crown of her head nearly touched the floor — something she had never been able to do before.

My human body is different, she thought, amazed. *Because of the change.*

She caught her lower lip. She saw herself auditioning for Cirque, imagined people gasping at the incredible things she could do. Her mind began to race with the fantasy. Werewolves only had to change on the full moon. She could still live a normal life. She could get out of Wolf Springs. Be what she was destined to be.

If it was the last thing she did, she would leave Wolf Springs. She would make her dream come true. She couldn't let what had happened to her, any of it, stop her.

"I swear it, Mom," she said, gazing at the bust of her mother. "I'll live enough for both of us."

Hot and thirsty, she headed downstairs for some water. She crept past the animal heads mounted on the wall and past the empty spaces where the stolen pictures had hung.

Outside in the darkness, the drums of the Inner Wolf Center were echoing off the mountains. A man named Jack Bronson had bought the old hot springs resort Wolf Springs had been named after, and now business executives paid small fortunes to learn how to let out their inner predators. Seen as a nuisance by a lot of the townsfolk, they mostly kept to themselves at the center. It was a good thing, too. Her one encounter with a couple of those executives in town had been less than pleasant. They'd gotten in touch with their inner *jerks* a little too much.

As she stepped into the kitchen, she thought she caught movement out of the corner of her eye. She turned her head swiftly, but there was nothing there.

Just my imagination, she thought, crossing toward the sink. Then she turned and jumped. Justin was standing outside the window, staring in at her. His thumbs were slung in the belt loops of his jeans, his head cocked beneath the moonlight. A jacket that he didn't need stretched across his shoulders and she remembered the dream, how he had caught her, trapped her. But now, looking out the window, she remembered riding on his motorcycle, and kissing him in the forest before she knew he had a girlfriend . . . or that he was a werewolf. He had been her first real kiss, and even now, despite everything — despite Trick — she still felt drawn to him.

He gave her a slow nod and she caught her breath, wanting, and not wanting, to go to him. They were two of a kind now, in so many ways.

She went to the back door, opened it, and stepped onto the porch, where he was already waiting. The drums matched the unsteady flutter of her heartbeat. She had to tip her head back to see into his penetrating blue eyes, but she defiantly met his gaze. He looked displeased, and she remembered that in the werewolf world she was the lowest of the low, practically an outcast. He was very high-ranking, definitely her superior, and she should show respect by lowering her gaze. She didn't back down, but she was afraid not only of him, but also of what she had done with him. Last full moon, the time of her first-ever change, they had hunted together. Taken down a deer — even though she was a committed vegetarian. And she hadn't remembered any of it.

He glanced upward, as if checking on her grandfather's window; then he blew air out of his cheeks and jerked his head to the side of the cabin. She had left a pair of sneakers by the door. She stepped into them and followed him, her footfalls crunching on frosty earth.

Shoulder to shoulder, they crossed the driveway. She didn't see a truck or his motorcycle anywhere, and she wondered how he'd gotten there. And when. Once in the woods, he turned to her.

"I didn't tell," she said in a rush. "I didn't say a word."

Without replying, he took her arm and pushed up the sleeve of her sweatshirt, examining the place where she had fallen into a silver animal trap that morning. When she'd been injured, Justin had carried her to his truck, intent on getting help, even though he had expected her to be dead by the time he'd reached it. Silver was incredibly poisonous to werewolves: even a small prick from a silver knife could make them horribly sick. More catastrophic damage could definitely kill them.

"How come you're still alive?" he whispered, though loudly enough for her to hear over the drumbeats.

She knew without looking that there wasn't even a mark on her skin. Werewolves healed amazingly fast. That was one thing to be grateful for.

"Maybe the trap wasn't made out of silver," she said. "Maybe you just thought it was."

"Oh, it was. Believe me. I smelled it. Felt it." He dropped her arm and studied her face. "If you were bit by one of us, how can you be immune? *We're* not immune."

"My point exactly," she shot back. "Maybe something *else* bit me."

"Oh, we're not back to that," he scoffed. "Darlin', the Hellhound is a myth."

Her temper flared unexpectedly. "Why? Why is it a myth and you're not?"

Katelyn had never believed in werewolves until coming to Wolf Springs. Who was to say the Hellhound wasn't real, too? Cordelia had told her that it was the werewolf equivalent of the Bogey Man, a story they told to keep each other in line, especially the youngsters. *Be good or the Hellhound will get you.* But even most of the adults seemed to believe that it could come for them if they broke any of the werewolf laws — like letting humans know their secret. Cordelia had believed the monster was real. And she'd broken the laws . . . She'd even thought she'd seen the Hellhound outside her house, but her father and the rest of the family had just laughed at her.

Justin shook his head and grinned. And angry as she was, Katelyn couldn't stop herself remembering what it had felt like to kiss those lips. And even though she cared deeply for Trick, she couldn't help the feelings that stirred inside her when Justin Fenner stood too close. Somehow it seemed different, even more intense, now that she was a werewolf, too.

"Getting riled up, aren't you?" he asked, smiling at her. "Biting back?"

The drumming stopped abruptly. She and Justin stood in the relative silence, though the wind made the pine branches scrape, and an owl hooted. There was a rush of wings. She was certain he could hear her heartbeat as it roared in her ears.

Justin leaned back against a trunk and crossed his arms over his chest. The moonlight slashed his face, giving it a sinister cast. "Damn it, this is such a mess," he said quietly.

"Hey, I didn't ask to be attacked, okay?" she flung at him defensively. "I didn't want this to happen to me!"

"Well, see, as I figure it, that's the only upside." He broke off a branch, then cracked it into two, running the ends along his palm. "That it did happen to you."

"Not seeing that," she snapped, moving farther away from him, although her mind flashed back to the big amazing life she was planning to escape to. "Not at all."

He dropped the pieces of wood onto the ground. "Being stronger and faster than any human ever dreamed? You will. You'd better. There's no going back, Kat."

"No one else is immune to silver, or so you've said," she reminded him. "So maybe it's different for me there, too. Maybe I can . . . go back."

"Keep your voice down." His own voice dropped an octave.

She looked quickly around. "Who else is here?" she demanded.

"The alpha's nervous about you," Justin said, ignoring her question. "Our kind are born werewolves. We hardly ever bring in humans changed with a bite. Uncle Lee said the last time someone was bit in without permission was in 'the homeland.' That's Scandinavia. The fjords. In the seventeenth century."

Four hundred years ago? That lent weight to Cordelia's refusal to believe that a Fenner werewolf had bitten Katelyn.

"Was he there when that happened?" she asked.

A fleeting smile appeared on his face, but just as quickly disappeared. "Oh, man. You don't know *anything*."

"Then enlighten me," she retorted.

He raised a brow. "Don't you have the sense to know you shouldn't speak to me like that? With such disrespect? You know how high-ranking I am. Do you do it because you're scared?"

She said nothing, just tried to look as if she wasn't afraid. She didn't want to appear fragile or needy in front of him. Werewolves despised weakness.

"You need to learn so much." Even in the darkness, she could feel him studying her, assessing her. "*So* much."

She remained silent, and he did, too.

"We're not immortal, Katelyn. Of course Lee — our alpha — wasn't around four hundred years ago," he said finally. "We heal up quick, as you've already noticed, but we do have a normal human lifespan. We make the most of the time we have, though. In ways you can't begin to imagine." He pushed away from the tree trunk and ambled toward her. "Kat."

Her name on his tongue was like a caress. Silky, sexy. She could feel herself reacting, and she glided out of reach.

"I'm not here to hurt you," Justin said, and she thought there was just the slightest emphasis on the first word in the sentence.

She scanned their surroundings: the woods, the road, the front of the cabin. Was that someone creeping through the shadows beneath the overhang of the second story? A person, or a wolf?

"Who else is out here?" she asked again.

"You need to get used to being watched," he said, still evading her questions. "You need to remember that Lee's got to look out for the safety of the entire pack."

"Then he needs to remember that someone did this to me. Without my permission, or his."

"Listen to me," Justin said, leaning forward. "You know about his dementia, that he's losing touch with reality. He knows it, too, and he's running scared. He can't be seen as losing control. He'll be challenged. He was going to pick Cordelia to succeed him but that's out the window now."

Katelyn couldn't believe Cordelia would have become the new alpha. Cordelia was just seventeen. Cordelia's two older sisters had bullied Cordelia mercilessly, and she spent half her time apologizing for things that weren't even her fault. How could Lee Fenner have ever thought she would be able to lead the pack?

"I thought it was odd, too," Justin said.

She knit her brows. "I didn't say that."

"You didn't need to. I read it. You'll get better at reading body language, same as us."

Us. She would have to be doubly, triply careful around him then. Just like with Trick. Justin could read her; Trick somehow just knew her.

"What happened to you happened on his watch," he continued. "Something so counter to our moral code it's never happened here in Wolf Springs, ever. You're proof that he's not in complete command of his pack. A source of shame. It might be easiest for him just to get rid of you."

Threatened, she reared back, and he lunged forward and caught her by the shoulder. His head lowered toward hers and she knew he was going to kiss her.

"I'm standing between that decision and your life," he said huskily. "You need me, Kat."

And you need me, she thought, fighting not to let him kiss her, ever. *I'm the only one immune to silver, and you're the only one who knows it.* He was planning something, and he needed her to pull it off.

His lips were brushing hers when she turned her head.

"Lucy," she said. "Your girlfriend, remember?"

He grunted. "I'm sorry, Kat," he muttered, and he let her go.

Katelyn took a sharp breath. Just being around Justin was like being hypnotized. It had to be something chemical, because they were both werewolves. It couldn't be that she was that weak.

"Hormones," he muttered.

"What?"

He huffed. "Look, I know you have to be going crazy right now. All the chemicals in your body have been shaken up, changed. The wolf side of you is fighting the human side and it's like being a little kid again. Everything will feel more extreme for you and when you're not with someone to remind you how to act, you're going to have to remember that your life is riding on your behavior. It's going to take a while to learn to handle it. Right now, the wolf in you is responding to the wolf in me but you don't even have the impulse control of a two-year-old human."

"Feeling like a two-year-old is not my current problem," she snapped. Her problem was that she wanted to kiss him like there was no tomorrow.

"When your body learns to adapt to everything that's happening to it, you'll feel fully in control again." He paused. "Until then . . . be damn careful around me or any other young wolf in the pack."

"Like being alone out here with you is being damn careful," she groused.

"Yeah, well, if we are truly alone."

He was trying to joke, she could tell, but it just fed into her paranoia, her feeling of being watched.

"*So* not funny."

He sighed. "Look. It's not a question of whether you're a human or an animal. You're both. And you're going to have to learn to live with that twenty-four/seven. There will be times when the animal part of you'll want to act on something and it will be wrong. Same with the other way. So deal with the human issues with human responses and the animal issues with animal responses."

"And what if the issue is both human *and* animal?"

His grin was evil. "Like making out?"

She nodded, completely humiliated to be discussing it with him like this. But she thought about Halloween when she'd gone from kissing Trick to kissing Justin while barely missing a beat, then hating herself for it.

"Then tread very, very carefully. You bite a human, draw even just a little blood accidentally, and they'll change."

Thinking of Trick, she swallowed hard. "*Maybe* they'll change. We don't know. Because I'm different."

"You willing to take that chance?"

He reached out to push a strand of hair back from her face and even though she wanted to step closer to him she forced herself to take a step back.

"What'd you do with the animal trap I got caught in?" she asked, wanting desperately to change the topic.

"Hid it," he said uneasily, as if he didn't want to discuss it. "You tell no one, hear?"

"Someone already knows," she insisted. "Knows enough to put out a trap."

"That thing was old. It didn't even spring. It would have taken your arm off when you fell into it if it had been working."

"But it doesn't matter *when* it was put out," she said, sensing she should shut up but not being able to. "It matters *that* it was put out."

"Kat, I'm not an idiot." When she opened her mouth to speak again, he said, "You should go back before your grandfather misses you." Then he added, "Lee wants you to come over tomorrow."

Cold chills washed down her back. She never wanted to see Lee Fenner — or any of them — again. She knew that was too much to wish for, but she had hoped for some kind of reprieve before it all started — learning to fit in, groveling like a kicked dog before that madman —

"I have homework," she said rebelliously.

He smiled grimly. "You're going to have to do better than

that if you want to stay alive. Make up some excuse to your grandfather. Say you have a project with Cordelia for school."

It had only been a matter of hours, but it was still hard to believe that Cordelia was gone. Nobody outside the pack knew yet, but sooner or later someone would surely have to say something, especially when she didn't show up for school. Wolf Springs was a small place. Once word got out it would spread like wildfire and as soon as her grandfather heard, Katelyn would no longer be able to use Cordelia as an excuse for going to the Fenner house. She felt a rush of hope. Maybe Justin figured Cordelia's banishment was only temporary.

"You should head on over around ten in the morning or so," he said. "We have a big Sunday dinner around noon."

She wondered if they chose to eat different foods when they were alone — but she didn't want to give him any more reminders that she didn't know anything about the way werewolves lived. Instead, she gave Justin a curt nod and brushed past him. After taking a few steps, she turned and watched him melt into the darkness. Then she could feel eyes upon her. Werewolf spies?

She felt a rush of wind and an invisible hand plucked at her sweatshirt. Something exploded against the tree just behind her and she jumped and let out a yelp. She clamped her hand over her mouth, ran toward the back of the cabin and then darted inside as quickly as she could.

She leaned against the kitchen door for a moment, then crossed resolutely to the window, meaning to shut the faded gingham curtains.

Then she glanced down. There was a hole in the side of

her baggy sweatshirt. She picked it up and felt the warmth radiating from the area. A perfect little circle. She stuck her finger in and then realized there was a hole in the back of the sweatshirt as well. Something had gone clean through.

She clutched her sweatshirt.

Someone shot at me.

She began to shake.

Someone just tried to kill me.

2

Katelyn pushed away from the door. She hadn't heard a shot. What did that mean — some kind of silencer? Maybe it wasn't a bullet hole after all.

She knew who would know. Her grandfather — Dr. Mordecai McBride. Katelyn had called him Ed when she had first arrived, after her childhood nickname for him of "Extra Daddy." When she didn't call him "Grandpa", of course — the name she knew he loved her to use.

But she stopped herself with a hand on the banister. She couldn't tell him anything. Mr. Fenner had told her he would kill her — *and* her grandfather — if she said a word about her new life.

Maybe the shot was just meant to scare her, remind her that she was being watched and the stakes were the highest if she made a mistake.

Had Justin known someone had been waiting out there in the darkness?

Her knees wobbled and she plopped down in the chair in front of the computer station she, Trick, and her grandfather had set up a few hours earlier. She could feel her heart pounding and she struggled to calm herself down. They'd only shot once. A warning, surely.

Listening to each creak and groan of the trees outside, she sat in the darkness, stiff and fearful.

Katelyn.
Katelyn.
You can't hide.
I know who you are.
I shall do thee mischief in the woods.
Soon.
Click.
Click.
Click.
Claws on the hardwood floor.
Click.
Katelyn.

She jerked awake, lifting her neck painfully. She had

fallen asleep at the computer. Had someone called her name?

She guessed it was early morning from the way the light was streaming in the windows. Stretching her neck left and right, she pushed back, and for an instant she thought she detected something else in the room, a clicking like toenails on the hardwood floor. She froze, listening. But she couldn't hear anything.

"Ed? Grandpa?" she called softly. "Is that you? Are you up?"

No answer. But the sense that she was not alone grew stronger.

Her hair stood on end as she rose and took a deep breath to steady herself. She looked at the rifle on the wall and walked over to it. Put her hand on it and listened.

When she'd first arrived in Wolf Springs, she would have flown upstairs to her room and hidden under the covers if she'd felt freaky-scared like she did right then. But now she had people to protect — her grandfather and Trick. And maybe, just maybe, Cordelia was in the house, seeking shelter.

The werewolves of the Fenner pack had been ordered not to help Cordelia in any way, on pain of death. Katelyn had been there when Lee Fenner had issued the command, and he had singled Katelyn out. In front of everyone, he had forced Katelyn to swear to be loyal to him as the alpha and to obey him no matter what. She knew she had to prove herself to Mr. Fenner, and to the pack, to survive.

It was crazy, especially since the reason Cordelia had been banished was because she had been protecting Katelyn. Cordelia had known there'd been a chance Katelyn was going to turn into a werewolf, but she had wanted to know for sure before going to her father with the shocking news. Swearing not to help Cordelia when Cordelia had sacrificed everything in helping her was just wrong.

But he had *forced* her to swear. Technically, though, she wasn't a Fenner werewolf. Mr. Fenner hadn't given permission for her to be changed, and there was no proof that a Fenner werewolf had done it. Ergo, she owed him no loyalty.

And he's not here. At least, that was what she told herself as she took the rifle down and made her way into the kitchen. And if Cordelia had come to her, Katelyn would do all she could for her. Cordelia was the one Katelyn was loyal to.

The back door flew open and she jumped back. Her grandfather stared at her, clearly startled as he stepped into the house. She sagged against the counter. "You startled me," she said.

"Seems like," he answered, eyebrows raised. He looked at the rifle.

"What — what were you doing outside?" she asked, then winced as she realized how paranoid and suspicious that sounded. And after all, Wolf Springs was a place of possible danger. Two girls had died this year, one of them killed in the forest just before her arrival and the other soon after. No one knew what had killed them, but it had people plenty shaken up.

Mordecai lifted one hand and she noticed that he was carrying a log. "Fire needed it," he said with a grunt. "Log's already dead," he added.

Katelyn felt like an idiot. He took the rifle and walked out of the room. She busied herself making coffee to hide how jittery she was feeling. She was exhausted and was beginning to think about having to go over to the Fenners. She didn't know how she'd stay awake to drive out, let alone make it back.

Which could be moot if they want to kill me.

The phone rang, and she grabbed at it.

"Don't come here today," Justin said. "Stay away."

Her grandfather walked back in the room and headed to the sink to wash his hands.

"Um, but, what about our project?" she said into the phone.

Justin hung up. She replaced the handset and stared at it for a moment. She was getting what she wanted, but why? Had Mr. Fenner decided to get rid of her? She wished she'd been able to tell Justin about the night before and being shot at. If she'd had his number she could have texted him.

"She still mad at you?" Mordecai asked as he dried his hands.

Katelyn jerked, startled. "What?"

"Trick told me you and Cordelia had a fight."

"When did you talk to him?" she asked, her voice shrill, and she knew she had to calm down. "Yeah, it's . . . bad," she amended.

"She seems like a handful. Hard to be friends with."

"Her whole family's kind of weird." She winced. She probably shouldn't have said that. And she felt a prick of disloyalty for it. She poured a cup of coffee for each of them, adding the cream and sugar.

He took a sip of his coffee and nodded. "I figured we'd go

into town in a bit. We'll check to see if your new tire is in, and you can go to that store you like and get something for the Cirque show."

Relief flooded her. She would much rather be in town with him than waiting here at the cabin wondering who was spying on her, and whether whoever had shot at her was going to try again.

After breakfast Katelyn hurried upstairs to shower and get dressed. When she came back down she was at least feeling a little better, a little more awake.

"I'm ready," she said as she hit the bottom of the stairs.

He was holding the sweatshirt she'd been wearing the night before. She felt shaky. How could she have been so stupid to leave it out?

"Oh, sorry for being a slob," she said, practically grabbing it out of his hand. She took it, ran back upstairs and tossed it on her bed. She had to get a grip. If she acted like nothing was wrong, he would assume that nothing was wrong.

Heading back downstairs, she forced a smile onto her face. "Let's go," she said.

They drove toward town in silence. Fortunately, she was getting used to silence around her grandfather. Today, especially, it was a blessing; she had too much going on in her head to chat.

They went through the dark tree tunnel; then, on the crest of a hill, she saw that the town of Wolf Springs had replaced the Halloween decorations with baskets of holly and ivy hanging from the lampposts. Many of the doors of the

Victorian buildings sported cheery winter wreaths. Thanksgiving was almost here; and after that came the Christmas vacation. A sign had gone up in a vacant lot announcing that Christmas trees would go on sale that weekend. To Katelyn there was an air of rebelliousness to all the festive cheeriness, as if Wolf Springs was fighting back against whomever — or whatever — had mauled those two girls to death.

"If we bought a Christmas tree in L.A. this weekend, it would be a brittle mess by December," she said.

Her grandfather surprised her with a laugh. "I know. Used to be day after Thanksgiving that we got a tree. But once the snow hits everyone becomes more isolated, so we get started a lot earlier around here. Better to have some festivity while everyone can enjoy it."

Isolated. A few days before, she wouldn't have believed it would be possible to be more isolated than she was. But with the loss of Cordelia, and the fact that she had to protect her grandfather and Trick from her secret, she felt more isolated than ever. If they were snowed in on a full moon night . . . she looked out the window and clenched the arm rest.

"What happens when the snow hits? I mean, with school and everything?" she asked.

He shrugged. "On the bad days? No school. Rest of the time, snow plows keep the roads cleared. Of course, it's easier for the folks who live in town. Everybody just takes it one day at a time."

One day at a time. She couldn't think like that. She had to make plans, contingencies. She would have to talk to

Justin about it. Surely he and the others knew what to do.

But why would they? In their world, the pack was made up of families. They didn't have werewolves living with non-werewolves. It was one more thing that made her different, one more way in which she was a liability.

One more reason for them to kill her.

The storefront blurred past, and then they pulled up outside Babette's. The store's windows still held memorial signs for Haley and Becky — the two girls who had died. Would there soon be a missing person poster going up with Cordelia's face on it?

"I've got some errands to do, and I figure you don't need me hanging around pressuring you to buy something with a longer skirt or a higher neckline," he said with a half-grin. "So, why don't we divide and conquer?"

"Okay. Meet at Cowffeine after we're done?" she asked.

"Sounds okay."

She slid out of the car and then stood on the sidewalk as he pulled away, before turning and walking inside the shop. Her grandfather was in control of her money, meager as it was, until she turned eighteen, and she had only a few dollars to spend.

Babette's was a funky consignment clothing store with fashions and disasters from several decades crammed in together. Cordelia had told her it was the place to go shopping and had taken her there a couple of times.

Babette, an attractive middle-aged woman, looked up from a crossword and then hopped off her stool and came around to Katelyn.

"Kat! How are you?"

"Good," Katelyn said, tamping down her rush of anxiety. It hurt to come into the store without Cordelia. And not to be able to tell a single soul that Cordelia's own family had driven her out.

"What can I help you with?"

"I'm just looking for a dress for a night at the theater."

Babette's eyebrows shot up. "A play, around here? I haven't heard of anything."

Katelyn shook her head as she surveyed the racks, mostly to cover her discomfort. "No, actually, it's in Little Rock. My grandpa is taking me to see the Cirque du Soleil. The tickets were a birthday present."

"Well, a belated happy birthday, dear!" She beamed at Katelyn. "I'm sure we can find you something special."

Katelyn tried to politely wave her off. "I can look on my own."

"Nonsense. Birthday girls get the royal treatment."

They moved among the racks and Katelyn felt awkward as Babette kept up a steady stream of chatter, pulling first one, then another dress out for her inspection.

"I'm surprised Cordelia isn't with you today," Babette said.

Katelyn inspected the price tag on a blouse she had no interest in buying. "She's . . . not feeling well." She didn't know what else to say. She wondered just how the Fenners planned on explaining her absence to people.

Babette pulled a sad face. "Oh, that's too bad."

"I think I'll try on this one," Katelyn said, reaching for a little black dress.

"Oh, I bet that will look just lovely on you, dear."

Katelyn headed back toward the front of the store and stepped into one of the two dressing rooms. She slipped off her jeans and sweater and piled them on the minuscule bench, then took the dress off the hanger. Just then, the bell over the front door chimed and she could hear footsteps.

"Hello, Babette," an older woman called.

"Well, hello, you two. Do you need any help?"

"Here it is, Mama," a younger woman said. "This is it."

"I think we're set, Babette," the older woman said.

Katelyn pulled on the dress and tried to look at herself in the mirror in the cramped dressing room. It seemed so strange that she had last been there with Cordelia and it felt weird to be picking out a dress when so much was going wrong. She nearly laughed at the thought — she had said nearly the same thing to her friend when they were trying to pick out Halloween costumes. Cordelia had insisted, though, that the show had to go on.

The door to the other dressing room opened. There was a lot of rustling, and then it closed again.

"What's wrong with Steve?" the older woman whispered. "He's a catch."

"*Catch?* Mama, please, are you serious?" the younger woman whispered back. "Besides, his daddy will make sure he marries up, you know?"

Katelyn paused. The only Steve she knew in town was Steve Berglund, a werewolf who had been one of Cordelia's suitors. They couldn't be talking about him, could they?

The older woman made a snorting sound. "Well, Dan's big plans for that died when . . . *she* . . . did."

Katelyn's heart stuttered. It *was* werewolf Steve they were talking about. Steve Berglund's father was named Dan, and he had wanted Steve to marry Cordelia. They were talking about Cordelia as if she were dead. But she wasn't, only banished. Unless they knew something she didn't. She moved closer to the wall, listening intently.

"Do you think Mr. Fenner will change his mind?" the younger woman murmured.

"I know you liked her, sissy, but I don't think that's going to happen. She's gone." Her voice rose a little. "And I'm certain Mr. Fenner knows what is best for his family."

Tears welled and Katelyn shut her eyes tightly, relieved that Cordelia wasn't really dead — not that they knew — and miserable because she lived in a world now where things like that were a real possibility.

"I'm still not going after Steve," the younger woman said.

"Then why are we here?" her mother replied with asperity.

There was a sudden knocking on Katelyn's door that sounded as loud as gunfire. She jerked, but managed to keep silent.

"Kat, honey, how'd that fit?" Babette asked.

"Umm, fine," she said, freaking out. The mother and daughter in the other dressing room would have to know that she'd overheard them.

"Well, come on out here and let us see," Babette insisted.

Katelyn opened the door and stepped out, smoothing down the dress. It was black, simple and elegant with white straps, a sweetheart neckline and a full skirt that swirled just above her knees. She knew it showed off her legs well. She executed a little turn, then smiled at Babette — a smile that faltered when the other dressing-room door opened.

"Perfect," Babette said, cocking her head, appraising her. "What do you ladies think?"

"Lovely," the older woman said, a chill in her voice. Katelyn recognized her at once: her name was Myrna, and she was a werewolf.

"Looks like everyone needs something special," Myrna's daughter said. Katelyn had forgotten her name, but they'd been forced to kiss each other's cheeks when Katelyn had been introduced to the pack — the standard method of greeting from werewolf to werewolf within the pack. She was pretty with tapered, curly hair that framed a cherubic face, big brown eyes, and cupid-bow lips.

"This didn't work," the girl added, fingering the fabric of the dress she wore.

"We'll find you the perfect dress, Hannah," Babette said.

Hannah. The name suited her. Hannah glanced sideways and gave Katelyn a hesitant smile and Katelyn smiled back.

"Ladies, you've all met, right?" Babette said cheerfully.

Katelyn nodded slightly.

"How are you, Kat?" Myrna asked.

"Good," she lied. "You?"

"Just fine."

And this couldn't be more awkward if we tried.

"You know, I think I'll take this," Katelyn said to Babette. "Let me just go get changed."

She hurried back into the dressing room and quickly put her other clothes back on, then forced herself to walk back out. She saw with relief that Myrna and Hannah were at the very back of the store so she hurried over to the cash register and presented Babette with the dress.

"You looked so pretty in this," the older woman gushed.

"Thanks."

Babette put the dress in a bag. "Tell Cordelia I said hello and not to forget about those winter formals I'll have coming in."

"I will," Katelyn said faintly.

She hurried out onto the sidewalk and lost her composure for just a second. She guessed it was to be expected. Sooner or later she had to run into other members of the pack in town by accident. She'd just hoped the day would come much, much later.

She walked toward the coffee shop, grateful for cold, crisp air that made her blood sing — a brief moment of pleasure. Before Wolf Springs, she'd lived her whole life in southern California where it rarely got this cold, but she liked it.

She walked inside Cowffeine, the cute little coffee shop that sported a cartoon cow wearing an enormous cow bell on its sign. She ordered herself a hot chocolate and sat down at a table near the windows on the far side of the café with her back to the door, not eager to encounter anyone else she might know while she waited for her grandfather to finish his errands. She made a mental note to ask Justin how she was supposed to handle accidental meet-ups with other pack members. Should she treat them like friends, strangers, or acquaintances?

"This is so screwed up," she whispered to herself.

People were talking around her, but Katelyn tried to focus on her hot chocolate, how it smelled, how it tasted. Then she heard footsteps behind her. They came to a stop.

"Hey, sexy. Whassup?"

She froze. *No way. Not now.* Then she pivoted and looked into the face of Mike Wright, resident asshat of Wolf Springs High, and his smarmy smile vanished.

"Oh, it's you," he managed, clearly shocked.

"Uh, yeah, who did you think it was?" she asked, her anger rising. He was a bully and a jerk who had dissed Cordelia at every chance, and he was always baiting Trick. She knew the two boys had been in a couple of actual fights and she was sure he was the one who'd slashed Trick's tires on her first day at Wolf Springs High.

He flushed. "Someone a lot hotter than you," he said, before turning and stalking toward the front of the café.

She forced herself to take a deep breath. Of all the people to accidentally hit on her. She felt her lips curl in disgust.

Shoot me instead. She was only half joking.

Suddenly there was a commotion outside and she turned around just in time to see Mike through the picture window. He was taking a swing at Trick, who must have been on his way in. Taller, panther-lithe, sinewy and agile, Trick easily ducked the punch, and Mike tried again. This time Mike connected with Trick's jaw and Trick's cowboy hat blew off as his head snapped backwards. Recovering, he swung back, hard, and socked Mike in his doughy midsection. Mike staggered, balled both fists, and lunged at Trick again.

A surge of heat rushed through Katelyn as she flew toward the door.

She wanted to see Trick beat Mike senseless. *She wanted Trick to kill him.* She really did.

Her vision telescoped, as it had been doing ever since the bite, and she could see Trick's green eyes blazing with anger and surprise. The bruise already forming on his square, mocha-brown jaw was ugly proof that Mike deserved a world of pain.

An arm came around Trick and grabbed him across the chest. Katelyn blinked and her vision went back to normal as, with a start, she realized that it was her grandfather who had hold of Trick. The muscles in the older man's arms flexed as he struggled to contain him. Another man was dragging Mike away from Trick.

Katelyn joined the coffee-house customers spilling outside. Her grandfather looked like he was now lecturing Trick. Trick was standing a few yards away, head bowed deferentially, hands stuffed in the pockets of his jeans.

Mordecai McBride looked up and saw Kat. He walked over and took her bag from her. "We're parked over there," he said, pointing across the street.

"I'll just be a minute." Katelyn looked over at Trick, and her grandfather grunted and headed for the truck.

She walked up to Trick, awkward and tongue-tied, although why should she be? He'd been in plenty of fights before. But she couldn't help but stare at the bruising around his jawline. A thrill ran through her and she took a deep breath. Apparently her inner wolf approved of the fight.

"Hey," she said. "Can I get you anything? Ice pack? Anger management classes?"

Trick looked at her, shoulders hunched and wearing a scowl that sharpened the angles and hollows of his face. Even sullen and tousled, he was breathtakingly hot.

"What happened?" she asked, more kindly.

Trick reached out, pulled her into his arms and hugged her tight. Over his shoulder Katelyn spotted Hannah and Myrna staring; Hannah had apparently found a dress because she was carrying a bag, and Katelyn felt a fillip of fear. She didn't want them reporting back to Lee Fenner that she had a boyfriend, and a human one at that. That would put Trick in even more danger than he already was.

She pushed him in the chest, just hard enough to get him to let go and step back. "We'll talk later," she whispered, afraid that the other werewolves would hear but knowing that she had to say something to him. Then, before he had a chance to respond, she walked toward the truck.

3

"Boys can be idiots, sometimes," her grandfather said after they had driven out of town and into the forest.

"Yeah, well," Katelyn muttered. She was still replaying what had happened in her mind, and how angry she had felt. Rather than stand by and watch the fight, she wished she could have joined in. It was as Justin had said — everything felt more extreme.

But I controlled myself, she thought proudly. *Better than Trick, that's for sure.*

"Your new tires haven't come in yet. The boy will have to

drive you to school tomorrow morning." He glanced over at her. "That going to be okay?"

"Yes," she said, because really, what was the alternative? Having her grandfather drive her? "I wonder why Trick can't just get along better at school?" It was a poor shadow of her real question.

"This is the last year. Then he's free and clear."

Wrong, she thought. *If he stays in Wolf Springs, he's not clear by half.* And then she reconsidered. Why *should* he stay in Wolf Springs? Maybe they could leave together.

Just . . . go.

On Monday morning, she was relieved to see Trick's vintage green Mustang pull up outside the cabin to drive her to school. He was wearing his sheepherder's jacket and his black cowboy hat against the chill, and except for an incredible bruise on his chin he looked good. As the sun rose, they shared coffee and toast with her grandfather, then left for Wolf Springs.

As soon as they were in the car he turned to look at her. "I'm sorry." He shrugged. "For whatever I did that got me big-time dissed."

"We're good," she said, but she had a struggle to know what to do or say after that. She couldn't pull him close, but the thought of pushing him away was a cold, sharp blade just under her heart. Finally she gave up and kept herself busy on the drive by texting Kimi, her best friend back in Los Angeles. But it was five in the morning in L.A. so there was no reply. And there might not be. When Katelyn had moved to Wolf

Springs, they had drifted apart, and she missed the contact.

Niki and the Dove was on Trick's iPod, filling the Mustang with quirky Swedish voices singing in English. Blasting through the forest as usual, he kept glancing at her as he drove. But whenever she looked back over at him, his attention was fixed on the narrow, winding road. He seemed to be on the verge of asking or saying something, but he was holding back; she fidgeted with her phone just for something to do.

She and Trick sped into the foreboding tunnel of trees that completely blocked out the sun. The space left for vehicles was impossibly narrow, yet Trick shot through it as if they were being fired out of a cannon. He seemed incapable of driving slowly.

Wolf Springs High consisted mainly of a large, two-story wooden building with a pitched roof encrusted with over-hanging turrets and dormer windows. There were wrap-around porches on both floors. On top of the building an LED sign glowed scarlet through the early-morning gloom, the zipper of letters reading W-O-L-F-C-O-U-N-T-R-Y.

Heads turned as they walked into school together and Kat supposed people were beginning to speculate that they were a couple. She wondered if Trick thought they were.

When she'd arrived in Wolf Springs, she'd been the five hundredth student. Now, by her count, they were down to four hundred and ninety-six. Two dead, one moved, one kicked out of the house. But it felt to Katelyn as if the entire remaining student body was crammed into the narrow corridor: the din of voices and slamming lockers, the body heat — it was oppressive, smothering. Before her change last Friday, she hadn't minded it all so much. But now every sound, every jostle from passing students, assaulted her like a body blow.

"Take care, darlin'," Trick said, and he bobbed his head closer, as if he were about to kiss her. Then he stopped himself, gave her a mock-cautious salute, and walked the other way. Part of her was still poised in hope, waiting for that kiss.

Katelyn had braced herself to see Cordelia's empty desk, but as she slid into her seat beside it, the reality of what had happened hit home. She heard the bell ring, but couldn't tear her attention away from the vacant space. Around her, people were still talking; life was going on. Moving on.

But that desk was empty.

Somehow, class hadn't started yet. Then Mrs. Walker, the office lady, came bustling in. She explained that she was subbing for Mr. Henderson, who was absent.

Katelyn rose unsteadily, gathered up her things, and went over to Mrs. Walker, who was putting her stuff down on the desk. Mrs. Walker smiled at Katelyn and lifted her brows.

"I — I don't feel good," Katelyn told her. Mrs. Walker was also Wolf Spring High's equivalent of a nurse. "Headache . . . possible migraine. Can I go lie down?" There was a sick room with a cot next to the principal's office.

Mrs. Walker pulled a concerned face and nodded. "Okay, but check in with me once you're feeling better, all right?"

"I will," Katelyn promised.

She left the room and trudged down the hall. Smells

rolled down the corridor like waves on the beach — perfumes, body odors, coffee. Now that she had said she had a headache, a real one was threatening to erupt.

She entered the darkened room, which contained an old wooden desk and matching chair, and a cot facing a blank chalkboard. The top drawer of the desk held a thin blanket and a fresh pillowcase for the pillow, and Katelyn got the cot ready and lay down. Staring up at the old plaster ceiling, she traced faint images the way she and Kimi used to do when the clouds rolled in over the Pacific Ocean. A seashell. A surfboard. A wolf. Another wolf.

Sighing, she closed her eyes and rubbed her temples to break the building tension, the cot creaking as she tried to get comfortable. And then she detected muffled voices on the other side of the wall. Then not so muffled, as she stopped moving and eavesdropped.

". . . don't know where he is," said a voice. It was Coach Ambrose.

"Well, he didn't call in sick. He didn't call in at all, and I can't reach him." That was Mr. Hastings, the school principal. "I'll send Pat Lewis over there to check."

Pat Lewis would be Sergeant Lewis, the man who had taken fingerprints at her house after the break-in.

"Wes did caution the kids not to go into the forest. So he knows better than to put himself at risk."

Katelyn guessed that Mr. Henderson's first name was Wes. And he still hadn't shown up for class. They must be talking about him.

"God, what if it's another murder?" Mr. Hastings

muttered, then sighed. "I don't mean to sound so heartless. Let's see what Lewis finds out."

"I have to get back to my class," Coach Ambrose said. "Oh, for your info, I've got Mike Wright for detention. I caught him loitering around Trick Sokolov's car after the second bell rang. With a box cutter."

Katelyn grimaced. Mike again, with his piglike nose and super-bad attitude. She'd made an enemy of him the first time she'd met him by sticking up for Cordelia when he'd started harassing her. Katelyn had had no idea, of course, that Cordelia could have crushed his windpipe and tossed him off the bridge over the river if she'd felt like it.

If I get that strong, I'll totally do it for her, Katelyn thought acidly. *For both of us. For Trick, too.*

The principal swore beneath his breath. "There was a break-in over at the McBrides'," he said. "I wonder if Mike had anything to do with that, too. He's said some choice words about that new girl, McBride's granddaughter."

Katelyn scowled. She just bet he had.

"Remember when Mike and his boys tried to pin those other burglaries on Sokolov?"

"Trick didn't do this one, either. Lewis already cleared him."

"Mike's just a bully. But Trick's a rich kid, bored, smart as hell," the coach said.

"Trick and I go way back," Mr. Hastings replied with a wry chuckle. "Wolf Springs can't contain a boy like that."

"Seems to be a few other things we can't contain," the coach replied. "I'm worried about Wes."

"I'll let you know what I find out," Mr. Hastings told him.

She heard a door close. There was another silence. Then the principal said, "Yeah, hi, Pat. Listen, can you go over to Wes Henderson's place? Brick house on the corner by the old stables? He didn't show up for work and my calls are going straight to voice mail. Given the circumstances . . . yes. Thanks."

Katelyn waited, but nothing more came from the office, leaving her to ponder what she'd heard, Trick's frequent run-ins with Mike, and the slashed tires on his Mustang the first day he'd taken her to school.

She woke to the sound of an incoming text on her phone. She was still in the sick room and she snatched the phone up, reading off an unknown number. Her heart skipped multiple beats when she saw the message.

RU alone? C

C, for Cordelia. Katelyn almost screamed in relief. Her friend was alive!

Yes! School. Where RU? Katelyn texted frantically, screwing up three times in her haste and having to redo.

Safe. For now.

Katelyn closed her eyes against an onslaught of deep, relieved joy.

A third text bubble popped up: *No thanks to you.*

It hurt, but Katelyn almost didn't care. Just to know Cordelia was okay was enough.

C, tell me where u r, she typed.

But there was no answer.

Then her glance ticked up to the chalkboard.

Coming home w/me today, it read. *J.*

J for Justin. The board had been blank when she'd come into the room. Deep, visceral fear propelled Katelyn off the cot as she stared at the board. *Justin had been in this room while she'd been asleep.*

She looked around for any other evidence of his visit. There was none. Then she grabbed up her backpack, got a pen and her English notebook, and copied Cordelia's new phone number into it. Next, with regret, she deleted the texts.

She stayed in the sick room past lunch, hiding, seemingly forgotten by a busy Mrs. Walker. She texted Cordelia four times, but there was no reply. Then she called and let her grandfather know she'd be going over to "study with Cordelia" in the afternoon. When she emerged from the school at the end of the day, Trick fell into step beside her. His cowboy hat was pulled down low over his eyes, giving him a mysterious air.

"Hey, where've you been?" he asked, taking her backpack, which she was carrying against her chest. They crossed quickly to the lot.

"I didn't feel good," she replied tersely.

"What the hell," Trick said in a soft, angry tone.

Dead ahead of them, in the lot, Justin had just ridden up on his motorcycle. He stopped and put down his foot. The engine still idling, he reached into a square fiberglass compartment attached to the side of the bike and showed her an extra helmet.

Trick stared at Katelyn incredulously.

"I have to go to Cordelia's for homework," she said in a rush. "We're doing a project."

"I could have driven you over," he said.

Justin raced the engine and impatiently held up the helmet. Trick looked from her to Justin and back again, and a purple flush worked its way up his neck. He pursed his lips into a tight frown.

"See you tomorrow." Katelyn gave him a little wave and Trick shrugged.

Justin flicked up his visor. He didn't smile. He just waited. Seething, Katelyn walked over to him. She took the helmet as he stowed her backpack in the compartment, then got on the bike and slid her arms around Justin's waist. As Trick walked past them and headed toward his Mustang, Justin flicked the visor of his helmet back down, gunned the engine, and tore out of the lot.

The ride was long and rough, but Katelyn held on grimly, glad that they weren't having to talk. Finally they made it to the Fenners' house.

"Lee's not here," Justin announced as the motorcycle rolled down the sharp incline of the driveway. "Truck's gone."

Katelyn was relieved. She examined the windows of the large, sprawling house to see if anyone was there. After Saturday night, she felt eyes everywhere, and she couldn't help being rattled.

The house was an eccentric multi-storied, castle-like building of stone, wood and glass. Trees grew in little court-yards specifically designed to accommodate them. When Katelyn had first seen the rambling house, she had envied

Cordelia for all the space she had — something sorely lacking in the McBride cabin — even though the Fenner house was also home to Justin and his older brother, Jesse, Lee Fenner's nephews; both of their parents were dead. Then she had met Cordelia's snide, nasty sisters. And her father Lee, who was so bizarre that Katelyn had entertained the thought of suggesting to Cordelia that she move back to Los Angeles with her as fast as humanly possible. Of course, that had been before Katelyn had even known the Fenners were werewolves.

Justin had told Katelyn that the pack alphas had come from Lee Fenner's direct family line ever since the move to Arkansas in the 1800's. But Katelyn also knew of Lee Fenner's recent health problems, his shaky grasp on staying alpha of the pack.

"No one's challenged him for leadership yet?" she asked Justin as he killed the engine, then waited for her to climb off the motorcycle, pointing again to the left.

"I didn't say that no one's challenged him," Justin replied. He pushed down the kickstand.

Katelyn took off her helmet and studied the house again. She hadn't done anything to deserve this.

I did this to myself. I drove into the forest alone. I got out of the truck.

No. There was no way she was going to blame herself for this, or allow anyone else to put it on her. She was carrying enough guilt already: guilt at having taken a painkiller for a gymnastics injury on the night of the earthquake in L.A. — the earthquake that had led to her mother's death.

Justin dismounted and took off his own helmet, shaking out his curly hair, and despite her anger, Katelyn couldn't help blushing at the remembered sensation of her arms against his six-pack abs on the ride from school. She was a dancer and an athlete, and she appreciated a well-taken-care-of human body.

Don't try to sugarcoat it. You think he's hot.

It had taken nearly an hour to get to the Fenner house and she had felt her phone vibrating in her jeans pocket with text after text. From Trick, she was guessing. *Hoping*, she had to admit. She pulled out her phone and checked. Five messages from Kimi made her smile in surprise. Then there was a single text from Trick.

Call your grandfather, he had reminded her. That was all; and she already had, keeping up the pretense that she and Cordelia were meeting to make up and work on their project.

Tnx, she texted back.

"Drop your stuff on the porch," Justin said. "Then let's go. Lee's asked me to begin your training."

Training? It sounded so weird, as if he were a gymnastics coach. But Katelyn knew she needed to understand more about her new life, so she did as he asked, slipping her phone into the pocket of her jacket. She didn't linger on the porch.

They began to walk into the woods, and Katelyn felt that as soon as they were in the forest, Justin relaxed slightly. It was funny. Everyone else feared the woods but those who were werewolves seemed far more comfortable there than elsewhere.

"Those of us, the families who make up this pack, come

from Norway originally. We Fenners are direct descendants of the Fenris Wolf."

"Like in Norse mythology?"

"Exactly like. Fenris was a supernatural wolf-being who would bring about the death of Odin, king of the gods. He was bound with magical chains and imprisoned in a cave."

"Why did you come here? Why not stay in Norway?"

He moved his shoulders. "We're people, too, Kat. Lots of people left the Old World for different reasons." He gave her a look. "I've always wondered if someone found out about us."

She quickened with anxiety. There was always that threat about spilling the secret. Always the worry that she and her grandfather could be killed to guard it.

Justin raised his chin. She could tell he was sniffing the air, and she tried to breathe in whatever he had detected. She smelled leather and spice, dirt, and the pungent scent of pine.

Then he blinked and looked at her, as if he'd realized he'd lost his train of thought.

"Some folks also said that the cave where Fenris had been bound might be around here."

Katelyn's scalp prickled and she thought of the silver mine that she and Cordelia had been looking for. What better way to trap a werewolf than surrounding him by silver?

"What?" Justin asked suddenly. "You're shaking your head."

She hesitated. She never knew what she should say, and what she should keep to herself.

"Tell me," he said, stopping her with a hand on her wrist.

"I just thought about the silver mine Cordelia and I were trying to find for our history project, that's all."

She expected him to make fun of her, but he just looked thoughtful. "I suppose anything's possible," he said after a moment.

"So is Fenris good or bad?" Could *he* be the Hellhound?

"Legend says that Fenris was just. He dealt swift punishment to those who sinned, and rewarded his good children with plenty of hunting and land. But Odin ruled based on whim. And he was moody."

"Like your uncle," she said before thinking.

Justin's eyes widened. He pursed his lips for a couple of moments, and then he just looked sad. "I guess that's what makes it so hard to take. Uncle Lee was always harsh, but fair. The rules were simple, clear. Now . . . now no one is sure where they stand."

When she realized he was including himself in that statement, it sent another rush of fear through her. And she could guess how hard it was for him to live in a world of shifting rules. Of course, everything that Lee did, that all of them did, made no sense to her because she didn't even know what the rules were supposed to be. But he looked so sad that it made her heart ache for him. His life hadn't been an easy one, she knew. Just like her, he had lost both his parents, and nothing since then had been easy. She decided to shift the topic away from Lee for a minute.

"So, if Fenners are direct descendants of the Fenris wolf, shouldn't all werewolves look up to you?"

Justin laughed, a bitter, hard sound. "Wouldn't that make

life nice and easy? No. Look at all the religions in the human world. All the special, chosen people."

"So . . . other werewolves were created in other ways?" She thought of her attack, the bite. How did all this get started?

"The Gaudins claim to be descended from the Beast of Gévaudan — a werewolf that terrorized the area of Gévaudan in France in the Middle Ages. It killed more than two hundred people and that's a source of pride with the Gaudins. They are savages with no honor, no morality."

And yet Katelyn knew that her friend Cordelia had had feelings for Dominic Gaudin — the alpha of the Gaudins — who had stood up to Lee Fenner for her on Halloween night. What she had seen of Dom didn't make him seem any more savage than the werewolves of the Fenner pack.

"They've been spoiling for war for a long time," Justin went on, and there was a hint of growl in his tone. "It makes no sense. North America is huge, so there's no need to fight over territory, but they do. They sneak on our land, poach our prey, spy on us."

The anger was back, simmering just below the surface. He was taut, as if ready to spring. "So it's you versus them," she said.

He shook his head. "No, there are other packs," he said. "Most of them are pretty small. But there's one big one." She waited. Emotions flashed across his face, but she couldn't read them. "The Latgale family. They call themselves the Hounds of God."

"That's so weird."

"They don't think so," he said. "The pack came from Livonia. They said they were warriors who went down into hell to do battle with witches and demons. They believed that when they died, their souls were welcomed into heaven as reward for their service."

"Do they still believe that?" Katelyn asked, thinking of the Hellhound again.

Justin shrugged. "I guess. I've never talked to one of them. Only Uncle Lee has, and he said their leader was crazy." He made a face. "And we're back to moody alphas." He stopped abruptly. "Okay, we're here."

Katelyn looked around. "Here" looked like every other part of the forest to her. "Where?" she asked.

He grinned at her. "That's what I want you to tell me."

"O-kay," she said, drawing the word out. "Just give me a second." She started to pull out her phone, but he stopped her with a quick shake of his head.

"No GPS, no phones. I want *you* to tell me where we are."

She looked straight at him. "The middle of the woods."

"Now is not the time to be sarcastic, Kat."

She sighed and bunched up her shoulders as she tried to figure out how long they'd been walking. Finally she pointed back the way they'd come. "We're about a mile away from the house."

"Good. Remember that."

She cocked her head.

"It's going to be up to you to find the way back later." Before she could ask what he meant, he slapped her lightly on the back. "Tag, you're it."

Then he set out running. Katelyn stared after him in surprise for a second before she began chasing after him, bobbing and weaving around the trees. "You're going too fast!" she shouted.

He turned his head over his shoulder and shouted back, "You're going too slow." And then he seemed to leap forward, his legs moving so quickly she couldn't see them.

Startled and afraid of losing sight of him, she reached deep down inside herself. And she found speed that she would never have dreamed of.

Suddenly *she* was the one who raced so fast she was practically flying. She vaulted a fallen log with ease, darted between the trees, and then she passed Justin. She reached out and slapped his shoulder, then jumped out of the way of his reaching arms.

She laughed and ran faster, the trees beginning to blur by, and she felt dizzy and breathless and wildly happy all at the same time. Wind stung her face. She felt Justin's hand brush her shoulder and she twisted in mid-stride, ready to tag him back.

But he wasn't there.

She slowed, stumbled over her own feet, then stopped, turning in every direction, but she couldn't see him.

"Justin!"

Only silence greeted her.

It was the first time she had been alone in the woods since her attack. And all the reasons she shouldn't be out there alone sprang instantly to mind. Nervously, she rubbed the places on her arm where the trap had cut her. She'd heard something whispering to her again that morning. Calling her name. Promising. Threatening. Stalking. Even now, just thinking about it, she began to tremble. And it wasn't just the Hellhound she had to worry about now. Someone had shot at her.

She began to jog back the way she'd come, but now her legs felt leaden, heavy. Her lungs filled with the smell of pine and mud and traces of the perfume she'd worn to school. She didn't smell Justin at all. Didn't see footprints, or broken-off tree limbs, or anything else to signal his route. The forest was just the forest, and she was wandering from one identical tree to the next.

She came to a stand of trees growing so closely together that Justin couldn't have possibly passed through them. She walked along it, huffing, growing more nervous, and turned around to go back the way she had come. But she faced a V in the path that she didn't remember. She took the left branch, but it looked unfamiliar, so she went back to the beginning and took the right fork. She didn't recognize that, either.

Birds took flight overhead, startling her, and she raised herself on tiptoes to see if she could locate where they'd been roosting before they bolted. Maybe that was where Justin was. But she was too short to see over the bobbing pine branches in her way.

"Oh, forget it," she muttered. She reached for her cell phone. The GPS would help her get her bearings so she could at least find the right way back to the house. But when her hand dipped into her jacket pocket, she realized that the phone was gone.

Ice water seemed to pour through her veins. Worse than being lost, she had lost the phone, her lifeline to civilization; the device that Cordelia had texted her on earlier that day and might contact again soon. She wasn't sure if she had been sweating before, but she became hyper-aware of it now.

Something moved in the corner of her eye, and she ticked her glance in that direction. She saw only the trees. But it had to be Justin, she told herself. Messing with her.

"Marco," she called out, a little mockingly, because she knew it would be uncool to sound afraid. But the truth was, she was getting more jittery.

"Marco Polo," she called.

Something cold and sinister seemed to settle across her shoulders and she whirled around in a half circle; finding nothing, she glanced anxiously around, then upward, squinting. Pinpricks of gray afternoon light were barely visible above the treetops, and she heard the plaintive cry of a dove, things stirring in the underbrush.

There could be many things in the forest. A werewolf pack of things. Maybe they were hunting her. Maybe Lee Fenner had decided after all that she was too dangerous to be allowed to live. Maybe there was a bounty on her head.

And I knew how dangerous he is, and I got on Justin's motorcycle and came here like an idiot anyway, she thought. But she hadn't really had an option, had she?

The weighty sensation pressed down and she shivered as if someone had just walked over her grave.

"Justin?" she croaked out.

A distant sound somewhere between a growl and a moan

echoed against tree against tree against tree. Katelyn froze. It didn't sound like a wolf. It didn't sound like anything she had ever heard before in her life.

The woods around her went deathly quiet. No chirping birds; nothing stirring in the brush. Then she looked down to see a little rabbit standing completely still. About five feet from that one there was another, and it, too, didn't so much as twitch its fluffy white cotton tail. They were so still that they both looked stuffed. Then she looked more closely and saw that the chest of the closer bunny was fluttering, as if it was panting. The other one, too. They were panicking.

The hair on the back of her neck rose. Not even the wind made a sound — it was as if it didn't dare move, either. The forest was holding its breath.

Another moan vibrated through the forest.

Closer.

The rabbits scattered in terror. Cawing birds shot across the forest canopy. And something began to crash through the heavy growth. Something huge.

In her direction.

She took off like a shot, running blindly. She came to an incline and skidded, tumbling end over end as her slippery boots lost their purchase. She scrabbled to her feet, charging forward. Dodging nooses of Spanish moss and spindly out-stretched twigs, she ran an obstacle course as the sound of breaking branches gained on her.

A squirrel skittered up the tree nearest to her. More birds burst from a tangle of vines and roots. The wind began to blow as if it had just woken up.

She kept going. And going. The crack and snap behind drove her faster. There was another growl, and she poured on speed. She twisted her ankle on a loose rock but managed to keep her footing. Then a strong smell filled her nose, almost like rot; and she felt something hot and moist against her shoulder, as if someone was breathing on her.

Oh, God. It's a werewolf. Justin couldn't change at will yet, so it couldn't be him. She ran faster, bobbling hard on her ankle, her breath coming in bursts. She came to a thicket of pines interlaced with each other. Wildly, she looked left and right. No way to pass. Her lungs on fire, she heaved in air as she dashed along the tree line. Then she spotted a low-hanging branch and jumped up to grab it. Tipping herself upside down, she thrust her legs up and over the limb and whipped herself right side up in a sort of modified gymnastics move like on the uneven bars. There was another branch above her head; she stretched and gripped it, and repeated the movement. Then she set her feet on the branch, wincing at the pain in her ankle, and grabbed onto an over-hanging bough. She pulled herself up toward it, and looked down to the ground below.

She heard the moan again, and her heart stuttered. That was not a werewolf howl.

Shadows seemed to crawl along the ground.

Katelyn.

She couldn't tell if it was spoken aloud or in her head. But it was the same voice that had been coming after her when she had fallen into the trap.

The Hellhound?

The shadows darkened as she stared at them. Impulsively, she tried to swing herself onto the next higher branch but it cracked, broke.

She screamed as she fell. If something was down there, it would get her. Acting on pure instinct, she tucked and did a flip, then managed to stick a landing as she planted herself in the center of cold, menacing darkness.

Katelyn, the voice said again.

"Help!" she screamed.

Something exploded through the wall of branches and grabbed her.

4

Katelyn began to swing wildly at whatever held her.

"Kat! It's me!"

Justin. He was there and he was shaking her by the shoulders. She batted crazily at him.

"What's wrong with you?" he demanded, dodging her hands.

"The Hellhound!" she cried, pushing away from him. "Oh, my God, Justin, run!"

"No way. Not that again." A flash of irritation crossed his face. "You just got turned around and freaked yourself out."

He grabbed her hands in both of his, jerking on them when she wouldn't stay still. "Damn it, Kat."

Panting, she looked back over her shoulder. The shadows were gone. "It was coming this way," she insisted. "I know you heard the groans." She looked down at her hands in his, and he let go. She almost grabbed onto him but he turned away and started walking. "Justin, there *was* something."

As she kept close behind him, she could practically feel that something was watching her.

Letting her go.

For now.

Seconds later they were back in the clearing. And there stood Lee Fenner with a stopwatch in his hand. Back from wherever he had gone, he was dressed in jeans and a long-sleeved chambray shirt. He was very tall, with a shock of white hair, and his tanned face was lined like a worn leather satchel. In human form, he had nearly torn the hair from her head in a fury when she'd failed to act properly obedient. Swallowing hard, she tried to stay calm, but it was very difficult to pretend that she wasn't scared to death.

He looked from the stopwatch to her, lids narrowing until his amber eyes were two golden slits. He clicked the timer and frowned at her. "Well, your leg's not broken," he said. "You're not covered in blood. So what the hell took you so long?"

"She got lost," Justin said before she could say anything. He squeezed her shoulder hard, a warning to stay quiet. "She'll get the hang of it."

Mr. Fenner grunted and trained his steely gaze on Justin. "That's up to you, isn't it, boy?"

"Yessir," Justin said. "But you should have seen her, Uncle Lee. She's a gymnast and she's got moves we can use when we hunt. She was up in the trees like a monkey. She can climb up, look for prey. I'm thinking when she starts keeping her memory, she could do great moves when she's changed, too."

Mr. Fenner cocked a brow. "Oh?"

Katelyn quavered under his gaze. Could he have been the thing trailing after her? He wasn't winded, and he was fully dressed. "I've been studying gymnastics for years."

He grunted. "Maybe you'll be useful after all." He held up a warning finger. "You don't say a word about any of this to your grandpa. Your training. Us. Not one word."

"I haven't and I won't." She tried to keep her voice steady. As he glared at her, she lowered her head to show respect . . . and so that he couldn't see her clamped jaw. He was a tyrant, and she hated him as much as she feared him.

"Now get her home," he ordered, and sauntered off in the direction of the house.

Avoiding Justin's gaze as well, Katelyn headed for the motorcycle. But Justin gently brushed her forearm with his fingertips. It was a soft, kind gesture.

"We'll take the truck," he said. "You're too tired to hang onto me for that long."

"I, um, lost my cell phone," she said. She didn't want to tell him, but neither did she want him finding it and investigating it too closely.

"No, you didn't," he said, pulling it out of his pocket and handing it to her.

She stared at him as she wrapped her hand around it. How had he gotten hold of it? Had he found something on there that would get her in trouble, like a new message from Cordelia? As much as she wanted to check the phone, she kept her attention riveted on his face.

"How?" she asked.

"Werewolves can move very fast, Kat. You're not used to it yet, but you'll get there. I programmed my number in," he added.

"Not cool," she said. And then before he could tell her to act more respectfully, she lowered her head.

He didn't respond, just headed for the truck, forcing her to follow. As they climbed into the vehicle, every one of Katelyn's senses went on alert and she moved as far away from him as she could, gripping the armrest. Then Mr. Fenner appeared at Katelyn's window, rapping lightly at it. Startled, she fumbled for the button to unroll it, but Justin hadn't turned the key yet and the electric function didn't work. She opened the door.

"Tell your mother to get home," he said. "It's going to rain."

Katelyn was stunned. He was talking to her as though she was Cordelia. She slid a glance at Justin, who cleared his throat and started the engine.

"Sure will, Uncle Lee," he said. "We'll go tell her right now."

"Good. Good." Mr. Fenner nodded and stepped away

from the truck. Katelyn shut the door and sat unmoving as Justin headed for the main road.

"He's stressed," Justin said. "You know Cordelia was his favorite." He glanced at her as he turned to the left. "You haven't heard from her, have you?"

Was he testing her? Did he already know the answer? Had Cordelia texted her again, and he'd seen it? She itched to check out her phone.

"I won't give up on finding her," Justin said, as if he could read her mind. "I'll make sure she's safe. I promise you, Kat."

She heard the caring in his voice, the concern, and tried to say thank you, but she was too upset. She leaned her head against the window, then thought of all that had happened and pulled away, half imagining that the Hellhound would hurtle itself at the window and crash through the glass.

"He thought I was her," she said, deliberately not answering his question. "And that Cordelia's mother — his wife — was still alive . . . I didn't know what to do."

"You did fine," he assured her. "Best thing to do is just say and do as little as possible."

"Why?"

He chewed the inside of his cheek as if considering his words very carefully. "Uncle Lee has always been a very dangerous man. His condition — this dementia — now makes him unpredictable as well as dangerous."

She swallowed. "All that talk of killing . . . it's not just talk, is it?"

Justin focused his sea-blue eyes on her. He looked so serious, dead sober. "No. He really *is* willing to kill you, and your grandfather. The secret has to be protected, and that's just him doing his job."

She shivered. She had known that was the answer, and she could tell that Justin was being completely honest. "Has he ever had to kill before?" she asked.

Justin was silent for a long time. "There have been challenges," he said softly at last.

The hair stood up on her arms. Challenges. Fights to the death. It was so awful and barbaric. So totally unbelievable.

"But, family, it's so important to him," she said.

"Not as important as his duty to keep the pack secure."

And somehow she sensed that they were no longer talking about her or Cordelia. His jaw was clenched, his chin raised. She traced his sharp profile with her gaze. The tension in the truck was nearly unbearable.

"What is it?" she asked quietly.

"Don't ever cross him, Kat. I couldn't bear to lose you, too."

"Too?" she whispered, barely remembering to breathe.

He hunched his shoulders. "When it was clear what was starting to happen to Uncle Lee . . . my father . . . my father went to have a talk with him."

She felt her heart skip a beat. "What are you saying?"

"I'm saying two men walked into those woods and only one walked out."

"You don't think . . . I thought your dad was killed in a hunting accident."

"That's what Lee tells everyone. I have my reasons to think differently."

"Justin," she breathed, "I'm so sorry. And now you have to live with him. How can you even stand to look at him?"

"He's my alpha . . . for now."

And those last two words hung in the air between them, and Katelyn knew in her heart that one day Justin was planning on making a challenge.

"You called me your secret weapon," she whispered.

"No one can know about your immunity," he said. "No one."

I bet I'd be Mr. Fenner's favorite if he knew I was immune to silver, she thought, but she just nodded as the truck slipped into the dark woods; as, in the blackness, the world disappeared.

Click. Click. Click.

Nails on wood.

Nails on glass.

And leering down at her.

Eyes.

Burning eyes.

Watching from above.

What big eyes you have.

The better to see you with.

Click. Click. Click.

Nails on the floor.

Hot breath whispering on her cheek.

Sleep, beast of silver.

Katelyn's new tires came in, and her grandfather put them

on her Subaru, which meant that Trick didn't need to drive her to school anymore. Seeing her riding with Justin had obviously pissed Trick off, but he couldn't quite keep his distance; Katelyn told herself it didn't matter what he thought of her, but it did.

Driving through the woods alone, though, she couldn't help but think of running through them as something called her name. She kept the car doors locked and seriously rethought her grandfather's offer of a gun. Would regular bullets work on a werewolf or a Hellhound, or would only silver bullets work?

She and Cordelia had researched the Hellhound when they had begun their history class report on the lost Madre Vena silver mine. According to legend, the Hellhound guarded the rich cache of ore and silver treasure deep inside the mine. Cordelia's father had been pushing her to find the Madre Vena, and Katelyn wondered if she had done so. After all, she had lied to Katelyn about having one of the books they'd been looking for. All that time hunting for it, and Cordelia had kept it hidden in her room all along. Maybe that was why Cordelia had been so certain that the Hellhound was real. Maybe she'd seen it.

Katelyn wanted that book. She wanted to know why Cordelia had lied to her.

And if the Hellhound's real, I want to know how to steer clear of it.

She didn't want to be its third victim. Whispers had gone around school that Haley and Becky had died horribly. Apparently Sergeant Lewis had said he'd never seen anything like it and the morgue technician had thrown up when he'd seen Becky's mangled body.

She thought again about just bailing. And then, as usual, her resolve crumbled when she imagined being hunted down. They might do something to her grandfather or Trick in retaliation. She didn't know if she was being a coward, or a hero, or a realist. At night, lying on her bed, she stared at the statue of her mother in the moonlight, and wondered what it felt like to completely give up. Her mom would never have given up.

But she wasn't sure where the line was drawn between giving up and giving in.

On Wednesday morning, her grandfather looked at her across the breakfast table with a strange look on his face. He took a sip of coffee and tapped the table idly with his fingertips. "You okay?" he asked.

She sat up straighter and pasted on a smile. "Yeah, fine. You?"

"Same."

But she looked at him more closely and realized that he seemed tired, more so than she'd ever noticed before. "Are you okay? Is something wrong?"

He paused while he sipped his cup of coffee. "The break-in is still bothering me," he admitted after he put the cup down.

She blinked at him in surprise. She wasn't used to him being so straight with her. Should she have somehow known that he'd been upset? Had the weight of what had happened to her made her oblivious to other people's concerns?

She sipped her coffee as she formulated her response, remembering her own feelings when she'd realized Justin had taken her phone.

"Were the paintings valuable?" she asked.

Mordecai took another sip of coffee, and light streaming through the curtains filigreed the gray stubble on his chin. "One of them was a landscape I painted for your grandmother. The other was just something my father picked up at an estate sale when I was a kid. No money in either of them."

He scratched his chin and rested his hand on the table. His face changed, hardened. "The silver belonged to your grandmother, and before her, my mother. I was planning on giving it to you someday when you got married." Pink rose in his cheeks. "Whole family heirloom thing, you know."

She stared at him, touched. She had nothing from her parents, thanks to the earthquake and house fire caused by it, and the thought of having something like that was beautiful. White-hot anger flashed through her as she realized the thieves hadn't just stolen from him but also from her.

"Do the police have any leads? Is there a place around here that someone would go to pawn something like that?"

"Pat already put the word out."

She reached across the table and gripped his hand. "I'm so sorry," she whispered around the sudden lump in her throat. "You know there's places online where you can buy old silver patterns and things like that. My mom sold some of her stuff after Dad died."

"Then I'm glad she never wanted your grandmother's," he said with a sad smile. "No, it's irreplaceable. My dad was a silversmith. He made each piece by hand for my mom."

Katelyn blinked in surprise. "My great-grandfather was a silversmith?"

"Your dad didn't tell you that? He was a fine craftsman. The shame of it is those pieces of silverware were the only things he made that I had."

That was when she realized just how much she and her grandfather had in common. They'd both lost everyone, everything that really mattered to them. Maybe fate had put them together for a reason. Maybe someday she could even find him something that his dad had made.

If Mr. Fenner didn't kill both of them first.

⊰⊱

Katelyn had hated leaving her grandfather alone in the cabin, but she finally did. She made it into her history class just as the bell was ringing. Mrs. Walker was substituting for Mr. Henderson again. A few minutes into the hour, Sergeant Lewis and Mr. Hastings strode into the room and Mrs. Walker looked up from her book as the students fell quiet and expectantly waited to find out what was up. Katelyn could feel her own chest tighten, and her skin prickled with anxiety. Had they found Mr. Henderson? Cordelia?

Mr. Hastings cleared his throat. The look on his face spoke volumes — something was terribly wrong. Katelyn's thoughts flew again to Cordelia.

"Students," he began, "I wanted to let you know that Mr. Henderson has officially been declared a missing person."

Gasps rose up from around the room. Katelyn tensed, in case there was more bad news. In her experience, it usually came in threes, or fours, or sixes.

"Now, if anyone knows anything, we'd appreciate you coming forward and telling us so that we can find him quickly, before anything . . ." He trailed off.

Before anything bad happens to him, Katelyn filled in. *But he knows that something bad might have already happened to Mr. Henderson.*

In the front row, a girl raised her hand.

Mr. Hastings acknowledged her. "Yes, Gretchen?"

"What about Cordelia? She hasn't been in school all week."

Katelyn had been wondering how long it would be before people started to question Cordelia's absence. When Katelyn had first moved to Wolf Springs, Trick had warned her that gossip and rumors moved with G4 speed — the only G4 there was to be had in town.

"Cordelia's family has contacted the school about her situation," Mr. Hastings said. "It's a private matter that we're not at liberty to discuss."

That caused several more ripples through the room. Katelyn wondered what story the Fenners had concocted.

Gretchen leaned sideways and whispered to another girl, "They were *close*, Mr. Henderson and Cordelia."

Katelyn's face went hot and she closed her eyes in dismay. No, she thought. *No, don't do this.*

"Are you okay?" someone murmured as a hand rested on her shoulder.

It was Beau, who had warned her to get out of Wolf Springs because of the killings. Of course, that had been before she had become a werewolf. Now she needed to tell him that she didn't want to investigate the killings around Wolf Springs; that she didn't want to investigate the current deaths, or the ones Beau said his own grandmother had told him had happened half a century before. A massacre, she'd called it. A killing field.

"I'm fine," she murmured, studying the varnished surface of her desk.

"I gotta tell you something," he persisted. "My grandma had a stroke. She was yelling something fierce the other night, said she saw a demon in her window."

Katelyn was stunned. A werewolf?

"She just screamed 'Demon! Sweet Jesus protect me!' and then she collapsed." Beau looked wan. "She's not doing too well."

She saw the unspoken plea on his face. He wanted her to help him find out what it was that his grandmother had seen. She'd been so intrigued about everything his grandmother had said about Wolf Springs before — that the town was "a banked fire," according to her, and that every forty or fifty years or so something happened, something terrible, something epically bad. That the animals went crazy, and then people died.

That it was starting again.

She'd asked her grandfather about it. But now, she didn't

dare involve Beau. If the answers pointed to the existence of werewolves, she'd be signing Beau's death warrant. She resolutely opened the book on her desk and stared at the words, but the letters swam before her eyes.

"Kat?" he prodded.

"Beau, I — I just don't want to talk about . . . things," she whispered.

Mr. Hastings and the police sergeant walked out of the classroom, leaving a buzz of whispers and texts in their wake. Gretchen was holding court, shredding Cordelia's reputation as she made insinuating remarks about cozy "meetings" with Mr. Henderson to discuss her "history project." Everything in poisonous air quotes, of course. Katelyn had been at those meetings and they had discussed their history paper and their bibliography and his interest in the silver mine. There was no more chemistry between Cordelia and their teacher than between Cordelia and Coach Ambrose. But the seed of a juicy rumor had been planted, and it was taking root. In a tiny town like Wolf Springs, it would be a tangled thorn patch before lunchtime.

I should speak up for her. I should say something, Katelyn thought. Or not.

"That's not true. They didn't. None of that is true," she blurted suddenly, and heads turned to stare at her. She looked hard at Gretchen. "You know it's not."

Gretchen just raised a brow and smiled knowingly. Then she turned her back on Katelyn and slid a sly glance at the girl sitting beside her. The other girl smiled back. There was more than one kind of wolf in Wolf Springs, and Gretchen was busily raising her status in the pack through the power of gossip. Katelyn had no idea if it was a battle she should take on, but she couldn't stand by and let Gretchen do that to her friend. And she was still Cordelia's friend, even if Cordelia was blaming her for what had happened.

"It wasn't like that," she said again.

Beau patted her arm. "It's okay, Kat. No one believes it."

And she felt even guiltier for not offering to help him find out what had frightened his grandmother, and what threatened their town.

What *did* they believe around here? she wondered. What did they know?

That afternoon, Katelyn told Justin about what people were saying about Cordelia. They were standing in the Fenner kitchen filling up two water bottles, and she blurted out the horrible gossip about Mr. Henderson. He blinked and guffawed, but when he saw how upset she was, he leaned forward as if to brush her cheek with a kiss. It was the way pack members acknowledged and comforted each other. But he pulled back before his lips made contact with her skin.

"You can kiss her," his older brother said, coming up behind them. "She's not a stranger."

Jesse Fenner had Down's syndrome and Cordelia had told Katelyn that one of the reasons for Justin moving the two of them into the Fenner house had been because he needed help taking care of his older brother — help that was often provided, Katelyn knew, by Justin's girlfriend Lucy, when she was there. For the most part, Jesse stayed at home because he couldn't be trusted to keep the family secret — he was so trusting and, left to his own devices, might talk to anyone. Sometimes, though, he got to go to the pharmacy to visit LaRue, the cat there, while a prescription was filled for some kind of medication he was on. Jesse wanted a cat in the worst way.

"I know she's not a stranger, buddy," Justin said. He smiled at his brother and screwed on the cap of his water bottle.

"I'm glad to see you, Kat," Jesse said. "Justin's glad, too." He pulled a sad face. "I miss my cousin. Say her name, he'll break your neck." He mimicked doing just that, putting his fists together, then turning them in opposite directions.

Katelyn felt sick to her stomach.

"No one will ever hurt you, Jesse," Justin said, and a fleeting expression passed over his features. It looked like anger, but Katelyn couldn't decipher it before it was gone.

"I'm going to Lucy," Jesse said. "She has some sour apple gum." He grinned at Justin. "If you marry Kat, I can marry Lucy. She loves me more than you."

"You're a heartbreaker," Justin said, feinting a punch at Jesse's chin.

"You're a neck breaker," Jesse said, giggling and squirming away. "You, Justin, you're a breaker!"

Then Jesse trotted out of the kitchen, leaving Justin and Katelyn alone again. Justin gave Katelyn a little eye-roll.

"What about Mr. Henderson?" she said, taking up where she'd left off. "What do you think happened to him?"

He shrugged. "Can't say."

"Or won't?" she pushed. "Justin, two people have died.

And a teacher at my school is missing. And I was attacked. And no one is doing *anything*—"

Before she realized what was happening, his hand was across her mouth. He pulled her hard against his chest and pressed his mouth against her ear.

"You don't know that," he whispered. "You don't know half of what's going on. And if you want to live through this, drop it. *Now.*"

It took her a moment to register that he was shaking.

"I can't protect you if they . . . if he . . . if anyone hears you saying things like that," he whispered. "Asking questions is dangerous. Please, don't risk your life . . . or mine . . . that way."

When he pulled his hand from her mouth, all she could do was stare up at him. He looked truly, genuinely afraid. She glanced toward the other room and thought about Jesse. Justin's brother was the sweetest person in the whole world and he'd never do anything to hurt anybody. But that didn't mean he wouldn't tell Lee or Lucy what he might have overheard. She swallowed hard and nodded. Justin worked so hard to make the whole werewolf thing seem normal, because it was, for him at least. Sometimes she actually relaxed enough to forget that she was living under the threat of death.

"I'll be more careful," she whispered, soft enough that she hoped only he could hear.

He bent down and brushed his lips against hers. She could taste the longing on his lips and felt herself respond to it. But she pushed away from him and shook her head.

Not careful, she mouthed to him. And Lucy — *his girlfriend* — was in the house. How could he come on to her like that when Lucy was about?

He hung his head, looking like a puppy who knew he'd done something wrong. And the expression was so endearing she wanted to kiss him again. What kind of girl was she? Hitting on another girl's boyfriend? *No.*

Before she could move he shook himself and exited the room, leaving her a bit dazed.

That did not just happen.

Katelyn's legs nearly gave way as she stood alone in the Fenner kitchen, her hand over her mouth, her heart thundering.

If you want to live through this . . .

She pressed her hand against her lips as her thoughts fuzzed away, leaving her in a stupor. What if Jesse had wandered back in and seen them kissing? Or Lucy?

Which was more dangerous: the nameless predator in the forest or the one named Lee Fenner? And did Justin really expect her not to do a thing to protect herself?

Maybe Justin was working behind the scenes to help her. Or maybe he was just out to help himself. She didn't know. She didn't understand how pack politics worked. It was even more complicated than high school! Back in L.A., while she and Kimi had always had friends, Katelyn had been too busy to figure out the rules of the popularity game. But the werewolves of Wolf Springs weren't playing a game. They were deadly serious about fighting their way up the social ladder of pack dominance. Cordelia's sisters had told their

father about Katelyn to bust Cordelia for hiding the news —
and a potential threat to the pack — from him; Katelyn was
certain of it. They must have known Mr. Fenner was planning
to name her his successor as alpha.

None of them seemed to be taking Katelyn's attack
seriously. Or maybe talking about it was forbidden because it
made Mr. Fenner look bad. She was expected to keep all of
them safe with her silence, but no one was doing anything to
keep *her* safe. All they did was tell her to shut up and do as
she was told.

All these strangers, including her grandfather, wanted to
control her. What on earth had he been thinking of in bringing her here? First he forced her to live in a cabin in the
middle of the forest; then he warned her not to go into the
forest by herself; but then he got her a car so she could drive
through there alone. His solution to the whole mess seemed
to be to teach her how to shoot.

She clenched her teeth. She was done with holding her
breath in case she did or said the wrong thing.

"Screw this," she said aloud.

She walked down the hall and went into Cordelia's bedroom. It was very pretty, decorated in green and lavender. On
the other side of the room, a sliding door led to one of the
courtyards dominated by a tree; and from there, to the forest.
Her walls were lined with cheerleading trophies and photographs. It all looked so normal.

Katelyn stood in the dim light. Her bravado was fading,
and she figured she'd get in trouble if she was found there.
But she needed answers.

Cordelia's bed was unmade. Her school textbooks sat in the center of the bed — she clearly studied the way Katelyn did, in bed, probably with earbuds in, too. The countdown to the full moon had been murder, but Cordelia had reminded her that even if her life changed that drastically, she would still have a life. That what she did day-by-day would still matter. That included high school and homework.

Katelyn quickly poked through Cordelia's pile of books. The first thing she wanted to locate was the book Cordelia had initially lied about having — a book by a man named Theodore Switliski. Mr. Henderson had asked her about it, too. And now he was missing.

No luck; she crossed to the desk and examined the spines of a few more books piled there. Nothing.

Then she heard Jesse's voice in the hall. "I pet LaRue softly, softly," he said. "Don't want to break his neck."

There was a beat. Then Lucy replied, "No, that's one neck you do not want to break, sugar. But there are others," she muttered.

Katelyn panicked. It sounded as if they were headed toward Cordelia's room. Well, what of it? Could anyone blame her for going into the room of her absent best friend?

Yes, they would blame her.

"I left my Halloween candy in Cor . . . in her room," Jesse said. "She gave me sour apple gum. And candy. I didn't get to trick or treat."

Katelyn looked around the room. Sure enough, she saw a plastic jack-o-lantern brimming with wrapped chocolate bars and lollipops.

"Sugar, we're not supposed to go in that room," Lucy said.

"*Please*," he begged.

Something slammed against the door, not too hard, but hard enough to make her jerk. Grimacing, she darted to the sliding glass door to let herself out. It was locked. But she was stronger than she used to be, right? Should she try to force it?

"Okay, Jesse. Please, honey, stay calm. You know your Uncle Lee doesn't like you to get too upset."

"I want my sour apple!" he whined.

The closet. Katelyn darted back across the room, opened the door, and popped inside. There was a skylight overhead, bathing her in sunshine like a spotlight and she cringed, feeling vulnerable. Standing on top of a row of shoes, she also felt monumentally stupid. People who were werewolves had enhanced senses, including the sense of smell, and Lucy might realize she was inside the room. But she figured her scent was already present since she'd been in Cordelia's room before.

The bedroom door creaked open and she pulled back into a wall of hanging clothing, then tried to breathe as quietly as possible.

"There it is," Lucy said. Katelyn heard her footfalls go past the closet door. "Happy now?" They crossed back.

"I didn't go trick or treating," Jesse said. "A man came to our house. He and Uncle Lee were yelling."

"Yes, well, they made up," Lucy said. "And look at all the candy you have. Oh, here's the gum."

Katelyn heard the rustling of paper. Jesse must be

unwrapping a stick of sour apple. "Is she dead?"

"I'm sure she's just fine. It's nothing for you to worry about. I don't want you to worry about anything, Jesse James."

"You love me. You love me more than Justin."

"Oh, honey, everyone loves you."

"Justin loves Kat."

Katelyn went numb. Without thinking, she sucked in her breath. Then she shut her eyes against a tide of panic, worried that she'd made too much noise.

"You know your brother likes pretty girls," Lucy said after a pause. "But they're, well, they're like candy. They're not all that good for your health."

What did *that* mean? Was she threatening Justin?

"I brush my teeth," Jesse said proudly.

"So does Justin. Now let's get out of here before we get in trouble, okay? Let's leave it a secret that we even came in here."

"I'm good at secrets," Jesse said.

"That's good, darlin'."

The bedroom door opened and closed. Katelyn exhaled slowly. She tried to step off Cordelia's shoes and wobbled to the right. She put her hand out to steady herself . . . and her hand went right through a poster of a wolf baying at the moon taped to the closet wall. Then she realized that there was an opening just behind it, like a little wall safe.

And there were some things inside. She reached in, and the first thing she pulled out was *Ozark Folklore*, by Theodore

Switliski. The "missing" book that Cordelia "didn't" have. Next Katelyn found what appeared to be a purple-bound blank book. Curious, Katelyn opened it.

... I don't know why he's so obsessed with finding the mine. I'm scared we will find it, and then he'll do something to Kat.

5

"Oh, my God," Katelyn whispered. It was Cordelia's diary. She shut it, wishing like anything for her backpack, then slid it under her arm while she pulled out a framed photograph of Dominic Gaudin, the leader — the alpha — of the Fenners' rival wolf pack, the Gaudins. It was like a studio portrait, very posed. His reddish-gold hair brushed the shoulders of a gray opened-neck shirt, and a golden pendant of what appeared to be some kind of wolf-like monster dangled from his neck. He had very straight, big shoulders and a broad chest. His forehead was high, his eyebrows brown, his eyes a crystalline blue.

The picture was inscribed *Pour toi, ma belle Cordelia. D.* Katelyn's mother was French, and the words were easy to translate anyway: for you, my beautiful Cordelia.

Katelyn had seen Dom Gaudin when she'd accidentally spied on the Fenners during their hastily arranged Halloween night meeting with him. Tensions had run sky high, and the meeting had fallen apart. He had accused the Fenners of invading his territory and dumping silver in his streams. He had humiliated Lee Fenner by saying that word had reached him that two human girls had been killed, and probably by werewolves. Lee Fenner had denied it all, but it wasn't until Dominic suggested that he would make peace by marrying Cordelia that Mr. Fenner went completely crazy and booted him. That had been the night Katelyn had first seen the Switliski book in this room. Cordelia must have hidden it away right after that. Maybe she'd been afraid that Katelyn had already realized that she had it.

That was the same night she said the Hellhound came onto their territory. Fenner werewolves had searched the property for invaders, but had found none.

She put back the picture of Dom and tried to smooth the poster into place again. Then she left the closet and faced the bedroom door, not sure how to leave with her loot. She looked around, then grabbed Cordelia's Wolf Springs High sweatshirt off the back of her chair and put it on. She slipped the books under the front and hastily darted into the hall. Then she hurried through the living room to the entryway, where she had left her backpack and purse, and slipped the books inside. For good measure, she took off Cordelia's sweatshirt and stuffed it in, too.

And then something amazing happened: she scented Justin — a bit of sweat and leather — and heard his soft intake of breath. Was that his heartbeat? It *was*. Rapid.

Her senses had kicked in.

She stiffened and looked his way. He was standing beneath the arched transom, leaning on his elbow, gazing at her as if he wanted to memorize what she looked like. She pulled her hands from her backpack, trying to keep her own heart from going into overdrive.

"Hey," he said.

She didn't answer.

He sighed, grimaced. "I know you aren't used to the way we are. We're aggressive."

That's one way of putting it, she thought. She made a show of picking up her backpack. She didn't want him to know she was affected by him, but she was pretty sure he could tell.

"I'm sorry. I keep forgetting . . . a lot of things that I should keep in mind." He started to reach toward her. "I get scared, for you."

"Okay," she said. "Thanks."

"I'm going to drive you home."

"No training?"

He shrugged. "Uncle Lee's not here and there's some stuff we can talk through while we drive."

She felt awkward as she climbed into his truck. He looked over at her and she swallowed, didn't return the look. He turned on the engine and started down the road in silence. Trick always played music. It was like his life had a soundtrack.

Same as hers.

"We act different from humans," he said. "We're much more physical."

"Yeah, I'll say," she blurted.

To her surprise, he laughed. She slid a glance over at him to see him shaking his head and chuckling to himself. The dappled sunlight kissed his face.

"Just listen to me," he said in a voice that was almost a plea. "Do what I say. Things are so messy in the pack. Just . . . stop rocking the boat."

"Me? I didn't ask for any of this. I didn't ask to be bitten. I didn't ask to be kissed by you."

"No, you didn't ask for either of those things, but they happened and now we just have to cope."

"So, teach me."

"I'm trying." He shook his head. "You are one of the most stubborn people I've ever met."

And hearing him say that made her feel good, made her feel like she was still her own person. Like she was on the right track to take care of herself. With a thrill, she thought of the books secreted away in her backpack. She would survive and figure this all out.

"Look, life in a pack is all about rules. And one of the things that keeps you alive is knowing your place in the hierarchy of things."

"And I'm at the absolute bottom."

"Given all the circumstances, you are. That means you need to show respect to everyone."

"You mean I need to cower in front of everyone."

He sighed. "I know it might feel like that sometimes, but really it's not bad."

"And you think that just because you don't know any other way to live."

"Tell me your old life was better," he flung at her. "The way they act at school. Someone murdered your father. Your mother was completely alone."

"She had me," Katelyn said. *And I got her killed. I took that stupid painkiller and couldn't save her from the fire.*

"We have a whole pack. We have folks, just like those people down in Wolf Springs. It's not all about domination and rules. It's about belonging. We're tighter than most families. Our heritage goes back generations, and we know who we are." He looked hard at her. "Cordelia said you never once mentioned any other relatives except for your grandfather. I have a dozen within shouting distance. And if I'm in trouble, they'll help me."

Her lips parted. "You said her name," she said softly.

"Of course I did. Cordelia is not dead to me. I told you I would help you find her and I will." He sighed again. "But you have to help me in return. Lee's going to be asking me about your progress," he said. "I need good things to say. That are honest."

"My senses kicked in again today," she blurted. "I could smell you when you were behind me just then."

A smile broke across his face. "That's great. That should

start happening more and more. When we hit puberty, and we start to change, all that shifting back and forth hits us hard. It's really hard to deal with. But it smooths out. My senses are always heightened."

"That sounds hard, tiring." And also, kind of . . . sexy.

"You get used to it." His face softened. "I don't really even remember what it was like before. Like the world was flat, or something."

She let that sink in. She heard the pleasure in his voice. He was genuinely happy for her. To him, she had won the lottery.

"So, what's next on the training schedule?"

"Swimming," he said.

She was startled. "It's practically snowing," she said, glancing out the window at the gray sky.

His teeth were very white against his tanned skin as he smiled broadly at her. "You won't be cold. You're a werewolf, Kat."

By the time they reached the cabin, he had managed to shift her mood so that she was actually looking forward to their afternoon tomorrow. After he drove away, she hurried into her room to look at the books she had taken from Cordelia's cubbyhole. She opened the diary first.

I think I have a friend! She's the new girl, Katelyn McBride, only people call her Kat. She's really sweet and funny. I know I can never tell her the truth, but it would be so nice to start over. I pulled away when Justin and Jesse moved in, and I can't seem to get back in good with my old friends.

Katelyn smiled wistfully and read on, reliving the story of their growing friendship. And then . . .

I don't know why Daddy hates the Gaudins so much. As soon as I mentioned Dom's name at dinner, he hit me across the face and told me to go to my room. He said he would rather see me dead than with Dom. Dom says he thinks something is wrong with him. And I can only be with Dom if our packs unite, and Daddy gives his blessing. Otherwise, that would be the highest disloyalty, and I'm a Fenner born and raised. The weirdest thing of all is that a couple of years ago Daddy was the one who suggested I should look to Dom as a possible suitor.

And then . . .

I know I saw it. I know the Hellhound was at my window. And I know it's going to kill somebody. And I think it might be Kat. She's a mistake.

"God," Katelyn murmured, shutting the book. She could barely speak. "Oh, God." Justin spoke of protecting her, but he didn't even believe in the Hellhound. As far as she knew, she was on her own.

She thumbed through the rest of the diary for more mentions of the Hellhound. Cordelia had written about so many things that it would take hours to go through her diary. Laying it aside for the moment, Katelyn picked up the Switliski book.

She opened it and came face to face with an old engraving showing a monster ripping apart a man. Enormous glowing eyes blazed from inky washes of blurred shadow, huge fangs dripping with the man's blood as it ripped open his stomach, and two front claws were wrapped around his neck, yanking his head off. Beneath the illustration, a caption read:

THE HELLHOUND.

The old-fashioned illustration picture was so graphic. The Hellhound. Violent. Savage. That was what it did to you if you couldn't get away. Tore you apart. Mauled you to death.

Was that what Cordelia had seen? Was that what had been outside Beau's grandmother's window? And that had mauled two girls to death?

Is that the thing that calls to me in the forest?

She forced herself to look at the picture. There was a reason Cordelia had hidden this book from her. A reason Mr. Henderson had wanted to find it.

And now they were both gone. Cordelia was in hiding and Mr. Henderson was missing, maybe even dead.

No; they hadn't found his body, yet they'd found the others so fast. He couldn't be dead. But she still had the sneaking suspicion that she would never see the archaeologist-turned-history-teacher again, alive or dead.

She picked the book up and began to read.

Many believe that the Hellhound is, or was, a real creature.

Some say it might have been a large bear, perhaps mutated or deformed in some way. The more colorful stories about it can be found in *In the Shadow of the Wolf*, along with a complete discussion of the dark and violent history of Wolf Springs.

She groaned in frustration. That had been another book that had been missing from the school library. She and Beau had been searching for it. Maybe Cordelia had had that one, too.

Or maybe . . . someone else had taken it.

And that someone else had paid for reading it.

In the morning she was up early. Way too early. She dressed in dark clothing, slipping on her sneakers so she could move quietly. She put on her black leather jacket and scrawled a note for her grandfather, telling him she needed to get to school early to check some books out of the library. Pouring fresh, steaming coffee into a travel mug, she crept out of the house as silently as she could and drove away.

Her heart raced the entire way to school. It was still dark out, but she hoped that someone — the janitor, the principal, someone — would have unlocked the school early. Some-body had to be the first one there in the morning.

The sign atop the steepled roof was on. W-O-L-F-C-O-U-N-T-R-Y burned in red across the sky like a brand. Wolf Springs really was wolf country. Did the werewolves of Wolf Springs laugh at the ignorant humans unknowingly advertising their secret?

As Katelyn neared the school, she felt her courage deserting her. She couldn't believe what an idiot she was to have dreamed she could do this. Then she thought of Cordelia, and Mr. Henderson himself, and started to pull into the empty school parking lot, but immediately realized that a car parked there would look suspicious. She swerved back out, nearly crashing into a utility pole.

She drove a block away and then parked. By the time she shut the engine off, her palms were damp and her hands were shaking.

She got out of the car, checking one last time for the flashlight she had brought. No cars meant no people at all. Maybe she should wait until someone showed up.

Or maybe someone forgot to lock one of the doors. I should at least check. I came all this way.

Nervously, she trotted toward the school, crossing the deserted parking lot, then slowing when she realized she had broken into a run. She was moving too quickly; if someone saw her streaking toward the front entrance, they'd notice. Wind whipped brittle leaves along her path as traces of dawn painted the horizon. She headed toward the back of the large wood building, scanning the veranda for signs of movement. There was nothing.

Guarded on either side by skeletal bushes, there was a break in the wrap-around porch about a third of the way down, and inside, a green wooden door. Katelyn tiptoed up to it and waited a moment to steady herself.

Determined, she touched the door latch. The metal was icy, and she jerked her hand away. Then she realized that it didn't really bother her. She wrapped her hand around the knob and gave it an experimental twist. There was a snapping sound, and then it turned.

Oh, God, she thought. *Did I break it?*

She pulled the door open. Darkness stared back at her, but she was afraid to use her flashlight in case someone was inside the building.

Crazy, crazy, she told herself, and then she stepped inside.

Feeling her way with her feet and hands, she encountered something solid at hip-level. A desk, maybe. Was she in a classroom? Something grazed her other hip.

Then, as her eyes adjusted, a dim, watery light beckoned beyond a rectangle of black — the entrance to the classroom — and Katelyn stepped into the main hall of the school. The light was a plate-sized dome glowing from the ceiling at the opposite end, in the direction of her history classroom— and Mr. Henderson's office.

Her destination.

And, all of a sudden, she could see well. In the dark. Everything shimmered in oranges and reds. She grinned, and began to walk softly on the balls of her feet. Posters lined the walls, and she read them easily. There was a canned food drive for Thanksgiving. Tickets were going on sale for the Winter Formal. Life at any high school.

The school buildings had once been a Spanish church, and to her left, a large stained-glass window of a saint with a blue-eyed pet wolf seemed to gaze down at her. The man wore a robe; there was a halo around his bald head. But there were no blue-eyed wolves in the Ozarks. Had the artist who had created the window known that? Was the creature really a werewolf?

If the saint knew, he wasn't saying.

She was spooked; she felt watched. Cordelia had told her the school was supposed to be haunted. Back then, Katelyn had privately made fun of the gullible locals. There were enough tall tales about Wolf Springs to fill a dozen books: a weeping banshee searching for the children she had murdered; a thief who made nooses out of Spanish moss to hang his unsuspecting victims as they walked through the forest. A man who had changed into a bear.

She'd thought they were all so stupid, proof that she had been exiled to "Banjo Land." But the laugh had been on her.

She felt the back of her neck prickle, swore that the blue eyes of the stained-glass wolf tracked her, and she ran-walked the rest of the way to the classroom.

The door from the hall was unlocked and light spilled into the room from the windows, saving her one more time from using the flashlight. She could see the black rectangle behind Mr. Henderson's desk that was the door to his office.

Hurriedly she crossed the room, remembering the first time she'd walked into it. Trick had just nicknamed her "Kat," and she'd told Mr. Henderson that was her name. Now everyone called her Kat except Trick, who had whispered her real name, Katelyn, over and over on Halloween night, when she had broken down in grief and fear and he had been there.

The door to the office wasn't locked. But as she pulled it open, there was something stretched across the transom, like a thick spider's web — yellow police caution tape. NO TRESPASSING, it read, and she shied backward. They had wrapped the ruins of her home in yards of that tape, after they found, when they found . . .

"Mom," she whispered.

Lifting one leg up high, she snaked her way through.

Mr. Henderson's desk, usually cluttered with textbooks and papers, was bare. A chair that had contained more books sat empty.

It hadn't dawned on her that the police might take away his stuff. Grimacing, she looked around the room, then squinted at a low-lying bookcase, which still had a few books piled haphazardly, as though someone had looked through and then discarded them.

Katelyn reached back through the tape and quietly pulled the door shut. Then she hurried to the bookcase, dropping to her knees so she could more easily read the titles. He had the teacher's edition of her textbook; and lots of titles about the Civil War; and then at least half a dozen on Arkansas history.

Then book after book after book about treasure hunting, shipwrecks, ancient civilizations, and lost mines. A fleeting smile crossed her mouth. It seemed that Mr. Henderson was Wolf Springs' answer to Indiana Jones.

Unsure of how much time she had, she satisfied herself that *In the Shadow of the Wolf* was not on the shelves, then stood and moved to his filing cabinet. It creaked as she opened it, and the first thing she saw was a large file labeled HISTORICAL DETECTIVE. That had been the name of the assignment that had led to Katelyn and Cordelia researching the Madre Vena mine. She pulled open the file and started thumbing through the papers, which were from her class, filed in alphabetical order. FENNER, CORDELIA/McBRIDE, KAT, came up quickly, and she pulled it out. They'd gotten an A. He had circled the letter and written "GOOD WORK!" beside it. A few sentences were marked, and in a couple of places in the margins he had written, "CONCLUSIONS DRAWN HOW? BACK UP ASSERTION!"

On the last page, he had written, "SWITLISKI?" and "YOU TWO ARE DEF. ONTO SOMETHING." She was about to put the paper back when something slipped to the floor. She squatted and found a paperclip.

And then she saw something wedged between the file cabinet and the book case. She used the paperclip to fish it out.

A business card for Fenner Construction, Lee Fenner, Owner. She stared at it as the wheels turned in her mind. Had Mr. Henderson been trying to find the mine for Mr. Fenner? Is that why Lee had pushed Cordelia to choose it as their project?

Is that why he was missing? Had he found it?

Katelyn thought of the Hellhound. Had it been guarding the mine?

Or had someone else done something to her history teacher? Did the police have any leads? Obviously, they had missed the business card.

Then someone called out, "Hello?"

6

She must have made too much noise.

Katelyn tucked the business card in her pocket and ducked down behind Mr. Henderson's desk. Then she looked up with horror at the open filing cabinet, sure to attract attention if someone came in through the office door.

She could make up an excuse, she thought, trying to stay calm as she braced herself for discovery. She could say that she had lost something valuable. *Something belonging to my best friend.* With all the rumors going around about Cordelia and their history teacher, no one would blame Katelyn for trying to learn the truth.

She heard the classroom door open. Every muscle in her body tensed. Then there was silence. Her hearing snapped into overdrive and she heard a voice murmur, "Hello? Huh. Weird."

Then the door closed.

Mike Wright. A wave of fury shot through her, and she was stunned by how fierce it was. It was like somehow he embodied everything that was wrong about her life, this place. She was sure all the kids at her old school that had seen therapists on a regular basis would know a name for it.

Breathe.

She shut her eyes and clamped her jaw. Her chest heaved. Very slowly, her emotions ebbed. She waited a few seconds to make sure she was in control of herself, then reached up and eased the file drawer shut. Then she snaked back through the caution tape, and tiptoed through her history classroom.

As carefully as a tight-rope walker, she opened the door and peered into the hall. Seeing Mike and one of his redneck homies messing around with Trick's locker, she almost took off along the hall after them. She looked down and away, overcome again with the desire to hurt Mike.

Permanently.

Mike and the other boy started snickering, then went trotting on down the hall. Katelyn hurried over to Trick's locker. From what she could tell, they had used lipstick to write the F-bomb and the worst homophobic insult for "gay" Katelyn had ever heard. What a moron! In Santa Monica,

Mike and his minion would have been expelled for what he'd just done. But here?

Katelyn looked around for something to clean off Trick's locker. She finally grabbed some paper towels from the girls' bathroom and set to work, smearing the lipstick until it was illegible. If she had her way, Trick would never see what Mike had done. Mike was a bully and a moron and the stereotype of every prejudice she had held about the south. He was mean and stupid. And he seemed to be getting away with more than his share of nasty pranks.

I could just kill him, she thought.

She finished, tossed the paper towels, then snuck back outside. She was halfway across the parking lot, which now had five cars in it, including one painted like the Confederate flag, when her phone rang. Startled, she glanced down at the number. She didn't recognize it, but she answered anyway.

"Are you alone, cher?" said the voice on the phone, deep and masculine, touched with a lilt of Louisiana Cajun.

Katelyn was so startled she almost dropped the phone. It was Dominic Gaudin.

"Yes. Hello. Do you know what's happened?" she said urgently, hunching over the phone as if to muffle their conversation. It dawned on her that someone might be watching — someone not connected with her high school. A pack member, reporting her every move to Lee Fenner. She pushed that to the back of her mind. *So what?* she thought rebelliously, gazing around.

"*Oui.* She has called me," he said. "I'm coming for her."

Katelyn caught her breath. "Where is she?"

"She's alone, and frightened," he said. "She has no one."

"Me," Katelyn said firmly. She searched the lot. And then she felt a fillip of anger. She could see Mike Wright through the windshield of the Confederate flag car. He was smoking a cigarette and, from the way he was nodding his head, listening to head banger music. He hadn't noticed her. "She has me."

"She's not sure of that. She knows that her father has threatened to kill anyone who helps her."

Katelyn gave her head a shake. "I'll help her." She started to walk in Mike's direction and realized that was a bad idea. So she slipped into the shadows of the trees, making her way toward her parked car.

"Or maybe you'll tell them where she is, if I tell you. To get in good with your new family," Dom said.

She was speechless. "They are *not* my family."

"They are who you run with."

"No way. They are who I run *from*." She laughed bitterly.

"Ah," he said. "Then you'll come with her, when I come for her?"

Her stomach did a somersault and she caught herself giving another quick shake of her head before she remembered he couldn't see her. Part of her raced ahead to how wonderful it would be to be free of insane Lee Fenner and his whole dysfunctional family. And as far away from Justin as possible. She would miss her grandfather and Trick a lot.

"What would your pack think of me?" she asked him. *The mistake?*

"It doesn't matter what they *think* of you, cher. What matters is how they treat you. I am the alpha, and if I accept you, they will, too. We're more disciplined than the Fenners. And I'm not losing my mind."

All plusses. And she and Cordelia could be friends again. She had no one now.

"I'm afraid of what would happen to my grandfather." She decided to leave Trick out of the discussion. She didn't need to go around advertising to werewolves which humans in Wolf Springs they could use as leverage to get her to do what they wanted. "They might retaliate."

"Did *he* think of *you*, forcing you to come here?" Dom asked her. "He knew a girl had been killed in the woods. There has been a second one since your arrival. Your teacher is missing. Does he send you home?"

"How do you know . . . ?" she began, then trailed off. Had someone told Cordelia about Mr. Henderson? Did Dom Gaudin have a spy in Wolf Springs?

"He's still my grandfather," she said.

"And Cordelia is your best friend. She's the only real friend you have. And you're the only friend she has. She risked everything to keep you safe. She could have *died*. Her pack has been her whole life, and she's going to be lonely in my pack, until she makes some friends."

"Tell me where she is," Katelyn asked.

"You say 'please' and 'thank you' when you speak to me, cher," he said, not unkindly. "I'm an alpha. You need to show me respect."

"*Please* tell me where she is." She tried not to sound

impatient. All this ritualistic-manners stuff was annoying when there were bigger issues at stake. "Please."

"I will send someone to take you to her," he said. "Tonight. Be ready."

Alarm bells went off. "Where? What time?"

"Your cabin. Midnight."

"No, wait. I think they're watching me."

"We'll make sure they aren't," he said.

He disconnected.

—·— ⚔ —·—

Lunch.

And Trick was studying her. Since it was a cold November day, everyone was crowded inside the lunchroom. She would be welcome to sit at his table — his arty, slightly nerdy crowd really liked her — but she kept to her spot in the stairwell of the unused staircase at the back of the room. She was going through the motions of eating the peanut butter sandwich her grandfather had made for her the night before. He had added an apple. It was the exact lunch he made for her every day, and she found it very touching. All she was missing was a juice box and she'd have the lunch she used to pack for herself in elementary school. But the truth was, she had no appetite. Her phone call with Dom was swirling in her mind. Could she really leave? Just go? And then what? What kind of life would she have? She'd be a runaway. A statistic in the growing population of Wolf Springs citizens who had met bad ends.

And if she went missing, her grandfather would go crazy. Could she do that to him?

The questions were drowning her, so she made a pretense of texting so she could keep to herself and try to figure out her next step.

Even with staggered lunch periods, students were packed in tightly and the place was steamy, making the wolf mural that filled one wall look like it was sweating. Beau was also looking at her from across the room, and she kept up the show of texting so she would have a good excuse for avoiding him, too.

Then Kimi actually texted her.

Yo!

Hi, Katelyn texted back. *How's it? Jane?*

Left me 4 a boy! came the reply.

Abandoning texting, Katelyn called her. "*What?*" she said once the connection was made. "Some friend she turned out to be."

"You know how some girls are," Kimi said. "Girlfriends are what you have until you hook up with a guy. And, hi."

"Ridiculous!" It felt like old times. She wondered if that was why Kimi had started texting her again. But it didn't really matter, did it? They were talking.

"It's no guy you know," Kimi said. "Doesn't go to our school. He's a total stoner, though, so boring."

Katelyn was nearly giddy with the normalcy of their conversation. She almost burst into tears, which made no sense, but she held onto the phone with both hands and tapped her toes happily on the stair.

"So, big news," Kimi said. "My mom told me to tell you that she met a family court judge at Pilates who said she'd sign off on your emancipation papers if the case came before her. Which, *hell*, yeah."

Katelyn was stunned. Before she had flown out to Wolf Springs, Kimi had been lobbying for her to file for emancipation so Katelyn could stay there and live with Kimi's family. Kimi's mom was an attorney and she'd been willing to present the case and assure the judge she would provide Katelyn a home. Until that moment, though, Katelyn hadn't been convinced it could actually work.

"Making deals outside of court like that, isn't that illegal or something?" Katelyn asked, as butterflies danced in her stomach. Another chance to leave Wolf Springs dropped into her lap?

She ticked a glance in Trick's direction to find that he was still looking at her, and she turned her head slightly and cupped her mouth.

"If you could offer some proof about why Wolf Springs is a bad living environment, that would seal the deal," Kimi continued.

"Well, there was a murder recently."

"Right on! I mean, oh, how awful and sad. Anyone you know? Or knew?"

"I guess she was in some of my classes, but no, I didn't. And my history teacher is missing."

"Jeez. Is there a guy running around with a chainsaw, too?" Kimi asked, and Katelyn snorted.

If only I could tell you what's really going on, she said. *You wouldn't believe any of it.*

Then she inhaled the mingled scents of soap and leather.

Not Justin. Trick. Up close, she could see the stubble on his cheeks and chin, and the flecks of blue in his green eyes. Without warning, her vision telescoped and she felt as if she were falling into his eyes, into their depths, and she felt incredibly dizzy. Then she blinked to try to pull herself out of it.

"The missing teacher is a nice addition," Kimi said. "I'll tell my mom." Then she added, "Are you okay? I mean, were you close to him or anything?"

"Close," Katelyn ventured, testing out the idea. Then she gave her head a sharp shake. "Kimi, I need to go. I'll call you when I get home."

"From the cabin in the woods, wa ha ha," Kimi said. "Kiss kiss. You'll be home before you know it."

"Mwah. Sounds *poifect,*" Katelyn said, and hung up. She closed her eyes and pressed her finger against the bridge of her nose. She inhaled slowly, then exhaled, then opened her eyes again.

The telescoping was gone. But Trick was standing right there, in living color.

"Yes?" she said.

"I'm coming over to your house after school," he informed her. "I'm going to help your grandfather chop wood for the winter."

"Quaint. I'll be home later. I'm going to Cordelia's house again, just for a little bit." She almost added, *I'm going swimming,* but she doubted that Justin had been serious. It was practically sleeting outside.

"No, you aren't," he said. When she frowned at him, he

added, "It's not Cordelia's house anymore, is it?" He wasn't asking. He knew.

"Trick, I don't have to explain myself to you." The words came out more sharply than she had intended. *How* did he know?

"Your pappy told me to watch out for you." He narrowed his eyes and pursed his lips in displeasure. "He's trouble, Katelyn. You're new here. You don't know about his past."

"I think I know who you mean, and trust me when I say this, Trick. He has a girlfriend. They're practically engaged."

"That's never stopped him before," Trick retorted.

Her cheeks went hot.

"Are you okay?" he asked, and she nodded. "You don't look okay."

"I'm fine," she insisted.

"Don't go over there this afternoon. There is absolutely no good reason for you to go."

"Got it," she said, and she took a big bite out of her apple. He shifted his weight on his hip, upset and pissed off, and she took another bite. Clenching his teeth, he turned on his heel and walked away. She stared at his retreating back — okay, his butt — and smiled.

I'll get out of here, she told him. *I'll take you with me.*

She devoured her apple like it was a rabbit.

⋯ ⋙✦⋘ ⋯

Afternoon.

Katelyn walked to the end of the high-dive and stared down at Justin. Treading water in the steamy pool, he was bobbing in the water. His hair was slicked back, accentuating the planes and angles in his face, and she felt awkward in the swimsuit he had brought for her. She wondered if it was Cordelia's — likely, since it was so baggy on her. Cordelia was taller than she was.

"Just jump," Justin said. "You're not afraid, are you?"

He had no idea who he was dealing with. She backed up, ran, then sprang off the board. She executed several axial twists before she slid into the water without a splash. When she came back up, he was staring at her open-mouthed.

They were at the Y, where her grandfather had found her gymnastics lessons, and while it was almost as bad as Trick had said, there was a woman on staff who had been a gymnastics coach at Cal State Long Beach, and taught private lessons. She wasn't in, but Katelyn took her card.

Justin had rationalized the swimming by emphasizing the need to stay in shape. Whatever condition you were in as a human directly affected your strength and stamina as a wolf.

"What about your mental health?" she had asked him, and he'd clouded over.

"You mean Lee? He's just as unpredictable in wolf form as human," he said shortly. "Something's got to be done, and soon."

She told herself that she didn't care about any of that. It wasn't her business. All she had to do was steer clear of Lee Fenner.

And wait until midnight, and see what happened next.

The hours dragged by. Her grandfather asked her if something was wrong and then offered to play a game of Scrabble.

Her heart was only half in it, but when he won by 400 points she had to admire his skill. When she went upstairs she passed the time by reading more of Cordelia's diary. After Cordelia's first transformation, they had had a party, like a werewolf bat mitzvah, orchestrated well away from the kids who hadn't yet changed.

Cordelia had once had her daydreams and crushes, and even tried to get her father to accept a human boy into the pack. She had been told to break up with him and wait for a mate to be selected. *Selected?* Cordelia had wanted to date and have a boyfriend, but it turned out werewolf teenagers — or at least the daughters of the alpha — lived much more circumspect lives than Cali girls. Or pretty much any other girl, period. Boys, too, since they were also half of the equation. So maybe Justin didn't love Lucy. Maybe it was simply that they were facing an arranged marriage. Maybe love was supposed to come in time.

I don't care, she told herself. *I don't want him.*

Katelyn was afraid she'd fall asleep in her room — she had to get up so early every morning to drive to Wolf Springs High — so she put the diary down and did some stretching exercises. She wondered where Cordelia was. She wondered if the Fenners were watching her right now.

And what would happen to her tonight.

Finally, at five minutes to midnight, a text came in: *I am coming. Porch.*

She grabbed her purse, crept downstairs, and tiptoed out onto the porch. Anxiously shifting her weight back and forth, she sucked in her breath when a black BMW crept up the drive.

The passenger window rolled down and a handsome younger man who resembled Dom Gaudin silently gestured for her to approach. The door opened. She got in and shut the door, sitting beside him. The Beemer drove away.

"I'm Luc Gaudin," he said. He was all crazy red-blonde curls, heavy eyebrows, and deep-set brown eyes. "I'm Dom's younger brother."

"The Fenners—"

"Are not a problem," he said smoothly.

"Where are we going?"

"There's a warming hut," he said. "Ma'amselle Fenner took shelter there."

"Is it far?"

"Far enough. Are you hungry? Thirsty?" He peered at her. "Nervous?"

"I'm freaking," she said honestly.

"You didn't pack any of your belongings," he observed.

She gaped at him. It hadn't even dawned on her. Somehow it hadn't occurred to her that they would leave immediately. But why would they stick around?

She fell silent. He looked at her kindly and said, "Cordelia told us what happened to you. That someone attacked you."

Maybe one of the Gaudins had done it, to make Mr. Fenner look bad. Maybe Luc himself. But no, he had brown eyes. The werewolf that had bitten her had blue eyes, and werewolves didn't change eye color when they transformed.

"Yeah, I'm supposed to be all joyous about it," she said. "No offense, but I'm not."

He cocked his head. "A great shock, *non*?"

"That's putting it mildly." She blew air out of her cheeks. "Is she okay? I mean, was she hurt, or—"

"I don't know," he said. "You must understand. For us Gaudins, being banished from the pack is a fate worse than death. I would rather have my heart torn out than suffer what she has suffered."

She nodded, but she couldn't imagine *wanting* to be a member of the Fenner pack. From what little she had seen of the Gaudins, the Fenners were kind of like the loser werewolves.

"Do you know if there's a cure for being a werewolf?" she asked him hopefully.

He cocked his head. "Ah, I am sorry. We don't have one. But we've never looked."

She leaned her head on the back of the seat. "Why are you helping us?" she asked and then regretted it. "I mean, there've been hints that there's not exactly — that maybe there's bad blood—"

He sighed heavily. "When first our two packs settled in this country there was already a rivalry. We wanted to protect our borders, our hunting grounds. It is no different than our wild brothers or even the lion packs of Africa. And to complicate things we are human as well. We have nothing in common with one another but the fact that we change. Our culture, our heritage, our way of life are different. Over the years a thousand slights or discourtesies created more and more friction. For our part, we avoided them at all costs."

"What happened?" Katelyn asked, sensing that there was more to the story.

"More people settled on both our territories, clearing the forests, decreasing our lands and the animals we take sustenance from. The packs have grown larger but the resources smaller. And then, about eighty or ninety years ago, before you and I were even born, some terrible things happened around here."

Katelyn sat up straighter, sensing the importance of what was coming next.

Luc cleared his throat. "Even worse, *forty* years ago, it happened again: there was a string of murders among the people here. Savage. Brutal. The Fenners accused us, but we knew none of us could be responsible. Then, when we were having a pack meeting and all members were present, three more murders were committed, but this time they were on our lands. The Fenners had a rogue werewolf and it was killing, threatening the safety of all."

She felt cold all over, as if someone had just walked over her grave. The Fenners had lied to her. Even Justin.

Unless he's been lied to, too.

"Who was it?" she asked.

"Which Fenner? We don't know."

"Well, what made it stop?"

"That was the strangest part. It just did. A short while later we were informed that Lee Fenner was the new alpha and we hoped that the pack had sorted it out, and that he could keep his people in check in the future. But the intrusions onto our land had only just begun," Luc said, his voice hardening. "They began to poison our streams with silver. As I'm sure you know, a werewolf may touch silver, though it is painful, but it must not pierce the skin and enter the bloodstream or one becomes incredibly sick and will probably die. We learned the hard way that drinking the silver would also kill us. I will never forget the day that I watched my sister die, screaming, as silver in our water burned her from the inside."

Katelyn shuddered. "That's awful," she whispered.

Luc nodded. "My brother, he wishes for peace, not war. He once thought that a union between him and Cordelia could end the suffering. But now those dreams are gone."

Which meant there was nothing else standing in the way of war, Katelyn realized. Dejected, afraid, she crossed her arms and looked out the window.

"You still haven't answered my question. Why are you helping us?" she asked.

Luc flashed her a smile. "Why does any man do anything?"

"I don't know."

"Love, cher. Dom is in love with Cordelia and he would not see her come to harm."

After countless twists and turns, the car pulled to a stop, and Luc smiled at her.

"We're here."

Katelyn undid her seat belt and jumped out, racing toward a narrow A-frame building sided with shingles. Smoke was pouring out of a chimney. There were no windows.

The door of the hut flew open and Cordelia stood framed in the doorway. Katelyn ran over and began to throw her arms around her, then stopped. Cordelia's face was puffy with crying, and she looked as if she hadn't eaten or slept in days.

"Hey," Katelyn said awkwardly, then raised her head as

Dom came up behind Cordelia and put a hand on her shoulder.

"Ma'amselle Katelyn McBride," Dom said. "A pleasure to meet you in the flesh."

"Thank you for finding her," Katelyn replied.

"She found us." He gave her shoulder another squeeze. "I'll leave you two to talk."

Cordelia stepped out of the hut so he could get around her. She gave her head a little bob and he inclined his head rather imperiously. He looked at Katelyn.

"You need to lower your head to me," he said.

"Oh." She tucked in her chin and mentally rolled her eyes. *God, if Kimi or any of her old friends could see her now* . . . But in her encounters with other packmates, she'd seen lower-ranked were-boys go all Geisha like this, too. Turned out you had to behave a certain way according to your rank, not your gender—aside from a certain amount of human-woman tending of the male ego that seemed more common in Wolf Springs.

He chuckled and walked to the car. "Luc and I will go for a drive."

Cordelia turned around and led the way into the hut. A fire was roaring inside a metal fireplace, and as soon as they were both inside, Cordelia threw her arms around Katelyn and began to cry. Katelyn did, too, feeling such tremendous relief that she had to sit down on the sleeping bag stretched out on the floor before she fell down.

Cordelia moved two grocery bags out of the way and plopped down next to Katelyn, burying her face in her hands.

"Oh, Kat," she said brokenly. "I want to go home!"

"Why?" Katelyn blurted, then caught herself and put her arms around Cordelia again, and her friend leaned her head on Katelyn's shoulder. "I mean, oh my God, Cordelia, look at your family. Your father's . . ." She trailed off, realizing that Cordelia already knew how bizarre her family was.

"You don't know what it's like to be born a Fenner," Cordelia said. "We have the blood of the Fenris Wolf running through our veins. In the werewolf world, we're revered. We're like gods."

Katelyn thought about Regan and Arial, overdressed and over made-up, slinking around like they were practicing for some Southern Gothic play. The delight they'd taken in ordering Cordelia to run away as fast as she could before they caught her. Justin said werewolves were aggressive, but the Fenners were flat-out extreme. That didn't sound very godlike to her.

"What's it like in Dom's pack?" Katelyn asked. "You'll be with him, and he's the alpha, right?"

"Kat, Kat," Cordelia hitched. Then she lifted her head. "I'm nearly eighteen years old, the daughter of the alpha. If I join another pack, I'll be a traitor. How would *you* treat an outsider who had been branded a traitor?"

The question was absurd. Katelyn didn't live in a world where thoughts like that occurred.

"I thought *you* called *Dom*," she said, a bit at a loss.

Cordelia wiped her face with both hands. "I did. I didn't know what else to do. But he wants me to declare my loyalty as soon as we get to Louisiana. In front of everyone. I — I need time." She dropped her hands to her lap and stared pleadingly at Katelyn. "I need my daddy to forgive me and take me back."

Katelyn played with the slick fabric of the sleeping bag, unaccountably disappointed. She didn't see leaving with Dom and Cordelia as a clearer path to her own happy ending. Cordelia might be the daughter of an alpha, but Katelyn was just a *mistake*.

Except . . . I'm immune to silver, she remembered.

"Maybe Daddy just needs time," Cordelia said, reaching into one of the grocery bags. She pulled out a packet of tissues and blew her nose. "If I can just go with Dom without declaring myself, and then Daddy asks me to come home . . ." She stared at Katelyn with huge, pleading eyes. "You'll come with me, right?"

Here it was, the time for her decision. Katelyn looked at her friend, and her mind raced.

And then it came to her.

"Cordelia, your father wanted you to find the silver mine," she began.

Cordelia nodded. "Kat, I — I hid some stuff from you. That book Mr. Henderson wanted? I had it. And my daddy had Mr. Henderson over for dinner and asked him to help him find the Madre Vena. I didn't tell you that, either."

Katelyn thought of the business card she had found. *Maybe Mr. Henderson is not around because he's busy looking for the mine.*

No, she didn't buy it.

"Mr. Henderson is missing," Katelyn said carefully. "Could something have happened to him?"

"Missing?" she asked, growing pale. "What do you mean?"

"He stopped coming to school. They don't know where he is." Katelyn would never tell her what people were saying about Cordelia and him.

Cordelia covered her mouth with both hands. Her eyes grew enormous and she went from pale to chalk white. "The Hellhound," she whispered. "It guards the mine. What if it got him?"

The door to the hut opened and Dom Gaudin stood in the doorway. Cordelia visibly jerked, and she grabbed Katelyn's hand. She looked even more terrified.

"Ladies?" Dom Gaudin said. "We can't risk staying here much longer. Is Ma'amselle McBride coming with us?"

"Don't leave me," Cordelia said under her breath. "I need you, Kat. I risked my life for you."

She did. Katelyn owed her.

Dom turned his head and spoke in French to someone who was still outside.

Her stomach in a knot, Katelyn took a breath and whispered in a rush before she lost her nerve, "What if I looked for the mine? And if I find it, you can tell your father that you found it."

"Oh," Cordelia murmured. "Oh, would you do that?" She looked over Katelyn's shoulder at Dom. "Maybe I should stay. Help you. But the *Hellhound* . . ."

"The time's come," Dom said, coming into the hut. "We don't want to linger on Fenner territory. It's time to go. With, or without you, Miss Kat?"

"Without," Katelyn said. "I have to stay and try to get the

others to see reason, to get Lee to forgive Cordelia. Then . . ." she thought of what Luc had told her in the car. "Maybe then there can be peace."

Dom sighed heavily. "Peace is a dream I once cherished. I would urge you to abandon it, but I can see that you have not lost hope. It is not an easy thing to leave all that you know behind. I must warn you, though, we cannot risk coming back for you."

"I understand," Katelyn said, even as she could hear Cordelia crying.

From a distance she heard a sort of whistling sound. Dom spun around with what Katelyn recognized as a French curse falling from his lips. "We will be found. Hurry."

He grabbed Cordelia around the waist and ran with her, propelling her toward the idling BMW. Katelyn ran behind, but before she could climb in, Dom held up his hand.

"I'm sorry — we must go and we cannot go the way you were brought. If you are caught with us you are dead. Your home is that way," he said, pointing through the forest. "Go quickly before they find you here."

Then Dom turned from Katelyn and jumped into the car as well. The wheels kicked up dirt and pine needles, then disappeared down the road.

7

Katelyn had never been a fan of conspiracy theories, but as she watched the car disappear, she began to believe. The Gaudins had told her the Fenners were nowhere near, but had they simply lured her to the hut, then dumped her there? Alone?

She realized she had no way home. All she had was her cell phone. She stared down at it, wondering if she dare call Trick or Justin. Now that she knew where Cordelia was going, she wasn't sure if there was anything to be gained by bringing Justin into the picture. Handsome and charming when he wanted to be, not entirely to be trusted. She was certain he would be able to tell that Cordelia had been in the warming hut — and that the Gaudins had been, too.

But if she called Trick for a ride, she'd have to explain what she'd been doing out there alone. Maybe he'd come anyway, if she could even manage to describe where she was. She tried her GPS function, but it wasn't working. Maybe the warming hut was a known landmark.

It was a bad idea to go into the woods by herself. If this were a horror movie, she'd tell that moronic girl on the screen that she deserved to die a hideous death because she was too stupid to live. But Gaudin had said the members of her pack were coming — and they would kill her.

Swallowing her pride and her anxiety, she texted Trick, but it didn't send. She winced and tried calling him. Another fail. So, no calling for help.

That left the "dying in the woods" option.

Her heartbeat picked up as she stared out at the vast expanse of trees, and jerked. There were some blotches on the trees and they were *glowing* a bright red. And she could see streaks of shimmering crimson in the dirt where the car had been.

She trotted to the closest tree and peered tentatively at the glimmering blob. It was a handprint. Maybe one of the Gaudins had touched it while making sure there were no Fenners around? The streaks of red on the ground were like neon tire tracks. Correction: they *were* tire tracks.

She didn't know how she was seeing them. Maybe they were heat-generated. If that were the case, they would disappear as they cooled. Now was the time to strike out, instead of waiting until morning.

But Dom had said they weren't going back the way they had brought her. Which meant at some point they would split from the trail they were on. And if she was very lucky there would be a fainter set of tracks showing the other path. Decided, she headed out.

The tire tracks were still glowing. In fact, the forest itself was glowing — branches, leaves, even pebbles and earth — shimmering, shining. It was like a fairyland. Entranced, Katelyn had trouble concentrating on the path of the tire tread as she took in the luminous night. Was this how werewolves saw the world? It was so beautiful it made her gasp.

Go, she told herself, and although she had planned to carefully walk the route, she broke into a run. She could almost see her entire body shining as she raced beside the orangish streaks on the ground. Instead of being afraid, she was exhilarated, and she ran even faster. She didn't know how she kept from tangling her feet together but she kept going. Her arms flew out to the sides and brushed silvery leaves as she flew past. Faster, and faster. She laughed and the sound echoed in her head.

Supernatural, she thought. *I'm supernatural.*

And it felt *good*. Wonderful. She had never felt so strong. Before she realized what she was doing, she vaulted over a tree trunk, did a flip, and stuck her landing. Then she started running again.

And finally there were two sets of tire tracks and she veered off to follow the fainter ones. She could barely see those but she ran as fast as she could through the dark twists and turns. And finally the glittering streaks were gone.

But as she slowed to a halt another sense took over. She could smell the faintest scent of wood smoke: it had to be a cabin, hopefully her grandfather's. She ran toward it, and just as she began to tire, she caught sight of the cabin itself. Somehow she had gotten around behind it and she was approaching from the back.

Am I busted? she thought, and cautiously approached, spinning various stories about why she had been out in the woods after midnight. Going for a walk?

When two girls had been murdered, and a teacher was missing?

She walked up onto the back porch and tried the kitchen door. Locked, but she had a key — her grandfather had made a duplicate for her because he had rarely locked his doors until she'd arrived. She kicked off her muddy boots and almost fell through the doorway. Grabbing a glass, she went to the kitchen sink. The curtains were open and she stared out into the back yard. If there were no Fenners on duty tonight, then why not? How had the Gaudins made sure she wouldn't be seen when she got into the BMW?

Maybe they lied to me. If Dom thought I'd be going with them, it wouldn't have mattered.

She gulped down glass after glass of water. She was starving, too, but she didn't want to risk waking up her grandfather and having him ask awkward questions. She went upstairs, pausing by Mordecai's door. She didn't hear him snoring. What if he'd done a bed check and found her gone?

Catching her lower lip between her teeth, she cracked open the door. Although the room was dark, she could see into it. There was his bed.

With no one in it.

Her heart sank.

What if he's out there looking for me?

She shut the door and went into her own room. Sweaty from her run — just how far had she traveled? — she decided to take a quick shower. She hastily shampooed her hair and put on an oversized Samohi — Santa Monica High — T-shirt and a pair of sweats. Time to sleep.

Taking her blanket and pillow, she went down the stairs into the living room. As usual, a fire was blazing away. Her phobia about fire had been so great when she'd arrived that she couldn't even handle being in the living room — a fact she had kept well hidden from her grandfather. But after struggling with her conscience, she hesitantly threw the business card in the fire to erase possibly incriminating evidence — thereby protecting the pack. Despite the fire, she felt a cold chill. She sacked out on the leather couch and stared at the blaze as she kept replaying the entire weird night.

I'm going to find that mine, she swore. *I'm going to find what's in it. And I'm not going to get killed by the Hellhound in the process.*

⊱ ⊰

She didn't realize she'd dozed off until she jerked awake to the sound of the front door opening. Footfalls crossed the room well behind the couch, then went up the stairs. A door opened and closed. Her grandfather.

I should let him know I'm home, she thought. She lay on the couch for a couple of minutes debating what to do. Maybe he hadn't realized she'd been gone. But maybe he'd been looking for her. Finally her conscience won out. Nothing in her wanted to, but she knew what it was like to worry. So she went and crept up the stairs, facing the music, and rapped lightly on his door.

"Grandpa?" she called softly.

"Katie?" There was a rustling, and then he opened his door. He was wearing pajamas. "Is there something wrong?"

"Oh." Holy cow, she *wasn't* busted. Now what? "I thought I heard a noise."

He frowned, looking concerned. "Like what?"

Like you? Maybe she'd awakened him when she'd come in, and he'd gone outside to look around. She shrugged. "Um, maybe like a car?"

He covered a yawn. "I'll go see." He took his rifle off the wall and she followed him to the front door. He opened it, peered around, shook his head, and closed the door. Then he went to the back yard. She started to get scared, wondering if there were Fenners out there. What would happen if he spotted one of them?

"Nope."

"I'm sorry," she said. "I didn't mean to wake you up."

"That's okay, honey," he said. "I've probably slept long enough for one night anyway. Old guys don't need much sleep. Anything ever bothers you, don't hesitate to come get me."

He went back upstairs, looking expectantly over his

shoulder. She followed him, and when he went into his bedroom she tiptoed over to the couch to get her blanket and pillow. In the silence, her hearing went into overdrive. She could hear the creak of her grandfather's bed as he turned over, and a moment later he was snoring softly. The crackling of the fire was as loud as thunder. And outside she could hear small noises from the engine of his truck as it cooled off.

He lied to me, she thought. He hadn't been home, either. She looked up at the second floor of the cabin as if she could see through the floor and ask him why. But apparently werewolves didn't have X-ray vision.

Gazing cautiously out the window, she thought she saw something move in the shadows. She locked the door and hurried back upstairs.

⊷ ⊱⊰ ⊶

Katelyn was tired when she drove to school the next morning. The crowded hallways seemed even harder to deal with. People had B.O. or were wearing so much perfume that she wanted to gag. The heat was on and it was sweltering. Miserable, she pulled in her shoulders and tried to get through the crowd as fast as possible. She had almost made it to the door of her first class when she collided with Mike Wright.

"Hey, bitch, watch it," he said, glaring down at her.

And without thinking she made a fist and would have punched him in the stomach except that someone jostled her from behind and instead of hitting him, her fist flailed at thin air.

Mike didn't see it; he just walked on, muttering about

stupid blind bimbos. Adrenaline coursed through her and she glared at him with hatred.

In all the turmoil, she had forgotten that it was a minimum day. Which meant no lunch period to get through, though at the end of it, Trick was standing beside her locker. An ambush.

Nervously she walked up to him and he said, "I was texting Sam last night, then chatting with her."

"How is she?"

Sam's party had been the site of their one and only date, the night that Katelyn had been attacked and bitten. Sam had moved to Little Rock soon after as her parents had split up and her mom had a new job. Before leaving, she'd given Katelyn some news clippings and a pen-and-ink drawing of a heart-shaped boulder and a waterfall that her mom had found when sorting out some old boxes. The image had struck a chord, but Katelyn couldn't place why.

"She's glad she moved." He smiled sourly. "I told her about Mr. Henderson and we got to talking about everything that's been going on. Her mom overheard the doctor talking on his phone when they brought Becky's body in." Becky had been the second girl to have been mauled to death out in the forest. Katelyn shivered. But Trick was continuing. "Apparently, the police said they had evidence that showed she'd been sneaking into the Inner Wolf Center. And that her body had been moved after she was killed."

"Sam told me the same thing," Katelyn said. Sam's mother had worked as a nurse at the local clinic.

"I think she told Beau, too, as he's been emailing her. Told her his grandmother saw something in her window and then had a stroke."

Katelyn frowned. She didn't know Beau had told anyone else.

"So now Mr. Henderson's missing. Though I guess Cordelia's family has accounted for her?" Trick looked at her, and she felt her face prickle. Did he know?

"She's not home," she said cautiously, "but no one has told me where she went. Some kind of family stuff, I think. Her family have talked to the school, apparently."

He shrugged as if that was a good enough reply. Trick really hadn't liked Cordelia.

"I'm not going to sit around and let more people die," he announced.

"What are you going to do?" She tried to sound casual, but she was afraid for him. He needed to stay well away from the secrets of Wolf Springs.

"Well, Sam got me thinking, and maybe there's something odd out at that Inner Wolf Center. I'm going to go check it out."

"What, just walk in and say hi?" A light, panicky sensation threw her off balance, and Katelyn nearly dropped one of her books. She and Cordelia had had a run-in with two slightly drunk executives who had been taking a seminar there. Jack Bronson, the man in charge, had arrived and booted their butts on the spot. But Katelyn still didn't trust him.

"Maybe, but we can sneak in around the back — there's a way through the old buildings," he said. "Anyway, I can't think of anything else to do. And I really liked Mr. Henderson." He paused, and then he said, "Do you want to come with?"

What she wanted was for him to walk away. But she knew Trick well enough to know that he wouldn't. And if he found out something that could help her, it would be good.

"What the heck," she said, and he smiled at her. He hadn't done that much lately. It was nice.

They took his Mustang. Soon they were speeding along a one-lane, back-country road. She rested her head against the back of her seat, remembering half days at Samohi when she and Kimi would pile into Kimi's convertible and drive to the beach. There was no beach in Wolf Springs.

Wolf Springs was situated in a valley, surrounded by heavily forested hills. As they crested the rise, she saw a battered old sign that said WOLF SPRINGS CLUB. She and Cordelia had read about the old hot springs resort. A man claiming to be the descendant of the Spaniard who'd first discovered the mine had died of a heart attack on the grounds. In his last, agonizing moments, he'd claimed he'd been attacked by the Hellhound.

The car drove into deep shadow, and then Trick whistled in appreciation, prompting Katelyn to peer up through the windshield. Above them, sharp silhouettes of steep Victorian gables, cupolas, and arches frowned down at them. As she moved her head, the sun glinted off squares of leaded-glass windowpanes, disappearing where the glass had been blown out. It was a craggy ruin, unwelcoming, and Katelyn felt the hair on the back of her neck rise up, like the hackles of a wolf.

"This is the back way in," Trick said. He waggled his brows at Katelyn. "We can just . . . help ourselves."

"See, this is why you get in trouble with the law," she said with asperity.

"You can stay in the truck," he offered.

She was tempted. The place looked very scary.

"Are you going to take your gun?" she asked him.

"Am I Southern?" he replied. "It's under your seat. Where it always is," he added.

She made a point of raising her feet off the ground.

"I thought your pappy drilled that nonsense out of you," he drawled.

"He taught me how to shoot, not how to like guns."

They got out and he retrieved the weapon. As he emptied out his backpack, she put a hand on his wrist. He looked down at it, and then at her.

"Let's think this through. You got in trouble for breaking into people's houses."

"*Allegedly.*"

"And now we are sneaking onto private property *with a gun?*"

"It's okay." He put the gun in his backpack and slipped his hands through the straps.

It was cold in the darkness; among the ferns and tall, brown grass, Trick pointed out a staircase of tumbled-down stone, and said, "I'll go first."

At the top of the stairs, a chain link fence sagged with NO TRESPASSING signs. Weeds had grown among the diamonds. Katelyn found herself listening for the telltale hum of electricity, in case the fence was armed. As far as she could tell, the coast was clear.

"This is the original resort," Trick said. "I remember some grumbling when Jack Bronson came in to build the center, cuz he didn't tear down any of the old buildings — I guess the town had expected him to. Said they were a hazard. Sam got all conspiracy theory on me on the phone last night. Said maybe there was something in them Bronson didn't want anyone to see."

As he spoke, Katelyn's vision sharpened. She covered her surprise with a little cough. Then she did a careful sweep for video cameras or guards while Trick worked on a stretched-out section of fencing, trying to make it big enough for them.

Just as they stepped through, the sound of drums filled the air, followed by howls, and she reflexively grabbed Trick's hand as his arm came around her, shielding her. Then they both exhaled, letting out some tension as the Inner Wolf executives did the same.

"Dang," Trick said without letting go of her, and she nodded.

Together they stomped through waist-high vegetation. They came to a three-story brick building — the tallest of the ruined structures — and Katelyn held back deliberately as they moved the rotted wood door, which had fallen off its hinges. Trick reached into his backpack and pulled out a flashlight.

They crept into a hallway littered with trash, old bottles, and remnants of upholstered furniture. Trick shined his flashlight on an old oil painting of beautiful grounds landscaped with bushes and statues: in the center, in front of a brick building — maybe this very one — was a beautiful fountain featuring a ring of statues of wolves with their heads thrown back. On the top of the fountain, a single wolf poised as if to attack.

They left the corridor to find themselves in the entrance to the building, a cavernous space with a vaulted ceiling and a grand staircase that led to the next two levels, fanning off into balconies on each of the two floors. Katelyn could almost see ladies in fine velvet gowns and men in top hats and Victorian suits strolling along the balustrades.

They tiptoed up the marble stairs, Trick angling the light so they could see where they were going. He reached behind himself and took her hand as if it were the most natural thing in the world, and she left her hand in his.

"I wonder how many people have died here," Trick said quietly. "I mean, I don't believe in ghosts, but this place feels . . . *busy.*"

She felt it, too. Like things sliding past them, around them — shadows, whispers. Then she remembered the name of the man who had suffered his fatal heart attack — Barry Cazman. She'd read about him during their research on the mine. He had died on the grounds in 1937.

And he had a drawing in his pocket, she remembered. *Could it be the drawing that Sam had given her? Sam's mother had found it with other old papers in their attic. There was a piece of weathered paper with the sketch of a waterfall and a heart-shaped boulder in it. Cazman described it as a map, and said it showed the entrance to the Madre Vena silver mine.*

Her mouth dropped open as she made a connection:

Which is exactly what's in one of the paintings that got taken from our cabin.

In all the chaos after the bite, she had never put the two — the paper and the painting — together. Had someone broken into their cabin specifically to get that painting? What about the other painting? Maybe they'd stolen a few other things — the silver — to cover their tracks. She'd put the clippings in her dresser drawer and hadn't thought to look for them when Justin had driven her home; she'd had a lot of other things on her mind.

"You okay?" Trick asked her. "You're trembling."

She shook herself. "Yeah, sorry," she said. It wasn't something she could share with him. Or anyone. For sure she wasn't telling Justin. It was a bad feeling to know how utterly alone in this she really was.

They reached the top floor, which was completely dark. Trick's flashlight revealed mounds of rubbish piled like haystacks. She heard squeaking. Rats. Her lips began to curl and she could feel a low rumbling starting in her chest. Horrified that she was reacting like a wolf and not a girl, she pressed her hand against her mouth.

Trick stopped, flashlight swinging back and forth. "Did you hear something?" he whispered.

She could feel panic rising in her but she forced it down. "My stomach growled. I missed lunch," she said.

"We'll get something after this," Trick said. "I'm hungry, too."

Mincing along, the two of them moved onto one of the balconies; then, drawn by watery light ahead of them, they walked toward a wall of leaded-glass windows so dirty the sun could barely penetrate them.

When they reached the glass, Trick rubbed one of the panes with a wadded-up paper napkin from his backpack. Layers of grime smeared away to reveal a blurry oval. Trick peered through it first, then grunted and gestured to Katelyn.

There was the old fountain, encircled by bits and pieces of wolf statues, topped by the headless statue of the alpha. Beyond, there was another chain link fence; and beyond that, they were staring at an amphitheater filled with bare-chested men whose faces and chests were smeared with crimson. Many of them were pounding wildly on drums. As if by a pre-arranged signal, they all threw back their heads and howled.

"Oh, my God," she said. "That can't be blood. That has to be red paint, or body makeup."

"Yeah," he replied, sounding unconvinced.

"That's it! Let out your inner wolf!" said an amplified voice.

Katelyn recognized it from their confrontation outside the Wolf Springs tavern. Jack Bronson himself was standing on the stage in a polo shirt and Dockers, wearing a headset.

"Be free! Feel the power of the wolf surging through you!"

"Bozo," Katelyn muttered.

Trick jerked his head toward her. "Did you hear that? Was that you again?"

She cocked her head, unsure what he was referring to.

"I heard a *real* growl," he said. "Like an animal." He took her hand again, clenching it hard. "*Kat, there's something in here with us.*"

Katelyn's heart began to pound as Trick stood statue-still. She hadn't heard anything.

Oh no, what if it was me? What if she had growled again and hadn't even realized? *But what if it* wasn't *me?*

Her heart pounded even harder and her hearing went crazy. She could hear Trick's breathing, fast, frightened; his heartbeat, strong and muffled. The idiots outside the window, as they howled for all they were worth, then stopped.

And in the silence she heard something else.

Click. Click. Click.

8

Dread caught Katelyn. It was the sound from her nightmares, claws clicking on the ground as a creature walked
through the darkness.

Trick was still clenching her hand and she yanked on it as
she ran-walked back across the room. Then she couldn't contain her instinct to flee any longer.

"Run!" she whispered.

She didn't need to tell Trick twice. He was right beside her
as they raced across the debris in their path. They made it to
the stairs and the beam from his flashlight bounced and

skittered across the marble. Katelyn wanted to tell him to turn it off, but realized that her werewolf senses were allowing her to see in the dark — he didn't have that advantage.

Trick gripped the handrail tight as they descended in a blur. Katelyn had always been sure-footed, an essential skill for a gymnast and a dancer, and as the old marble was slippery and covered with layers of dust, her shoes slipped against the stone, but she was able to adjust her weight to keep herself from sliding.

Somewhere in the darkness, a growl echoed off the walls.

It was followed almost immediately by the crash of splintering wood as the ancient railing gave way beneath Trick's hand and plummeted into the darkness. Trick began to fall as well, yanking Katelyn off balance. She landed hard on her knees, throwing out her free hand to stop herself from nose-diving over the edge while the flashlight cartwheeled end over end, casting crazy shadows over the walls and ceiling before shattering on the floor.

Trick was trying to cling to another part of the banister but it, too, gave way with a crack, and a moment later he was dangling above the inky darkness, holding tightly to Katelyn's hand. He was going to fall — probably die — if she couldn't save him.

Adrenaline surged through every cell, every nerve, and she stretched out her legs, testing the base of the banister with her feet, trying to find a solid section to brace herself against. Finally she found one and she reached down and caught Trick's free hand, then arched her back, pulling for all she was worth.

Trick practically came flying and he landed on top of her with a grunt. He quickly rolled over and sat up.

"She shoots, she scores," he said. "Thank you, gymnastics."

"And a lot of adrenaline," she added quickly, covering for the fact that she had just shown far more strength than she should have.

He jumped to his feet and helped her up. "Superkat, you saved my life."

Before she could say anything, the hair on the back of her neck raised as another growl erupted close at hand. Menacing, threatening. She turned slowly.

A large German shepherd was crouched a few steps below them, fangs exposed, eyes flashing. It was a guard dog, she realized with renewed panic, which meant there were probably people from the Wolf Center on their way to catch the intruders.

The dog growled low in its throat; a warning, a challenge. "Easy, boy," Trick said.

It snapped its jaws at him and he drew back his hand.

"Not easy," he said. "What are we going to do?"

Katelyn heard more growling, lower, deeper. *It's coming from me.* She didn't know what to do but she went with her gut. Hoping the darkness concealed her actions, she curled her own lips up, revealing her plain, ordinary human teeth.

At least, she hoped they were human. She had been told that older members of the pack could change at will, but that couldn't happen to her, could it? Impossible. She was young and she'd only been a werewolf for a few weeks. But she shouldn't be able to touch silver, and she could.

What if Trick sees? What if I hurt him?

She could feel her mind racing into overdrive as she allowed her wolf-part to begin to show, to project itself toward the German shepherd, her low growl still rumbling in the back of her throat. And the dog whined and dropped his head and tail.

She blinked in shock. He had backed down. *From me.* She held her hand out and he came forward and licked it.

"Let's get out of here," Trick said, edging around the dog.

She nodded. She gave the dog a gentle pat on the head and trailed after Trick, running her tongue over her teeth. They still felt human. And she was no longer growling.

They made it to the ground floor and were almost at the front door, the dog trotting next to them, submissive. Something pricked at the back of her mind. Something was still wrong and she suddenly realized what it was: the dog's nails weren't making a clicking sound on the marble. They must have been clipped short.

But she had *heard* a clicking sound.

That meant that something else was stalking them.

With a cry she grabbed Trick's arm, tore through the door and flew back toward the Mustang. When they reached the fence, she shoved him through and his sleeve tore on one of the corners. She stopped, trying to collect the incriminating fabric, but it just shredded into a smaller piece. And there was no time, for in the back of her mind she could still hear the clicking of phantom nails.

Trick had reached the Mustang and was yanking open the driver's side door.

Moving on, Katelyn caught the glint of something silver on the ground in the bushes and her eyes seemed to zoom in on it: a piece of flatware — a knife — with a shield and a rose on the handle. It resembled the McBride stained-glass coat of arms in the cabin window. A piece of the silver stolen from her grandfather's cabin? For a moment she thought about grabbing it and going back to use it on the fabric stuck in the fence, but she could *feel* something watching her so she left the knife where it lay and jumped into Trick's car.

"Go, go, go!" she shouted as soon as she'd closed the door.

He took off fast, the truck fishtailing around the first turn. "What happened, Kat?" he panted, sucking in air. "What did you see?"

"I think . . . I think there was another dog," she said.

"Damn, girl," he said, sliding a glance at her as he chuckled. "You handled that like a superspy."

"My friend back home raised dogs," she lied.

"Kimi?"

"Different friend."

They drove in silence for a minute or two. Finally Trick spoke. "Okay, next time front door."

"We have a problem," she announced.

He looked at her.

"We left part of your shirt behind, and fingerprints and stuff. And I saw a piece of my grandmother's stolen silver by the fence."

His brows shot up. "Let's see it."

"I left it." She made a face. "I freaked out and I just kept running." She looked at him. "I can't exactly tell the police I found it whilst breaking and entering."

"Which side of the fence was it on?" He started to turn the car around. They would fishtail again if he wasn't careful. "Inside is trespassing, or B and E. Outside is happening by. And how freaky is that? So did one of those crazy bastards break into your house?"

Kat paused to think on this. Then, "Does the sheriff have an anonymous tip line?" she asked.

He blinked. "I have no idea. Despite the rumors, I'm not all that knowledgeable about my friendly law enforcement agency." He looked at her. "We have to go back." At her disbelieving expression, he added, "Soon."

Katelyn felt like an idiot for not grabbing the knife as they fled, but she was still buzzing with adrenaline on the way back to the school parking lot. She didn't really know what Trick had hoped to accomplish, but it had been a daredevil thing to break in in broad daylight. What had Cordelia liked to say about Trick? That he was unpredictable?

And I went along with it all, she thought. *What if we had gotten caught?*

"You're thinking very hard over there," Trick said. "Processing our walk on the wild side? Or looking forward to your weekend?"

"My . . . ?" She caught her breath. Her grandfather was taking her to the Cirque du Soleil show in Little Rock. She had completely forgotten about it, impossible as that seemed since the Cirque had been all she had dreamed about for years. Dreamed about joining.

"Yes," she said. "Can't wait."

His smile was intense, and his hand brushed hers as he shifted gears. Alone with a boy, in a car, danger. But Trick was Trick. An exception to all rules.

They pulled into the school lot. There was a scattering of cars — probably teachers — and Trick came around to the side to let her out, but he suddenly seemed distracted as he walked her to her car, looking around, frowning, while she got out her keys.

"Is there something wrong?" she asked.

Then she saw the Confederate flag car skulking from around the back of the school. Mike Wright. Her vision telescoped and she could see through the windshield the pig-faced jerk behind the wheel. She felt a sudden wave of extreme fury and balled her fists, barely under control.

"You should leave," Trick said.

She gritted her teeth, then forced herself to remain calm. "*We* should leave." She looked at him. "C'mon, Trick."

Mike revved his engine. Trick tensed and glanced over at his Mustang. A muscle jumped in his cheek as if her temper flare were contagious.

"Oh, my God, are you thinking of racing him?" Katelyn blurted. "Are you as much of a Neanderthal as he is?"

Then the roar of a motorcycle overshadowed Mike's engine as Justin rode down the street toward the lot. Trick's mouth dropped open and he looked from Justin's motorcycle to Katelyn.

"No. Kat, really?" he said incredulously.

As Justin approached, Mike peeled out, making a show of swerving around Katelyn and Trick and heading in Justin's direction. Justin kept coming. So did Mike. At the last possible moment Mike swerved — and wound up driving onto the sidewalk, bumping his front end against the tarmac. Katelyn felt a momentary flash of dark glee, then glanced over at Trick. He'd missed Mike's clumsy exit; his gaze was focused laser-like on Justin as the motorcycle rolled to a stop a few feet away.

"Okay, well," Trick said, and walked to his car.

"Trick," Katelyn called, but Trick got in and slammed his car door. Katelyn reached out a hand in his direction, but he started the car and peeled out much the same way as Mike. She watched him go, feeling guilty, angry, sad . . . and relieved. What had she been thinking? She couldn't feel this way about Trick. She was a werewolf.

"Lee wants you over now," Justin said. "He's going to train you himself today."

She realized Justin had shown up just as the normal school day would have ended. He hadn't known about minimum day. She made a face.

"Here's the thing. My grandfather bought tickets for a show in Little Rock for my birthday. It's this weekend and we're leaving as soon as I get home."

Justin stared at her as if she'd spoken to him in a foreign language. She forced herself not to cringe or apologize and waited for him to say something.

"You can't just *leave*," he said. "The alpha didn't give you permission."

"Um, I'm not *leaving*," she said hotly. "I'm going to Little Rock."

He turned off his motorcycle, kicked down the stand, and got off. He walked toward her and, without thinking, she took a step away from him. He stopped.

"I know you're new at this," he said.

"There's no way I can tell Grandpa I'm not going so I can go over to your house," she said. "Justin, he's my grandfather. I live with him. I'm a minor and he's in charge of me. Legally. He also knows what a big deal this is to me so he'd be sure to guess something is wrong. Be suspicious. Of the Fenners."

He stared at her for a long moment. Then he said quietly, "Maybe we have to change things. Maybe you shouldn't be living with your grandfather any longer."

"What is that supposed to mean?" she cried. She made a fist and shook it at him. "Don't you dare touch him!"

"You," he said, grabbing her fist. Then he pulled her against his chest. All she could see was his blue eyes. "You are my pack inferior. You *never* tell me what to do."

"Fine!" she shouted at him, but her voice shook. "Whatever!"

He took a breath and lowered his head toward hers, then stopped at the last moment and released her, breathing hard. He stepped back and whipped out his cell phone. Punched in a number. Brought it to his ear.

"Hi, Uncle Lee," he said. "We got a bit of a situation today." He quickly explained. "I know, sir." He held out the phone. "He wants to speak to you."

"Kat," Lee Fenner said on speaker. "This time, it's okay. Next time, it's not."

"Okay," she said. Justin mouthed *Yes, sir* at her. "Yes, sir."

"One word, *one*, and your grandfather won't come back from Little Rock."

She felt as if he had punched her in the stomach. "Yes, sir."

"I'll be home soon, Uncle Lee," Justin said.

"Get some ice cream," Lee Fenner said. "Your daddy loves mint chocolate chip."

Color rose in Justin's cheeks. "Yes, sir." He disconnected.

Katelyn said, "I'm sorry."

"You check in with me while you're gone. Text me. Tell me where you are."

"Okay," she said, and he looked meaningfully at her. She blinked in disbelief. "*Yes, sir.*"

"And, Kat?" He looked in the direction Trick's Mustang had gone, and his face became guarded. "Remember the way it works? If you bite someone, even a little love nip, and accidentally draw blood, they change. And if they change, they're dead for sure."

She was floored. He was talking about Trick. About making out with him.

"For sure," he repeated. There was anger in his voice. Jealousy. He started up his motorcycle and roared off.

"Jerk," she said, as tears welled in her eyes. "Like I would."

⊷ ⬛◆⬛ ⊶

Everything looked strange, foreign, as Katelyn drove home through the woods toward the cabin. The trees were all different, but not in any special way. Even though there was only one route, she kept wondering if she was going in the right direction. She felt weirdly light, as if she were floating.

She remembered after her father died, her mother had curled into a ball on the floor in a corner of the living room and said something in French over and over again. Katelyn couldn't understand her, but she had crept down beside her and they held each other. After a long time, Giselle had said in English, "Is this still our house?"

Detective Cranston, one of her father's police friends — he had many friends in the force — had taken Katelyn aside and explained that her mother was disoriented from the sheer amount of stress she was under. He told Katelyn that she needed to take care of her. And Katelyn had.

But who is taking care of me? she thought now, trying to shake it off. *I don't need taking care of. I'm seventeen.*

But the entire exchange between Lee and Justin had freaked her out. Permission? To go to Little Rock? *How* was she ever going to get out of Wolf Springs and have a real life? Was her future really going to be so strictly controlled?

She took a deep breath and said aloud, "You will get out. You will make it happen." Things would change. Lee Fenner would be replaced. She would earn that new alpha's trust, and then her freedom. She'd get out.

She had just about calmed herself down when she rounded the last corner before coming into view of the cabin and saw Trick's Mustang parked out front. She flinched. What was he doing there?

She got out slowly and walked up the steps onto the porch. Opening the door, the first things she saw were an old, battered suitcase and a duffel bag by the front door — her grandfather's luggage, she supposed.

Trick and her grandfather were bustling around in the kitchen, Trick rinsing dishes while her grandfather gave her a wave with a kitchen knife.

Mordecai looked at her inquisitively as he finished cutting a sandwich — she smelled cheese and salami — and laid it on a plate. He'd made two. One for him and one for Trick.

"Oh, hi. I—" she babbled.

"Hi. Sandwich?" Mordecai asked.

"Yes, thanks. Just cheese." Even though she wanted the salami. But she was on record as being a vegetarian and didn't want to raise any more red flags.

She glanced at Trick, whose face was turned as he scrubbed a coffee cup as if getting it clean was a matter of life or death. Apparently he hadn't told her grandfather about the piece of silver she'd seen. That surprised her, since the two seemed so close. He set the cup down and looked at her with hooded eyes.

"Surprise," he said.

Her grandfather started making the sandwich. "I thought you might like it if we took a friend with us, so I got another ticket to the show. I figured you'd invite . . ." Mordecai drifted off, and cleared his throat. "I just asked Trick."

Cordelia. He'd thought Cordelia would be going with us. Katelyn's chest tightened. She'd be going with Trick now, instead. She told herself that given what had happened in the parking lot, she wasn't sure she wanted to spend a weekend with him. But who was she kidding? And what could she do about it anyway?

She turned to Trick. "I — I'm glad you're coming," she said, her face going hot.

"Thanks," he bit off. "Me, too." So there was to be a truce, but they weren't in the best of places. That was better than having to salute him and call him "sir."

Sheesh.

Her grandfather looked from one to the other, and then occupied himself with getting something out of the fridge, grinning slyly. "We should head out soon." He glanced out the kitchen window. Clouds had rolled in, and the day was gray. "Might rain."

"Gimme five," she told him. "Ten," she amended. She hadn't packed and she still wanted to look at that old drawing again.

She spun on her heel and dashed upstairs. She took a moment to retrieve the old parchment from her underwear drawer and unfolded it. There was the rock-shaped heart and behind it, a waterfall, just like in the painting that had hung downstairs: it had to be the location of the mine.

She quickly threw some clothes into her father's leather suitcase engraved with his initials SKM — Sean Kevin McBride — on a brass plate, making sure to pack her new dress from Babette's very carefully. Then she slipped into clean jeans and a turtleneck the color of her light blue eyes. After running a brush through her hair she trotted back downstairs.

"All set," she said, as she picked up the cheese sandwich

her grandfather had made. She devoured it while her grand-father put away the dishes Trick had washed and they all then piled into her grandfather's truck, Katelyn sitting on the front seat between them. She had thought about suggesting that they take her Subaru, but that would have meant Trick would be in the back seat.

I shouldn't care, she thought.

Her grandfather put the truck in drive and a moment later they were rolling away from the cabin.

"We're off," he announced, sounding more excited than she'd ever heard him. Maybe he needed this trip just as much as she did.

"And as an added bonus," Trick said, "I mixed a playlist."

"Remember the rule," her grandfather growled, though the corners of his mouth twitched.

"Don't mess with the driver," Trick said. "I think you'll like what I picked out, though, Doc."

"Not very likely. Your taste in music hasn't been good since you were five."

Trick had brought a portable speaker, which he set up on the dash. He plugged in his phone and a moment later "Thank God I'm a Country Boy" was blaring. It was so unlike his usual choice of music that Katelyn couldn't help laughing out loud. Her grandfather actually cracked a smile.

Trick moved his leg, maybe by accident, maybe so he could rub it against hers, and something in his face shifted. She thought about unpredictability and his assumption that she was going over to the Fenners to chase Justin. Best to let him think so. Life was too complex. But it hurt in a strange new way and she found herself changing her mind once again and adding two words to her vow to have a normal life: *with Trick*.

Maybe Mr. Fenner wasn't the only crazy one.

The drive took a little over four hours, but they finally reached their hotel, got their suitcases, and trooped inside a welcoming Victorian lobby decorated with brass pots of ivy. A couple of minutes later, they were upstairs in their one-bedroom suite with two twin beds in the bedroom and a sleeper sofa in the living room.

Her grandfather tapped the key card against the knuckles on his other hand. "I figured I'd give you girls the room, but—" He stopped abruptly.

"Don't worry, Dr. M. I'm all about the couch," Trick said quickly.

"Sounds great," her grandfather replied.

Katelyn was a bit weirded out at the thought of sleeping in the same room as her grandfather — it wasn't like he felt totally like family yet — but he took his suitcase into the bedroom, and she followed.

"I call window," she said, dropping her bag on the bed nearest lacy white sheers giving way to a view of the street. It was dark, and she could already see stars glittering over the tops of brick buildings and a white marble cupola.

"Fine with me. I always like to sleep closer to the door." He lowered his voice. "I hope this is okay."

"Oh, yes. It's fantastic, Grandpa," she replied, sounding

maybe a little too chirpy in her eagerness to reassure him. "Thank you."

He gave her a measured look, pleased at the "Grandpa." "Did I invite the right guy?"

She reddened. So he thought she was hanging out with Justin, too.

"How much do you know about Trick?" she asked instead.

He raised a brow. "Such as?" When she didn't say anything, he crossed to his suitcase and opened it. She saw that he had packed a suit, and she was touched by all the trouble he'd gone to to make this a weekend to remember.

"I've known Trick since the day he was born," he said. Then he added softly, "And I met Justin the day he risked his life to save a little girl."

Katelyn remembered that day very well; a little child — just a toddler — had run in front of her grandfather's truck. Justin had leaped off his motorcycle and grabbed the girl, rolling to the side of the road with her and saving her life. It had been amazing. Fast. Quick. Brave. *Werewolf speed*, her mind told her. But now Mordecai's comment gave her pause that her grandfather hadn't dismissed Justin out of hand. Was it because he thought she might like him better than Trick?

"Let's go have a nice dinner and turn in," he suggested. "We've got a full day tomorrow and that was a long drive. I'd like to beat Trick about the head for sliding in a few heavy metal nightmares once I was lulled into complacency."

She laughed and gave him a quick, impulsive hug. He flushed and patted her back in return. The grandfather/

granddaughter relationship was growing stronger day by day, but neither felt totally comfortable about it yet. After all, Katelyn hadn't seen Mordecai for over five years before moving to Wolf Springs to live with him. Soon it was time for dinner; she kept up the pretense that she was still a vegetarian, and then they went back to the suite and climbed in their beds.

But Katelyn was too wired to sleep. She felt odd sleeping in her grandfather's presence, and wished she'd asked for the pullout couch instead. She remembered trips up to Tahoe with her parents when she was a kid, how they'd always slept together in the same room. But with her parents it had been normal; she'd been used to it and them. Then a text message came in, and she jumped, hoping it was from Cordelia. But it was Justin, and she remembered with a jolt how he had told her to keep in contact. Oh, God, she really wasn't all that good at being a werewolf, was she? Following the rules.

Everything OK? he had sent.

She texted back a *yes-sir* — her version of an apology — and decided to try Cordelia again. Then, even though the phone was on vibrate, she heard her grandfather clear his throat. She wished even more fervently that she'd asked for the couch, but sighed and lay on her side looking toward the window, staring at the stars. When she closed her eyes, she kept seeing Cordelia's face as she got into the Gaudins' car, and then the glowing forest. And she wished there was something she could do not just to save herself but also to save her friend.

Katelyn woke in the morning and it took her a moment to remember where she was. She checked her cell phone to see if any new texts or calls had come in. Nothing.

The shower was running. She rolled over to find her grandfather's bed empty, just as the water turned off. A minute later, the bathroom door opened and she rolled back toward the window to give him privacy. After she'd allowed him some time, she rolled back over again.

He was wearing a pair of trousers with a towel across his shoulders, and just as she was about to wish him a good morning, he turned to get a fresh shirt hanging in the closet and his towel slipped. Suddenly Katelyn could see his back. She stared, startled.

Deep, hideous scars ran from his shoulder blade nearly to his hip on his right side.

Scars that looked like claw marks.

9

"Grandpa, what happened to you?" Katelyn blurted before she could stop herself.

He jumped and turned to her, eyes wide, nostrils flared. He shrugged his shirt on quickly and began to button it. "Good morning. Didn't know you were awake," he said gruffly. "You sleep okay?" he asked.

She bit her lip as she nodded her head, her skin tingling with anxiety. He was avoiding her question. Maybe she should let it go, but his scars looked exactly like the gouges the werewolf had left on her. Scratch marks that had miraculously healed within a couple of days. *One of the first signs that something had changed about me.*

"Happened a long time ago," he said curtly, tucking the shirt-tails into his pants.

"*What* happened?" she persisted.

He was silent for so long that she wasn't sure that he was going to answer her. Just as she was about to give up and head for the shower herself, he answered.

"I got attacked while I was hunting," he said. "Long time ago."

Her heart pounded in her chest as she stood up. "Did it bite you?" she asked, voice tense.

He gave her the strangest look and she swallowed, panicky. Did he know why she was asking?

He shook his head. "Nope. I was cocky, and I got too close. It just scratched the hell out of me."

"Did you, did you kill it?" she asked, hating the fact that her voice was quavering. She didn't want to betray anything she knew about the things that attacked people in the forest.

"Never saw it again." He walked out to the living room. "Hey, Vladimir, you vampire. You up?" he called.

She made it into the bathroom and got into the shower. It took her forever to figure out the faucet controls; she was high-strung, jumpy. Something had left those scratches on her grandfather's back.

Wait. He never said what kind of animal it was. He just said he never saw it again.

A thousand questions raced through her mind as she tried to focus on the feel of the water pounding on her face, the heat. His back explained so much. Why he knew the woods were dangerous.

It wasn't just about what happened to Becky Jensen before I arrived. It's about what happened to him.

When she finally left the bathroom, she dressed swiftly and then walked into the living room, where Trick sat on the edge of the couch, muzzy and all bed-head — for someone with short hair. He was wearing a pair of black sweatpants and his chest was bare. She felt herself blushing.

"Did you use all the hot water?" Trick asked, rolling his shoulders and cricking his neck. She blushed again as she looked harder.

"Find out for yourself," she said tartly.

When he walked past her she couldn't help but sneak a peek at his retreating back.

No scars on him.

She grimaced, mortified, when she saw her grandfather taking it all in, no expression on his face.

⊰ ⊱

A day of sightseeing flew by, and before she knew it the three of them were standing in line for Cirque. She was in her new black dress, her grandfather had on his suit, and Trick was wearing a white formal shirt, black jeans, and a really nice black jacket. He had on polished black cowboy boots, and she was sorry he'd left his hat back in the hotel.

"I couldn't get the third ticket in the same row, but it's close," Mordecai said, squinting at the seat numbers. "You and Trick can sit together."

"Are you sure?" she asked.

"I'm sure," he said. He wrinkled his nose. "Figure he'll probably appreciate it more than I will."

The moment they sat down, Trick began to reach for her hand, then put his hands in his lap. She was bereft, and the kaleidoscope of feelings inside her twisted again.

"Your grandfather told me what this means to you," he said, voice serious. "I'm glad I can be here."

The green of his eyes pulled her in. "Me, too," she said, not trusting herself to say anything else.

Then the lights dimmed and the music began; music she knew, music she had moved to. Beautifully costumed performers defied gravity — and reality — and she was swept up in the magic of it. Everything in her yearned to be up there, to move like that. The conversation with Mr. Fenner and Justin chafed at her, and only made her want it all more as her heart swelled and ached with every moment. She felt as if she was watching her life, the life she had dreamed of, rushing by, and she wanted to reach out and catch it, make it go more slowly, beg it to wait for her to figure out how she could still be a part of it.

"Incredible," Trick whispered, and she looked — really looked — at him. She saw how moved he was, and looked at the planes and angles of light and dark playing on his face.

He understands; he sees the other world that this is. Surely she could tell him about her new world. She could.

Her breath wouldn't come.

He wanted to help. He would help. He was already involved.

She closed her eyes. Could she risk Trick's life over this?

Was she risking Cordelia's life if she didn't?

If she didn't tell him, and he discovered the truth anyway, what would happen?

The room began to spin and she could barely see. Her heart was beating too fast and sweat beaded on her forehead. She felt incredibly sick and she could barely force herself to sit in her chair. Something was happening to her. All the objects in the room — the people, the seats, the stage, the rigging — burst into white light, then reds and oranges. It looked like fire. And then a girl appeared, high in the sky, seated in the center of thick, fibrous ropes. Katelyn began to tremble, then shake. Her ears began to buzz.

Then the girl on the swing performed the final movement, the leap.

And she began to plummet toward the ground below.

"No!" Katelyn screamed.

It all happened so fast: the girl, falling; Katelyn, screaming; and Trick's arms around her, tightly, as the crowd burst into laughter and applause. They had assumed her scream was part of the act.

Trick pressed her face against his neck as he put his lips up to her ear. He said, "I'll get you out of here." He put his arm around her shoulders and pulled her up as he stood.

Then he was cradling her against himself as he hurried her up the aisle, out into the lobby. She was biting her lip to keep from sobbing aloud, but she couldn't stop the tears. He kept walking, and she felt a blast of cold air. They were outside, and a sullen moon and gray-fisted clouds hovered overhead. The chill stung her face and she was dimly aware that Trick was taking off his coat and wrapping it around her. Then he was wiping her face with a piece of cloth — a handkerchief — and pressing her body against his. Her face fit into the space between his clavicles and his chin, and she shuddered against him as he held her in his arms.

"It's my fault that she died," she told Trick in a rush, and she was surprised she said it. And yet, she couldn't stop herself. "My mom. I was on painkillers when the earthquake happened, and I was so doped up that she couldn't get out in time when the . . . fire started." She felt tears on her cheeks.

"And now I'm *here*," she said, anguished, "and there's so much. Oh, *Trick*—"

"I'm here, darlin'." Trick brushed his lips against the crown of her hair. His heart was thundering and she felt icy, unwell. But then she had the sharpest sensation of being watched. Almost as if someone were poking at the back of her neck with one long, cold finger. She stiffened and darted her gaze left and right.

Oh, my God, she thought, freaking out as her knees buckled. Trick was already holding her so tightly that he probably didn't even notice. She had to get it together. If Lee Fenner had sent a spy to watch her . . .

"I'm okay now," she said. "I'm fine."

"Katie," her grandfather said. She didn't know when he'd come up to them. Maybe he'd been the one watching. She hoped so.

"I'm sorry," she said. "I just . . . it was . . . I — I was dreaming of the Mexican cloud swing when the earthquake happened. It just hit me all over again. But I'm . . ." she took a deep breath. ". . . monumentally embarrassed." She raised her voice and forced out what she hoped was a convincing laugh.

Just then, people poured out of the doors and walked toward them, talking, laughing. The performance had ended.

"Good timing," she said, trying to make a joke. She smiled at Trick.

But he didn't smile back.

Katelyn didn't know who made the decision, but when they returned to their hotel suite, she had the rollout couch and the two guys shared the bedroom. She was relieved; it had been awkward to sleep in the same room with her grandfather and she didn't want to repeat the experience. The rollout had been made up with fresh sheets, and as she crawled beneath the covers, she realized she could still smell Trick all around her. *One of the advantages of having heightened senses*, she thought with a smile. She pulled up the sheets and curled inside them like an embrace.

She knew it made sense that she'd had a meltdown. She was under terrible strain and if anything besides an earthquake could set off her emotions, the Cirque show was it. But if the Fenners had sent someone to spy on her, she hoped they counted it as "normal" that a teenage girl whose mother had died less than three months ago might lose it. In fact, she would seem less normal if she hadn't. But would Lee Fenner see it that way?

Should she text Justin again? Be an obedient young werewolf? Avoiding trouble certainly made sense. She didn't want either her grandfather or Trick to suffer just because she didn't like to bow down to rules she couldn't understand.

Biting her lip in annoyance, she sent a brief message to let him know they were back at the hotel for the night, then she texted Cordelia again. There was no response.

The hotel offered an elaborate brunch in the morning, and everyone ate like pigs. Then they piled into the car. Trick and her grandfather were cautious around her, chatting about inconsequential things. In a weird way, Katelyn was glad Mordecai had seen just how torn up she really was inside. She didn't think he had understood what he had asked of her, forcing her to move to Wolf Springs. Now he had seen her pain firsthand.

When they arrived back at the cabin, she wondered if she might also be PMSing werewolf-style as she felt so un-believably restless. Wasn't menstruation linked to the phases of the moon? So would werewolf girls notice it more? After Trick left and her grandfather went to bed, she had to go out-side and stand in the fresh air. The Inner Wolf guys were at it, beating their drums, their howls echoing off the mountains. Instead of irritating her, the noise steadied her. Was that what she had done at the Cirque show — let out her inner wolf?

A text came in from Justin: *Are you back?* and feeling daring, she called him.

"Are you all right?" he asked, and she heard the tension in his voice. She felt her throat tighten; she was afraid he knew what had happened.

"Yeah," she said. "It was great."

"Any problems?"

Was Trick being there a problem?

"No. It's all good."

"Okay. G'night, darlin'," he said, and disconnected.

She stared at her phone. He had called her "darlin'." Well, Trick called her "darlin'" too. It was just a Southern thing. And yet she fixated on it — how his voice had sounded all sweet, as if he had really meant it.

Doesn't matter, she reminded herself. He was taken, and werewolves fought to the death if a rival tried to move in on their mate. She wasn't that kind of girl, anyway — one who would try and steal a guy from a girl once he was taken.

He's not mated. But from what Cordelia had told her, he might as well be. And she didn't really want him either, did she? Trick was who she wanted, wasn't he? Justin's near-irresistibility was just about her wolf hormones; once that all settled down, she'd be okay. Wouldn't be attracted to him anymore. *Are you kidding?* a voice inside her head persisted. *A guy that hot?*

The phone rang, distracting her from her dangerous train of thought. Speak of the devil: Justin again. She took the call.

"I missed you," he said, and hung up again.

The drums and howls echoed in her ears. She looked down at her phone, and then up at the moon, which had been sliced into shards by the obsidian silhouettes of the trees. Her heart picked up speed.

If she was completely honest, she had missed him, too.

⊰ ⊱

Monday came way too early, and Katelyn felt tired and achy. As she sat through history, which Mrs. Walker from Admin was actually trying to teach, she stared at the back of

Gretchen's head and then at Cordelia's empty desk. She refused to so much as look at Beau, who seemed to know that he should keep his distance.

The hour from hell was finally over, and it was time for P.E. She slammed through the open door to the gym, and nearly collided with Mike Wright, who frowned at her, then smirked, and looked over her shoulder in disgust. She looked to find Trick close behind her. She didn't know what he was doing there. It wasn't his hour for P.E.

Mike's piggish face stretched into a sneer and he planted himself in front of Trick with crossed arms.

"Where you going, freak?" he demanded.

Trick said nothing. He gave Katelyn a nod and started to walk past Mike as if he weren't there.

"Hey, I got detention because of you." Mike flailed at the air, too far away from Trick to actually hit him.

"You got detention because you're a psychotic moron," Katelyn said.

Both Trick and Mike stared at her, and she narrowed her eyes at Mike. "A moron, and a bully, and a jerk."

Mike's mouth dropped open. Then he lunged at her, as if to scare her, and everything inside her snapped. She lunged forward, too, then brought up her knee and rammed it upward into his crotch. He let out a howl, doubling up, and she slammed her fist against the side of his face.

"I hate you!" she shouted at him.

"You're gonna die!" Mike shouted back at her. "Just like your trashy slutbuddy—"

She threw herself at him again, only this time Trick

grabbed her and dragged her backwards. She struggled against him, getting one arm free. He wrapped his hand around her wrist.

"Katelyn, stop," he said. "*Stop.*"

"What's going on?" The coach stuck his head out of his office, then walked up to the group. Students were coming over, too. In L.A., people who fought on campus were considered bigger losers than stoners, and clearly fighting must also be a big deal at Wolf Springs High.

"Chill," Trick murmured in Katelyn's ear. He let go of her and stepped toward Mike. "Just got me some payback, sir," he said calmly.

"No, it was Ka—" Mike said; then he fell silent as he took stock of the other kids gathering to catch the drama. He clenched his jaw and glared at Trick, as if Trick really had attacked him.

"Okay, you two, come with me *now*," the coach said.

"Trick, no," Katelyn said to him, unable to believe what she'd just done. Trick made as if tipping the brim of an invisible cowboy hat and followed Mike and the coach through the exit.

Katelyn took a step toward them, then hesitated. She had to stay under the radar. She remembered back to her first day of school when Cordelia had lost her temper in gym class and nearly bested Mike at chin-ups before she pulled herself together and pretended to be weaker than she was. At the time, Katelyn had thought Cordelia was pulling some Daisy-Mae routine to look feminine and helpless, and it had irritated her. But now she understood that Cordelia had been hiding just how strong she really was. She had to learn to do the same.

Fresh rage roared through her and she shut her eyes tightly, trying to maintain her composure until it passed. Finally, admitting defeat, she lurched toward the girls' dressing room, her nerves sizzling like livewires.

"You okay, Kat?" asked Dondi, one of Cordelia's friends from her cheerleader days. She laid a comforting hand on Katelyn's shoulder as Paulette, from Katelyn's art class, looked on. "Did Mike say something to you about Cordelia?"

Katelyn chewed the inside of her cheek. So others had seen her go after him. It would get around. Justin might hear about it.

"Yes," Katelyn said. "You don't want me to repeat it."

"No, of course I don't." Dondi said firmly. But her eyes were glittering with excitement. Katelyn knew she wanted all the gory details so she could tell everyone.

Some friend you are, she thought. "Good," she said, leaving the locker room and heading for Mr. Hastings' office.

After Katelyn explained to Mrs. Walker that she had information on the fight that had just taken place, Mrs. Walker told her to go on in. She pushed on Mr. Hastings' door, to find the principal seated behind his desk, Coach Ambrose leaning against the wall, and Trick and Mike in chairs facing the principal. Trick looked over his shoulder at her and his eyes widened. He gave his head a shake and she just shrugged.

"Well, here she is, so you can apologize to her right now,"

Mr. Hastings said to Mike.

"No f'ing way," Mike blurted.

"Or you can get expelled for defacing school property and starting fights," the principal said.

"Damn it," Mike grunted, his face going blotchy and purple. He took a huge sigh. "Okay. Whatever. I shouldn't have said Cordelia and all them Fenners are inbred cannibals, and they probably ate Mr. Henderson for breakfast."

Katelyn stared at him in shock. Substitute another word for "inbred cannibals" and add her own fearful suspicion about what might have happened to Mr. Henderson, and Mike might have been perilously close to the truth.

"Okay. Go on back to class, Mike," Mr. Hastings said to him.

Mike pushed back his chair furiously, and the coach dismissed him with a smile aimed at Katelyn.

"Kat," he said, "have a seat."

As she and Mike crossed paths, he flashed her a look of pure, undying hatred. He mirrored exactly how she felt.

Bring it, she thought. *I'll gut you.*

But she couldn't let them know she was thinking like that, so she ignored him and took the chair he'd vacated.

"Now let's talk about this gymnastics equipment the Sokolovs want to donate to the school," the coach said, pushing away from the wall. "Which, I must say, Trick, is very generous of your folks."

"And well-timed," the principal said dryly, leaning his elbows forward on his desk.

Trick just smiled pleasantly; Katelyn gaped open-mouthed

at him while he kept his attention on the principal. She could tell Trick knew she was staring at him and a little smile played over his face.

"Well, Katelyn here's a world-class gymnast," Trick said. "Did you hear tell of that? Professional level, and my folks have some connections in that world. They said they didn't want all that talent to go to waste."

"Well, that's mighty fine. You could start a team," Coach Ambrose said to Katelyn.

She felt a rush of excitement at the base of her spine that nearly took off the top of her head. Yes! It would be like home. Training other people had always helped her stay on top of her game. She'd already had hours and hours of teaching classes, and she was good at it. She'd have a place among her schoolmates. And it would be something that was hers.

Then she checked her enthusiasm. Maybe the Fenners would object. After all, Cordelia had had to quit cheerleading because of Mr. Fenner, she reminded herself. And Jesse. But Katelyn didn't live with them so school was her business, not theirs. Screw them. She wouldn't let them take this away from her.

"Sounds great," she told the coach. Trick looked pleased.

"What sort of budget were your folks thinking about?" the principal asked Trick, practically salivating. Good gymnastics equipment could be pricey.

"We'll sit down after school and figure out what to order," Trick replied. "Unless you're too busy today, Katelyn." He focused his sea-green eyes on her and raised a brow.

She heard the challenge in his voice. She knew very well

he was testing to see if she'd blow him off in favor of Justin. For gymnastics equipment, yes, she could be bought.

"Sounds completely great," she repeated, looking steadily at him, and his slow smile appeared. She couldn't help but smile back. It actually *was* completely great.

"The coach and I will talk," Mr. Hastings said, nodding at Coach Ambrose. "We'll confer about what kind of setup the gym can accommodate. We'll be sure to thank your family properly, Trick." He reached out a hand. Trick rose and clasped it, and they shook. Then Trick shook hands with the coach.

This is so cool, Katelyn thought.

As she and Trick pushed back their chairs, she wished she could ask the principal what Cordelia's family had told him about her absence. And if he'd gotten any news about Mr. Henderson.

Yes, the gym equipment was cool, but she couldn't forget that there were a few things in Wolf Springs that were definitely not cool. Including her.

10

U have to come over after school, Justin texted Katelyn as she sat in art class. The class were making ceramic story pots, 3D interpretations of a favorite work in another medium. Katelyn was busily making her own little figurine in a red leotard swinging on a Mexican cloud swing. Paulette smiled over at Katelyn as she worked on her version of *Where the Wild Things Are.* Katelyn wondered if Paulette knew the wild things were in houses and art classes as well as the forest.

She texted Justin back. *Can't today. OK? Don't feel good.*

Then she grimaced as if she could see him lose his mind at her mutinous disrespect. *That time.*

? he wrote back.

"C'mon, connect the dots, Justin," she muttered under her breath. "Please."

"Is that Cordelia?" Paulette asked, not concerned, just being snoopy. Paulette was on record as disliking Cordelia intensely. Paulette had warned new-girl Kat McBride that Cordelia was a two-faced, mean snake, someone best shunned.

It's that *time*, Katelyn finally texted back, flushing.

Got it, Justin said. *Good that you stay away. CU in a couple days.*

"Okay, that's embarrassing," she thought to herself. She typed in *KK. And good to know that w. girls get a break once a month.* She didn't dare type out the full word "werewolf," but figured he'd get the point.

She said to Paulette, "It's not Cordelia."

Paulette nodded and added a blob of clay to the side of her pot. "I wonder what happened to Mr. Henderson," she said in a low voice. "I can't believe he's gone."

"Not gone," Katelyn said, and then she stopped. Because what did she know?

"He must have family," Paulette went on. "I wouldn't be surprised if they don't show up here, asking questions. I'd be going crazy."

"I know," Katelyn murmured, feeling guilty even though she'd done nothing to Mr. Henderson. Werewolves didn't hurt people. Didn't attack them.

But someone attacked me.

"This isn't turning out the way I wanted," she blurted suddenly. She reached out a hand toward the figure.

"Kat, leave it be. It's really sweet," Paulette protested. "Besides, if you start over now, you won't finish in time."

Katelyn sighed and looked out the window at the parking lot; rain was pouring down at a sharp angle, pushed by the wind, the sky hung low, and overhead lightning crackled. She stared at Trick's Mustang and reminded herself that a good thing had happened today. An awesome thing. But she was near tears.

Werewolf hormones, she reminded herself. *Get a grip.*

She smiled at Paulette. "You're right." She gave the figure a little push, and Paulette smiled back.

⊶ ⊷

That afternoon, after school, Trick was waiting for her at her locker. She was tired from monitoring herself and he lifted a brow as she got out a few books and shut the locker door.

"Hey?" he said.

"I'm fine," she said. "I mean, hi."

They began to walk toward the lot, which was shimmering with rain puddles. He reached in his backpack and held out something wrapped in a gray cloth. As she touched it, she had a strange sensation in her mouth, as if she was chewing aluminum foil. Unwrapping it, she saw it was a knife — by the looks of it, the silver knife she'd left behind at the Inner Wolf Center.

"I went back last night, after we got home," he said. "It was bugging me. Wasn't it bugging you?"

"Yes. It was bugging me." She touched the handle. The metal gave off a tangy, burning odor. She remembered how positive Justin had been that the trap she'd fallen into was silver. Now she knew why. Her senses must have been duller back then. "Maybe if we told my grandfather we found it *off* the property." She hesitated. "But I don't want to get you in trouble."

"Tell you what. If the police don't get anywhere, I'll fess up. How about a week?"

"Oh." Saying anything felt intense and confining. But a week would give her time to think it through. "Okay, yes."

"Good." He hefted his backpack over one shoulder. "Let's go to Cowffeine to talk about the equipment. They have free wifi. We can drive over together and I won't keep you long."

"And you won't beat anybody up."

"No, ma'am." He tipped an imaginary cowboy hat.

They drove down Main Street in his Mustang, Katelyn wistfully admiring the Christmas decorations hanging from the lampposts — candy canes and jingle bells — and the holly wreaths on the doors of the Victorian buildings. Wind buffeted the finery. Nearly all the leaves on the trees were gone, and it began to rain again.

"Looks like an early snow this year," Trick said as he peered through the windshield. "Your pappy's laid in lots of supplies, yes?"

"Yes," she said faintly. A little less than three weeks until the next full moon. Surely it wouldn't snow before then. She'd have to figure out a way to justify staying out all night.

"Don't be scared," he said. "Getting snowed in is kind of fun."

"If you don't live in the middle of the forest."

"You and the doc can come stay with us if you want. We've got lots of room."

"Oh." She turned to look at him. "Thank you."

"No big," he replied, but he looked happy.

They drove past Babette's. Mr. Henderson's missing person's notice was taped beside the one commemorating the two girls who had died, Haley and Becky. Katelyn thought about what Paulette had said, about loved ones going crazy with worry.

Thinking of that, she checked her cell phone as she climbed out of the Mustang. There was nothing from Cordelia or Dom. But there was one from Justin.

Hope you feel better.

"Whoa," she said aloud. *That* was unexpected, the sequel. Trick raised a questioning brow. "Sorry. It's nothing."

"How's Kimi?" he asked, as if he assumed that was who she was talking to.

"Good. Great," she told him, and she felt a tightness in her chest as she imagined the beach and L.A. with Trick in it. Just a few days ago, she'd actually begun to dream that Wolf Springs would become a distant memory.

"We'll get you a bunch of cool equipment," he said as they went into the coffee house. There was a large display of *Discover Your Inner Wolf* merchandise, and beyond that a place to order coffees and pastries, and some wooden tables.

"You probably know the best websites to order from. We —
Shit," he murmured under his breath.

Katelyn looked in his direction. Jack Bronson was coming
out of the restroom.

She stopped dead and Trick murmured, "It's okay."

"How have you been?" Bronson asked Katelyn as he
walked up to her. His voice was way too friendly. "Katelyn
McBride, isn't it?"

She cleared her throat. "Yes. Fine. Thanks."

"No more trouble?" he persisted, and she felt Trick jerk.

Smooth, she thought.

"It's all good," she said tightly.

"Good, good." He patted the shelf holding the display of
his books, some T-shirts, and coffee cups. "Would you like a
copy of my book?"

"We have one, thanks."

"Your grandfather and you." He said it almost as if
he were making a joke. "Well, good. I hope you like it." He
smiled at her a beat too long, and then at Trick very cursorily,
and walked out the front door.

"Yikes," Trick said. "*Trouble?*"

"Two of his guys tried to hit on Cordelia and me," she said.
"He stopped them."

"Whoa." Trick looked out the door, then at the books.
"And yet you never mentioned it."

"Was I supposed to?" she asked, flaring. Then she softened. "I'm sorry. I'm short-tempered. I — I didn't get enough
sleep last night."

"Then we'll get you something to wake you up," he said.

"Caffeine is always my first drug of choice."

The gym equipment was ordered. Among the amazing haul: uneven bars, parallel bars, a vault, a balance beam, a trapeze, and a cloud swing. Trick put it on a black credit card, which meant either that there was no limit or the sky was the limit: a few kids at Samohi had been given black credit cards — and, usually, chauffeurs, if so.

Katelyn's reprieve from the Fenners ended two afternoons later when Justin told her to drive over to the house to resume her training. She went immediately after school, telling Trick only that she was busy. Which he did not like.

When she got out of the car, Mr. Fenner came over from the house and stared at her car so long she was afraid he had forgotten she was coming over. He growled deep in his throat and pulled back his lips.

"How many bodies does this make, six? It has to end," he told her.

Katelyn stared at him in shock. There were only two dead people that she knew of. Possibly three if Mr. Henderson was truly gone.

"Excuse me?" she asked.

Lee Fenner looked at her. "I may be only eighteen, but I'm not stupid. I can see what's happening. Someone has to put an end to it."

Katelyn's heart began to pound as she realized he was having one of his episodes, reliving something from when he was about her age. Her mind instantly flashed to everything

Beau and her had heard about the rash of killings forty or fifty years earlier. Was six a rash?

"Do you know who's doing it?" she asked, hoping that her voice didn't shake.

He stared at her for a long minute, and the hair on the back of her neck stood up. Then he turned without another word and went back into the house, slamming the door so hard the windows rattled.

Justin ambled toward her from the yard, looking from the front porch to Katelyn and back again. "You okay?"

"Yeah, he um, startled me. He was baring his teeth."

"Don't let it throw you when he makes wolf gestures in human form," Justin said. He lowered his voice. "It's a symptom of his . . . condition. Our pups are taught from the cradle to cut out that kind of nonsense."

"Oh," she said quietly, thinking of how she had started growling when she and Trick had snuck into the Inner Wolf Center.

"It's never happened to you, has it?" he asked, studying her.

"No," she replied, trying to sound earnest, crossing her fingers that he couldn't hear her heartbeat speed up. But of course he could. Of course he would know. The only question was, would he let it go?

"Hmm," he said. He walked into the trees and she followed. The darkness and gloom descended.

"Soon we're going to work on focusing your hearing, your vision and your sense of smell."

"Soon, but not today?"

"No, today, we're going to see just how strong you are," he said with a smirk.

"Shouldn't I be focusing more on social stuff? You know, what to do and not do around the others so they don't want to kill me for breaking some rule I don't even know?"

"We need to work on that, too," he acknowledged. "But you have to test yourself, find limits of your new abilities so that you understand them. Because understanding what you're capable of and learning how to control it will help the rest of the world not figure out who you are and want to kill you."

"So, basically it's all about not getting killed."

"Pretty much," he said, pausing under a tree. The lowest branch was about twelve feet off the ground and Justin looked up at it. "Jump up there and grab that branch."

She gazed at it. "I'm springy, but not that springy."

"How do you know unless you try? After all, that's only about two feet higher than the rim on a basketball hoop. It should be easy for you now."

She crouched and jumped as high as she could, but came up about a foot short. She landed back on the ground and glanced at him.

"Again. And this time actually try."

"I did try," she said, feeling irritated. She crouched back down and stared up at her target. She felt all the muscles in her body coiling and then releasing as she sprung upward. Her hands wrapped around the branch and she gave a triumphant shout and looked down at Justin.

"Good! Now do chin-ups," he said.

She started and couldn't help but think about the

Cordelia and Mike contest on her first day of school.

"So, the most important thing to know about the pack is that as the bottom member you have to be subservient, you have to drop your eyes when someone is talking to you and make sure to give them those 'ma'ams' and 'sirs'. You have to be quiet and polite and respectful to everyone."

"See, I have a hard time seeing that happen," Katelyn said, struggling to keep the sarcasm out of her voice as she worked her chin-ups.

"Those are the rules, Kat. Being bottom-ranking sucks."

"So, how do I move on up?" she asked.

"Just like the rest of the world. You marry up or fight your way up tooth and nail."

"No way!"

"Well, Kat, sometimes you have to fight. And sooner or later you'll understand that."

She was thinking of hitting Mike and realized that Justin had missed her point. "I meant marry up. I'm not doing that."

She heard a chuckle and glanced down. "What's so funny?"

"The fact that you think you have a choice."

She let herself drop back to the ground, bending her knees to cushion her fall. She suppressed the urge to throw her arms backward when she had stuck the landing.

"What do you mean?" she asked. She thought of some of Cordelia's diary entries, about her dad telling her he'd choose her mate.

"Everyone marries in the pack, and younger than you're probably used to, being from California. It's your duty."

"I'm not marrying a werewolf," she said.

He gave his head a weary shake. "You're not going to have a choice about that. In fact, it's likely you won't even have a choice as to which werewolf. These things can be complicated and given how you came to be here . . . Uncle Lee will probably be choosing your mate." He flushed slightly and glanced away. She wondered why. Was he jealous? She wondered again if his uncle had arranged his romance with Lucy.

"You're kidding, right?"

"No, I'm not."

"I won't do it."

"We'll see," he said, effectively shutting down the conversation. "Now, jump to the next branch over, the one that's a foot higher."

An hour later Justin declared that training was over for the day. They headed back to the house and reached it just as Jesse trotted from around the back. He was holding a mud-encrusted action figure in one hand and a gardening trowel in the other.

"Hi, Kat, hi," Jesse said, hurrying up to her and giving her a kiss on her cheek, as all the pack were supposed to do. She kissed him back, and he giggled. "Did you marry Justin now? Because then I can marry Lucy."

"Justin is going to marry Lucy," Katelyn said carefully.

"My Uncle Lee says you're going to get married," he reported, nodding seriously at her. "He says you need a man."

"He— he *did*?" Aghast, she stared at him, then at the Fenners' house, where the alpha was.

"When you get married, I can wear my suit. You should stay for dinner. Lucy says I can have a drumstick. You can have the other one." Jesse looked past her and waved. "Hi, little brother." He cracked up. "Did you kiss Kat?"

"No, sir," Justin said.

"You should kiss her cheek. We don't kiss strangers but Kat is not a stranger."

"I'll kiss her next time."

"See you later," Katelyn managed, hurrying toward her Subaru. Then, lightning-fast, Justin was beside her with his hand wrapped around her forearm.

"You need to say goodbye to the alpha," he said. "Show respect."

She looked up at him. "Justin, he's talking about me getting *married*. I'm a senior in high school! Did you know about this while we were talking in the forest?"

"No, but I'm not surprised."

"I'm not getting married."

"All you need to do right now is say goodbye," he reminded her. "Don't stir the pot when you don't have a spoon."

"Oh, that's so quaint," she flung at him. If she saw Mr. Fenner, and he told her he wanted her to get married—

"Kat, I've got your back," he said quietly. "Just go say goodbye."

He walked her to the front door and it opened before she could turn the knob. Arial, one of Cordelia's older sisters, stood on the threshold with her arms tightly crossed. Her blonde hair had been pinned up in a messy bun, but one section had come free and coiled loosely around her shoulder, as if she'd been doing something physical. She looked warily at Katelyn, then visibly relaxed just a little when she shifted her attention to Justin.

"No," she said to him. "We can't have visitors."

"Kat is a member of the pack," Justin reminded her. "She wants to pay her respects before she leaves."

"I'll tell him." Arial reached for the doorknob, charms on her bracelet jingling.

Justin put his hand around hers. "No. You know that's something she should do," he said in a quiet but firm voice. "The alpha deserves her respect."

Arial sucked in a breath. "The alpha," she began, then toyed with one of the charms. "Daddy's resting before dinner." Then, as if she had to explain, she added, "He's been through so much. You know what I mean."

Justin grunted. "I surely do. And I'm wondering who it was that put him through most of it."

She gave him a wicked scary smile, seductive, dangerous. "Careful, Jus. Remember who you're talking to." She still didn't look at Katelyn as she added, "I'll tell him she said goodbye."

Then she shut the door in their faces.

"*Sure* you will," Justin muttered.

"I heard that," Arial said through the door.

Justin smiled sourly. "Knew she would," he said to Katelyn. He walked her back to her Subaru and politely opened the door. Southern men had manners; she had to give them that.

"Why does she blame me for getting bitten?" she asked him flat out. "I didn't do anything wrong."

"You remind her that he didn't pick her to succeed him," he said, as she got into the car. He shut the door and she rolled down the window. "And that her alpha's not in control. Packs are only as strong as their leaders. When the alpha shows weakness, it throws everybody off."

"So I'm a source of shame to her, too." Katelyn jabbed the key in the ignition.

"In a word, yes," Justin said.

"When won't I be?"

He leaned his elbows on the car door and gave her a sad smile. Then he dropped his arm toward her and tugged on a tendril of her light blonde hair.

"When you're settled," he said. "When you fit in. You're the omega — the lowest-ranking — but the alpha and I are both paying attention to you. That elevates you, and that's confusing everyone." One half of his mouth curved up in a cynical grin. "It'll be less confusing when you're not such an oddball."

"Oh, *thanks.*" She tried to jerk her hair out of his grasp.

He held it tighter, chuckling. "Try to have a little compassion." He tugged. "Our whole lives are built on pack order. And we're in disorder. It's not good for us."

"*Compassion?*" Katelyn cried. "For *her*? She made sure Mr. Fenner knew about me. She nearly got Cordelia killed."

"Her loyalty didn't lie with Cordelia. It lay with her father. You know that's a strong bond."

"No, I wouldn't know," she said hotly. "My father was murdered when I was twelve years old." She swatted his hand like he was a pesky fly and he released her. Then she started the engine and put the car in reverse, barely giving Justin time to get out of her way.

She sped through the forest, eager to be safely out of it, replaying her conversation with Justin. Remembering that his father was dead, too, and that he suspected Lee had killed him on purpose. Either way, his father was dead. There were a lot of deaths within the pack, so maybe that was why Justin didn't cut her any slack about what had happened to her.

Her thoughts drifted to her father's funeral, and how everyone had kept asking her if she was okay. No one had asked her mother, and it was obvious that Giselle Chevalier — her mom — hadn't been handling it okay at all. And Katelyn had suddenly understood that anyone who asked didn't really want to know. They just wanted to feel as if they'd done the right thing.

Thunder rumbled through the forest, and the trees shook their gnarled fists at her as she wiped her tears away and fought to pull herself together.

Even though she had wanted to be through the woods as fast as possible, she still wasn't ready to be back at the cabin when she parked outside. Grateful for the rain, she let it run down her face to hide her tears before going inside.

A sharp odor hit her. Her grandfather was at the table beside her computer, cleaning a gun. He looked up at her and gave her a nod, almost a smile, and she smoothed back her soaking wet hair.

"I forgot an umbrella," she said, even though that was pretty obvious.

"I was just fixing to make hot chocolate," he said, and she

felt a rush of pent-up tenderness toward him. There was no way in the world Mordecai McBride drank hot chocolate when he was alone.

"I'd love hot chocolate," she managed, her voice cracking slightly. "Thanks, Grandpa."

He put the gun on the table and went into the kitchen. She sank down beside her computer and powered it up. Mail from Beau. The subject header was *Anything?* with no message content.

She thought about Mr. Fenner. How old had he been way back then? Cordelia had told her that her father was approaching sixty, so he could have been a teenager then, or a young man. Were they his fault? Six murders. How many had there been, all told?

Nothing, she typed back. Then she shut her computer down.

Taking a breath, she walked into the kitchen. Mordecai was stirring a pot of milk and spooning cocoa mix into it, and Katelyn picked up the container and inspected it; the expiration date was five years old. Given how long hot chocolate mix kept, it was possible that he'd bought this jar before the last time she'd been there as a little girl — with her father, not long before Sean McBride had been murdered.

"You have a fight with that boy?" he asked her.

She set down the jar. "Trick?"

"The other one." He gave the milk a stir. "Still wondering if I invited the wrong one to Little Rock."

"No," she said in a rush. Then she realized there was no way she wanted to talk about boys with her grandfather, and let out a heavy sigh. "I just . . ." Fresh tears spilled down her cheeks. "I miss my parents." Words started rushing out of her. "It was so amazing of Trick to make that bust of Mom for me, you know? But I don't have anything of Daddy's, except for that suitcase. It's all gone, from the fire." She cried harder. She just couldn't stop herself.

Looking pained, her grandfather stirred the milk. He poured in the cocoa slowly, deliberately, then ventured, "I've got some stuff of your dad's. Out in the garage. Your grandma kept it."

She caught her breath and looked at him hopefully. "Really? Like what?"

"Probably everything he ever touched," he said. "He was our only child. Doted on him so. You never dream you're going to bury your own son." A stricken expression clouded his face. Then he shook himself and reached for two cups out of the cabinet. "We'll go through it. There's a lot of stuff out there, but I'll find it and bring it in for you. Don't go in there, Katie, though — some of the boxes aren't stacked too safe."

"Oh, thank you, Grandpa." She hugged him, putting her arms around his surprisingly brawny body and squeezing tightly. He patted her back, and she did the same, feeling ridges beneath the fabric of his shirt. His terrible, deep scars.

His showed. Hers didn't.

She watched as he measured out the steaming liquid into two cups and handed one to her. She clinked cups with him, the way she and Kimi used to do, whilst wondering privately if they'd get sick from drinking such old stuff; but she didn't want to spoil the mood, so she took a tiny sip.

So did he. And then he looked out the window and said, "We might have a white Thanksgiving this year. Gotta warn you. When the snow comes, we'll be holed up."

"Trick invited us to his place for the winter," she said.

"Did he?" He took the spoon to the sink and rinsed it. "Is that where you want to be when the storm hits?"

She wasn't sure what he actually was asking, and she wasn't sure she would have known the answer anyway. "Better there than here, I guess. He's closer to town."

"Sokolovs own a snow plow," he remarked. "I never got that fancy." He put the spoon in the dish drainer. He seemed to be moving slowly, as if he was in pain.

"Are you okay?" she asked.

"Just tired. Do you have homework?" he asked, and she nodded, grateful for the excuse to escape to her room. She was feeling edgy again.

She crossed the kitchen and was just about to make her way to the stairs when she impulsively turned back around.

"Guess who I just met," she said. "The Inner Wolf guy. Jack Bronson."

Her grandfather's bushy gray eyebrows shot up. He looked as if she had hit him in the stomach. "How? Where?" he demanded.

"Just in town. At the coffee house. I think he was in to sign some more of his books or something." She had no idea what insanity had prompted her to bring it up. Maybe because she hadn't told Trick she'd met him. And she'd never told her grandfather about the run-in with the two drunk guys.

"That man is crazy. He's ruining Wolf Springs. Don't ever go near him or talk to him again."

They passed the rest of the evening knocking around in the little cabin. Her grandfather finished cleaning his gun and then he read a hunting magazine. Feeling contrite, Katelyn emailed Beau and told him she was sorry she'd been so standoffish, telling him she had "family stuff" and when she'd taken care of it she'd be back to investigating the history of Wolf Springs with him. A small white lie. He'd written back that he was sorry for her troubles, but glad he hadn't caused them.

When she finally went to bed she couldn't relax. She lay staring at the skylight, then over at the bust of her mother that Trick had sculpted. There were things of her father's in the garage. Photographs of him as a little boy, probably. His school papers. But most likely pictures of him and her mom and Katelyn, too. All kinds of things that she'd thought were lost.

Her grandfather had said he'd bring some boxes in for her to go through, told her not to go in there, but Katelyn wanted to look now. Her parents had always laughed on Christmases when she'd forced them to get up at three- and four-o'clock in the morning, unable to wait another second. "So impatient," her mother had chided her, but her dad had said she was driven.

Maybe if she nosed around just a little, opened a couple of boxes, she'd be able to get to sleep. Her grandfather would understand, right? He'd made the offer. She was just taking him up on it a little sooner than he had intended.

She got up and a minute later, flashlight in hand, she hurried down the little path to the garage and went inside. There was his canoe, and there, the tower of boxes of food, antifreeze, and other supplies he had purchased for the winter. He had his workbench; on it lay more weapons in various stages of disassembly.

And then she faced dozens of boxes — a garage full. Most were cardboard, sealed with packing tape; others had just been folded closed. She ran her flashlight along them and read off labels gracefully written with a black marker: her grandmother's handwriting, she guessed. *Sewing Room. National Geographic. University Files.* There were just so many. Sighing, she wandered between two tall stacks, telling herself that if she didn't find anything in half an hour or so, she'd go back to bed.

Cookbooks. Taxes.

The life of an elderly married couple. Her parents would never have such a life. She wondered if she would, herself.

She kept poking around through dust and cobwebs, getting a little grossed out. She really shouldn't be doing this. Then the beam of the flashlight passed over a single word:

Sean.

Her heart skipped a beat. She stood in front of the box and placed her hand over her father's name. Then she lifted the boxes from on top of it and set them on the floor.

The packing tape along the seam was yellowed and dried up, so that it wasn't really holding the box together. Katelyn picked at it with her fingernail, wincing guiltily when the brittle tape crumpled away. Slowly, methodically, she peeled it off, keeping the strip intact as best as possible so she could at least lay it back over the seam. Then, with a deep breath, she opened it.

Sheets of gritty tissue paper made crumpling noises as she pushed them out of her way, revealing a carefully folded blue and white crocheted baby blanket. Her heart tugged as she unfolded it and put it against her face. It was as soft as rabbit fur but she smelled no trace of anything but dust.

She shook it out, refolded it reverently, and held it against her chest. There were more baby clothes inside — little shirts and booties. And photographs of her dad as a baby. She saw her own light blue eyes staring back at her. Her own small mouth, pulling a smile.

"Daddy," she whispered. "I miss you."

She went through the box slowly, gently, unfolding each item, admiring it, refolding it. Then, finally, knowing it was getting very late, she made sure everything was put back as she'd found it, picked up her flashlight, and turned to go. One box wasn't enough, but she should wait. And besides, there was a knocking little hollow place where her heart should be, and it hurt.

Then, as she replaced the tape, she dropped the flashlight. She crouched down to pick it up and a smell hit her. Metallic. Like tin foil. She shone her flashlight over an untouched row of boxes and sniffed the air. Her eyes began to water.

Silver, she thought.

But the side of the box read AMMO.

Weird, she thought. But it was time to go. She straightened and was about to leave when the smell drew her back, and she decided to have a look. As she moved a couple of cartons out of the way, dust lifted, ghostlike, and she sneezed. Then she opened the box and peered in.

Inside sat a rectangular metal olive-green box. It really was an ammo box. Her grandfather had carried out a few of those when he'd taught her how to shoot. But there was definitely silver inside.

She unthreaded the black strap wrapped around the box, then opened the lid and aimed her flashlight at the contents.

She gasped. Her heart triple-hammered in her chest, then skipped beats as her pulse roared in her ears and she staggered backwards into another stack of boxes.

There were dozens.

Gleaming in the light.

Silver bullets.

11

"It can't be!" Katelyn blurted aloud, but she knew she was right. She covered her mouth with both hands. The boxes behind her teetered, threatening to fall, but she could do nothing but stare at the bullets. In her grandfather's garage. Silver bullets.

Before she knew what she was doing, she bolted. Still clutching the flashlight, she flew out of the garage and across the road, into the forest, as if it was safe. Branches tore at her pants, at her hair.

Thunder rumbled. Lightning crackled above the treetops,

lighting up the forest, and she saw a shadow thrown against a trunk that was not hers. It was black and thin, the hands elongated, unearthly. She couldn't make sense of it. Her heart was beating too fast and she staggered left, right, as the rain bucketed down on top of her head.

There are silver bullets in the garage.

There is something out here with me.

The shadow slid along the tree trunks in strobe-like flashes of light and she threw herself away from it in a half circle and slammed hard against a tree. The flashlight rolled away and framed a face beneath a cowboy hat.

Justin's face.

"Kat?" he asked, hurrying toward her. "What's wrong?"

"What — what are you . . ." She couldn't talk. She was terrified. Maybe she'd imagined it and they'd only been normal bullets — her senses were off-kilter because of all the changes and the stress.

He put his arms around her and she burst into tears. She shouldn't be doing this, shouldn't let him see; but she couldn't stop herself.

"Did something scare you?" he asked her.

"Why are you here?" she asked shrilly, pulling herself back out of his embrace. There was so much rain everywhere, and she could barely see, and nothing was making sense. Had she gone crazy?

Justin's face glowed through the sheets of rain, white like a phantom, As she blinked at him, the forest came alive. There was a squirrel on a branch above his head; an owl still higher, preparing to dive at it. Farther on, there was a beautiful tawny wolf. Justin was not alone.

She began to run as fast as she could, pushing past branches and slipping in the mud. Lunging at ropes of Spanish moss, grabbing onto pine branches, she scrabbled and struggled. All she saw was a field of red and blinding white as her werewolf senses kicked in. Everything was giving off its own heat. It was like the other night trying to come back from having seen Cordelia, only five times more powerful.

Then Justin grabbed her and held her even though she flailed at him. She panted hard.

"Let me go," she said.

"What the hell is wrong?" he asked her.

"Nothing," she said. "I — I just got spooked in the garage." She jerked as he took off his cowboy hat and put it on her head. Then he picked up her flashlight and started walking her out of the woods toward the cabin.

"Spooked, hell."

"I — I'm so emotional." She threaded her hair away from her face. "I've been really short-tempered." She tried to peer through the trees. "Who's with you?"

"No one. I came alone."

She slipped, and he grabbed her hand. She was galvanized by his touch. "I saw a wolf."

"Then you were seeing things, darlin', because we're the only wolves here."

They stood at the edge of the road. The garage door hung open, and Justin headed toward it.

"No," she said quickly. "I found some things of my dad's, and it just freaked me out. But I'm not supposed to go in there. My grandfather asked me not to, but I did anyway."

"See what comes from not listening to your elders," he chided her gently. "Your father is partly why I came. I didn't know your pa was murdered. I didn't know much about you at all, except that you were new in town and Cordelia liked you. I did a little digging, and then I got to thinking about you being changed and all, without a hell of a lot of guidance."

He straightened the hat on her head. It was miles too big, and she could barely see beneath the brim. She clenched her fists, sure that she was about to burst apart — which was his point, she supposed.

"Digging," she said. "Digging where?"

"Girl, you're all over the internet," he drawled. "Your daddy's murder. Your mother's death. Didn't they teach you how to be careful about your information back in L.A.?"

"I can't talk about this now," she said tensely. "I'm supposed to be in my room. If my grandfather finds me out here, he'll ground me. And then I won't be able to come over for my 'guidance.'"

He was silent for a beat. Then he said, "Being a female werewolf's different from what I know. You were smart to stay away for a few days. That's our rule, too. I think my uncle's forgotten that we've got an extra complication here."

If she could have spared any more emotions, she would have felt embarrassed. But she was already overloaded; she wanted him to go away. She wanted to go back into the garage and make sure she hadn't been seeing things.

And . . . she didn't want him to go away. She wanted help. She didn't want to be so alone right now.

I can go to Trick, she thought. But she could tell him even less than she could tell Justin.

Cordelia. The right answer. Her friend. She pressed her knuckles together beneath her chin and exhaled, as if to get rid of how much she missed her.

"If we brought someone in to guide you — a female — she'd have to be high-ranking," he continued. "Which would mean someone like Arial or Regan . . . or Lucy."

She shook her head. "No way."

"But—"

"Don't be an ass," she said hotly. She let her hands fall. "I have to go. Stop stalking me."

"I told you to get used to being watched," he said. "And don't talk to me like that. *Ever*. Not even when we're alone."

"Or what?" She raised her chin. "You'll hurt me?"

He pressed his lips together, and she wanted to slap that scowl off his face. Who put him in charge? Who could decide he was high-ranking?

"Go in the house," he snapped. He handed her the flashlight.

"I have to straighten things out in the garage. By myself," she added pointedly, taking it. She couldn't leave the bullets out. Her grandfather would know she'd found them.

So what? she thought hotly. *He doesn't know.*

Does he?

She quaked. "All right, then," he said. "But this isn't over. We need to talk." He took his hat, and the rain blasted at the crown of her head.

Katelyn used that as her excuse to duck into the garage. And shut the door in his face.

The bullets.

Most of them were tarnished, but some were still shiny. She stared at them queasily, trying to convince herself she was in some kind of waking nightmare, then she picked one up, turning it over in her palm, studying it. Finally she dropped it back into the box, reached out and closed the lid.

Suddenly cold, she wrapped her arms around herself and thought about the scratch marks on her grandfather's back, her fears that they had been made by a werewolf.

She thought about someone shooting at her in the forest. "No way," she said aloud.

After she stowed the bullets and tried to replace the tape, she hovered on the threshold of the garage and tried to pick out Justin from the shadows. It weirded her out that he was there.

And I did see a wolf, she insisted.

The storm pushed at her as she hurried back inside the cabin, then closed and locked the door. She stood for a moment, her back pressed to it, listening for a sound, any sound, that would let her know if Mordecai was awake.

The house was silent. Her head spun, and her stomach churned as if she were going to throw up. Fear and revulsion collided, and also the tiniest flicker of hope. If her grandfather knew about werewolves, then maybe she could actually tell him, confide in him.

With the very next heartbeat, she knew that wish was

foolish and suicidal. Mr. Fenner had been clear that if she told her grandfather anything, he would kill them both.

Not if Grandpa kills him first.

She trembled as the thought took hold of her. Her grandfather was a hunter and he had a whole box of the right kind of ammunition. He could shoot Mr. Fenner and then . . .

What? she wondered. The rest of the pack would rip them to shreds. Or at least her, since her grandfather might already be in jail for murder.

She stared at the wall of trophy animal heads. What happened to a werewolf when they died? Did they look like a wolf, or a human? For one crazy second she imagined Mr. Fenner's human head mounted on her grandfather's wall and she was sickened by the thrill that rushed through her.

I hate him, she realized. *I hate him for sending Cordelia away, for threatening me and my grandfather and Trick.* A low rumble started in her chest and she shook her head hard, trying to calm herself down.

She moved swiftly into the kitchen and poured herself a glass of water. She was completely losing it, torn between rising fright and a wild, hysterical giddiness. The rumble was getting louder as she brought the glass to her lips.

She downed the glass of water and then stood for a moment, spooked by her own reflection in the window. White face, black holes for eyes. The growling seemed to have died down, but the hatred for Mr. Fenner still burned bright.

And she wanted so badly to tell her grandfather everything. He was strong; maybe he could protect them both.

Head thrown back, she gulped down another glass of water.

What if he shot Justin?

Her heart stopped for a moment.

I'm crazy. If he knows about werewolves, he has those silver bullets for one reason and one reason only. To kill us. How do I know he wouldn't kill me, too?

She thought of the silver trap in the forest that she had fallen into. Had her grandfather put it there?

The room tilted crazily and lightning billowed against the gingham curtains. She put her glass in the sink and made her way upstairs. Shivering, she changed into dry pajamas and lay down on her bed, misery coursing through her as she stared up at the skylight.

It was just too dangerous.

She couldn't tell him.

Not ever.

⊶ ⊰⊱ ⊷

Click.

Click.

Click.

Silver girl, silver girl, let me come in.

Peering down through the skylight.

Creeping down the hall.

Opening the door.

Click.

Click.

Click.

⊶ ⊰⊱ ⊷

"What?" Katelyn said blearily as she sat up. She could see her breath, and when she looked up she saw that the skylight was completely covered with snow.

She had taken off her soaking wet pajamas and laid them on towels on the floor; they were still ice-cold and still wet. If she had hung them in the bathroom, her grandfather would have known that she'd gone outside.

She dressed in jeans and a sweater, realizing she felt the cold, and raced downstairs. Mordecai was putting a log on the fire, which crackled and roared. She was surprised that she felt the cold so intensely and it drove her over to stand in front of it next to him. The radiating warmth began to thaw her slightly.

"Good morning," her grandfather said.

She nodded. "Why is it so cold?" She walked over to the window and stared outside.

Snow, everywhere. The dreaded winter had finally come.

She leaned her head against the window pane and strangled back a sob. *What happens when the full moon comes in a couple of weeks?* She took a moment to steady herself. Her grandfather came to stand beside her and she stole a glance at him. *What do you know? What's going on?* she wanted to scream at him. But she stayed quiet.

"Are we snowed in?" she asked.

"Naw," he said with a chuckle. "Higher up the mountain got a lot of snow, but this isn't bad. Just means it's time to put chains on your car. You ever done that?"

She shook her head. She'd seen her dad do it once when she was a kid on a trip to Lake Tahoe, but that was it.

"I'll teach you," he said.

A low rumbling sound reached her ears. *Oh no, why am I growling?* she thought. It took her a breathless moment to realize that the sound wasn't coming from her, but from outside.

"What's that sound?" she asked.

He cocked his head as though listening. She mentally smacked her forehead. *Of course, he probably can't hear it. He isn't a werewolf.*

A moment passed, then another. The rumbling grew louder, sounding mechanical in some way.

Finally he nodded. "Sounds like Trick's car." He looked at her intently. "Sharp ears," he muttered.

Trick was coming. There were silver bullets in the garage, Justin was spying on her, and now Trick.

A minute later, his Mustang pulled up outside the cabin. Katelyn watched from the window as he got out. He was wearing a black sweater and black pants, and he looked sleek, like a panther.

He walked up the steps and she went to answer the door. Despite everything, she felt a tingle of anticipation as she let him in.

"Mornin'," Trick said. He kicked the snow off his boots on the mat, took them off, and walked inside.

"Coffee?" Mordecai said, appearing from the kitchen with a mug.

"You know I never refuse free coffee," Trick said, taking the mug and sipping the hot liquid. "Or free food."

It was such a blatant hint about breakfast that Katelyn

cracked a smile. Her grandfather shook his head and disappeared back into the kitchen.

"So, what's up?" Katelyn asked, sounding brisk and curt. If Trick noticed, he gave no indication.

"You ever been sledding?" he asked.

"They had a snow hill at the L.A. Zoo at Christmas," she replied. "It was killer."

He snorted. "That was just stunt snow. This is real snow. *First* snow, and we're going farther up the mountain to take advantage of it."

"No clothes," she informed him.

"Brought some."

This is crazy, she thought, but it was just her insane double life come calling again.

He must have seen her make the decision to go, for he grinned at her and said, "I should warn you, I pack a mean snowball."

"Bring it, Vladimir," she taunted him, using his hated first name.

"Oh, I will, Katelyn. I'll go get your stuff."

She watched him from the porch. He really was gorgeous; she let herself stare and couldn't help but feel the corners of her mouth tugging into a smile.

⸻

The world was snowy and beautiful, tree branches frosted with ice and sprinkled with powdery white. There were chains on Trick's tires and the trunk was half open, exposing two old-fashioned wooden sleds secured inside with bungee cords.

Her grandfather waved from the porch. "Come back in one piece."

"I will," Trick said as he moved to the car.

"Wasn't talking to you."

Katelyn couldn't help but snicker as she got into the Mustang.

A minute later they were on their way. She sat back against the seat and looked out the window at the receding cabin. *Silver bullets. In our garage.* Were there also werewolf pelts?

She shuddered hard. Trick must have seen her do it.

"Yo?" he said.

"Just thinking." She looked over, trying to read him.

"You don't have to be this nervous," he said. "Packed snow only leaves minor bruising."

"I'm not nervous."

He didn't reply.

"How well do you know my grandfather?" she asked, trying to keep her tone light.

Trick raised a brow. "He's my godfather. I was born in your cabin. And what with my folks being away on business so much, we've spent a whole lot of time together over the years."

She stared at him, assuming he was joking. She didn't know anyone who had a godfather. Images of Mafia guys in trench coats rose in her mind. "C'mon."

He shrugged. "I'm serious. My middle name is Mordecai."

She gaped at him, thrown, not sure what to do with the new information. Aware of how little she really knew about

Trick. And now she realized it, he rarely mentioned his parents. She knew they were rich, very rich — but they were also very busy, flying all over the country for his dad's design business — and she had been amazed when going to Trick's place for a party to discover that he had his own building on their property. "How come I didn't know this?"

"I don't know. I guess I thought you did know." He smiled at her. "We're practically related. But luckily, not technically." He cocked his head. "Does it bother you for some reason?"

"No," she said quickly. "Why would it?"

"You tell me." He winked at her. "Because, hello? It is bothering you. It's cool, Katelyn. We share no common genes. Our offspring will be healthy."

She made a show of sputtering with indignation and gently punching his shoulder. But that was all it was, a show. Inside, she was working things out. That helped explain why he came over all the time, and all the conversations they'd had on the porch. And why her grandfather trusted him to take care of Katelyn.

If only my grandfather knew that I got bitten by a werewolf on Trick's watch, she thought. *After he hid out in his car at Sam's party and told me to go away.*

Then they were driving on a road she'd never been on before, climbing toward the mountaintops. Snow flurries fluttered against the windshield, and glittered in the sunshine.

"You're having so many private conversations you could be schizophrenic," he drawled.

She was saved from having to answer as Trick guided the

car to the side of the road and killed the engine. Back in California they wouldn't have just stopped wherever it struck their fancy. There would be a formal park, with a blacktop lot for the car, and drinking fountains and signs.

He opened the door and put on his cowboy hat. As he went around in front of the Mustang, he held up his hand, signaling for her to wait in the car, then when he got to her side of the vehicle, he stomped his boots hard and she realized he was tamping down the snow for her. Satisfied, he opened the car and held out his hand.

She took it, and as he helped her out he grabbed a hand-ful of slushy snow from the roof of the car and slid it down her back. She shrieked and batted at him, laughing as he trotted backwards. He yanked his cowboy hat off and used it as a shield as she gathered up snow with both hands and flung it at him. He jockeyed back and forth, taunting her, guffawing as she kicked snow at him, then headed straight for him.

"Crazy girl on the loose!" he cried, easily sidestepping her.

"Who are you calling crazy?" she demanded as she wheeled around for another attack. She started to put on a burst of speed, then reined herself in as she remembered that she couldn't draw attention to her enhanced abilities.

Trick raced up a hill, cackling in triumph. Then, as she pre-tended to struggle to catch up with him, he hung a U-turn, soaring back down on the other side of a stand of evergreens. She tried to get to him, but he was too fast. He reached the car and unfastened the sleds, loping back to meet her as he trailed them behind on the ground.

Panting, she fell in beside him. He reached in his jacket and handed her a pair of black waterproof gloves.

"Forgot to bring you some," he said. "Use mine."

"Oh, no, I'm not—" She was about to tell him that she wasn't cold. Just this morning, she'd been very chilly in the cabin. But now, she was just fine. Of course, she should be freezing, plus it was so sweet of him. "Thank you." She put the gloves on, which were miles too big for her hands, and wiggled her fingers at him.

At the top of the hill, he set the sleds down side by side. They were made of wood standing on wicked-looking curved blades to cut through ice and snow. The incline sheered downward, and she caught her lower lip between her teeth.

"You're not scared, are you?" he asked.

She scoffed. "Preposterous," she said.

"That's a mighty big word, little lady," he drawled. "Care to back it up with some runs down the mountain?"

"Mountain, hah. This is a bunny slope." She cocked her head. "Do you sit down or lie down?"

"Whatever it takes. Not a lot of rules in sledding."

He sat on his sled, then chuckled as she hesitantly copied him. She picked up a loop of rope.

"That's how you steer. Pull this way, you go to the left."

She pulled on the rope, then jerked her head over at him. "Don't, like, give me a push to get started or anything, okay?"

"Don't think that's how it works with you," he teased. Then he dug his snow boots into the whiteness and pushed off, and began to angle down. Watching him, she decided it didn't look so bad, and did the same.

And she went fast, very fast; she left silver bullets and the Hellhound and the Fenners behind as she screamed with a combination of alarm and exhilaration. The sled picked up even more speed, and Trick shouted out, "Whoa, whoa, Katelyn!"

Faster.

"You're on ice!" he bellowed. "Just steer straight!"

She shrieked, laughing, realizing she was going to fly past him. How the heck was she going to stop?

He cupped his hands around his mouth. "Lean backward. Try to drag your feet!"

Instead she reflexively yanked on the rope, way too hard. The sled zoomed sharply to the right and Katelyn tumbled off, face first, into the snow. She burst into a cascade of relieved guffaws, laughing so hard she couldn't move.

"Oh, my God," Trick said, stricken.

She kept laughing, helplessly, until he reached her and cautiously rolled her onto her back. All she could see were his green eyes as he bent over her and wiped the snow off her face.

"Are you okay? Are you all right?" he demanded.

She nodded, still laughing. "Ice on my side of the hill, huh? How *convenient*—"

Trick slid his hands under her neck and upper back, lifting her from the snow, and kissed her. His lips pressed against hers and he gasped, then he eased his tongue into her mouth. Pleasurable explosions burst at the small of her back and fanned out everywhere — her toes, her cheeks, the top of her head. She couldn't believe how good it felt, but it went beyond physical sensation to a sweet, deep joy. This was Trick, smart and quirky and yes, scary and unpredictable, but it was Trick. She hadn't kissed him in almost a month, and she had missed him, missed this. So much.

Trick's breath was hot against her cheek, her earlobe. He kissed her closed eyes, returning again and again to her mouth. He was raising her head, shoulders, and upper back above the snow, cradling her, holding her as if she were the most precious, adored girl in the world. She put her arms around his neck, clinging to him, never, ever wanting to stop kissing him.

He covered her face with kisses, then whispered her name into her ear over and over: "Katelyn, Katelyn."

And there was something about his voice that stopped her. Something familiar, and dangerous. Something that reminded her that when she was with Justin, she wanted him to kiss her like this, too. It made her feel two-faced and she understood how it would hurt Trick if he knew. And even though she knew the attraction to Justin was only physical — something to do with the wolf part in her reacting to the wolf in him — it still made her feel ashamed.

I'm not part of Trick's world anymore. I'm not human. And my grandfather has silver bullets in his garage.

"Trick," she protested, turning her face.

He didn't answer, just craned his head and kissed her mouth again. Her lips parted and her head fell back. It felt so good. And so right.

I'm not human.

"Trick, please." She pushed gently at him, feeling his heartbeat beneath her hand, and then she said, "No."

He stopped immediately. His breathing shallow, he cradled her head and laid his cheek against her forehead. Then, with a sigh, he pulled her up to her feet. His face was full of color; his cheeks were red and his lips were slightly swollen from their kisses. And his pupils were so dilated they almost looked black.

If only she could explain. But she couldn't.

As if he could read her mind, he cupped her chin and chastely brushed his lips against hers. Then he took her gloved hand in his and splayed it over his heart, which was racing so fast she couldn't count the beats.

"No's the magic word," he said. "I want you, Kat. But it's not just physical — I'm not some kind of animal."

But I am, she thought. Part of her wanted to take back the no. But she had to sort everything out.

"And I won't just be friends," he added. "I can't be your best androgynous pal in the friend zone while you sample what Wolf Springs has to offer." When she opened her mouth to protest, he shook his head. "You don't owe me anything, darlin'. Not even an explanation. But if I keep kissing you, you will. That's how I'll see it."

"Trick," she said, and he cocked his head, the sun glistening on his high cheekbones. He was so amazing-looking. Check, beyond that, *he* was amazing.

"When — *if* — you're ever ready, you know how to let me know."

Shaken, she lowered her gaze. He began walking away

toward the car. All too soon, their morning together was at an end. She was so sad. It had felt like a reprieve.

Then something hard and wet smacked the back of her head. A snowball. She whirled around to find him bent over, already packing another one.

As fast as she could, she grabbed two handfuls of snow and smacked them together. There was no snowball, only an explosion of icy crystals. She shrieked, defenseless, as Trick's second snowball hit her on the shoulder. As she yelled in protest, he picked her up and carried her to her sled, plopped her on it, and grabbed the rope. He began to drag her up the hill.

"No!" she cried. He kept pulling. "Trick, I said no!"

"It's all in the context, darlin'," he said, and kept going.

"Fine. Wear yourself out." She dug her heels into the snow to add to the drag. He kept pulling and she kept dragging. Then she leaped up and yanked on the rope he held so tightly, throwing him off balance. As he fell, she took off running down the hill, arms flailing as she laughed in triumph.

She tried to keep herself from running flat out, but her competitive streak got the best of her. Stumbling over her boots, she put on a burst of speed, heading for a copse of trees at the slope's edge. Her laughter echoed against the hill. She was giddy. It felt so good to put everything on a shelf and just *be* in the moment — to be a kid, to flirt with a hot guy who was into her. It was exactly what she needed to burn off all the tension.

"I'm coming for you!" Trick bellowed behind her. "Better run, girl!"

She burst into the trees and tore through them, laughing like a crazy person. Then she came to a rise before the next hill and stopped to catch her breath. As she panted, she looked back over her shoulder, but Trick's approach was hidden by the trees. Then she looked down the next hill, planning her escape.

About a hundred feet away, something dark was lying on the ground. As Katelyn studied it, a funny feeling tapped at the base of her skull and lifted her hair from her neck. She began to run toward it. It was a person.

"Hey!" she cried. "Hey, are you okay?"

As if in answer, a bird trilled. She heard something behind her crashing through the trees. She didn't wait for Trick.

It was a man. Or rather, what was left of him.

12

Katelyn stared down at the man's body. His eyes gaped wide in shock, his mouth an O of horror, pain. And his chest and stomach . . .

Katelyn covered her mouth with both hands as she fell to her knees beside him. The hunter-green parka he wore was soaked with blood and . . . and there were things . . . pieces.

"Mister?" she said, reaching a shaking hand toward him. His eyes didn't blink; the cavern that had been his chest didn't rise and fall. She took a deep breath and pressed her fingertips against his neck. His skin was ice cold. Recoiling, she pulled away for a moment and then forced herself to take another deep breath as she wondered how long he'd been dead. She clasped his wrist. Clammy flesh did not give way; it was frozen.

I'm touching a dead person.

The crevices in his chest revealed something white protruding from mangled piles of bloody, dark objects. His ribs. On his parka, an embroidered patch bore the emblem of a wolf's paw. The writing said *The Inner Wolf Center, Wolf Springs, Arkansas.*

"Oh, my God," Trick said above and behind her. Then he moved past, bending over the man, checking his pulse the same way she had. She watched numbly, shaking all over. Then she scooted away and got to her feet. "Call 911," Trick said, pulling his phone out of his pants pocket and handing it to her. "God, there's so much blood."

There was. The man lay sprawled on an incline, and the blood had pooled beneath him, then run down on the side farthest from Katelyn. A river of blood had gushed out of him, then frozen.

His left knee was bent backwards. And his left foot . . .

His foot was missing.

"Trick," she said wildly, but she couldn't make herself say anything but his name.

"Here," Trick said, taking the phone from her. He looked down and swore. "No service. Did you bring your cell? Katelyn?"

Part of her couldn't stop scanning the area, searching for

his foot. The other part of her was praying she wouldn't see it. When her mother had died, there had only been ashes. And memories.

I'm looking for a foot.

She took off the jacket Trick had lent her and put it over the man's face. Trick turned on his heel and headed up toward the car. Wincing, Katelyn moved away awkwardly from the dead man, crossing her arms over her chest. Her breath came in labored little gasps. After a couple of minutes, when she realized Trick hadn't returned, she backed away from the man, feeling irrationally guilty for leaving his side, then pushed through the trees. She hadn't wanted to shout for Trick. Didn't want to disturb the — the *body.*

Trick was standing on top of the hill beside his sled, her phone to his ear. Then he saw her, picked up the sled when it would have been easier to let it slide down, and came over.

"Yours doesn't work, either. Let's go to the cabin." He looked past her and she turned quickly, half expecting to see the man stumbling out of the trees. Trick chewed the inside of his cheek as if debating something.

"Do you want the jacket?" she asked him, feeling ill.

"Oh, girl," he said mournfully, reaching out and holding her against his chest. "I just don't like leaving him there."

"I know what you mean." She closed her eyes tightly, losing herself in his warmth.

"What if it comes back?" he said.

"What comes back?"

"The animal that killed him."

She let out a sob. *Please, let it be just an animal.*

They rushed back together to the Mustang, and drove back in taut silence, Katelyn checking both their phones for service. Even though Trick drove with a seeming disregard for safety, it took forever to get to the cabin. To Katelyn's shock, Sergeant Lewis's squad car was already parked behind her grandfather's battered blue truck.

"Did we get through?" she asked.

"Oh, God," Trick whispered, stricken. The wheels had barely stopped rolling before he and Katelyn were running up the steps and bursting into the cabin.

Her grandfather and Sergeant Lewis were at the kitchen table, bent over some objects covered with what appeared to be wet sawdust, spread out on a layer of plastic trash bags. Beyond the wet, muddy odor, she detected the unmistakable smell of silver. She froze.

"Sergeant Lewis found some of our things that were taken in the break-in," her grandfather said, looking up at her. "Dumped in the Wolf Springs bog." Then he looked at her again. "Katie?"

"We found a man," she blurted. Trick came up beside her and put his arm around her waist. "Dead."

Sergeant Lewis was instantly all business. "Where? Can you show me?"

"The sledding hill," Trick answered, then launched into a detailed explanation of how Katelyn had found him, and that there was nothing they could do to help him.

"Katelyn put a jacket over his eyes," Trick said faintly.

"I think you're going into shock, son," Katelyn's grandfather said. "Katie, get him some water."

But Trick was rushing after Sergeant Lewis, who was already halfway to the door with a big radio phone to his ear. Her grandfather grabbed his rifle from the wall rack. "Stay in the house," he told Katelyn. "Don't go outside."

She was about to insist that she should go back, too, when she realized she needed to make some calls of her own. As soon as she heard the three of them drive away she called Justin, but his voice mail answered.

Urgent!!! she texted him.

She tried Cordelia next, then Dom. No one responded. Trembling, she went into the kitchen and splashed water on her face, then looked through the window at the snow-covered yard.

"Did one of you do it?" she demanded.

Her phone dinged, signaling the arrival of a message. It was Beau.

"Not now," she said aloud, as if he could hear her.

Then as she poured herself a glass of water, movement in the yard blurred in her peripheral vision. Before she even knew she was going to do it, she slammed down the glass, threw open the kitchen door, and raced outside. Something was running down the side yard. Snow came showering down in its wake and Katelyn ran straight through the cascaded curtain of white, charging from beneath the frosted branches to the road, where her Subaru and Trick's Mustang were parked. Footprints — they looked human — had cut a path across the road into the forest. The trees were quivering. Katelyn kept going.

And then she wondered what the hell she was doing. This

could be the person who had shot at her, coming to finish the job now the coast was clear. Or the monster that had killed that man.

She kept running, unable to stop herself. But the force of her momentum threw her forward as a terrible pain squeezed her knees, ankles, and spine. She could hear her joints popping and a growl tore out of her throat.

She was transforming.

The forest shimmered and gleamed; snow falling in loud bursts from the trees looked like fireworks sparklers. She loped instead of running. Her thoughts began to dissolve. It couldn't be happening. But it was, and she was caught in a grip of unbelievable agony. Pain stabbed her everywhere, bone-deep. Then her foot caught on a root and she arced into the air, her body twisting, and she fell face-first into the snow. Her ears rang and her nose and forehead stung. She was so stunned she couldn't move. She lay there, exposed and vulnerable to whomever had been in the yard. She didn't know if she was wolf or human. All she knew was that she was hurt.

She had no idea how long she lay there, braced for an attack. Woozily she raised her pounding head. Her cell phone was going off. She grunted and awkwardly fished in her half-torn pocket — with a human hand — and drew it out. Then she made the connection.

"Do they know who did it?" a voice asked.

Katelyn's eyes popped open. It was Cordelia.

"No. Do you?" Katelyn replied.

"But *you're* okay."

"I guess," Katelyn said. "Oh, my God, I was so scared I

would never talk to you again!"

"I want to come home," Cordelia whispered. "Have you figured out anything about the mine?"

"Still working on it," Katelyn said. She pushed herself to a sitting position and pulled her legs underneath her. Then, clinging to a tree, she got to her feet.

She heard sniffling. Cordelia was crying. "I'm here alone. Dom is pressuring me. He says if I don't declare my loyalty soon, I'll have to leave. But if you found it, and we told my daddy . . ."

"I'll keep trying," Katelyn promised.

Picking up speed as she headed across the road, she tried the front door. Locked. Her key was in her purse, in the house.

"How did you know someone had been killed?"

"Dom told me," Cordelia replied.

"How did he know?" Katelyn asked, suspicion flooding her as she ran around to the back door and looked at the snow to see if there were any prints leading back inside. There weren't. Cursing herself for being an idiot, she let herself in and quietly closed the door. Standing still, she listened. Nothing. She began to creep through the kitchen.

"Cordelia," she said into the phone. "Listen, something happened." All she heard was static. "Cordelia?"

The connection had been severed, or lost. Maybe it was just as well that she'd had a minute to reconsider her impulse to confide that she'd begun to transform. Katelyn dialed back but the call was blocked. Dom must have spies. And if they could come back for Katelyn, then the Fenner territory was not secure from invaders.

Do I care?

Her grandfather called; then he and Trick came back. They were grim-faced and her grandfather said he didn't want to talk about it. Instead, he began to inspect the items Sergeant Lewis had retrieved from the Wolf Springs bog.

"There's about half of the good silver and one of the pictures," Mordecai said as he picked up a framed mountain landscape. It was warped and covered with mud — and it wasn't the painting with the waterfall and the heart-shaped boulder.

"And you say he found this in a bog?" Trick asked.

Mordecai nodded. "Why anyone would throw sterling silver in a bog's beyond me," he said angrily.

Katelyn picked up a serving knife and glanced at Trick. He looked back at her with a neutral expression.

"Careful with that, sweetie," her grandfather warned her. "It's sharper than the dickens."

And it's silver, fatal to all werewolves, she thought as she looked down at the knife. *Except me*. And, thinking of the silver bullets in the garage, she "accidentally" pricked herself in the thumb with the tip of the blade. It felt so weird to do it, as if she were lying.

She knew very well that she *was* lying.

I am not a werewolf.

Blood bubbled up from the wound. "Ouch," she said. She felt as if she had just walked across a chasm on a rope bridge, then cut it loose so that her grandfather and Trick couldn't follow. It was a horrible, frightening feeling and she swayed.

"Katie?" her grandfather said, his expression unreadable. "What happened?"

"I just pricked myself," she said. "It's barely a scratch."

"Sometimes those hurt worse than the big ones," he replied, taking her hand and examining the wound closely. "That knife's probably covered with bacteria."

"I'll get the first-aid kit," Trick said, leaving the room.

"Tell me what happened," Katelyn said to her grandfather as she sucked on her finger. "To that man."

"Animal mauling, like those two girls," he said. "Maybe you should start driving back and forth to school with Trick again."

"Um," she began, thinking of how she'd manage going over to the Fenners. And looking for the mine.

Then Trick walked back into the room with the first-aid kit. Katelyn cleaned the cut and applied her own bandage while Trick looked on. Another text came in. Justin. He must have heard. She glanced down at it.

Killer not one of us.

So he said.

But somehow, like Dom and Cordelia, he already knew about the dead man and about why she was calling. She glanced at her grandfather and Trick from under her lashes. The terrible news was traveling so fast. People — correction, werewolves — were hearing about it more quickly than they should. How? She might be keeping secrets from them, but it was clear the werewolves were keeping secrets from her, too.

⊶ ⊨⊨ ⊷

Word of the death of the Inner Wolf executive spread

through school like wildfire. Katelyn's classmates didn't hold each other and weep the way they had when Becky Jensen had died. But they did walk around looking shell-shocked, and tributes for Mr. Henderson began to appear at the door to his office — silk flowers and candles, and handwritten notes. *We hope you're okay, Mr. Henderson.*

The police imposed a curfew — no one out on the streets past 8:30 at night. No one really complained. Everyone was afraid.

Beau cornered Katelyn at lunch, his face peaked, shifting his weight as he held a lunch tray in his hands. She was sitting in the stairwell. Across the room, Trick watched.

"The cops came over and asked my whole family a ton of questions," Beau began. "I think because of my grandma. She couldn't give the police much information, but last night in the hospital she began to make a little more sense. The doctors are really happy about her progress."

"That's great," she said.

"She keeps saying there was something at her window. And I think there was, Kat." He looked at her with hurt in his eyes, and she felt herself giving in to the inevitable. If she didn't help him, it would make him curious and he might ask questions she couldn't answer. And if his grandmother had actually seen the Hellhound, Katelyn wanted to know.

"Maybe we could go see her together this weekend," she suggested.

Clouds of worry rolled away from his face. "That'd be good. Thanks. Have you found anything? Heard anything?"

She didn't tell him about the Switliski book. She just

shook her head and picked up her peanut butter and jelly sandwich, even though she had no appetite. Beau got the hint and said, "She's all the way in Bentonville. It'll be a drive."

"I'll square it with my grandfather," she promised. But a moment later another thought sprang into her mind: *Do I have to clear this with the Fenners, too, like when I wanted to go to Little Rock?* An instant later, this was followed by, *Screw that; I'm not going to have my freedom curtailed completely.*

Gratified, Beau walked away, giving Katelyn a clear view of Trick watching her.

⋯ ⫯ ⋯

When she pulled up outside the Fenner house, she sensed that something new was wrong. Usually Justin stood outside waiting for her, but there was no one there. She walked around the back, her boots crunching on a layer of crusty frost, and took inventory of the parked vehicles. Apparently, Arial and Regan had come over.

Her throat tightened. She was so not in the mood to deal with Cordelia's bitchy sisters.

Straightening her shoulders and lifting her chin, she knocked on the door. There was no answer. She tried calling Justin's phone, but he didn't pick up. She stood there, wondering what she should do. And then she heard raised voices from inside.

Someone was arguing.

I shouldn't be here, she thought. *Not if they're having family problems.* She started to back away from the door.

Without warning, it flew open and Arial stood framed by

the doorway. Dressed in scarlet and gold and wearing heavy makeup, she crossed her arms and sneered at Katelyn.

"Well, speak of the devil," she said, raising her voice only slightly, for sensitive werewolf ears to hear.

"What's going on?" Katelyn asked, taking another step back. Fear pricked at her scalp and her body started to quiver. *Run*, it told her. *Flee.*

Trembling, she ticked a glance toward the tree line, wondering if she could make it there before the others caught her. A moment later she realized that was foolish. Some of them could shift into wolves at will and they would hunt her down and maul her to death.

It's just a primitive response, she told herself. *Fight or flight. The animal part of me.*

Except . . . the people in the house were animals, too.

Justin appeared in the doorway behind Arial. "Kat, come in," he said, voice tense.

She didn't want to, but she didn't see that she had any other choice. When Arial didn't give way, she had to push past her and she saw the anger flicker on the face of the higher-ranking girl. Justin led her to the living room where the rest of the Fenner clan was gathered, except for Jesse.

"Jesse's with Lucy," Justin said, as though reading her thoughts.

"What's going on?" she asked.

"Too much, that's for damn sure," Lee Fenner said, voice hardly more than a growl. The others glanced his way, but no one commented. Katelyn knew now that it was considered a sign of weakness or immaturity to display wolf behaviors when in human form. That their alpha was doing it was a symptom of his dementia.

"We're discussing the murder," Doug — Regan's husband — said, sounding kind as he acknowledged Katelyn's entrance into the room with a lifting of his finger.

"An invasion of our territory, that's what it is," Mr. Fenner snarled.

"We're still not sure that Dom's pack is behind this," Albert, Arial's husband, pointed out, his posture deferential, his tone cautious. Katelyn translated: no one wanted to contradict the alpha.

"They must be. It can't be one of us," Justin argued.

"It's her, of course," Regan said, tilting her head toward Katelyn.

All eyes were on her.

"What?" Katelyn gasped, stunned.

There was a moment of terrible silence and she could read the fear and hostility in the body language of those around her.

"But *I* was attacked. And I can't shift at will," she finally managed to say.

"And the first girl was killed before Kat got here," Justin pointed out with a heavy sigh. "So it *can't* be her."

She felt as though she had been slapped in the face. From the tone of his voice he sounded like he *wanted* it to be her.

"Only one thing is certain," Doug said. "Someone's disloyal."

"Maybe they're spying on us, going to the Gaudins and telling them all about us," Regan said.

Katelyn thought of Dom and his brother. They had managed to sneak into Fenner territory to extract Cordelia unobserved.

"Yes. We need to find a way to flush the traitor out," Mr. Fenner announced. "And then rip out her . . . or his . . . throat."

Katelyn went cold all over. They were discussing murder. She thought of her lawyer father and what he would have thought of her standing there listening to them. *If they kill someone, I'm an accessory, guilty as well*, she thought, anxiety pouring through her. *I have to get help. Find a way to stop all this madness.*

She could hear the others talking, but she was no longer paying attention to what was said. The image of the silver bullets in her grandfather's garage blazed into her mind. She knew how to shoot a rifle. Could you just put silver bullets in a normal rifle? Could she do that? Her heartbeat roared in her ears. Could she kill these people?

They are not people.

And neither am I.

She trembled so hard she couldn't see, couldn't hear. She couldn't feel her shoes against the floor.

"So, it's settled then," Mr. Fenner said.

"What is?" She could have kicked herself when he glared at her. She couldn't afford the luxury of fuzzing out around him.

"You'll have Thanksgiving dinner with us," Justin said.

She blinked again. How had they gotten from talking about murder to Thanksgiving?

"But my grandfather expects to have dinner with me . . .

er, sir," she said, desperate for a way out. She couldn't imagine sitting down to turkey dinner with the Fenner clan and struggling to pretend that she was thankful for anything in this whole mess.

There was an exchange of looks that didn't bode well. Then Justin said, "We'll work something out."

"You can go, Kat," Mr. Fenner announced imperiously.

Her lips parted in surprise. She'd come all the way out and now there'd be no training? She dipped her head, grateful for the reprieve, and hurried to the door.

Justin followed her out to her car. When she started to open the door, he laid his hand over hers. His dark brows met over his deep blue eyes.

"Things are bad now, Kat. Suspicions are running high and no one wants this police investigation to go forward."

She nodded, trying not to focus on the touch of his hand and the way her skin was tingling. He leaned forward and brushed her cheek with his lips.

"Don't worry," he whispered. "I'll protect you."

"Please, don't touch me," she said, aware that heat was starting to flash through her, burning in her veins like fire. It was how it always felt when he was this close. His breathing had changed, become more ragged, and she knew he was feeling what she was. She pushed the feeling back down — this was *not* who she was.

With a small grunt of frustration, he stalked up the steps and went back to the house. Katelyn got into her car and drove away as fast as she could.

That was close, she thought.

Too close.

⇥ ❧ ⇤

Saturday morning, Katelyn went with Beau to see his grandmother. It was a long drive to Bentonville, and both of them were nervous. Beau kept music on to fill the void.

"They've moved her to the convalescent wing," he told her as he angled his truck into a space in the parking structure.

She wrinkled her nose as they entered the building. She had always disliked hospitals, but now the smell of antiseptic and sickness burned into her pores like acid.

As they walked down the hall toward his grandmother's room, Beau took her hand and gave it a squeeze. "Thank you for coming with me."

"No problem," she said. "I just hope that she can tell us something useful."

They made it to the room and walked in. Katelyn recognized her as the elderly lady she'd met the first time she went in to Babette's. Beau's grandmother, Mrs. Nelson, had looked very elegant then, in a black dress and feathered hat, but now the hospital bed engulfed a sunken old lady, frail and wispy-headed, and fearful. She had warned Katelyn and Cordelia to go home and lock their doors. But for her, her home had not been safe.

"Grandma, how are you? This is my friend, Kat, the girl I was telling you about," Beau said, planting a kiss on her forehead.

The older lady smiled wanly at him and picked at the edge of her hospital sheet. She didn't even look Katelyn's way.

❧ 220 ❧

"You're my good boy, Beau," she said in a warbly, uncertain tone.

Beau flashed a smile at her, then glanced over at Katelyn, as if he weren't sure how to get started.

"I love you, too, Grandma. Ah, we were hoping you could tell us what you saw that night at your window," he said.

"My . . . window?" the old lady repeated, worrying the sheet more rapidly.

"Yes, Grandma, remember?" Beau prompted. "You saw something that frightened you?"

"We don't want to upset you," Katelyn said.

The old lady turned her head toward Katelyn, and her eyes bulged. She cowered, pushing herself against Beau.

"*You!* I saw *you!* Get away from me, demon!"

13

Katelyn stared in shock at the old lady, who was grabbing at her grandson. Then Katelyn met Beau's astonished eyes.

"No, I wasn't there," Katelyn said.

"Get away from me!" the old lady shouted.

Katelyn fled the room, and rushed down the hall, then back the way she'd come. She could hear Beau's grandmother screaming. A nurse hurried across the hall, saying, "Now, Henrietta, what's the matter?"

"She's the one!" Mrs. Nelson shouted. To Katelyn it sounded loud enough to be heard by the entire building.

Whether or not that was just her enhanced hearing she didn't know. "She's a monster! She's killing them. Beau, you have to shoot her," she said, lowering her voice. Katelyn could still hear her. "I got a gun under my bed at home, honey. You take it and you shoot her in the heart."

"You have a *gun*, Grandma?" Beau said, his voice laced with disbelief.

Katelyn wanted to be out of there, but her car was back in the school parking lot. I could just leave. *I could walk there, or better yet, run.* Her heart was pounding in her chest and she ducked her head to avoid meeting anyone's eyes.

But leaving will just make me look guilty. And I'm not. I didn't hurt anyone and I certainly didn't appear in her window.

She forced herself to sit down in the waiting room. She put her head between her knees, feeling dizzy. Slowly her thoughts cleared and she pushed back upright in the chair.

She couldn't hear Beau or his grandmother anymore. Maybe the old lady had calmed down. She picked up an out-of-date *People* magazine and forced herself to flip through it even though she couldn't focus on the words. Instead she stared at the pictures. All the pretty people of Hollywood. And all she wanted to do was go back home and have a shot at being one of them, and not a monster.

She heard steps and looked up to see Beau hurrying her way.

"Oh, my God, Kat, I'm so sorry," he said in a rush. "I don't know what set her off like that." He blanched. "I guess the stroke has messed up her mind even more than we thought."

"Let's hope it affected her aim, too," Katelyn said, then

winced and shut her eyes. "I'm sorry, Beau. I did not just say that."

He managed a gallows laugh. She put down the *People*; they got a couple of sodas out of the machine in the waiting room and then they hit the road.

"Maybe she made it all up," Beau said. "Maybe she didn't see anything at her window." He sounded rattled. He had believed his grandmother. He frowned thoughtfully. "And maybe there haven't been rashes of deaths every forty to fifty years in Wolf Springs." He nodded, as if to himself. "We haven't seen any articles about it, no news accounts, nothing."

And this was her moment to steer him away from murders and monsters and all kinds of things, pin it all on some random person and ignore the connection with the town's past. To protect him.

"Yeah," she said, trying to sound enthusiastic and con-vinced. "Good point."

Failing.

"But my grandmother also said that Wolf Springs was a lot more isolated back then. That people didn't talk about things. They kept to themselves," he pointed out. "And three people have died."

"Yeah, but she also said I was the demon she saw. Maybe it's like some people are saying, that those Inner Wolf guys are frightening the wildlife."

He frowned. "Maybe one of those guys murdered Becky Jensen. Say she went to meet somebody, and it went wrong, so he moved her body and then the animals got to it?"

"Or he did it himself, to make it look like an animal

attack?" she said, shutting her eyes hard against a rush of anxiety. None of this was remotely what she had expected when she'd agreed to visit his grandmother. She'd been hoping for a description, some useful clues. Not to have any fingers pointed her way.

"Sam said her mom heard the doctor talking to Sergeant Lewis. He said he'd never seen anything like what had happened to Becky. That her injuries didn't add up."

Because a werewolf caused them? Katelyn pondered.

"Kat," he said, glancing over at her from behind the wheel, "you know, maybe you should stay out of this. You're new, and you've got to find your way with everybody. You know, make friends and stuff, not lurk around asking questions. The only other new kid I've ever known was Sam, and she didn't last here."

"Just six years," she said dryly, morbidly amused by *his* attempt to protect *her*. "And she left because her parents are getting divorced."

He moved his shoulders. "Yeah, okay, but trust me when I say that people at school are sizing you up. In town, too."

Talking about me, she translated.

He hesitated. "I know you're planning to move back to L.A. when senior year is over, but a year is a long time."

No, I'm not moving back, she thought, feeling lost and sad. People were going to wonder about her when she stayed. They would think she wimped out. Or maybe they'd decide she was devoted to her grandfather and didn't want to leave him.

Or maybe Mr. Fenner would make her marry some guy.

She nearly burst into uncontrollable, nervous laughter at the thought. She never, ever in a million years had thought she would have to worry about marriage when she had gotten on that plane in L.A.

If only she could rewind time. She wouldn't have come there. She remembered how Kimi and her mother had begged her to file for emancipation so she could move in with them. *Why* hadn't she done it?

Because I was stupid, she thought. *And how dare Mordecai bring me here, to a cabin in the middle of the woods, cut off from everything, when he* knows *about werewolves?*

Unless the silver bullets in the garage weren't his. Maybe someone had hidden them there. Maybe they were part of the estate from his friend who had died a few weeks ago — the one whose Subaru she was driving. Maybe that guy was the one who had set the trap in the woods. How could she know? She couldn't just ask.

⸱—⸱⧓⸱—⸱

When she got back home she was surprised to find Trick there.

"Hey," he said as he met her on the porch. "Your pappy told me you'd gone with Beau to visit his grandmother."

"Yup," she said, not eager to explain herself. It had been nice to be able to tell her grandfather exactly where she was going, but she hadn't counted on having to explain to Trick why she cared about Beau's grandmother.

He raised an eyebrow and looked at her quizzically. She just forced herself to smile at him. His T-shirt was drenched in sweat and he had on a beat-up pair of jeans. Still, he looked good and she could feel tingles at the base of her spine as she stared at him.

"So, what are you doing here?" she asked.

He shrugged. "Getting y'all winterized, since it looks like you guys won't be staying at our place. Making sure the roof's in great shape, all the weather stripping is in place on the doors. And, of course, chopping even more wood."

"Oh," she said. It would be easier to keep her secret if she was sequestered in the forest. Her grandfather, though, would be at higher risk.

And so would she.

Trick ended up staying for dinner, and afterward they all gathered around her grandfather's new flat screen to watch a movie. Her grandfather sat in his chair and she and Trick shared the couch and a blanket. She thought she caught Mordecai smirking before turning his attention fully to the screen. As the opening credits rolled, Trick reached out and took her hand and she let him.

The fire crackled cheerily; the movie was dumb but easy to watch. Trick held her hand all through the movie and she marveled at how good it felt, how comfortable. She didn't have the overwhelming need to kiss him, to be closer; it was somehow warmer, nicer. It made her feel even closer to him. And although she knew that was dangerous, she was enjoying it too much to put an end to it.

When the movie was over her grandfather excused himself to the kitchen and they lingered in front of the door.

"I liked this, Kat," Trick said.

"Me, too," she said.

"Thanks for a nice evening." Trick brushed a strand of hair away from her face.

Her cheek tingled where his fingers had connected and she leaned into him a little, not wanting him to go.

"You know, you still owe me a snow fight. I was winning."

"You were not," he said with a smile. He looked deep into her eyes. "I think I was."

She shivered as he stepped closer. Then, instead of kissing her, as she half expected, he wrapped his arms around her and hugged her tight.

"I'm always here for you," he whispered. Then he broke away and let himself out the door.

After Trick left, her grandfather said, "Maybe we *should* go to the Sokolovs' when it snows."

She didn't know what to say, so she just smiled non-committally and went up to bed.

Sunday morning after breakfast her grandfather got out the silver that had been recovered from the bog, some silver polish, and a rag, and set to cleaning them. Katelyn drifted over to the table and sat down. "You have an extra rag?" He nodded and handed her one and she picked up a piece of the silver. She could smell it and her skin felt warm where it touched, but she forced herself to ignore it. She thought about Trick and wondered what he was doing. "Last night was nice. Does Trick always help out like that?"

Her grandfather flashed a rare grin. "Yeah. The boy's good for something."

"He told me you're his godfather."

"That's true."

"Do you trust him?" she asked bluntly.

He stopped and gave her a funny look. "He's a teenage boy. I'd trust him with my life. I wouldn't trust him with a pretty girl."

"Then why do you let me hang out with him?" she asked, smiling.

"Because he knows I'd skin him alive if he hurt you."

She was touched. There was a bond, a loyalty between her grandfather and Trick. And yet he cared about her getting hurt.

"What if I hurt Trick?" she asked him, working at a patch of tarnish on a spoon.

He concentrated on his polishing. "You talkin' about Justin?"

She was talking about so much more than matters of the heart. There were too many ways she could hurt Trick even if she didn't want to. She felt dizzy at the thought of what could happen to him if he was ever around her when she changed.

"I guess," she said finally, dipping the cloth into the gray, pasty polish.

He cocked his head, appraising her. "Then I'd tell Trick to take it like a man. A young woman's got the right to do as she wishes. That's nature's way."

"Well, that's forward-thinking," she said with a smile.

His face crinkled with a grin. "It's the truth. You can't walk through the forest without seeing male birds trying to get the attention of the female. Or a pair of bucks knocking antlers while the doe just watches."

"And yawns," she added, and he grunted.

"I figure the human animal shouldn't be any different. It makes me sad sometimes to see girls throwing themselves at guys who don't want them. That's not how things should be."

Katelyn remembered Becky Jensen, the girl who had died just after she had arrived in Wolf Springs. According to Sam, Becky had invented an entire relationship with Trick — one which ended when he dumped her. Had she been telling the truth?

Now Sam was gone, and Becky was dead, and there was no way to know exactly what the real story was . . . except that Katelyn just couldn't see Trick doing something so heartless.

But maybe he'd grown up since then, she thought. *Maybe I'm seeing a new, improved Trick.*

"You and Trick are close but you've never pushed me to pick him over . . . anyone else." She wiped the polish over the back of the spoon and began to rub it. Soon she would see her reflection. How could it not be different, now that she was such a . . . a . . .

Monster.

He looked startled. "There's no rush, honey. You're only seventeen. I'd be just as happy if you don't pick anybody until you're, oh, fifty-seven."

That was refreshing.

"But if I *did* like someone, you'd be okay with it?" she asked.

Her grandfather chuckled. "Your grandmother's father hated me, but it didn't stop how she felt. And in the end he was smart enough to see that if he tried to keep us apart, she'd just run away with me."

"Wow, really?" She was impressed. Her grandparents had been intense. She wished she'd gotten to meet her grandmother, or even better, that she was here now.

"Love is a powerful thing," he replied. "And it can't be denied any more than it can be tamed."

That gave her pause. Back home in L.A. most kids talked about hooking up, not falling in love. Was it different there in the hills, or was her grandfather talking like a person from a different era?

"Why didn't Grandma's father like you?"

He chuckled with a faraway look in his eyes. "He thought I was too uppity. I don't think he had much use for philosophers. College boys either, for that matter."

Katelyn bit back a smile, trying to imagine how anyone on earth could think of her cabin-dwelling grandfather as "uppity."

Their conversation died away, and they polished the silver together in companionable silence. The odor was so strong; it was incredible to her that he couldn't smell it. She wondered why silver was so poisonous to werewolves. And why it didn't bother her.

It took a couple of hours, but the silver was finally shiny. The rest of Sunday passed quietly, almost too quietly. Katelyn found herself growing more and more agitated, as though she were waiting. For the snow, for more deaths.

⋅⋅⊰⬩⊱⋅⋅

Monday after school she found herself again at the Fenner house, doing more training with Justin. There was more running, jumping, but he also worked on her sense of smell and trying to use it to track him through the woods. It went better than she expected. When they finished he offered her his cheek. "See you tomorrow," he said. "We'll do some more."

"Can we skip tomorrow and meet Wednesday?"

He shook his head. "I'm taking Lucy Christmas shopping Wednesday, and I don't think she'd cotton to waiting in the car while I teach you how to howl," he said. "Me, I like to order things online. But you know how the female of the species is — always on the prowl for something shiny."

"You're so sexist," she said.

He raised a brow. "Is that the way they talk in Santa Monica? Here in the hills, them's fightin' words."

Katelyn sighed. In some ways, she and Kimi had been right about calling Wolf Springs "Banjo Land." Around here, women still tended to cater to the male ego, and so far, in the pack, the alpha-*male* held sway. But with three daughters and no sons, Lee Fenner had been planning to hand over leadership of the pack to a female.

Had been. Until Cordelia was banished. Now she guessed it was anyone's guess who was going to get control of the pack.

"Hey," Justin said, jostling her. "I'm just teasing you. Sorta."

"Is it a problem that Lee doesn't have any sons?" she asked. "Are there people in the pack who are unhappy about possibly having a female alpha?"

"Yes," he said, losing his lightness. "But the female of the alpha pair holds a lot of power. She can boss around the other males."

"Just not *her* male," she said, and he nodded. "Would you be okay if the alpha was a female, maybe even Lucy?"

"It won't be Lucy, but I'll play along with your question. My alpha is my alpha," he replied. "Once the alpha's declared, my loyalty instinct kicks in."

Loyalty instinct. She had never heard of such a thing.

He must have seen her confusion. "As far as I can understand it, humans have to work at being loyal, and staying loyal to each other. But we have a natural impulse to figure out the chain of authority and respect it. It makes life a lot easier."

"But you're bucking the system," she argued.

He winced as if she'd hit him. "Here's the thing, Kat. 'Alpha' means the highest-ranked, based on being the most dominant. And 'dominant' means exerting the most control. Our alpha is our king, and he's on the throne only as long as he guides and protects the pack. In the old days, there was a lot more fighting to become alpha. A lot of challenging. But that was before civilization encroached on us."

"Or vice versa," she said. "You encroached on civilization."

"Even out here, there are a lot fewer wild places," he said. "We used to run for miles and miles and miles. We're too bunched up now. It puts added pressure on everyone."

"So why don't you spread out?" she asked. She took a chance. "Some of us could move to L.A."

To her surprise, he reached over and tousled her hair in a friendly, big-brother sort of way. It was a side of him she hadn't seen, at least where she was concerned. He was like that with Jesse.

"L.A.," he said. "We'd be like the Beverly Hillwolves, gawk-in' at them big-city folks."

"You'd do great," she insisted. A fleeting microfantasy raced through her mind in which she and Justin headed a pack that moved to L.A. Or maybe even Montreal. She could get a job in the Cirque du Soleil and just not work on full moon nights.

But that meant a life with Justin, not Trick. And though Justin affected her in a physical way — wolf to wolf — Trick was the one she wanted to sit on the couch and watch movies with. Or maybe that was just as farfetched as imagining Justin without Lucy beside him.

"Kat," Justin said seriously, interrupting her reverie. "Don't get ideas. I don't see a move to L.A. in anyone's future."

"It's not up to you," she snapped. Then she jerked. "I'm sorry," she said quickly, backtracking. Because if he challenged Lee and assumed leadership of the pack, it *would* be up to him. He could give her back her life. Could she talk him into it?

"Listen, the packs are what they are and we don't split off, make new ones. Us, the Gaudin pack, the Hounds of God, and the others, we're all vying for territory while trying to survive in this world. So, tomorrow after school," he pressed.

"If you say so," she replied.

"I say so." He bent forward and offered his cheek. As she rose on tiptoe to kiss it, he swiveled his head, as if he was going to try to kiss her on her mouth. Then he stopped himself and, sighing, accepted her gesture of pack kinship.

Tuesday, Beau was looking pretty tired during history. After class she stopped him.

"Everything okay with your grandmother?"

"She was a little worse, but she's doing better now."

"Did you find a gun in your grandmother's room?" she asked, trying to force a smile. Mostly she wanted to figure out if he'd had any time to think about what his grandmother had said and get suspicious of her, Katelyn.

"No." He flashed a disbelieving smile. "Granny wasn't loaded. I did find something else interesting, though."

"What's that?"

"The missing book."

She stared at him, mind racing.

He grinned. "Yup, like some crazy old hoarder, my grandma was the one who had *In the Shadow of the Wolf* out from the school library. Heaven only knows how she got it or when. For all I know she checked it out when she was still *in* high school."

He was trying to be funny, she registered that, but she couldn't connect on that level because all she could think about was the book and what it might say about the Hellhound. "What did you do with it?"

He reached into his backpack. When he handed it to her, she swore her fingers tingled on the old leather cover.

"You can take it home and start reading," he said. "I didn't know where to start, but you did that paper."

"Thanks," she said quickly, tucking it against her chest.

"Let me know what you find."

"Of course."

Never.

All through training with Justin she was miles away, thinking about the book in her backpack and praying that no one went snooping and discovered it. They were working on her sense of hearing and she just couldn't get it to go into overdrive, too busy focusing on what she might find in its pages. Justin seemed distracted, too, and sent her home early. When she finally made it into her room, she slipped the book out of her backpack. It was dusty and worn, the white letters stamped into the blue cover practically illegible.

She flipped it open, eager to read the secrets it kept. But the print was tiny and there didn't seem to be any kind of table of contents. No index, either. She was going to have to read from the beginning.

The entire first page was one paragraph.

Welcome, Gentle Reader, to the myriad stories of the founding of Wolf Springs. This bucolic town, nestled in the beauteous mountains of the Ozark Region, was first settled by Spanish missionaries, in hopes of converting the local savages to the joys of the Gospel, as set down by our Lord, Jesus Christ. Ah, what a task lay before the good padres, faced with the stubbornness of the primitive innocent—

"C'mon, c'mon," Katelyn muttered, skimming the rest of the long-winded introduction. She turned the page.

— for is it not true that salvation can only be found in a society based on Christian values?

With a groan, she flipped back to the first page and picked up where she had left off.

And as many have often surmised, the soul of the childlike native must also be brought to the Lord—

The book progressed from describing the attempts of the missionaries to convert the natives to a detailed description of the building of each structure in the town. The dry goods store. The barber shop.

The blacksmith also ran a foundry, kept busy by hunters who requested peculiar casings for their ammunition. Horses for hire were stabled there as well.

She remembered that when she'd been in the sick room at school, Mr. Hastings had called Sergeant Lewis about Mr. Henderson's absence. And he had described Mr. Henderson's house as "by the old stables."
She made a second mental note, and kept on reading. And then . . . a secret.

The Lost Mine of Wolf Springs. A Discussion.

The author laid it all out — the Madre Vena, the claims

by Xavier Cazador to have found it in the nineteenth century. The outlaw, Jubal DeAndrew, who had threatened to kill him if he didn't reveal where it was.

It is said that a painting of the mine's entrance was created by Xavier Cazador for Jubal DeAndrew. In the foreground stood a heart-shaped boulder, and in the background one could view a silvery waterfall. But the true artistry of the painting lay in this: a false signature could be scraped away, and beneath it one could learn the longitudinal and latitudinal co-ordinates for the mine.

Her mouth dropped open. She had been right about the sketch, and the painting of her grandfather's that had been stolen showed the mine's entrance. Was it possible that the stolen one had been the original and had the coordinates on it?

It is said that although Cazador created this painting for DeAndrew, it was never given to its intended recipient. Cazador died, and DeAndrew went missing. One surmises that foul play might be blamed, perhaps by a rival interested in the painting.

Her head swam with the possibility. People were born, lived, and died in Wolf Springs. Their attics had to be bulging with things that might hold the key to unlocking so many of the town's dark secrets. Her grandfather might have had a fake — a replica — or it could have been the actual painting. He said his father had picked one of the paintings up at an estate sale. Was that the one? And was it the original?

The question was: had someone else figured out that he had it? Had they stolen the silver and the other painting only to cover up the theft of this vital clue?

She tingled all over and eagerly turned the page.

The mine is said to be guarded by a monstrous beast, a Hellhound, who keeps thieves at bay and protects the treasure as if it is his own. A notable detail about the legend surrounding the Hellhound is that the creature shows up in historical accounts of the area years before there is any mention of the mine. Whether this is an oversight is unclear. It is possible that when people learned of the mine they connected the creature to it as a means to scare others away.

To her disappointment there was nothing else she didn't already know about the Hellhound, at least not in that section. Her eyes blurred, as she realized that she had to be more tired than she thought. She kept trying to read the tiny words, but her head bobbed. With a reluctant sigh, she closed the book. It would have to wait until the morning.

Click. Click. Click.
The clicking mixed with the sound of drums. Both getting closer. Both in time with the beat of her heart.

"I found this for you, a perfect fit," Babette said, holding up some coveralls.

"But I won't be digging in the dirt," she protested.

"Don't think you won't before it's over."

Click.

She turned around, but no one was there. Just the walls of the cave. They were closing in on her and she smelled . . . something.

Aluminum.

No! Silver. Far more precious. Lovely but deadly.

"Just like you," Justin whispered in her ear.

His breath was hot; it tickled.

But then he was gone and the cave was shrinking around her. The walls were closing in and she knew that they were going to bury her.

And in the darkness something growled.

Laughed.

Cried.

"Katelyn," it whispered.

Click.

Click.

Click.

⊱ ⊰

Katelyn opened her eyes with a gasp. She was in bed and something was scratching at the skylight above her head. Nails on the glass going click, click, click.

She looked up.

There: a shadow darker than any shadow, and eyes that burned like the fires of hell.

She screamed.

14

As she screamed, the eyes disappeared. She leaped for the door at the same time her grandfather barreled in, wild-eyed, a gun in his hand.

"Katie, what is it?"

"I saw it," she whispered.

"What? What'd you see?"

And as her senses came back to her, she realized she couldn't tell him. She was sure that what had been on her skylight had been more than just a werewolf: she was certain it had been the Hellhound. But either way she couldn't risk her grandfather going to investigate.

"What?"

She wiped her forehead and managed an embarrassed, if extremely forced, smile. "Sorry. I — I guess I was having a nightmare." She crossed her arms. "I feel like such an idiot."

He visibly relaxed. "You need anything? Drink of water?"

"No, I think I'll be fine," she managed to say.

She strained her ears, listening for the sounds of something walking around on the roof, but heard nothing. Was it possible she *had* just imagined something staring down at her?

"Okay. Let me know if you need anything."

"I will," she barely managed to choke out around the sudden lump in her throat.

As soon as he closed the door, she wrapped her arms around herself and leaned against it. She thought of Beau's grandmother stroking out because she had seen "a demon" at her window. Why would she and Katelyn both be getting visits? As far as she knew, Beau's family had no connection to the werewolves.

Maybe it was because she knew there was something wrong and she told people.

Katelyn hugged herself even tighter. It was one more reason not to endanger those she loved. But she couldn't just roll over and stay ignorant instead of asking questions that someone needed to answer.

Like who is killing people. And what happened here forty years ago.

A sleepless night led to a difficult day trying to focus at school. As soon as it was over, she drove over to Babette's. Cordelia had once said that Babette was "gossip central," that the store owner knew everything that was going on in Wolf Springs. Katelyn wanted to know what Babette knew about the killings — or even what the woman *thought* she knew.

Babette waved at her from behind the register as she entered, and Katelyn's stomach tightened at the thought of talking to her. Katelyn didn't know her well, but Babette had seemed very shrewd the first time they'd met. Katelyn was anxious that she'd reveal too much of herself from the questions she asked.

To her surprise, though, Babette turned away from her. It was then that Katelyn saw that the store owner was talking to a police officer in a khaki uniform — not Sergeant Lewis, so it had to be Wolf Springs' other one, whose name she didn't know. She was a woman, about five-eight, with heavy dark eyebrows, a round face, and brown hair pulled back in a bun.

A bolt of unease shot through Katelyn. Something about the woman was off and it was all she could do to keep herself from walking backwards out the door onto the street and running for her car. Babette's brow was furrowed and she was drumming her fingers on the countertop. Babette was nervous, too.

Pretending to examine a couple of Fifties poodle skirts, Katelyn surreptitiously studied the shop owner. She could see the pulse in the woman's throat beating hard and fast and she could smell the tantalizing scent of fear coming off her. What on earth could Babette possibly have to hide?

"Becky was in to buy a new dress just before she got killed. She didn't say or do anything strange," Babette said to the police offer.

"A new dress? Special occasion?" the officer asked sharply.

"A party, maybe. I heard that she was dating Trick Sokolov."

The officer nodded. "Yeah, I heard that, too."

No, no she wasn't. She made that up, Katelyn thought, afraid for Trick. Except . . . that was what Sam had told her. Maybe Sam had been covering for Trick because Sam knew he liked Katelyn. Maybe Trick *had* been dating Becky, and *did* heartlessly dump her.

"Okay. What about Haley?" the officer was asking. "Did she say or do anything out of the norm?"

Babette shook her head, unconsciously running her fingertips back and forth along the counter. "You knew those girls, Luanne. They were lovely young ladies."

Intrigued, Katelyn drifted from the skirts to some neon-colored fringed Sixties purses, which were hung on a display closer to the register.

"Well, thanks, Babette. I'll be in touch if I have more questions," the policewoman — Luanne — said.

Katelyn kept her head lowered, hoping Officer Luanne wouldn't take the opportunity to interview the rest of the people in the store. There were only a couple of other shoppers, older women Katelyn didn't recognize.

But the policewoman left, and Katelyn sagged with relief. She set down a lime-green purse as one of the two women scurried over to Babette.

"Was it awful?" she asked, and Katelyn blinked at the weird question.

"It sure wasn't pleasant," Babette said with a humorless laugh.

"I just know they're going to ask me questions I can't answer," the other woman said, wringing her hands. And she, too, smelled of fear.

Katelyn blinked, surprised. The women weren't werewolves. She had met the entire pack. What secrets could they be hiding that were terrible enough to cause them to be afraid of talking to a cop that at least one of them knew on a first-name basis?

Did they know about werewolves, or were there skeletons in their own closets they didn't want seeing the light of day?

Welcome to Wolf Springs, she thought.

"Now, Estelle, you have nothing to worry about," Babette reassured the other woman. "I'm sure none of us have," she said, much louder and more pointedly.

Katelyn didn't flinch. She wouldn't let her know she'd been eavesdropping. She set down the purse and glided soundlessly to a rack of dresses.

A glorious red dress caught her eye, strapless with a long, flowing skirt. Red was the color of boldness. And right now she felt she could use some. She took it into the dressing room to try it on and attempted to listen in on more conversation, but the bell on the shop door tinkled. She assumed the two shoppers had left.

The dress fit and she hurried to the register to pay for it.

As Babette rang it up, she told herself to ask questions. That was why she had come.

"So, um," she said, and she smelled Babette's fear again. It was contagious. Katelyn didn't want to do or say the wrong thing around this woman. So much for bold. "Thanks," she said. She told herself she could come back another time, when she wasn't so rattled.

"Of course, honey," Babette said, without looking at her.

Katelyn's cell rang. She fished it out of her pocket and realized when she saw that the number was blocked that it must be Cordelia or Dom. She grabbed her purchase.

"Thanks," she said again as she struggled to get out the door.

"We have better reception inside the shop than out there," Babette said.

"Thanks, it's okay," Katelyn replied, practically tripping over a mannequin in her effort to get somewhere private in time to answer the phone.

Once on the street she had to risk it. "Hello?" she answered, her voice barely more than a whisper.

"Kat." It was Cordelia, sounding tired and upset, nothing like the girl Katelyn had first met. Being away from her family — from all she had ever known — was changing Cordelia. Turning her into someone far weaker. *Or was it from being around the Gaudins?*

Katelyn wrestled her Subaru's door open and threw the bag inside, following it quickly. She slammed the door closed.

"I'm here," she said.

"Have you found the mine yet?"

"No," she said, hating to admit it. "But I have that sketch of the heart-shaped rock and the waterfall that shows the entrance to the mine. Now I just have to figure out where they are."

She had only spent a couple of minutes staring at the sketch, just enough to realize they were identical to the elements of the painting that had been stolen from the cabin. She was fairly certain that that, and not the silver or other valuables, had been what the thief had really been after. But who else knew that her grandfather had owned the painting all this time?

"Kat, you *have* to find it. You *have* to help me."

It was too much. Katelyn was sick of other people telling her what she had to do. Everyone was threatening her, telling her the way she had to act, the things she had to say. And all the while something was stalking her and she still had no idea who it was that had shot at her.

"You know, I'm doing my best, but I don't understand what exactly the urgency is. I mean, you *like* Dom. You told me so. Do you hate him now? Has he hurt you?"

Cordelia sighed. "You don't understand. How could you? This world is so new to you. Of course I still like Dom — I wouldn't have called him if I didn't. Even if it meant dying on my own. But this is so messed up. I don't want to be cut off from my family, from my father and everyone I've ever known. Every minute I'm here I feel like a traitor. And that's how everyone thinks of me. I'm going to have to declare loyalty, and I — I don't know if I can do that." She said the last words in a whisper.

"Didn't you tell me your dad used to be into you marrying him?"

"If we formally allied the packs," Cordelia said. "If I was alpha of our pack, like Dom is the alpha of his. Then it would have been sort of like one pack. But obviously, that's not the case."

"I'm doing everything I can," Katelyn said, hearing her own misery.

"You need to do more and you need to do it soon. So, um, Dom . . . Dom wants you to spy on my family for him."

Katelyn's stomach did a flip. "No way," she said.

"I know you want to be loyal—"

"This has nothing to do with loyalty. This is purely about self-preservation. They don't trust me and they threaten to kill me every other day. Really don't need to give them a reason."

"You need to do this for me," Cordelia said. "That's reason enough." Suddenly she sounded more like the old Cordelia — surer of herself, clear about what she wanted. My — our — pack is in trouble. Our family."

"They're not my family," Katelyn insisted. The change in Cordelia was remarkable. When she thought of herself in terms of belonging to her pack, she was stronger.

"Even if I can't be there, you're there. And you have to be there for me."

Katelyn heard a muffled sound and then the call ended.

The entire drive home she just kept replaying the conversation in her mind. When she made it home she headed straight upstairs, got out the sketch again and stared at the heart-shaped boulder in frustration. The real painting was supposed to have coordinates underneath the signature. Who had it? She thought of the piece of silver dropped outside the Inner Wolf compound. And the rest, simply dumped into a bog. Why? It seemed highly unlikely to her that one of the executives who was there for a few days would have managed to leave, break into her grandfather's cabin, steal things, and sneak back into the center. Besides, they would take the silver, wouldn't they? Why dump it in a bog — was that some kind of implied werewolf threat that they could poison Fenner land? They wouldn't know about the painting. They'd be strangers to the area. So who would know there was a painting to steal?

Mr. Henderson.

Or . . . Jack Bronson?

⊷ ⊱⊰ ⊶

Let the tire have a flat now, Katelyn intoned. *Let the truck break down here.*

She sat beside her grandfather in the cab of his truck as they bounced along the road, heading to the Fenners' house for Thanksgiving. Mordecai had on the suit he'd worn to Cirque du Soleil and she was wearing the same black dress. She felt as if they were going to their own funerals. She'd briefly considered wearing the new red dress, but red was the color of blood as well as boldness and she didn't want to give anyone any ideas. Every nerve was strung tight; she could feel each molecule of air touching her skin.

This is sheer insanity.

Mr. Fenner had ordered her to attend Thanksgiving

dinner with the family. When she'd protested, explaining that her grandfather would expect her to have dinner with him, he had told her to bring him along.

"It'll be like the old days," he'd said happily. Regan, Justin and Doug had been in the room, and all they did was slide glances at each other and agree with him. Because he was their alpha.

Untroubled, her grandfather was whistling a Christmas carol. For all he knew, they were just going over there because Katelyn had a thing for Justin. She'd asked him to go, and with Trick spending the day with his mom and dad for once, he'd said yes, and here they were.

Finally they angled down the steep driveway, revealing the Fenners' fantastic house, and Katelyn thanked the gods when she didn't see a bunch of cars. She hadn't known if the whole pack would be coming or not. Apparently, though, it was just "family."

And us. If she asked her grandfather to leave, no questions asked, what would happen?

"Here we are," her grandfather said, shutting off the engine.

They got out of the truck and walked up to the front door. Her grandfather was carrying a bottle of red wine. She rang the doorbell and Jesse, in a suit with his hair slicked back, opened the door.

"Kat's here!" he hollered.

Katelyn winced, hoping he didn't do or say anything that would raise a red flag with her grandfather who, after all, might or might not already know about the existence of werewolves.

"Hey, Jesse," she murmured and let him kiss her cheek as he whined in her grandfather's direction.

"You remember my grandpa?" she asked, heart in her throat.

"Not a stranger," Jesse said slowly, almost questioningly.

Before either of them could answer, Justin appeared in the doorway. He, too, was wearing a black suit that fit him beautifully. Black was definitely his color.

"They're our guests, buddy," he said. "We talked about this. Let them in."

She could hear the tension in his voice. He was nervous, too.

"Happy Thanksgiving," her grandfather said, offering his hand.

Justin shook it, and after a moment, so did Jesse.

"Brought this." Her grandfather held out the bottle of wine, and Katelyn glanced around, expecting Mr. Fenner to appear. He was their official host. Shouldn't he answer the door to his home and welcome them in?

Maybe alphas don't do that, she thought.

"Thanks," Justin said to her grandfather. He held the bottle up to the light. "Wolf Creek Vineyards. That around here?"

"No, but I like their wines," her grandfather replied.

They've brought us here to kill us, she thought, and then she tried to tell herself that that was crazy.

Justin and Jesse moved aside to let Katelyn and her grandfather in. A moment later, Katelyn found herself introducing her grandfather to Arial and Regan, who were both dressed up. Arial had chosen shiny gold to show off her blonde hair and her curves, while dark-haired Regan opted for a red cashmere sweater and black skirt. Katelyn's heart began to pound, hoping the nasty, mean sisters wouldn't do or say anything that would set off alarm bells.

Amazingly, though, they were both polite, seemingly on their best behavior. Their husbands were very cordial, and Katelyn couldn't help but wonder if the alpha had ordered the good behavior, or if Cordelia's two laid-back brothers-in-law had been able to wield some influence over their wives. Either way, Katelyn was grateful.

Lucy came out of the kitchen in a gray velour sweater and a black pencil skirt, looking much more sophisticated than Katelyn had seen her before. She gave Katelyn a hug that could not have been more awkward, and Katelyn forced herself to smile in response and hug the other girl back.

And then, finally, Mr. Fenner entered the room, also wearing a suit. His shock of white hair and tanned, leathery face belied his age. No one would have been able to tell that he was roughly the same age as her grandfather.

Wolf Springs was a small place and everyone knew about everyone else, but Katelyn had learned weeks ago that that didn't necessarily mean everyone had actually *met* everyone else, and she had discovered that her grandfather had never met Lee Fenner before.

"Mr. Fenner," her grandfather said, holding out his hand.

Lee took it. "Dr. McBride."

Justin casually sidled over to her. "It's okay, Kat," he whispered.

"It's not, and you know it," she whispered back.

"So, it's a good day to give thanks," Lee said.

"I don't know of a bad day to give thanks," Mordecai replied with a smile.

Mr. Fenner slapped her grandfather's back with a roar of laughter. They seemed at ease and Katelyn watched as Justin carried the wine bottle out of the room, then returned without it.

But this is still such a bad idea, she thought.

"Well, let's eat," Mr. Fenner finally said, leading the way out of the foyer to a formal dining room. The table and chairs matched the wood paneling of the simple but elegant space, punctuated by a fireplace and a large oil painting of an icy landscape.

Please let it be a normal Thanksgiving dinner with a cooked turkey, Katelyn silently thought as they were directed to their chairs by Regan. Mr. Fenner was seated at the head of the table and her grandfather took the seat at the foot. She sat next to him.

Because I'm the lowest-ranking pack member, she realized. It put her close to Lucy and Jesse. Arial and Regan flanked their father. Doug sat next to his wife, but Justin was placed next to Arial, with Albert on his other side, farther away from the alpha.

Interesting. The husband who had been chosen — Doug — ranked above the husband who'd been born a werewolf — Albert. She wondered what that was about. Maybe as Regan was older that gave her husband higher status. She didn't actually know.

"You might know our family's Scandinavian, originally," Mr. Fenner said to Katelyn and her grandfather. "We say a traditional Norwegian table grace at Thanksgiving."

Everyone bowed their heads, and all the Fenners, even Jesse and Lucy, murmured words in lilting language. Then Lucy, Arial, and Regan brought the food in from the kitchen. Soon the table was laden with white china serving platters of standard Thanksgiving fare. Katelyn had completely forgotten if the Fenners knew she was pretending to be a vegetarian, so she put a few small pieces of dark meat turkey on her plate and she could feel herself starting to salivate just like some kind of animal. Maybe she could pretend she was just being polite by eating it.

Conversation around the table was light-hearted, mostly gossip about people in town, but nothing vicious, just comings and goings. Her grandfather participated and didn't once mention Cordelia's name, for which Katelyn was thankful.

Maybe that was why Doug had been moved closer to Mr. Fenner — Cordelia's spot at the table had had to be filled.

The adults were drinking wine, but she noticed no one drank very much of it. Her grandfather hadn't even touched his and Katelyn wondered if they had opened his bottle of Wolf Creek.

She began to relax slightly, enjoying the banter and the gossip, and most especially the turkey. Then she glanced toward the head of the table where Mr. Fenner was presiding, sitting in his chair as if it were a throne. Without warning, the hair on the back of her neck raised. Something felt wrong.

Regan was now staring toward Lee with her eyes practically bulging. Katelyn swung her eyes to Mr. Fenner and gaped in disbelief — his chin whiskers seemed to be growing into a beard right before her eyes. She blinked and realized it wasn't hair, but fur that was sprouting, and his jaw was beginning to elongate. He was shifting into werewolf form right there at the table for everyone to see.

She twisted to look at her grandfather, who was turning to say something, and did the first thing that came to mind — she swept out her hand, knocking his wine glass into his lap.

"Grandpa, I'm so sorry!" she cried.

He pushed back from the table as Katelyn half rose out of her seat to obscure his view of Mr. Fenner. Grabbing a napkin, she risked a glance over her shoulder and saw that Justin and Doug had both leaped to their feet. The werewolf form of Lee bared its teeth at them. Jesse began to bounce up and down in his chair and clap his hands in delight.

"Not at the dinner table!" Jesse shrieked.

"Oh, it's everywhere," Katelyn babbled, determinedly placing herself in her grandfather's line of vision. "I — I spilled the whole glass!"

"No harm done," her grandfather said, grunting as he took the napkin from her, bent down, and dabbed wine off his pants leg. And when Katelyn glanced up again, Lee Fenner was back in human form, rushing from the table, having burst the shoulder seams of his jacket.

"It's really okay, honey," her grandfather said, clearly assuming she was upset about the wine.

But it wasn't okay. The entire table had gone silent. Lucy had a hand over Jesse's mouth.

Her grandfather looked around, surprise on his face. "It's fine, everyone. If you can just show me to a bathroom . . ."

"Of course." Regan practically jumped out of her chair and headed in the opposite direction to that which her father had taken. "Just follow me, Dr. McBride."

"Jesse, sugar, can you help me in the kitchen for a moment?" Lucy asked. "Arial, can you get some paper towels? Or maybe that's where your daddy went?" she added pointedly.

Jesse got up and followed Lucy out. Regan left with Katelyn's grandfather and Arial dashed from the room, obviously going to check on her father. That left Justin, Doug, Albert, and Katelyn.

"Lu, do you need me?" Justin called. He had gone white.

"That would be nice, sugar," she called back. Justin pushed back from the table and left the room.

Coward, Katelyn thought, realizing she had new-found respect for Lucy. The young woman had taken charge. It was Lucy who was dealing with Jesse, not Justin. Lucy, who had prompted Arial to deal with Mr. Fenner.

"Damn," Doug grumbled. "*This* is going well."

"Doug, be careful what you say," Al murmured.

Katelyn could feel the thick, underlying tension. And anger. Fury, even.

"It happened because he's stressed," Al added. "Having company. A stranger."

"Should we leave?" Katelyn asked. She was positive her grandfather hadn't seen anything, but was that good enough for the pack? What was going to happen to them now?

"Not for us to say," Al told her. "Maybe you should go check on your grandfather."

She hesitated, not wanting to move out of earshot of the two Fenners. If she and her grandfather were in imminent danger, they needed to get the hell out of there.

"Then who *does* say? Who should I ask for permission to leave?" she persisted.

They both regarded her with carefully blank expressions.

"I mean, I know I should usually ask Mr. Fenner, of course, but if he's not feeling well . . ." She trailed off, confounded by their neutral faces.

"He's the only one who can give you permission to do anything," Doug replied, and his voice was kind. "It's not like you're used to, Kat."

Justin reappeared. His face was grim. "Go check in on your grandfather," he ordered her.

She heard a lot of shushing. Then Jesse's giggle. Lucy's quiet voice. Craning her ears, she heard the word, "*Secret.*"

Just as she was about to head off to the restroom, her grandfather reappeared with Regan. He was dabbing at his suit jacket.

"All better," Regan said. "Luckily he didn't get any wine on his nice white shirt." There was a glimmer of what almost looked like grudging respect for Katelyn in her eyes. "Nice aim."

"It's okay, honey," her grandfather assured Katelyn. He

began to sit down, but Arial finally appeared with a roll of paper towels.

"Wait, Dr. McBride. Let me make sure there's no wine on your chair," she said.

"I'll help you," Katelyn murmured.

She bent down beside Arial, who glared at Katelyn, tore off a couple of paper towels with exaggerated care, and handed them to her. Arial's hatred came off her in waves, and Katelyn did her best to ignore it.

"All better," Arial said. "Have a seat, Dr. McBride."

No, Grandpa, no. We need to get out of here, Katelyn tried to telegraph. But Arial gathered up the paper towels and walked out of the room again.

Mordecai sat down and Justin appeared with the uncorked bottle of Wolf Creek wine and a filled wine glass. Justin placed both before him with a flourish.

Katelyn opened her mouth to tell her grandfather that she wasn't feeling well and needed to go. She'd just have to risk Mr. Fenner's wrath by leaving without his say-so. But at just that moment, Mr. Fenner reappeared, his torn shirt replaced by a turtleneck sweater.

"Spilled," he said briefly.

"Lots of that going around," her grandfather joked.

"We have fresh rolls!" Jesse announced, bouncing on his heels as he carried in a wicker basket steaming with the fragrant odor of yeast and dough. "You eat them with butter! You can have honey!" He snickered. "We call people honey! But you don't eat them!"

"Good joke, buddy," Lucy said serenely. She smiled at Mr.

Fenner as Jesse approached him with the basket. "Uncle Lee, fresh out of the oven?"

"Thank you, darlin'," Mr. Fenner said, reaching in as Jesse beamed at him.

And just like that, the dinner in hell resumed.

15

They'd lived through dinner. Everything had gone well, considering, and as soon as the pecan pie had been served and eaten, Katelyn begged to leave. Her grandfather said, "Nice folks," in the truck, and she managed a nod. Then he reached over and gave her hand a pat. "I'm thinking, though," he said, "you might want to cross that one off your list. Seemed pretty taken."

She nodded a second time. She never wanted to go to the Fenners again. Ever. But she knew that wouldn't happen.

He paused and she steeled herself, dread filling her. There

was a question coming, she could feel it. She could practically *hear* it.

"Have they ever told you yet where Cordelia has gone?"

She clenched her jaw, wishing that Justin or someone else had at least told her whatever lie they had told the principal at school. She shook her head slowly. "No one wants to talk about it. She told me a couple of times that she wanted to move out. She's got an aunt or something in Colorado." She felt ashamed at how easily the lies tripped off her tongue. "I know they had a big fight. Jesse told me."

"I'm sure she's okay, though?" he asked, his voice questioning.

"She hasn't gotten in touch," Katelyn said, struggling to figure out what to say, how to act, so as to shut down further questioning without herself seeming like she was behaving suspiciously. Finally she said, "I, um, thought she would . . ."

Mordecai nodded. "Kids don't stick around here after they graduate. No future. Every once in a while someone can't wait even that long. Just sad that you had to lose a friend that way. Maybe she'll get back in touch after things calm down."

"Yeah, I miss her," she murmured.

"And maybe you'll make some more friends at school," he suggested.

She didn't want to talk about it anymore, even though she was touched by his obvious concern. "There's a girl in my art class who's really nice. Paulette."

"That's good. Maybe you can have her over some time."

Katelyn nodded. "Thanks." And in the back of her mind

she filed that away. Maybe someday when she needed an excuse for being out — like the next full moon — she could say she was staying over at Paulette's. And now that her grandfather was convinced she should give up on Justin, he might not turn as blind an eye to her going over to the Fenners' all the time.

When they got home they watched some television and then her grandfather finally headed to bed. Katelyn stayed up, reading more of *In the Shadow of the Wolf* and wishing again that it just had an index so she'd know she wasn't missing anything. She finally put it down again and went to get herself some water. As she padded into the kitchen, goose bumps broke over her body.

This time when she saw Justin staring in the kitchen window, she managed not to act surprised. She went out the back door, slipping into her shoes, and headed with him into the trees. She rubbed her arms.

"You shouldn't be cold," he said with a frown.

"All that stuff comes and goes," she said, unwilling to tell him that she hadn't been feeling the cold, but had been remembering her brush with a bullet.

Finally he stopped walking and she leaned against a tree.

"What?" she asked when he didn't speak.

"Kat," he said, placing his fingers over her lips. "Thanksgiving dinner was a nightmare. He should never have invited your grandfather over. And then when he started to change at the table . . ."

He closed his eyes and shook his head. "We watched that damn train wreck and we couldn't do anything about it. But this behavior endangered the pack. And, frankly, it endangered you." His voice softened and he cocked his head, studying her. "And that's not something I want to go through again."

She agreed with everything he was saying. It had been a terrible decision to invite them over.

"Does that mean you're going to challenge him?" she asked him.

Ashen-faced, he didn't answer.

She could almost hear questions buzzing around her head like wasps. Had he discussed challenging Lee Fenner with Lucy? How would he do it? Would they fight as wolves? What if Justin lost?

"Settle down, darlin'," he murmured. "You're not involved."

"I'm not stupid, Justin," she retorted. "Don't treat me like I am."

"Fair enough." He reached out a hand, and pressed his fingertips against her cheek. Then he jerked back and stuffed his hand in his pocket. "You've got to stay well away from me," he reminded her, cocking his head, staring at her hungrily. "*Well* away."

She scowled at him. "I did not touch *you*."

"I know." He sighed. "God, I hate this."

Finally, very quietly, he murmured, "I'm hoping it won't come to that. I'm hoping he'll just pick me." He pressed his fingertips against the bridge of his nose. "Oh, God, Kat. There is nothing in me that wants to challenge him. But how can I let this go on?"

She didn't say anything. After a minute he seemed to pull himself together. He looked at her intently. "You've kept the secret about your immunity to silver, right?"

"Yes."

"You haven't told anyone?"

"No, of course not. Who would I tell?"

He nodded. "We're going to get through this. It's going to be okay. I promise you."

He leaned down and kissed her cheek and then disappeared into the night.

Katelyn hurried back to the porch and made it inside without anyone seeing her or shooting at her. She stood in the kitchen for several minutes, staring out the window into the darkness.

She was immune to silver and in the garage were a whole lot of silver bullets, enough to take down the entire pack. Certainly enough to take down Mr. Fenner. She felt a twinge of guilt for not having told Justin about them.

Grabbing a flashlight, she headed back outside and crept into the garage to investigate the box with the ammo case in it. She opened it again and picked up one of the bullets. If she kept it, would her grandfather notice? She debated for a long time, and finally decided to leave them exactly as she had found them.

Then she continued her systematic search through the other boxes in the garage, half expecting to find a special rifle or handgun made to fire silver bullets. But she found nothing to tie the silver bullets to anything else. The other boxes were filled with old pots and pans, clothes, and a lot of books and papers from Dr. Mordecai McBride's years as a university professor. Sighing, she closed one box and opened another. She didn't know how to tell a gun that shot silver bullets from a regular one, anyway. She didn't even know if there was a difference.

She was getting tired. One more box and then she'd give up for the night. She opened up the next box and discovered that it was full of old pictures, many of them on thick cardboard. She picked up a handful and scrutinized them by flashlight, then smiled, charmed. They were of her grandfather and a young woman with her father's dimpled chin and long, straight nose. This had to be the grandmother she had never met.

"Hi," she whispered.

The couple had gone hunting together. And fishing. There was the same kind of canoe that was in this very garage — maybe the same one, even. She tried to remember what she'd been told about how her grandmother had died. An illness? She couldn't remember.

There weren't very many photographs — not enough for an entire lifetime — and soon she was finished. There had to be more, somewhere. But they would have to wait.

She was just about to put them back when she caught sight of a yellowed bit of paper at the very bottom of the box. Setting down the stack of pictures, she picked it up and unfolded it. It was a clipping from a newspaper article. She flipped it over, shining her flashlight on it and the title jumped out at her.

RARE WOLF SIGHTING IN TAHOE?

Her heart skipped a beat. There was some faint writing in the margins that she couldn't quite make out.

She began to read the article:

Tahoe — A visitor hiking yesterday claims to have encountered an injured wolf. The animal appeared to have been shot but when the man attempted to help, the wolf bit him and ran off. Wolf sightings are extremely rare in the Tahoe basin. Since wolves are migratory it is likely that this creature is not native to the area but traveled down from Oregon.

"We believe this was a coyote sighting," said Fish and Game spokeswoman Georgia Fullerton. "Because of habitat encroachment, our coyotes are becoming more brazen in their encounters with humans."

However, the hiker, attorney Sean McBride from Los Angeles, vacationing with his wife, remains adamant that his attacker was a wolf. The injury was not deemed serious, nor was the wolf assumed to be rabid. McBride was treated at an urgent care facility, and then released.

There was a roaring in her ears as Katelyn stared at the article, reading, rereading. Swaying, she reached out a hand and steadied herself against a pile of boxes. Her chest squeezed hard, and she grabbed her side, afraid her ribs were going to crack; she stumbled and leaned against the boxes.

Her father, bitten by a wolf? How come she'd never heard

anything about it? In a daze, she located the date of the article, and saw that it was the same year that he was killed. They'd come home from that trip without saying a word about an attack to her. Or maybe she'd forgotten. She'd only been eleven years old. But would she actually forget being told that a wolf had bitten her father?

Maybe they didn't want to scare me.

Or . . . maybe they didn't want her to know.

But people did get bitten by wild animals. There were mountain lion warnings all over L.A. She remembered a story about a six-year-old boy who had been killed by a coyote in a park in Long Beach.

Just because it had happened to her, it didn't mean anything had happened to her father.

Oh, yes, it does.

Quivering, she tried to straighten the pictures and put them back into the box; but she dropped them and they scattered on the floor. In the nearest photo, the face of her grandmother smiled up at her. Surrounded by trees, she was calmly holding a hunting rifle. Groaning, Katelyn dropped into a squat to gather them all up. She couldn't feel them in her hands. She was numb.

She replaced the box lid and threaded her way out of the maze of boxes, clutching the article in her hand. She made it upstairs to her room, heart thundering, and shut the door. She sank down on her bed, clicked on her reading lamp, and shoved the article underneath the light, where she could make out the words scrawled in the margins in red pen.

See, I told you.

It was her mother's handwriting.

Katelyn stared at the words, clutching the newspaper article until her knuckles were white. Her mother's distinctive loops and swirls blazed like neon. Why would her mom have sent the article to her grandfather? *What* had she told him? That there were wolves in that part of the country, that her husband had been bitten?

Her father.

Attacked by a *wolf*.

She felt like she was drowning, being sucked down into a whirlpool of pain and fear and darkness that she didn't have the strength to escape. In her mind, she heard the rumbling of the earthquake, the staccato tapping of the couch against the hardwood floor. The fire, already devouring the downstairs of their house.

Her mother's voice, penetrating the fog of the painkiller Katelyn had taken to ease her injury. Katelyn, so out of it she'd barely been able to function. Slowing her mother down, ruining her chance to escape. Killing her.

Wheezing, she spun around on her bed and came face-to-face with the bust that Trick had made for her. She stared into the cold, unseeing eyes and felt the dam inside her break.

"Mom, *what* did you tell him?" she whispered. "*Please.*"

Rage, fear of the unknown dragged her under. Tears rolled down her face. Barely breathing, she stared at the article.

"No," she whispered, over and over and over again.

⊶ ⊷

Full sunshine roused Katelyn and she bolted upright. A glance at her phone told her it was nearly ten. Moving like someone in a dream, she dressed and stumbled downstairs.

I can't ask Grandpa about the article, she thought. *I'll say the wrong thing.*

And she couldn't face him, either. She had to get away, be alone, make sense of this, make sense of anything.

She stepped off the last stair and fixed her eyes on the front door. She didn't know where he was, but if she could go—

"Hey, sleepyhead."

She jumped. Her grandfather was standing in the entryway to the kitchen, sipping coffee with a look of amusement on his face.

"Didn't mean to startle you. Want some scrambled eggs?"

"I have to go over to someone's house to study," she blurted. "I have to leave now."

"You can't work on an empty stomach. C'mon. I'll whip 'em right up." He gave her a wink. "That's an order, Private."

Defeated, she joined him in the kitchen, plopping down at the table.

He opened the refrigerator and pulled out the egg carton, the butter dish, and a quart of milk. "I've still got some coffee left." He opened the cabinet for a cup, and she spotted another one on the counter. "I could use some more myself. I couldn't sleep last night."

Alarm bells clanged. Had he heard her go into the garage?

She hadn't been very careful about how much noise she'd made when she'd come back in, because she'd been so upset.

"Want some milk in your coffee?" he asked her. "It's a mite on the strong side."

"I was going to leave early, stop by the library and grab some research books," she said. That wasn't what he had asked her, he'd asked about milk. A normal, rational girl would have just answered yes or no. But she wasn't normal and the whole world was irrational.

"I'll make it quick." He grabbed the other mug from the counter, filled both mugs with coffee, and poured a dollop of milk in one.

She bit her lip, really wanting to leave, but she took the cup and held it, tracing the swirl of milk that hadn't been mixed in. Maybe it would be good to have a late breakfast with him.

Because . . . maybe she shouldn't leave.

Maybe she should ask a few questions.

Don't, she warned herself. *Stop.*

"You okay?" he asked, cracking an egg into a bowl and dropping the shells into the trashcan under the sink. "You seem a bit jumpy."

"I had a bad dream," she said, gaze fixed on the coffee.

He grunted and she heard him moving around, then whipping the eggs.

"Dreams are your brain's way of telling you stuff that you're too busy to pay attention to during the day."

"I didn't know that."

"Yeah, we see and hear so much during the day that we

don't consciously think about and our brains just catalogue it all when we go to sleep." He got out a pan and put it on the stove. She heard the whoosh of the gas as he lit the burner.

She took a sip of coffee. It was as strong as an espresso.

"I didn't dream about anything from yesterday."

"Not in any way you would recognize normally. The brain's all about metaphor, imagery, when you're asleep." He added a pat of butter to the pan.

And suddenly she had an in for asking him what she wanted.

"I dreamed about my dad and playing in the snow with him in Tahoe."

"Happier times," her grandfather said with a grunt, pouring in the egg mixture.

Much happier.

"I remember he and mom used to love to go up there. Sometimes they took me. But sometimes they left me home."

He nodded. "Moms and dads need some alone time now and then. It didn't mean they didn't want you around."

"No, it was all good," she assured him, glancing up, then back down as her resolve began to waiver. "I always got to sleep over at a friend's house. I was just remembering this morning, though, I didn't get to go with them the last time they went. Daddy told me he was hiking in the woods and he found a — an injured wolf. And it — it bit him. He showed me the stitches."

Lies. No one had ever said anything to her about a wolf. But now her words hung in the air, and she clutched the cup hard as she waited to see what effect they had.

At the stove her grandfather's back stiffened.

Oh, God, she thought, lowering the cup to the table. Feeling her chest hitch, her muscles tighten. Cold sweat beaded on her forehead. Her mouth tasted like acid.

"Did he ever tell you about that?" she pushed.

"No, he didn't." He grabbed a plate and scooped the egg on it. Then he took it to the table and set it down in front of her. But he didn't look at her.

"Maybe Mom told you? I mean, it was a pretty big deal."

"No," he insisted.

More lies. This time from him. And she could tell that he hadn't simply forgotten, because he still wouldn't meet her eyes.

"Your pa should have known better than to approach a wild animal like that. I thought I taught him better." He was staring off into space. "Damn fool," he whispered.

There was so much anger and bitterness in his voice that it felt like a slap against her cheek. But it wasn't directed at her, and she knew it.

Ask him. Tell him. Her blood roared in her ears. She braced herself.

Stop.

Every survival instinct she had clamped down on her, ordering her to be silent. If she did this wrong, if she screwed up—

"Gotta run," she said, sounding agitated even to herself.

He didn't seem to notice. He was lost in his own thoughts.

"Have a nice time," he said from the sink.

She headed for the front door and ran to her car as horrible suspicions rushed in to fill the numb void in her mind, in her heart. The aching chasm. She looked at herself in the rearview mirror.

She wanted to go away. She had a car; she could take the road to Bentonville. And do what? She didn't have enough money for a plane ticket. Maybe she could call Kimi and ask her mom to buy her one. Or Trick—

"You stupid, stupid . . ." She was yelling at her reflection, but in her mind's eye, she saw her father. Her father, and a wolf.

And her mother's handwriting.

⋯ ⋯

Justin insisted on leading her into the Fenners' forest, then blindfolding her so that she would have to depend on her hearing. She protested, and he just laughed it off. He was in a better mood than he had been the night before. Somehow it made it that much harder to deal with her own drama, the fears that had latched hold of her and wouldn't let go.

Dad, what happened to you? she kept thinking over and over again.

"Katelyn, do what I say," Justin prodded, as they tracked into a stand of maples that had lost all their leaves. "Put this on."

He held out a black scarf. She made no move to take it. He narrowed his eyes at her, tapping his cowboy boot against a fallen tree trunk.

"I'll be nearby," he promised. "I won't let anything happen to you."

Defeated, she positioned the scarf over her eyes and tied it at the back. Then she heard twigs crackling as he walked away.

"Listen to the forest," he said. "Tell me what it tells you."

She stood quietly, her heart pounding, raising her chin as smells swirled around her: pine needles, underbrush, wet earth, and the delicious collection of odors that made up Justin's nearly-irresistible scent. She even smelled her own smell; she had been using a bar of lavender soap she'd bought in a gift shop in Little Rock.

And leather and soap: Trick. Was his scent on her?

Then she heard a voice, echoing and dreamy, as if it were coming from inside her head:

Katelyn.

You are mine.

Marked.

Click.

Click.

Click.

And someone breathing near her.

"Justin?" she called, reaching her hands to pull down the blindfold.

"Cordelia?" Mr. Fenner said.

As Katelyn peered over the scarf, she saw Mr. Fenner not five feet away. He was holding a rifle in his arms. She took a step backwards.

"Honey," he said, walking toward her, and she stood statue-still, terrified. "What are you doing out here by yourself?"

"Um," she said, scanning their surroundings. "Justin?" she called softly. "Help?"

"I've been hunting for you everywhere," he said. As she stared at him, he came up to her and offered his cheek. Her knees rubbery, she tried to rise on tiptoe to kiss him, but she was rooted to the spot.

Then he gathered her in his arms, embracing her, and rocked her back and forth. "Remember when you used to dance on my feet? My little gal. My gal." He sighed against her hair. "Where've you been, Corry?"

"Um, oh, here and there," she said hoarsely. He was lost in one of his delusions.

"I've missed you. I can't sleep when you're not home." His voice was whiny and petulant. "I worry so much about you. High time you got yourself a mate, so someone else can do the worrying for me." He chuckled. "They're all so scared of me, no one wants to declare for you."

"Right, Daddy," she managed to say.

"I didn't know you were sweet on Justin," he said, pulling back. His eyes were glazed, like someone in a bad movie pretending to be hypnotized. It was terrifying.

Did you bite me? In secret? Is it because you're crazy?

"Yeah, too bad he's my cousin," she said with a fake laugh.

"Why should that stop you two kids?" His chuckle was deep and warm. "Didn't stop me and your mama."

"Oh, well, that — that's great," she stammered.

He beamed at her. "Justin is perfect for you. You two could mate and lead the pack."

"Wow, yeah." She pushed tendrils of her hair away from her face and licked her lips. "We'd both like that." She was playing along, and playing for time, expecting Justin to check in on her soon. Surely he had detected the arrival of their alpha.

"You go find him. Bring him here." Mr. Fenner raised a hand as if in blessing. "I'll make it official."

"Sure, okay," she said, seizing her chance to escape. "Back soon."

She whirled on her heel and took off running.

And collided head-on with Lucy as the other girl stepped from behind a tree, her lips pulled back in a grimace of attack.

16

Katelyn took an involuntary step backwards, giving Lucy a wide berth. Lucy's eyes were practically glowing, and she bared her teeth at Katelyn as if she were in wolf form — losing control, Katelyn translated — and she swept back her arm as if getting ready to slap Katelyn as hard as she could. And even though Katelyn had dreaded seeing this side of Lucy, she was so terrified of what was happening with Mr. Fenner that relief flooded through her like a river.

"Lucy, oh, I'm so glad you're here," Katelyn said in a rush. "You have to help me. He — he thinks I'm her, I'm Cordelia."

"Don't say that name," Lucy snapped. But she stayed her hand, and uncertainty flickered in her eyes.

"He kept calling me by her name. And saying he's been hunting for me. I tried to play along because I didn't know what else to do." Katelyn could hear the panic and misery in her own voice and she wondered if Lucy could, too.

A moment later Mr. Fenner called out, "Cor, where are you? Let's go and tell Justin the good news. Your wedding. I'm so happy."

Consternation washed over Lucy's face and she whined softly. Lucy was just as distressed as Katelyn was.

"Let's get out of here," Katelyn whispered.

Lucy stood silently for a long moment, and then shook her head. "You go. I'll deal with this." She smoothed her hair, then made a wide berth around Katelyn and started walking in the direction of Mr. Fenner's voice. "Uncle Lee, there you are," she said, sweet as honey.

Katelyn didn't stick around to hear what was going to happen next. She took off running toward the house. She'd made it to her Subaru and was reaching for the door handle when a hand closed around her wrist and spun her halfway around.

It was Justin, eyes wide. "What the hell," he muttered.

"Did you see?" she demanded. "He thought I was *her.*"

"He's getting so much worse," Justin said, more to himself than to her.

"I've got to get out of here."

She expected him to argue with her. But he didn't. He just

nodded and let go of her wrist, then walked slowly back toward the woods.

Katelyn got in her car and blew out of there as fast as she could, her tires fishtailing as she swerved onto the main road. Her heart pounded as she imagined what was happening with Lucy and Justin and Mr. Fenner. A fight? A challenge? What if Arial or Regan caught wind of it? Neither of them seemed willing to take the title by force. Were female werewolves just as physically strong as their male counterparts?

Blinking, she cranked her radio sky-high and clenched her hands around the steering wheel. If something happened, they'd call her, wouldn't they?

She got home and brooded until dinnertime, braced for a phone call, an email, something. Nothing came.

"Everything okay?" her grandfather asked her over a piece of fried chicken. She was eating steamed vegetables and they tasted like cardboard.

"Do you believe in ghosts?" she blurted.

He blinked at her. "Haven't given it too much thought. This something for school?"

She pushed wisps of her blonde hair away from her face. "I've just heard a lot of people say there are a bunch of ghost stories around here." She studied him while she took a sip of water. "A friend back home said she saw a ghost when we were kids and I — I was just thinking about it while I was driving home," she lied.

"I'd like to think people move on when they die instead of being stuck here," he said.

His choice of words made her want to laugh. *Stuck here. Like me. Maybe I'm a ghost.*

"I know people believe in all kinds of things like Bigfoot, the Loch Ness monster," she said, trying desperately to sound casual as she pushed some peas around her plate. "What do you think? You think vampires and werewolves might actually exist?"

She counted off the seconds before he chuckled and set down his fork. "I know they're popular with the kids and all, but I just don't see vampires as being real. I mean, think about it. The undead?"

More silence passed. He didn't say a thing about werewolves. She wanted to persist — to make him speak — but she was afraid that if he wasn't suspicious already, then he'd know for sure something was up.

So she just nodded and focused her attention back on her meal. Later, when she went to bed, she couldn't remember eating a single bite.

⊰⊱

Monday morning rolled around and she still hadn't heard anything from Justin. The silence was driving her crazy. Despite their twisted relationship, she cared what happened to him. Though she tried to remind herself that he was pretty much her jailer, and that their attraction to each other was just physical, she also remembered how he had risked his life to save a little girl; that he was kind to Jesse; and that he was suffering over his uncle's deterioration.

And he came from a world of high passions and brutality. Katelyn was beginning to grasp that the many dead parents of the werewolves she had met weren't "hunting accidents," not in the way she had originally assumed. Had they died challenging each other? Or had they been killed for violating the rules of the pack?

The thought that death — murder — might be so commonplace sickened her. What difference would it make to them if a few humans died, too? Mr. Fenner had talked about six dying back when he was eighteen. The three recent deaths — possibly four, if Mr. Henderson had been killed — had to have been caused by werewolves.

Or the Hellhound.

She got in her car and drove through the forest, seeing shapes that weren't really there. Or weren't there *currently*. Wondering about Justin. About what would happen if he became the alpha. About what would happen to Mr. Fenner.

And to her.

She got to school early, which was her plan. Trick's Mustang was there and she took deep breaths for courage as she walked through the main hall, looking for him. He had gone silent as soon as her grandfather had told him that he and Kat were going to the Fenners' for Thanksgiving. She had let him have his snit.

Finally she saw him about ten feet ahead of her, ambling along in boot-cut jeans and cowboy boots. She was about to call his name when he turned around. He was scowling, and she took a step back, which he didn't seem to notice.

"Yeah, hi," she said.

He made no reply.

"So Thanksgiving sucked," she said.

"Stop. Don't even," he said harshly. "What do you want?" He shifted his weight, impatient, huffy.

"'Stop. Don't even,'" she mimicked. Then she grimaced. "This is stupid. They invited us and Grandpa said yes without asking me. Just like he decided we'd stay in our cabin instead of going to your house if we got snowed in. He didn't ask me about that, either. But he did agree that Justin is Lucy's boyfriend, and he doesn't need to do any more background checks on my known associates. We'll do Christmas." She raised her brows. "And I'll unwrap thousands of dollars in gymnastics equipment."

"Sure," he said, but he still looked completely furious with her. And his hands were trembling badly. In fact, scrutinizing him, Katelyn saw shadows under his skittering, bloodshot eyes; he almost looked like someone on drugs.

"Mr. Sokolov."

Mr. Hastings was standing in front of the door to the office, his face somber, arms crossed.

"Yeah?" Trick asked, in the exact same surly tone he'd used with Katelyn.

Mr. Hastings didn't like it, either. "I need to see you in my office."

Trick headed off toward the principal without even a parting word.

Katelyn turned and set off for her history class, glancing up at the stained-glass window of the saint with the wolf. Patron saint of Haunted High. Katelyn's secrets were making her invisible. Cordelia had had to disappear into the woodwork, too, losing all her friends. The one time Cordelia had held out her hand — to a stranger, to someone aching with homesickness and reeling from the death of her mother — it had backfired on her. And the rest was a terrible nightmare.

I wish I'd never met her, she thought mournfully.

A text came in, and equal parts of relief and dread washed over her when she saw that it was from Justin.

We need to talk. See you after school. Our house.

No part of her wanted to go back to Psycho Land, but she knew she had no choice.

Trick didn't show at lunch, so she didn't know what was up with him, either. When the final bell rang, she kept a lookout for him as she hurried to her car. Then her phone rang. Justin.

"Don't come," he said, voice tense.

She went cold. "What's happened?"

"Nothing. Don't worry."

"Right," she said sarcastically. "How *is* your uncle?"

"He's not the issue," he said. Then he hung up.

"Well, thanks for the update," she said to dead air.

And the reprieve. But it wouldn't last long.

The full moon was coming.

And Trick, already in his Mustang, was driving away.

⊷ ⊱⊰ ⊶

The next few days flew by. Trick stayed moody and distracted. And distant. He didn't tell her why Mr. Hastings had invited him in for a chat, but things had definitely cooled between Trick and the administration. Coach Ambrose told her that the gym equipment would arrive during the winter break and they'd get the team started during second semester. Whatever Trick had done, the goodwill he had bought with the equipment had been used up.

Questions about Trick would have to wait. The moon was waxing, and it would be full on Saturday night. Her aggression levels were rising at an almost uncontrollable rate as she'd been warned they would. After a lot of worrying, she'd finally just told her grandfather that she was going to spend Saturday night at Paulette's house, that their friendship was progressing nicely, and she crossed her fingers that he wouldn't find a way to check up on her. She wished she could let Paulette in on her cover, but she was sure the other girl would ask too many pointed questions about where Katelyn was *really* going.

Friday, she was tense and irritable, as if at any moment she was going to burst apart and a wolf would throw back its head and howl. She was a wreck. This time she knew for sure she was going to change, and she knew it would hurt. A lot. She also knew that she'd wake up with the taste of blood in her mouth.

When the final bell rang, she grabbed her books and hurried to the parking lot. She had just dumped her belongings in the back of the Subaru when she heard a familiar laugh.

"What's the matter, Sokolov? I told you if you kept driving that way, sooner or later there'd be an accident."

The hair on the back of her neck lifted. A few spaces away, Trick was standing open-mouthed, staring at his car. All the windows had been shattered, and there were dents in the body.

And on the sidewalk, doubled over with glee: Mike.

The one who had hurt Trick over and over.

The one who made so many lives miserable.

Before she realized what she was going to do, she found herself standing in front of him, practically nose to nose. From the way he blinked in surprise, she realized she must have moved fast, faster than she should have.

No matter. All she cared about was stopping him from hurting anyone again.

He saw her. Gave her a sexy smile. "What do you want, sweet—"

She balled up her fist and rammed it against his pig nose. She heard a satisfying crunch sound even as pain radiated up her arm. As he reeled, blood spurted from his nostrils and she could smell it, sharp and clear and it called to the wolf deep inside.

She growled and lunged closer. She felt hands grabbing at her, dragging her back, and she turned and snapped, barely missing biting Trick's hand as he jerked it away from her. She saw the surprise in his eyes and it penetrated the growing fog in her brain.

Don't bite him.

"You bitch!" Mike shouted, holding his nose. "I am gonna kill you!"

She had almost bitten Trick. Stunned, Katelyn stopped struggling and let him pull her away, beginning to shake as the adrenaline dissipated as suddenly as it had come. She could hear Mike screaming and swearing behind her, but he wasn't her problem anymore.

"I'm sorry," she whispered to Trick. "So, so sorry."

He shook his head. "Look, it's fine. Just come here with me."

She came out of her daze as he was leading her into a small park. The place was deserted. It was cold enough that she could see her breath. Framed by glowering clouds, Trick was watching her closely. Then he led her over to one of the swings and sat her down on it.

"Easy there, slugger," he said.

She wrapped her hands around the icy chains and tried to force herself to just breathe in, deep and easy. After a moment Trick wrapped his hands around hers. They were warm and strong.

"Thank you," she whispered.

"I'm right here," he said.

She leaned her head against his chest, breathing him in. After a minute he circled behind her and gave the swing a little push. She lifted her feet off the ground and he gave her another push.

"Dang," he said after a minute. "I'd hate to see what would happen to him if he trashed *your* car."

She smiled wanly. He pushed her again. Without thinking, she pumped her legs.

"How high do you want to go?" he asked, his voice gentle.

"I want to fly."

And he pushed so hard she nearly fell off the swing, but she kept her balance and swung her legs back. He kept pushing and she kept swinging, shifting her weight back and forth, building up speed and momentum. She flew toward the sky and then fell back to earth over and over.

The rush of wind was exhilarating and she felt like her old self. She *could* fly. She could escape all the violence and stupidity of Wolf Springs. And she could do it with Trick.

At the height of the arc she let go, launching herself into the air. For a moment she hung, weightless, and it was everything she had ever dreamed it could be. Then she began to fall. She could hear Trick yelling, but she would show him what it was really like to fly. She did a back flip and prepared to land on her feet as the ground came rushing up to meet her. She could do it. She was agile as a cat and strong as a werewolf.

And then she saw Trick beneath her, arms outstretched. She twisted at the last moment so she would land in his arms, parallel to the ground. He caught her and dropped to one knee. She looked up at him and there were too many emotions colliding in his dilated eyes.

"How was that?" she asked, breathless.

"You shouldn't scare me like that."

She tilted her head sideways and gave him a little grin. "Why not?"

He didn't smile back. "Because I'm crazy about you," he said simply.

The words hung between them in the cold air, shimmering, sparkling.

"I'm crazy about you, too." Her heart was soaring and breaking at the same time. There was a terrible kind of agony admitting it out loud, but there was also the most wonderful sense of release, as if the words had been bottled up for so long that they had just exploded out of her.

"I know things have been crazy. That I've been . . . there's something wrong with me," he said, dropping his voice down to a whisper.

"There's something wrong with me, too," she whispered back.

They contemplated each other warily, hopefully, as if each one was daring the other to go first. To confess. To reveal.

"You're seventeen. Life can't be this tangled up for you," he said.

"Can't it?" she asked him, letting him see all her misery and pain. "Look at me."

He hung his head.

He thinks it's because of him and all his drama.

She kissed him. He responded, and she could feel all his yearning. She twisted in his arms so that she could wrap herself around him. He was on his knees, still holding her.

He loved her. She knew he did. Knew that he would do anything for her. She wanted him, wanted to be with him, couldn't imagine her life without him.

And I don't have to. One little nip, that's all it would take, and then we could be together.

She put her teeth on his bottom lip.

I could do it right now.

She froze. She quickly let go and pulled away.

"What is it?" he asked.

She leaned her head against his shoulder and sobbed. He held her, rubbing her back. He was Trick.

"Trick, there's something I need to tell you."

"Anything." He kissed the crown of her hair.

"I need you to know." She took a deep breath. She knew what she wanted him to know, but what exactly did she need him to know? "I need you to know that I *want* to be with you."

"Works for me," he said, giving her a squeeze.

She lifted her head and forced herself to stare him in the eyes. "But there's stuff about me, terrible stuff, that you don't know. I just *can't* be with you. I can't risk hurting you anymore."

He didn't blink. Didn't smile. "Katelyn, if you care for me I'm willing to risk anything, do anything. Just let me help."

"I can't."

She twisted so she could get her feet on the ground and she stood up, feeling light-headed. He was still kneeling, looking stricken. "Trick," she said, her voice strangled. "If I were free . . . but I'm not. And you're better off without me."

She hurried away before he could stop her. She had only made it a few steps before the tears started gushing down her cheeks. Any delusions she had harbored that someday she and Trick could somehow be together were gone. In the span of an hour she'd almost bitten him twice, once in anger and once in passion. If she tried to be with him, it was only a matter of time before an accident happened.

And she loved him too much to curse him as she'd been cursed.

"Darlin'," he called after her.

"Please, I need to be alone," she cried, without looking at him.

"No way."

"Please," she said again, and as she walked away, he let her.

She wandered around for nearly half an hour before finding her way back to the school parking lot. Trick's vandalized car was still there, but there was no sign of him. She figured he was hovering nearby, giving her space, and she climbed into her Subaru and left as quickly as she could. She tried to force herself to calm down, but even after she had put the town behind her and driven well into the forest she couldn't.

Her cell phone trilled and she snatched it up. The number was unknown.

"Hello?" she asked carefully.

On the other end of the line all she heard was very gentle breathing.

"I'm alone," Katelyn said, clearing her throat and hoping that that hadn't been the worst thing in the world to admit.

"Kat?"

It was Cordelia, but her voice was strangled, barely recognizable.

"What's wrong?" Katelyn asked, all senses on high alert.

"It was never supposed to happen like this," Cordelia said with a sob.

She's crying. She felt a terrible chill. Cordelia had been so cautious about communicating at all.

Something's very, very wrong.

"What is it? What's happened? What can I do?"

"It's Dom."

"Has something happened to him? Has he hurt you?" she asked, her mind racing to different extremes.

"My time's up," Cordelia whispered. "I have to do it."

"Do *what*?" Katelyn shouted into the phone. "Cor, tell me."

"Please. I am — I was — your pack sister."

"Cor—"

"I have to *marry* him. If I don't, I have to leave. And I have nowhere else to go."

"No, that's crazy. Don't. Wait. I'll think of something."

"Then do it *now*," Cordelia said.

And then the phone went dead.

Katelyn tried calling back but the call went straight to voice mail, the automated robotic female voice informing her that the mailbox hadn't been set up, so she couldn't even leave a message.

She became aware of a rumbling sound that seemed to grow louder. Was it thunder? She frantically tried calling again. Straight to voice mail once more. Before she could hang up something slammed into the side of her car, sending it careening out of control, and Katelyn stomped on the brakes, sending herself weaving as something flashed by her on the narrow road. It was a truck.

Her Subaru slowed and rolled against a tree, which groaned under the impact. *They hit me*, she thought, shocked.

Ahead of her the truck had also pulled over, and the driver was getting out. Katelyn started to reach for her insurance card in the glove compartment when her hand froze.

Mike was sauntering toward her, a huge triangular-shaped apparatus on his nose, a leer on his arrogant face, and a tire iron clutched in his hand.

17

Katelyn stepped out of her car in a rage. "What the hell?" she screamed at Mike.

"Payback's a bitch, *bitch*," he said, snarling.

"What, you want to break my nose?" she demanded. "You really think you need a tire iron for that?"

His smile broadened and there was something so terrible about it, so leering, that an awful suspicion crept into her mind.

"I was thinking of taking it out on you a different way," he said, eyes moving down her body.

His look and tone confirmed her suspicions. And while the Katelyn she used to be screamed at her to get in her car and run over him, the new Katelyn began to growl.

Mike cocked his head to the side. "What the hell—"

She leaped at him, kicking the tire iron out of his hand before he could even move. She hit him in the eye so hard it snapped his head back. She growled again, an angry, throaty sound that started to turn into a howl. She kicked him in the stomach, doubling him over, and slammed her fist into his chin with everything she had in her. His eyes rolled back but she kept him upright, hitting him again and again in the stomach.

He was wheezing when she finally let him fall to the ground. Blood was pouring out of his nose and mouth. Both his eyes were already turning black and his breathing was uneven. She stood over him, waiting for him to get back up.

A few seconds later, his eyes flickered open and he stared up at her. He looked like something out of a horror movie, and she couldn't stifle her satisfaction.

Panting, she leaned over him. "This ends now, do you hear me?"

He nodded, almost imperceptibly.

"You leave Trick and me alone and I'll leave you alone. Understood?"

He nodded again. Sheepish, scared.

She left him there, got into her Subaru, and roared away.

When she pulled up in front of the cabin she flexed her fingers on the steering wheel. There was blood on them. Mike's blood. She'd have to make a break for the bathroom to try and clean it off before her grandfather could see it.

She left her backpack in the back and headed inside. As soon as she had opened the door she ran to the stairs. "Hi!" she called out when she was halfway up them.

"Katie, you okay?" her grandfather called.

"Fine," she yelled back just before she closed the bathroom door behind her.

A couple of minutes later she emerged, having gotten all the blood off. Her hands had stopped aching, which was an added bonus. She went back downstairs. From the living room her grandfather looked at her expectantly.

"Sorry, bathroom," she said with a grimace.

He nodded as she went back outside to grab her backpack. Somewhere in the distance she heard a wolf howl and it took all her willpower not to join in.

⊰ ⊱

Katelyn.

Katelyn woke with a start, a dream fading too quickly from her memory to hold onto. The nearly full moon poured light down through her skylight, bathing her room in silver. Every nerve sizzled. Branches tapped impatiently against the glass above.

Wearily, she picked up *In the Shadow of the Wolf.* There hadn't been any more information on the mine or the Hellhound and she was beginning to think there wasn't any more to find. She had finished Cordelia's diary, a litany of disappointments and excuses for the erratic behavior of her father. She and Cordelia had one thing in common: they hated Regan and Arial.

She put the book away and took out the paper with the picture of the heart-shaped boulder again. And she wondered for the thousandth time if the real painting had been hanging on their wall all that time.

⊶ ⊷

She spent the next morning pretending to study and surfing the net for aerial photos of Wolf Springs — there were none — but mostly just freaking out. Full moonrise would occur in less than ten hours.

When it was finally time to head over to the Fenners' she made it downstairs with her duffel bag.

"Have fun at Paulette's," her grandfather said, his smile strained. "And be careful."

"I will," she promised.

She kept forgetting to breathe. It was only her second full moon, and the first one as a full-time pack member. Her skin was tingling; she felt different compared to the day of the previous full moon, as if she was even more hyper-aware of everything around her. The sun was too bright; the wind whooshed with the rush of heavy breakers. An owl seemed to shout into her ear.

When she reached the house, dread wrapped around her as she took in the sight of the vehicles parked in the driveway. Arial and Regan were there. As she got out of the car, the front door opened and Justin came down the steps, his expression somber.

"What's wrong?" she asked, queasy and anxious.

"Nothing," he muttered, offering her his cheek. She kissed it, and he returned the kiss on her cheek. She felt nothing, no desire, just the certainty that something else had happened. Something bad.

"Let's go," he said.

He headed for the trees and she had to pick up her pace to stay beside him. He dodged a branch; not as quick, she pushed it back with her hands, nearly catching her foot on a gnarled tree root.

"Where are we going?" she asked.

"To rendezvous with the rest of the pack. Everyone else is gone." He gave her a look. "You were late."

"I'm sorry," she said.

"Don't be late again."

"Okay."

As he passed a pine tree, he broke a twig and pulled off the needles, then let the bare branch fall to the ground. "I guess you've probably noticed that we get on edge a smidge the closer it gets to the full moon," he said.

She nodded, so uncomfortable around him that she took a couple of steps away, trying to make it appear as if she were avoiding a couple of large rocks in her path. His scent followed, and she stumbled. He reached out a hand, and steadied her.

Flashfire.

"Yeah," she said, trying to mask her reaction. "Like hyperdrive."

"That would be the wolf, clawing to come out." He held her hand for an extra beat, and then he let her go.

"Wow, that sounds so awful." Her voice broke on the last word, and she cleared her throat. "Awful," she tried again.

"It's not, Kat," he said, exasperated. "I swear it."

They were deep in the forest now, weaving between trees. He seemed to be following a path only he could see. She smelled the air but there was nothing she could pick up on that might be guiding him.

"Come on, Justin," she said. "I know something's wrong."

"More evidence that the Gaudins have been paying us visits. Uncle Lee is convinced they've got a spy here."

"In the pack?"

"No, but here, possibly in Wolf Springs."

"How does he know?" she asked.

Justin shrugged. "I'm not sure. But I know we've got a spy or two on the other side ourselves."

She felt her throat closing up as she wondered if any of those spies knew that Cordelia had been in contact with her.

"How much farther 'til we get there?" she asked. She wanted to know if they were going to the same clearing where Cordelia had taken her for her first change, but she remembered that the pack was supposed to hunt far from there. That was why they had both been so shocked when the others had appeared, just as Katelyn was shifting. Uncovering her terrible secret. Ruining Cordelia's life.

"About two hours," Justin replied.

"Two *hours*?" she asked, coming to a standstill.

He huffed. "Our pack hunts deep in the forest, Kat, far away from people. That's what keeps everyone safe."

She shuddered when he said *our pack*. She wanted to protest, to tell him that it wasn't *her* pack at all. But off in the distance a wolf howled and the urge to howl back was nearly undeniable.

"They're calling us," he said. "Let's go. We can run if you like."

"No, I'm good with walking," she said hastily. She still didn't want to join up with the pack, no matter that she couldn't stop herself from walking faster and listening intently for another howl.

They trudged together for a while in silence. The blue of the sky faded to gray, and Katelyn sensed a change deep within her. With every minute that ticked by, her senses sharpened. The last few autumn leaves were brighter, more vibrant, even as the forest grew darker. She could hear tiny creatures scuffling under the bushes and the wind sighing in the trees even though the branches stood still.

And the more she saw and heard and smelled the more she wanted to run away. The heightened senses, the feeling of power that coursed through her body — all of it terrified her more than she could even give voice to.

Beside her, Justin walked as though nothing in the world was wrong, as though they were just out for a hike and they weren't werewolves, and their leader wasn't insane, and he didn't have a girlfriend, and it wasn't death to get between them.

A twig cracked somewhere to her right. A deer bounded in front of her, startling her, and she jumped sideways, slamming into Justin.

The deer ran off and Katelyn's heart raced. She wanted to urge it to run far and fast. *Because tonight we hunt and I don't want to kill you.*

"Kat, it's just a deer. Relax," Justin grunted.

"Don't tell me to relax," she hissed. "Imagine for five seconds that this wasn't the life you were born into and suddenly you're facing all this."

"It's not that bad," he said, sounding tense.

"Oh, really? Mr. Fenner wants me to get married. And if I piss him off he'll kill me. So, where does that leave me?"

"In a pack, and behaving like a pack mate," he replied.

"I'm barely seventeen. I'm too young to even think about any of this stuff."

"No, you're not," he said, voice husky. He reached out and took her hand again. And the contact sent fire running through her veins. But she had something to say, and she needed to get it out, no matter how hot he was. She forcibly removed her hand from his.

"Yes, I am!" she shouted. She couldn't stop herself. There was too much pain, too much change, and if he didn't understand, she would make him understand.

"You're overreacting." He moved his shoulders. "Even though my uncle's got his . . . problems, he knows enough to give you some time to adjust. He's not making any wedding plans for you."

"You know he is," she insisted. "You heard him." She didn't know what had happened after she'd left. What had been said. What had been done.

"That was only because he got you mixed up with . . . her."

"But what about *her*? He was pushing her to get married and he wouldn't even let her choose the guy."

Justin frowned. "You mean the football player she was

dating? He wasn't pack material. And wolves can only marry other wolves. She knew that. She probably would have married Steve."

Katelyn shook her head fiercely. "No, she wouldn't have."

He grabbed her by the arms. She could feel his fingers curled around her biceps and they seemed to burn into her skin. His nearness was making her head swim.

She stared at his lips and struggled to focus on what he was saying, but it was becoming difficult. She was having trouble thinking and for a moment she wondered if the change was happening already.

The wolf is trying to claw its way out.

"What makes you so sure about that?" he demanded.

"Maybe he was the one who started all this, trying to discredit her because she was going to reject him," Katelyn said, feeling like she was babbling.

Is that right, is that what I meant to say?

She stared at Justin. His pupils were dilating and the way he was looking at her, she knew she should back away.

Run away.

"How do you know she was going to reject him?"

Let go of me. Now, she thought. *Please.*

"Because she didn't love him."

He smiled. "It's not always about love, Kat."

He's right. This isn't love. This is just desire. The wolf wants him . . . and I — I don't.

But she did. She felt horrible about it, but there it was.

"Is that why you're with Lucy?" she snapped before she could stop herself. She was trying to push him away with her words. She just didn't know how far she could push. Her fuse was shortening. Darkness was falling. The moon would soon rise.

He made a strangled sound in his throat and his hands tightened on her arms. "I care deeply for Lucy."

"But do you love her?" It seemed like the only question in the world.

His gaze took on a faraway cast, the muscle in his jaw working. "We can't always have who we love."

Like Trick, she thought in despair.

His eyes bored into her very soul. He wrapped his arms around her and pulled her close.

"Kat, I'm only so strong," he whispered against her cheek. "I think about you constantly and I don't know what to do about it."

Her pulse was skittering out of control at his touch. And she could hear his heartbeat, strong and fast. And then his lips were on hers and the world seemed to tilt and spin around them as she tried to turn her head. This was wrong. No matter how good it felt, it wasn't a good thing to do.

But she could smell the ocean and the soap on his skin and . . .

. . . somebody else in the forest.

She broke away from him with a start and covered her mouth with her hands.

"What is—" He stopped, sniffing the air. "It's Doug," he said in an undervoice. "Doug!" he shouted.

A few seconds later Regan's husband came into view, jogging toward them, mouth drawn, eyes hooded.

"What's up?" Justin asked.

"Lee's looking for you. I told him I'd send you on in a hurry."

Justin turned to Katelyn, flushed and sweaty. "Guess we're going to have to run after all."

"No, it's okay. I'll walk her there," Doug offered. "Just go."

Justin nodded and took off without looking in her direction.

A moment later Doug began walking, and she walked beside him. She tried to check her hair. A few seconds passed, and then he turned to her.

"We need to talk." There was an intensity to his voice that put her on her guard.

"What about?" she asked, hating the way her voice quavered.

"I think you know," he said, casting a significant look after Justin.

"I don't know what—"

"Spare me, Kat. I saw. Hell, a blind man could see what's between the two of you."

She licked her lips, not sure what he expected her to say.

He walked steadily, head down, watching the path. Avoiding her. "No good can come of this."

She lifted her chin, struggling to have an ounce of courage, of defiance. "Why talk to me?"

Then he did look at her. "Because I take you for the smarter of the two . . . and the one more likely to get hurt."

They walked a few moments in silence and Katelyn struggled for composure.

"You know that he's spoken for. Lucy would be within her rights to challenge you. To the death."

"The code of the hills," she said sarcastically, but she was afraid. And ashamed. If Doug had noticed, others must have, too. And in real life, she would never have poached on another girl's guy.

She reminded herself that this *was* her real life.

Doug was silent for a moment. "You and I have a lot in common," he said at last, blowing air out of his cheeks. "I was nineteen when Regan was allowed to tell me the secret, offer me the choice of joining the pack. And as much as I loved her, it was one I wrestled with. And there were months and months of training before her daddy bit me in."

Bit him in. How could he have chosen that? She tried to imagine how it had been accomplished. Like a vampire bite? Surely not an attack in the middle of the night, deep in the forest.

"It was what I *wanted*," he emphasized, "but after I became a werewolf, oh my Lord, was I lost. Overwhelmed. There were so many physical changes going on that I felt like I'd lost my mind, my identity, my life. I couldn't control myself and for six months I felt like I was walking around in a fog, except for the nights when I changed." He ran his hands through his hair, and she saw that they were trembling. "Those nights saved me," he said, and then he fell silent again.

"Why are you telling me this?" she asked after a beat.

He faced her dead on. "Because I had months to get ready. They let me see them when they changed. I ran with them when they hunted. I knew what I was getting myself into. I can't imagine how hard it's been on you. No choice, no warning, no preparation."

Here was someone who understood. Someone who was being kind to her. It was almost too much.

"It's been a nightmare," she conceded.

"And that won't change, not for a while." He cocked his head. "And it never will if you don't leave Justin alone."

Mortified, she looked down at her hands. "I know. But it's not just me."

"I know, Kat. And for his part in this, I'd like to call him out for his disloyalty to Lucy and his alpha." His voice was tense, hard.

Frightened, she raised her head, not exactly sure what he meant. "But . . . you're not going to?"

He shook his head. "Because then one of them might kill you and I don't think you deserve that."

"Thank you." Her throat closed up and she worked to clear it. "Thank you, Doug."

He clicked his teeth. "I want to tell you, Kat, that Justin Fenner's been good to Lucy all these years. You've seen him. He's exactly the kind of guy women fall all over. Looker, biker, cowboy. Bad boy." He grinned lopsidedly. "Recipe for infidelity. I know there's gossip, but I know that good ol' boy. He has not strayed one single time. Until you."

She caught her lower lip between her teeth, feeling guilty for just . . . being. But thrilled, too. She couldn't help it. She was special to him, not just some random conquest. He'd been telling her the truth.

"Love is a tricky thing, trickier by far when you add all this mess of wolf hormones into the equation," Doug continued. "Then trying to figure out your place, you need all the help you can get."

"Regan hates me," she reminded him, wincing even as she did so. If he had an angle he was playing, she wanted to know now before things got messier.

"Regan is unbelievably self-centered," he said bluntly, and then he chuckled. "I love her, though. I'd die for her. I'd kill for her, though I surely pray it never comes to that."

Lee Fenner, she realized. *He's talking about the alpha.*

"I don't want Lee to mate me off to someone," she said. "Justin said I'll be given some time to adjust."

He made a face. "Not so sure of that, Kat. Your lupine instincts will kick in better if you're in a relationship. That's how wolves are. Focus on the group, and you'll worry less about yourself."

She felt a twinge of desperation. "Doug, there's a guy, a normal guy—"

He lifted a hand to cut her off. "A few years ago before his . . . condition . . . you might have been able to talk to Lee about this guy, but not now. Regan and I were lucky. Every once in a while someone gets bit in to the family, to bring fresh blood, widen the gene pool. It's a practical thing but still a very rare thing. Right now, something like that would be forbidden. Lee's our alpha — and that business with . . . you know . . . has meant he can't afford to be seen to back down from any decision."

"Not even one that concerns his own daughter?" she asked. "Her safety? If he's her alpha, isn't she his responsibility?"

"That's why he banished her. So that she wouldn't be his responsibility," Doug replied. "So he could avoid putting her to death."

"But he could choose not to. He's the alpha."

"We live by forcing her. So, if you value both your lives, keep your mouth shut. And I will, too."

She nodded. She was grateful for Doug's understanding —and for his discretion. But he was a member of the pack, loyal to Lee and married to Regan. How much of an ally could he be? And if Lee's own daughter, high-ranking Cordelia, wasn't going to be allowed back into her family, into her pack, what choices did *she* have?

She cast a sidelong glance his way. He seemed to be a good man. Al, too, who was married to Arial. How did two such nasty women end up with decent guys? It was a mystery.

After a while he spoke again. "The clearing's just ahead." He peered up at the sky, which was almost dark. "We should get a move on."

He broke into a run and she raced with him. Even though it was shadowy and dim beneath the trees, she could still see the way. It felt good to stretch out her legs and to let loose, running so fast she marveled at the feeling of the speed.

Birds scattered as she and he burst into a clearing and came to a stop. The rest of the pack had gathered. They were wearing underwear, T-shirts, and tank tops, and she averted her gaze, embarrassed. Someone chuckled.

Clad only in track shorts, Justin was standing next to Mr. Fenner, who had on a bathrobe. Doug touched her elbow almost imperceptibly and then walked over to Regan. Lucy was holding hands with Jesse, and Arial and Albert were talking with their heads close together.

Mr. Fenner raised his head and lifted a finger in the air. "Get ready," he told her. Then he tossed off the bathrobe, revealing a pair of boxers and a cheap white T-shirt.

He meant for her to undress, too. She'd put on loose shorts and a T-shirt beneath her clothes, and she looked around for a good place to stash her stuff so she'd be able to find them again in the morning.

Hopefully before anyone else wakes up.

Her skin was beginning to tingle. They had cut it close. The change was coming.

In the next instant, Katelyn found herself surrounded by several half-dressed young men, including Steve Berglund. They ringed her, walking slowly around her, acting as though they were sniffing the air. Her chest tightened. What was happening? Was Mr. Fenner going to choose a mate for her tonight? She opened her mouth to scream a protest and it came out as a howl.

She could feel the moon pulling on her, calling to her. Fire traced its way through her veins and she could hear her bones cracking. Her clothes ripped at the seams as her body changed.

She glanced up and saw everyone changing around her, and fresh horror flooded her.

I'm lost.

18

Running
 Bounding
 Yipping and howling
 with the pack
 with the group
 with the family
 One among many
 The pack is mighty!
 Who do you run with?
 Wolf girl, wolf boy

Dashing, soaring, flying
unfettered, free, released, unleashed
freedom in unity
the hills, the woods, the deer, the deer, the deer
the blood
the waterfall
the heart of rock
the waterfall

The males were loping around her, singling her out, and the wolf that was Katelyn rejoiced in her attractiveness while she snapped her jaws at them. But it was the waterfall that caught her attention, that and the rock; there was something about them that was important. Did predators lurk there?

A danger.
A monster.
A promise.
An answer.

Then the wolf that was Katelyn lost her name, as she was lost in a river of fur. In the pack. And all thoughts vanished in the hot, steaming blood.

⋅⊶ ⫚ ⊷⋅

Katelyn awoke and felt the frosty dirt beneath her cheek. She sat up swiftly. *My clothes. Where did I leave my clothes?*

But she and Doug had only just made it to the meeting site before everyone started to change. She'd still been wearing all her clothes, which meant they were ruined, the shredded remains scattered who-knew-where.

Mortified, she rolled over onto her stomach. Drowsing scatters of naked people surrounded her. Jesse lay sprawled unashamedly on his back with his arm over his eyes. Farther on, Mr. Fenner was lying with his back to her, a clump of forest tangle shielding his backside from view. Past Mr. Fenner, Steve Berglund lay beside an older woman Katelyn knew she had met, but she couldn't remember her name.

She saw blood in the grass and tasted some in her mouth. The air smelled of a deer they had taken down. She remembered washing Mike's blood off. She'd be taking another shower before she saw her grandfather.

Behind a tree, someone was shushing someone else and giggling. Katelyn scooted behind the next one over, trying to cover herself.

What was she going to do? She had no idea how to get back to the Fenners' house, where she had a change of clothes in her overnight bag. Then she heard a soft step behind her and crossed her arms over her chest, hunching forward, before twisting to look over her shoulder.

Hannah, the young woman she had seen in Babette's, held out a T-shirt and a pair of sweatpants. She herself was dressed in a jog bra and bike shorts.

"Thank you," Katelyn said, gratefully taking the clothes.

"You're welcome," the other girl murmured, eyeing Katelyn — the new girl at school, the new girl in the pack.

"I'll give these back as soon as I can," Katelyn said as she yanked on the T-shirt and then pulled on the sweats as fast as she could.

"Don't worry about it. I once got caught too close to the change. I know how it feels," she said, wrinkling her nose. Then she bent down to offer her cheek to Katelyn. It still didn't feel natural to kiss total strangers on the cheek, but Katelyn did it, remembering to offer her cheek to Hannah in return. Hannah brushed Katelyn's cheek gently.

Before she could say anything else one of the women called out, "Hannah!"

"Gotta go," Hannah said, disappearing into the underbrush.

Katelyn stood up, stepping from behind the tree. Most of the two dozen or so others were awake now, chatting as they dressed.

"Kat." Mr. Fenner approached her in a light blue, long-sleeved shirt and a pair of jeans. He was carrying a pair of cowboy boots and had a tall, younger guy trailing after him, maybe early twenties, hands stuffed in his jeans pockets, lower lip pushed out in a childish pout. His name escaped her. He had a scruffy beard and moustache, and an overabundance of dark bangs that swept across a high forehead.

"This is Quentin Lloyd," Lee said.

"Hey, Quentin," Katelyn said, checking his eye color.

Amber. *Not the one who bit me.*

"Quentin *Lloyd*," Mr. Fenner corrected her. "That's his whole first name. Last name is Oskarsson."

There were a lot of Scandinavian last names among the members of the Fenner pack, which made sense, since they'd originally come from there. Katelyn opened her mouth to say hello again, but then it dawned on her that the alpha wasn't introducing Quentin Lloyd just to be sociable.

"Kat," Quentin Lloyd said, looking over her slowly. Inspecting her. Undressing her with his eyes. In a bit of push-back, she folded her arms across her chest, and Mr. Fenner chuckled.

"I'll leave you two to get acquainted," he said, before walking over to speak to Doug. Doug caught her eye. His expression said *Be nice.* Then he redirected his attention back to Mr. Fenner.

Quentin Lloyd cleared his throat. "I don't like this any more than you do. My family's line is almost as old as the Fenners' and I thought the alpha thought better of me than this. I don't deserve to be paired with a bit-in nobody."

Even though she wanted nothing to do with Quentin Lloyd either, Katelyn couldn't help but be completely offended.

"If you're so upset, why don't you challenge him?" she snapped.

"Shut up," he said, and spat at her face. Stunned, Katelyn wiped her eyes with hands shaking with rage — *how dare he!* She could hear growling. "Maybe I'll just take you out instead," he said. "You're worthless and he'd probably thank me for it."

She opened her eyes again, blinking. Steve Berglund and two other guys were advancing on Quentin Lloyd. Their teeth were bared; they were the ones making the growling sounds, and past Steve she could see Justin standing bare-chested with a T-shirt in his hand, expressionless, tracking every movement.

Quentin Lloyd flicked his head toward the others, as if not deigning to face them outright, and he growled as well.

Every fiber of Katelyn's being urged her to take him on. Hit him back.

Challenge him.

What was it Justin had said about gaining higher status in the pack and having more control? You married up or clawed your way up. And she was getting ready to do some clawing.

As if he sensed what she was feeling, he narrowed his eyes at her, face twisted in fury. "They all think you're some kind of prize. Let them have you."

"One thing's for sure," Katelyn shot back. "You never will."

"What's going on here?" Mr. Fenner demanded, striding up in his boots.

"She spoke treason against you," Quentin Lloyd said.

"*What?*" Mr. Fenner whirled on her. His eyes — his human eyes — began to glow. Katelyn had never seen that happen before, and it chilled her to the bone. Things were different. More dangerous. She began to sweat.

He was standing on the balls of his toes; his large hands wrapped into fists. He was about to spring.

"She asked me to challenge you," Quentin Lloyd said, sneering at her.

Terror washed over Katelyn, tugged at her, a fear so deep she could only sense its fatal grasp on her. She was in mortal danger. Lee Fenner had banished his own daughter. He had threatened to kill her, Katelyn, numerous times. This might be the only excuse he needed. The pack would be rid of their problem.

Barely able to move her head, she glared at Quentin Lloyd, who was smiling sourly at her, certain that his accusation had hit home, and that Mr. Fenner was about to kill her.

It's either him or me, she realized over the howl of fear stuck inside her throat. *Think. Say something.* She bowed her head submissively to Lee, then looked up.

"He spat on me because he doesn't want me," she said, her head still ringing from the accusation. "He went on about how his family line was just as long as yours and that I — that what you were doing to him was — was outrageous."

Mr. Fenner scowled, first at her, and then at Quentin Lloyd. She sensed his uncertainty and knew she had to buy some time. She had to save herself.

"I did not!" Quentin Lloyd shouted, but even she could hear the quaver of deceit cloaked in his indignation.

She seized on it and faced Lee again. "I told him you were his alpha. I said you knew what was best. And if he didn't agree, and he was man enough, then he should challenge you to your face instead of going behind your back."

Gasps arose from the onlookers.

Lies. And more lies.

Life-saving lies.

"I didn't say that, alpha," Quentin Lloyd protested. "She said I should . . ." He backed away.

Lee Fenner pivoted on his boots, eyes blazing brighter, and locked his sights on Quentin Lloyd. "You dare, boy? We got more than one traitor in this pack?"

"No! That's not — not what I . . ." Quentin Lloyd

stammered, taking a step back and lifting his hands as though to defend himself. "Alpha, I, *please!*" The last word burst from deep in his chest, an anguished cry that just seemed to infuriate Lee more. "She's lying to you. She's just an uppity bitch, don't know her place—"

Lee Fenner changed into a wolf, the transformation swifter than Katelyn would have thought possible. He was completely white, like an albino, a huge, monstrous beast with his glowing eyes, and he leaped onto Quentin Lloyd like a whirlwind.

Quentin Lloyd slammed backwards against the ground, the wolf on top of him. Then he himself began to change, and she could hear the snapping of his bones.

"Quentin Lloyd!" someone screamed.

Howls filled the air, like screaming, and disbelief, and cheers. Blood sprayed in all directions. It splattered Katelyn's face, hot and thick, and she clapped her hand over it and staggered backwards, falling to the ground.

Now she could hear a horrible, gurgling sound. The white werewolf alpha tossed his head, jaws dripping blood. And slowly he changed back until he was Mr. Fenner again, half-naked in tattered, bloody rags.

Quentin Lloyd lay on the ground, eyes wide, mouth open. Blood pooled around his head and streamed along the ground, steaming in the cold.

Katelyn let loose with a scream that echoed off the mountains. She kept on screaming.

Everyone else went silent.

"Shut up," Mr. Fenner ordered her.

She pressed both hands across her mouth, forcing herself to stop. Then she vomited all over herself.

In a mirror action, Mr. Fenner wiped his hand across his lips. Then he leaned over the corpse and spat on it.

"Anybody else got anything to say?" he yelled. "Well?"

The pack shrank backwards. Shoulders hunched. Somewhere in the part of her that still functioned, Katelyn heard whining, groveling. She clutched her sides with her hands and cried silently, rocking herself.

Lee Fenner walked imperiously away. A moment later, Justin crouched down next to her and grabbed her hand. He squeezed it.

"Kat, you have to calm down," he said, his voice low and urgent. "*Now.*"

"I knew," she wept. "I knew he would take it out on him, but I said it anyway. I — I just . . . he *killed* him."

"You had to. Or it'd be you lying there." Justin was whispering, but his words sounded so terribly loud to her ears. "It was rage," he said. "It's what we feel."

"It was him or me, and I knew it. I'm a monster."

"No, darlin', you're not. You're a werewolf."

And the fact that Justin made a distinction between the two made her want to laugh hysterically. Instead she just cried harder.

"Come on, let's get you out of here," Justin said, firmly hoisting her to her feet. She dangled in his grasp, and he peered into her face. "You've got to stop. Right now."

He practically dragged her out of the clearing and into the forest. Her feet felt like lead weights and she was freezing.

The images played over and over. Mr. Fenner. The spray of blood. The blood that was on her now. The screams.

How much she had hated Quentin Lloyd. The fury inside her, barely banked even now, like a separate, wild creature. Her terrible, terrible remorse.

And finally, a realization, and she stopped short.

"Kat, what?" Justin asked, tugging on her.

"It wasn't Mr. Fenner."

"What are you talking about?"

"The wolf who bit me. It wasn't Mr. Fenner."

Justin cupped her chin and bent his knees so that he was at her eye level. "Are you sure?"

She nodded, feeling the wetness of the blood on her cheek and wiping it off with the back of her hand. Quentin Lloyd's blood. The blood of a dead man. Her stomach protested, but she forced down the bile in her mouth.

"He's the wrong color. His fur is white. My wolf was gray."

Justin's knees actually buckled, and he grabbed onto her shoulders to keep from sinking to the earth. As he pulled himself back together, she stared at him.

"I was so worried it was him," Justin said. "Any werewolf doing those things would have to be beyond reason." His meaning was clear: he believed that his alpha was insane. Not just delusional, but mad. "This means somewhere out there, there's another insane werewolf," he murmured. "And we still don't know who it is."

⸻

Katelyn couldn't remember most of the walk back to the Fenner house. At Justin's insistence, she took a shower, watching the water run red as blood swirled down into the drain. Moving like a zombie, she changed clothes again. Someone had gotten rid of the bloody shirt.

"You need to get out of here," Justin murmured, as she stood before him with her wet hair hanging over her shoulders. "Before he thinks about blaming this on you."

She started to cry again, and Justin shook his head. He walked her to her car and made her get behind the wheel.

"No," he said, "don't do that, Kat. Stay strong, and go." As if he could read her mind, he added, "I can't go with you."

As if she were watching a movie, she saw herself starting up the car and pulling out of the driveway. The morning sun rose in the sky, but the woods quickly smothered all trace of daylight. Alone with her thoughts, she struggled against breaking down again. All the talk of killing. The actual killing. *Killings.* Haley, Becky, the man from the Inner Wolf Center, and now Quentin Lloyd.

Death.

It was the dark specter that hung over all the lives in Wolf Springs.

And over mine, she thought with a shudder.

She pulled over to the side of the road and buried her face in her arms, clinging to the wheel. It was wrong to stop in the forest, but she was afraid she'd drive herself off the road.

It was him or me, she thought, but was she so sure of that?

She shook. Cried. Tried to stop, but the tears kept coming. And she couldn't stay in the forest. She had to get as far away from Mr. Fenner as she could — and any of Quentin Lloyd's loved ones, who might be looking for payback.

The images of Quentin Lloyd were replaced with those of her father, at his funeral. Open casket, with everyone staring at his body. His face coated with makeup. The police officers, the other attorneys, her mother on tranquilizers. Her grandfather had flown in, but at the last moment, he had decided not to attend the service, and stayed at their house.

The house that had shaken apart and burned to the ground five years later.

"The death of one's child is a parent's worst nightmare," he had said at the reception, weeping as he accepted a shot of whiskey from Detective Cranston, who had been in charge of the case. "Whoever did this, I hope to God he suffers in hell."

"We'll get him," the detective promised. But they never had.

On impulse, Katelyn pulled out her phone. Cell coverage in the forest was always dicey, but she saw that she had three bars. With trembling fingers, she dialed L.A. information and got the number for the Harbor substation of the Santa Monica P.D. She gave her name and asked for Detective Cranston.

And miraculously, he picked up.

"Katelyn, how are you?" he asked kindly.

"Um," she said, struggling to keep her voice steady. "I — I'm okay."

"I was sorry to hear about your mom," he said, genuine regret tinting his voice.

Katelyn stared into the darkness through the windshield, clutching the phone in both hands. *Hold it together,*

Katelyn, she coached herself as fresh tears stung her eyes. "Thanks."

"What can I do for you?"

She plunged on before she lost her nerve. "I — I was going through Mom's things," she said, which was a stupid thing to say because there were no things of her mother's left. "Was there anything unusual about the — the bullet that killed my dad?"

There was a moment of silence. "Is there a reason you're asking?"

Not now, please don't go into cautious cop mode now, she begged silently.

"Well, ah, I remembered overhearing something she said . . ." She drifted off, hoping it was enough. "Maybe to you. I don't know . . ."

There was a long pause on the other end and she caught her lower lip between her teeth, hoping she hadn't just overplayed her hand.

"I didn't realize anyone had told her," he said, his voice soft. "But, yeah. The bullet was really odd. Non-standard. There was silver in it."

Oh, God.

Katelyn's hands tightened so hard around the phone she thought she might break it. "Thanks," she managed to whisper. "That's what I thought I heard."

"We kept it out of the news," he said, "to see if anyone would come forward. You know how these things work."

She nodded without speaking. Her father had been killed with a silver bullet after he'd been bitten by a wolf. Time seemed to stand still. Because it was too awful to think about. Her father must have been a werewolf! Must have gone through what she was facing right now. And her mom must have known or suspected. Why else would she have sent that article to her grandfather?

See, told you so.

That he was a werewolf. Or at least someone thought he was.

Katelyn didn't want to know anything more. She couldn't deal with it. If she thought about it for another second, she would go insane.

"Katelyn?" Detective Cranston queried. "Are you still there?"

"Mmm," she managed to answer.

"Listen, if something breaks, I will let you know. I promise. I'm sorry nobody told you about the . . . unusual evidence we collected. But you're older now, and if I hear *anything*, I'll give you a call. Is this your number?"

She covered her mouth and nodded silently again. "Hmm-mmm," she said.

"Okay, Katelyn. You take it easy. I'll check in on you soon."

"Yeah," she rasped.

Then she hung up.

Almost immediately, her phone rang again.

"Katie," said her grandfather, "are you and Paulette—"

"I'm on my way home," she interrupted.

"Okay, see you soon."

She hung up and focused on driving, and when she finally parked in front of the cabin she climbed slowly out of the

Subaru. Somewhere off in the woods she heard a branch crack and she turned her head toward the sound.

And a low growl met her ears.

Someone was out there. Maybe it was one of Quentin Lloyd's relatives, already coming for revenge. She ran up onto the porch. She threw open the door and was startled to find her grandfather waiting just inside, face strained. As soon as she stepped inside he closed the door behind her.

"What's wrong?" she asked.

"Did you know Mike Wright?" he asked, voice tense.

Panic flared through her. Mike had told on her. She could get into trouble for having hurt him.

"Yes, he's a big bully, why?" she blurted out.

"Well, honey, he's dead."

She stared at him incredulously. It was impossible.

When I left him he was alive and conscious. There's no way I hurt him bad enough for him to be dead. What if it was the pack, hunting? What if — oh, God, what if I helped kill him?

What if I did it on my own?

He wrapped an arm around her. "Oh, Katelyn, I'm sorry."

"What happened to him?" she asked in a strained, anxious voice. She couldn't take any more. She just couldn't.

He took a deep breath. "From what Pat said, same thing that happened to those girls and that Inner Wolf guy."

She blinked, not sure she had heard him correctly. "You mean he was mauled by an animal?"

His face was hard to read. "Something like that, it appears."

"That's — oh, that's terrible." She felt dizzy. "Where was — where did they find him?"

"In the forest, on the road here."

She slumped with relief. That was far away from the pack's established hunting grounds — too far to hunt him down and then return to the meadow before sunrise, even accounting for superior werewolf speed.

A beat. He looked toward the front door. "Look, I've got to go into town for a little while."

"Can I come with you?"

He shook his head, then looked at the rifle on the wall.

"Not this time."

"Why, what aren't you telling me?" Her voice was shrill.

He sighed, low and long and sadly. "Well, the sergeant's got to do some investigating, ask questions." He paused. "Everyone knows there was bad blood between Mike and Trick."

She stared at him in disbelief. "He can't think Trick had anything to do with this!"

He half raised his hand. "No, he just needs to ask him some questions. And since Trick is a minor and his folks are out of town again, I have to go down there."

She tried to make sense of what he was saying. She wouldn't have dreamed that a godparent would count as a legal guardian. Perhaps in this part of the world it did. Maybe it was just the relationship her grandfather seemed to have with Trick and his family.

"You know Trick couldn't have had anything to do with this." She was having trouble staying in control.

"I know, Katie," her grandfather said.

He still wouldn't look her in the eyes. She was stunned. "You think he did!"

"I never said that. Look, it's just bad business all around." He pushed out a deep, heavy breath. "Pat's talking about forming some kind of hunting party to try and find whatever's doing this."

Fear knifed through her. "And you're going to join it?"

He shook his head. "Try to stop it. Everyone's so on edge they're more likely to shoot each other than any animal."

Was that what happened a few weeks ago? Did someone take a shot at me by accident?

He grabbed his keys. "Now I have to go."

She nodded.

He paused. She could see the wheels turning in his mind. "I think you need to be indoors. With the doors locked. Don't go out."

"I won't."

"Rifle's loaded," he said, "and you know how to shoot it." He looked uncertainly at the door, as if trying to decide if someone could knock it down.

"Just a minute," he added. He went outside and she could hear him going into the garage. She checked the windows in the living room to make sure they were locked. Then she went into the kitchen and tested the back door.

Two minutes later, he was back. He held out an old-fashioned revolver, and she didn't take it, instead crossing her arms over her chest.

"We haven't practiced with it," she murmured.

"It's easy. Point and shoot." He held it out, and she finally took it.

And her world blew apart.

"Use it. In case anything gets in the house. Or if you see anything . . . odd."

"Odd, how?" she asked, her voice barely above a whisper.

He wiped his face and exhaled slowly. She could see his agony. Feel his tension, smell his fear.

"Just . . . odd. Keep it close. Promise me."

"I will."

He kissed the crown of her head and then walked out the door. And her world crashed down. It shook and it burned and she was inside it, writhing in mental anguish.

And now she knew one thing for sure, because she could smell the silver bullets inside the gun.

Her grandfather knew about werewolves.

19

Twisting inside, terrified, and yet oddly composed, Katelyn stared at the gun in her hand. Why was she surprised? She had seen the bullets.

I could pretend they weren't his. I could lie to myself.

Shaking, she ran to the door to call her grandfather back, make him talk. Spill it all. Then she flopped her back against the door and slid to the floor, gazing upward at the ceiling as huge tears rolled down her cheeks.

How long has he known? What does he know? And who does he know about?

Wiping her face, she raised the gun to eye level and studied the ends of the bullets in the circular chamber. The odor of silver wafted like incense, mingling with the smoke and ash in their fireplace.

She sniffled hard and let out a shaky breath. She shouldn't have let him go out there.

No. I should have gone with him.

He had left her there because she was safer home alone than wherever he was going. She was stuck. There was nothing she could do to help Trick, who had told her he cared for her.

"I'm sorry," she said brokenly. Because he was in trouble, and she was afraid for him, and she knew he was innocent.

Right?

"Oh, God," she blurted. Of course she knew. She believed in him.

And I need someone to believe in me.

She thought about Quentin Lloyd's body. How would they explain that? Would he be seen as just another victim of the same monster? And was that monster the same one that had bitten her?

Mr. Fenner hadn't bitten her. She knew that now. But he was crazy. He had killed someone before her eyes, would probably do it again when he lost his temper.

He couldn't remain alpha forever. Everyone had seen: everyone already knew that he was crazy.

But they're all terrified of him. Because he's still strong and fast and ruthless. And even though he's losing his mind, that just makes him more dangerous, not less. They put up with it, like at Thanksgiving. Because it's their "instinct."

Another thing she couldn't do anything about.

But it's not my instinct, she thought. *I don't feel any loyalty to him. I don't have to sit here and meekly let him ruin our lives. I have to do something. I can't just sit here.*

Outside she heard a wolf howl. It was close. She clenched her jaw and wiped at her eyes. If it was coming for her, better that it did now while her grandfather was safely away. This way he couldn't get hurt. This way, maybe he wouldn't have to figure out she was a werewolf.

"I'm not afraid," she said aloud, and then she picked up the handgun and molded her hand around it.

She was not helpless. She had power no one else did. She was immune to silver. If a werewolf came near her house, she could shoot it.

And kill it.

She heard the crunch of gravel outside and she moved to a window just in time to see Justin getting out of a truck.

She blinked rapidly. She couldn't let him see the gun with the silver bullets. She ran into the kitchen and hid it in a drawer and then flew back to the front door, opening it just as he knocked.

"I came to check up on you. Make sure you were okay."

She nodded swiftly. And then over his shoulder she caught a flash of something moving in the woods. She jerked. "What's that?" she asked, pointing.

Justin spun on his heel and looked. "I don't see anything."

"There was something there a second ago."

"Maybe you're just jumpy."

"No, I'm not," she said.

Justin stepped off the porch and started walking toward the trees. When he got close something exploded in movement. With a yelp he began to give chase.

Katelyn bolted out the door, running toward him.

"It's a wolf!" he shouted.

And the wolf was running away from them. Savage heat filled Katelyn and she leaped ahead, running past Justin. She crashed through the trees, following the creature. She swept her arm low and snatched up a rock. She flung it with all her strength and it hit the creature in the head. It turned on her, all snapping jaws and saliva. She tried to see the color of its eyes, but couldn't tell in the gloom beneath the trees.

"Show yourself!" Justin commanded in a booming voice as he ran up next to Katelyn.

The wolf spun around and focused on him. Katelyn took a step to the side, but it didn't look at her. She took another step, then another. Justin and the wolf were closing in on each other, fixated on each other. Neither of them was paying attention to her.

It could be the wolf that bit me.

I can't let it hurt Justin.

Katelyn circled to the side and then grabbed hold of a thick tree branch and swung herself up into the tree. She moved carefully from limb to limb, maneuvering herself until she was over the wolf.

This is crazy. What am I doing?

And as the wolf snapped its jaws she realized exactly what she was doing. She was saving Justin.

Aimed like a missile, she dropped silently from the tree. Her boots struck the wolf hard just at the base of the neck. It collapsed onto its side.

"Did I kill it?" she asked.

"No, knocked it out," Justin said, giving her an admiring glance. "Quick thinking."

"Thanks." She tried to slow down her breathing, her heart-beat.

The wolf began to transform into a human and Katelyn stared intently at the face. As the wolf snout turned back into a human nose and mouth, Katelyn gasped.

"Babette!"

"You know her?" Justin asked.

Katelyn nodded. "She owns the boutique clothing store downtown. I didn't know she was part of the pack."

"She's not," he said grimly. "I think we just found our Gaudin spy."

⧏ ⧐

An hour later they pulled into the Fenners' driveway. Justin was at the wheel of his truck, Katelyn beside him, and Babette was wrapped in chains in the back. Justin had called ahead and it seemed the entire pack was waiting for them. Doug and Al hurried forward and picked Babette up, carrying her around to the other side of the house, with the rest of the pack trailing behind.

"You did good," Justin said.

"Thanks."

He looked around. "I just wish I could figure out why it smells like silver in here."

She shrugged as she had half a dozen times on the drive. He didn't know that she had a gun with silver bullets, or that she had taken it and stashed it under her seat while he was busy making sure Babette couldn't escape. Maybe it had been foolhardy.

Maybe not.

Reluctantly Katelyn got out of the truck and followed Justin to the back yard. The pack was in an uproar, the air vibrating with jeers and growls.

"What the hell," Justin muttered.

Pack members in human form were gathered in a semi-circle. Lee Fenner's back was to Katelyn, and he was kicking something on the ground.

Not something, *someone.*

Babette.

She was curled up in a fetal position, arms covering her head as he drew back his booted foot and kicked her in the back. Justin's hand went across Katelyn's mouth as she cried out. Oblivious — or unconcerned — Mr. Fenner bent over Babette and pushed her onto her back. Then he grabbed her by the hair as if he were going to scalp her and lowered his face toward hers. His face sprouted hair; his jaw jutted forward and his teeth morphed into huge, white fangs. Drool roped off them onto the woman's neck, and he opened his mouth to tear out her throat. Babette's face flickered in and out of her human face and the she-wolf within, her jaw slightly elongating and her ears lying flat against her head.

Justin yanked Katelyn hard towards his chest, his hand so tight against her mouth that she couldn't breathe.

"Not a word," he whispered.

"Go ahead," Babette snarled between clenched teeth. "Do it. Then you'll never know."

With a ferocious growl, Mr. Fenner's face became mostly human again. Katelyn tapped on the palm of Justin's hand and he loosened his grip.

"Know what? Tell me," Lee growled.

"Why don't you ask her little friend about your daughter?" Babette growled. "They were always whispering in the store about their boyfriends — about my alpha Dominic Gaudin, and the boy Trick Sokolov." She threw back her head and howled, beginning to change fully, but another lunge from Mr. Fenner sent her sprawling semi-conscious on the ground.

"So," Mr. Fenner said over his shoulder. He looked straight at Katelyn. "My girl was talking treason all that time, and you never told me?"

The crowd quieted for Katelyn's answer. On the ground, Babette lay unmoving. Dizzy with fear, Katelyn remembered to duck her head to show submission.

"Mr. Fenner, I didn't know anything. This was . . . before. She said she liked this guy who was older, and that you didn't like him." She prayed she could deflect Mr. Fenner's focus from Trick. She didn't want any of this to come near him.

He glared at her. "You should have told me, girl."

She started to sweat. She didn't know if he was following what she was saying. If he even knew who she was.

He gestured to Babette. "All these years, she's been spying

on us for the Gaudins. Listening to every stupid thing *she* said in that store. Stupid, careless. You *both* deserve to die."

"Mr. Fenner, I didn't," Katelyn began, but behind her, Justin whispered, "Ssh."

"I'll do better," she said, changing course, raising her chin but staying low, maintaining the respectful body position she knew he would expect. "Now I know. I swear it. If you'll just give me a chance to prove myself."

He blinked at her. And then smiled. "All right. Take this piece of garbage out in the forest. Kill her, and bury her. Come back and tell me that you've done it."

"Let's kill her here, Uncle Lee," Lucy called out, baring her teeth and snapping toward the semi-conscious Babette. Clearly this was an occasion when it was okay to let out a bit of inner wolf.

"Now *there's* a good girl," Mr. Fenner said, smiling. "Lucy knows her place. You're going to go far, darlin'. But no one has ever died at our home, and I mean to keep it that way. Justin, make sure Kat gets it done."

Justin gripped Katelyn's arm tightly, silently begging her to agree. Although she wanted to start screaming, she dipped her head again. Then Justin left her, walked to the inert woman, and picked her up in his arms. As he approached Katelyn, she had to look away.

"Follow me," he said through clenched teeth. She fell into step behind Justin: dazed, disbelieving.

Bypassing all the Fenner vehicles, Justin carried Babette up the driveway, lingering at the road for Katelyn to catch up. There was never any traffic on their country lane, and Justin crossed into the forest without even looking. Katelyn thought about running; he must have sensed it, because he glanced over his shoulder at her and slowed down.

Time slipped away from her. She was so lost, inside and out, and when he stopped and lay Babette on the ground, Katelyn crossed her arms over her chest and gave her head a quick shake.

"She's healing," Justin said. "It'll be better if you do it now while she's still barely conscious."

Katelyn looked down at the ground. "I could *never* do it. I'm not a killer."

There was a beat. "Yes, you are. You're a werewolf." His voice was steady, firm. When she didn't respond, he said, "And you have done it before."

She whipped up her head. Babette was lying at his feet, and she saw that he had put her facedown. Katelyn's stomach contracted hard as Justin stepped over Babette and came toward Katelyn.

"Quentin Lloyd," he said.

Her heart leaped into her throat. She felt icy, and unaccountably abandoned. "No. You said—"

"I said what I said. But was it really very different?" He cocked his head. "You knew what you were doing."

"No." She tried to take a step backwards. But something inside her was beginning to respond to Justin's approach — interest, warmth. She was shocked.

"Katelyn, you already have to lie to so many people. But you don't have to lie to me. I'm like you. We're predators. There's no shame in that. Hell, humans eat meat."

"I didn't," she rasped, "before I got here."

There was silence. She peered up at him through her lashes and she was sure she caught the shadow of a fleeting smile on his face. Outraged, she turned her back on him.

She took a deep breath. "I'll help you."

"No, you're the one he wants to kill her."

"No, I mean I'll *help* you."

He turned her around. "What are you saying?" he asked, face intense.

"I will support you. All the insanity, death, it has to stop. I will help however I can." She rubbed her arm that had been injured in the silver trap, not wanting to mention her immunity in front of Babette, worried that she'd already said too much in front of the Gaudin werewolf.

Justin got the message and she could see the thought quickening in his eyes. "Your price?" he asked.

She ticked her gaze over to Babette, now crouched on the ground in her human form, clearly terrified, and he grimaced. She held her breath, waiting to see what he would do.

Then he chuckled deep in his throat and said, "Run, Babette."

Katelyn jerked, hard, as Justin shifted his weight so that she could see around him. Babette was ready to run, but first the Gaudin werewolf stopped and tears rolled down her bruised face.

"I swear I will never, ever set foot on Fenner territory again," she whispered, all her earlier bravado gone. "*Please.*"

"If I catch you," Justin said, "I *will* kill you."

As an answer, Babette nodded, then dashed into the

forest. Katelyn could scent her, hear her crashing through the underbrush.

"If Lee finds out, there will be hell to pay," Justin said. He smiled. "Now, where were we?"

"Thank you," Katelyn said, throwing her arms around him in a tight hug.

He held her tight for a minute and then stepped back. "Let's go home."

Justin had blood on his shirt and, looking down, she realized that she did now, too. Babette's blood might be on her clothes, but at least her death wouldn't have to be on Katelyn's conscience.

When they finally trudged out of the woods and made it back to the house, Katelyn saw that everyone was still gathered. Heads turned at their arrival and she forced herself to try and stay calm. There was no reason to panic.

She felt a text message come in on her phone but she kept it in her pocket — she couldn't read any messages until she was alone. And as she and Justin came to a stop before Mr. Fenner and the rest of the pack, Katelyn had never felt so alone.

Lucy was staring at them both, fire in her eyes. "How could you!" she demanded before anyone else could speak.

Katelyn froze as her mind tried to process what was happening.

"I can smell you all over him!"

Katelyn blinked in shock. All the times that Justin had kissed her and they'd never been caught, and now, over just a simple hug, Lucy was coming unglued. She opened her mouth to say something, anything.

"Lu, you're just upset," Justin said soothingly.

"You go to hell, Justin Fenner! You lying, cheating bastard!" Lucy shouted.

Then Lucy leaped at Katelyn, knocking her to the ground, and wrapped her hands around Katelyn's throat. Katelyn felt her phone fall out of her pocket as she flailed at Lucy, arms windmilling, trying to bat at her. She was too panicked to remember how to defend herself.

Over Lucy's shoulder, Jesse was screaming and Justin was holding him back.

Holding him back from helping either one of us. This is a challenge.

To the death.

Then Katelyn's vision swam before her eyes. She needed oxygen. Everything hurt; she couldn't breathe.

They rolled to the side and in the confusion, somehow Katelyn drew up her right leg and slammed her knee into Lucy's body. She didn't know where the blow landed, but Lucy grunted and loosened her grip. Katelyn hit her in the face and got to her feet, preparing to run. The rest of the pack was keeping their distance, as Jesse cried and Justin held him, and Katelyn half ran, half staggered toward the driveway. Her ears were ringing.

I don't have my car, she thought, lurching forward, dizzy and disoriented.

"Kill her, Lucy!" someone shouted.

They've come to watch her kill me, Katelyn realized in a

panic. *I'm going to die and Trick and my grandfather will never know why.*

"I'll get you, bitch!" Lucy screamed, yanking Katelyn by the hair. Then they heard roaring, and Lucy spun her half around.

Katelyn blinked and slowly realized that Mr. Fenner was standing alone, hands on his hips, and he was speaking.

"— going on here?"

Before Lucy could say a word, accuse her of stealing Justin from her, Jesse shouted. All eyes swiveled toward him and in horror Katelyn realized he was holding her phone.

"What is it, Buddy?" Justin asked.

"Cordelia married that no-good Dom," Jesse said, waving the phone in the air.

"No," Katelyn whispered. "Oh, no."

That must have been the text she got. Now everyone would know she'd been in contact with Cordelia.

"Ssh," Justin warned her. "Not a word."

The silence was terrible. Katelyn braced herself for Mr. Fenner's fury. The entire pack held its breath.

Then, with icy calm, the patriarch of the Fenner clan, leader of the descendants of the Fenris Wolf, squared his shoulders and raised his chin.

"War," he said, his voice ringing out. He looked at his daughter, Regan.

"War," Regan replied.

He looked at Arial.

"War," she concurred.

Then Doug: "War."

And Al, Arial's mate: "War."

And then it was Justin who said, "War."

Then Justin slid a knowing glance at Katelyn, who was heaving, trying to catch her breath. They had a secret, just them two. She was his secret weapon. But he wasn't planning on making his move then.

A thrill of pure, unadulterated horror shot through her. So much had changed in the past few hours.

And she knew, with crystal clarity, that right there, right then, so much was about to change again.

Trick, she thought, her heart breaking. *Take care. I love you.*

"I can be your secret weapon, Mr. Fenner," Katelyn said in a loud voice as she took a deep gulp of air.

Justin's knowing little smile broke. She read his expression — *What the heck are you doing?* — but she ignored him, staring straight at Lee Fenner.

"I'm immune to silver," she announced. "It can't hurt me."

A ripple of shock and a few strained laughs of disbelief went through the crowd as Mr. Fenner strode past Lucy, forcing her to get out of his way or get slammed into, and grabbed Katelyn by the hair. He yanked back her head and glared down into her eyes. His eyes began to glow as the wolf took him over. She forced herself not to betray any fear.

"I'm not lying," she said. "You can test me."

"Right, because we're always testing each other for that," Lucy said between clenched teeth. She was practically pawing the ground. "She'll do *anything* to save her skin. Let me finish what I started. It's my right."

"Lucy, shut up," Justin said quietly.

"Justin, go get the sword," Mr. Fenner ordered him, staring down into Katelyn's eyes. Her scalp was on fire. She was dizzy, and in pain, but she forced herself not to blink at the mention of a sword.

It seemed her entire life flashed past as Mr. Fenner held her in his agonizing embrace. She heard footfalls, and then the unmistakable odor of silver. Chills rushed through her as the odor grew stronger. Were they actually going to cut her, stab her? She was immune to silver, but she wasn't invincible.

Mr. Fenner pushed her away and she fell down hard on her knees. He was holding a silver sword, its hilt wrapped several times in some kind of cloth, in his right hand. She started to panic, imagining he was going to cut off her head.

"This sword is our most priceless possession," Mr. Fenner said. "It's the silver sword that the gods used to attack our father the Great Fenris Wolf, but they failed to cut him down. In retaliation, the Great Wolf devoured his enemy. He was forever after called Moon Snatcher, and we were born of his blood. For that, the gods cursed all silver that we touch."

"Don't hurt Kat!" Jesse shouted, and there were a few ripples of nervous laughter. Katelyn couldn't move her head, couldn't see what was going on. Her heart was nearly leaping out of her chest.

"Alpha," Justin said. "If it will save her life, then I—"

Katelyn felt a sharp cut across her right bicep. Jesse screamed, which covered her own cry. Then Mr. Fenner yanked her up to her feet and took a step away from her, pointing the sword at her heart. Tears stinging her eyes, she clasped her hand over the wound, but she quickly realized he hadn't cut her very badly. Just enough to make her bleed.

Blood trickled through Katelyn's fingers, and Jesse started sobbing. Katelyn looked around and saw horror on the faces of most of the pack, but a few cruel smiles of anticipation as well.

Though she was swaying, Katelyn stayed on her feet. Mr. Fenner pushed her hand away and inspected the wound. Then he looked down at the sword. After a beat, he raised it upward to the sky.

"It's true!" he bellowed.

"Kat, Kat!" Jesse shouted, rushing over and throwing his arms around her. Then he planted a big wet kiss on her cheek. "Kat is so awesome!"

20

That seemed to be the signal for the rest of the pack to touch her, shake her hand, kiss her cheek. Everyone wanted to see her cut and marvel at the fact that she wasn't dead. She was soon surrounded by Fenner werewolves throwing back their heads and howling for joy. Some approached her cautiously, reverently. She heard the words "miracle," "game changer," and "mutation." At Mr. Fenner's order, Justin cleaned the cut and put a bandage over it. He smiled at her but Katelyn could tell there were mixed emotions in that smile — fear, pride, and maybe a little anger — and he kissed her cheek just like everyone else.

"Well played," he whispered softly, giving her hand a quick squeeze.

Arial, Regan, and their husbands approached. Arial was white-faced with shock; Regan looked like she wanted to grab the sword out of her father's hand and run Katelyn through with it.

"You *freak*," she whispered in Katelyn's ear. "Don't think this changes *anything*."

Pack politics might confuse Katelyn, but she knew her immunity changed a lot. She wasn't the least important member of the pack anymore, a fact Mr. Fenner confirmed as he came up to Katelyn and possessively put his arm around her shoulders. The well-wishers moved away, forming an impromptu circle in anticipation of more revelations.

"I believe a challenge was made," he said, almost jovially. "Lucy, where do you stand on that, darlin'?"

Lucy blinked and looked at Justin. He was standing closer to Katelyn than he was to her, and he stayed there. Shock flashed over Lucy's face, then anger, then hurt. But she cleared her throat and squared her shoulders, clearly making the best of a severely altered situation.

"I'm willing to put that on hold until we take the Gaudins down." Her voice was shaky. The wind had been taken out of her sails, and Katelyn nearly howled with relief. She would lose to Lucy in a fight. She might be immune to silver, but Lucy was still stronger and faster than her.

"Good girl," Mr. Fenner said. He walked over to Lucy and patted her cheek. She went scarlet and clenched her fists.

"Softly, softly," Jesse said, also patting her cheek.

"So how did you find this out?" Mr. Fenner asked.

Justin looked stricken. She let her gaze pass over his face without any expression, but she'd thought this through and there was no way she was going to implicate him.

"I was cleaning my grandma's silver, and I cut myself." She surreptitiously waited to see if Mr. Fenner — or anyone else — reacted. She was still trying to figure out who had broken into the cabin. No one did, not even Justin.

"You could have died," Mr. Fenner said.

"I thought I was going to."

"But you didn't say anything to your grandfather?"

She shook her head. "He wasn't home. I didn't say a word."

"Good. Very good. A quick thinker," Mr. Fenner said approvingly. "You *are* our secret weapon."

Oh, yay, she thought bitterly, but that was exactly how she wanted him to regard her. Indispensable.

"War council in the house, now," he said. "Justin, Arial, Regan, Doug, and Al. And Kat." He beamed at her. "Lucy, you take care of Jesse."

"Yes, Uncle Lee," Lucy muttered, looking even more downcast. Locked out of the action. Katelyn would have gladly traded places.

With that in mind, Katelyn made another decision. She said to Mr. Fenner, "I have something else to show you. Just you," she emphasized.

When he raised a brow, she began to walk toward Justin's truck. She heard him grunt in amusement, then trail after her.

She was violating some kind of etiquette by having him follow her but she didn't know what else to do.

"I smell silver," he said, and she nodded.

She opened the passenger's side door and fished the gun from underneath her seat. Taking a deep breath, she held it pointed to the ground so he would know that she wasn't threatening him and that she knew how to handle a gun.

She said, "I found this, Mr. Fenner. It's loaded with silver bullets."

For a moment, she thought he was having a heart attack. His lips moved but no sound came out — he was truly speechless. Then he moved as if to shield the two of them from prying eyes, reaching out for the gun before jerking his hand away.

"Where?" he demanded.

"In the forest," she lied. "I was out running and I smelled it."

"Did you see anything else?" he asked excitedly.

Now would be the time to tell him about the trap. Obviously, Justin hadn't. Mr. Fenner was not her friend. He was acting normal at the moment, but in her experience, that didn't last. He could turn on her in a heartbeat, just as he had turned on so many others. She thought of Quentin Lloyd with a shiver.

And besides, Justin was . . . Justin. She had a split-second fantasy where they got together and led the pack. But she didn't want to lead anything. And she didn't want Justin. She just wanted her life back. And she wanted to bring Cordelia home.

And be with Trick.

Always.

Never.

But before she could lie to him, he said, "That's from the mine. The Madre Vena. That's what's in it. It's not just a silver mine, it's also a stockpile where those who used it stored guns that shoot silver bullets. And more swords and knives, made out of silver."

Mr. Fenner regarded the gun. "Show me the bullets."

She blinked down at the gun. There was more? Is that where her grandfather had gotten the box of deadly ammo? She cracked open the weapon and let the shiny bullets fall into her hand. She wished she'd replaced them with tarnished ones; that would have added a touch of realism to her story.

"I shined them up," she said. "At first I wasn't sure if they were silver."

His face changed. "I know how it happened. *She* dropped it. She found the mine and told the Gaudins and they've stolen everything. It belongs to us. The mine is on our land."

She? Did he mean Cordelia? Was he blaming her for this whole mess?

"But who . . . who made the bullets?" she asked, her voice quavering as she thought of her grandfather inside the mine. Knowing all this time where it was. Did *he* know? "Did they come from the mine? Where is it?"

"That's something only Fenner alphas should ever know," he said. "It's a secret."

Did he know? *Tell me. Tell me, please,* she silently begged him.

Had Mr. Fenner killed Mr. Henderson after he had told him all he knew about the mine? Or because he had failed to find it? She doubted she would ever see Mr. Henderson alive again.

He pulled back his lips from his teeth and hair sprouted on his face and the backs of his hands. "We'll hunt them down and take what's ours. I'll have her pelt."

His jaw began to elongate. Katelyn's heartbeat picked up and her joints seized with pain; her instinctive fear of him was ratcheting up her adrenaline and beginning to force the change on her, too. She fought to stay calm, not wanting him to know that she had partially transformed once without the full moon. She knew now that that hadn't been a one-time event.

One secret at a time.

"I found it a while ago," she said. "When I first moved here. I didn't know what it was as I couldn't smell silver back then. But my grandfather was teaching me how to shoot. So I cleaned it up to see if I could use it. The bullets were covered with tarnish."

"Did you show it to him?" he asked urgently. "Has he seen it?"

"No," she said. "I wasn't supposed to be out in the woods. So I hid it."

"It was wrong of you to deceive him," Mr. Fenner said, knitting his brows. "But you saved his life."

She knew that. And if it was true that the mine was filled with silver bullets, then finding it would give her even more status. Maybe even enough to make sure no one ever tried to harm her again . . . and to bring Cordelia home.

"Sometimes, when it seems like we're being disobedient," she said cautiously, "we're really the most loyal."

"Does Justin know about this?"

"No. I brought the gun with me in case Babette started fighting us. I didn't tell him about it, though, and when he kept thinking he smelled silver in the truck, I pretended that I didn't."

"Show me *exactly* where you found it. Now," he ordered her. He pointed at the driver's seat, indicating for her to get behind the wheel. Then he jogged around to the passenger side and climbed in.

She looked from him to the pack. They were milling and watching. From his place at Lucy's side, Jesse bounced on his heels and waved at her while Arial gaped open-mouthed as she watched her father get into the truck. Justin's face was a neutral mask. Katelyn wanted to reassure him that their secrets were still their own. She had never told him about the gun — he would be stunned when he found out.

He had left the keys in the ignition so she started the engine and the two drove away. She could feel everyone's eyes on them. Mr. Fenner hadn't explained or told them what to do and obviously he expected them to wait for further orders.

Lee seemed to take up all the room in the truck. Although he was just a man, he was larger than life. Her hands on the wheel were sweaty, and Katelyn had to concentrate hard on her driving. He held out the gun and she almost screamed.

"This thing is making me itch," he said. "Take it."

The gun was heavy in her hand. *I could shoot him*, she

thought. For a second or two, she gave it serious thought. Then even more serious thought. Sweat beaded on her forehead. If he was gone . . .

She couldn't kill him in cold blood. She just couldn't do it.

What do you think he's going to tell you to do with this gun? she asked herself. *Shoot people.*

All she had been thinking of when she gave him the gun was protecting herself. But there were consequences to her actions. Dire ones. And killing Mr. Fenner would only bring on more of them.

Unless I ran. If I went to the Gaudins.

Right. The same pack Cordelia had been forced to join?

She put the gun under the driver's seat, one of the usual places for keeping guns in Wolf Springs.

Taking a huge breath to force down her aggression, she turned off the road into the meadow where she and Justin had found the silver animal trap. She reasoned that Mr. Fenner might smell silver residue on the earth where it had lain, confirming her story that she'd found the gun there. She pulled to a stop and they got out.

They began to wade through waist-high ferns and undergrowth. "It's been a long time," she began, "but it was somewhere around—"

He cupped his hand over her nose and mouth and threw both himself and Katelyn to the ground. She began to panic but he whispered into her ear, "Intruders."

He drew his hand away and she inhaled. There was something subtle in the air that grew sharper with the next breath. It was a pungent scent like sweat — the smell of other people.

Then she heard a male voice speaking in French. The Gaudins were French-speaking Cajuns. She listened intently, but she couldn't make out a single word. Giddy hysteria threatened to bubble out of her. If only she'd known she'd grow up in a world where bilingual werewolves were her sworn enemies, she'd have asked her mother to teach her the language properly.

Mr. Fenner pressed his finger across her lips and she nodded: *stay quiet*.

"Where's the gun?" he whispered.

"Truck," she whispered back.

The French-speaking man said something else. Katelyn assumed he was on his phone. Then she remembered that she hadn't been able to get cell reception, just as a second voice replied to the first.

Mr. Fenner raised himself on his elbows and looked back at the truck. It sat in plain sight. The voices drifted closer and she could see the frustration on his face.

Closer.

She darted her gaze in their direction. With barely perceptible gestures, Mr. Fenner tapped her arm and pointed to his own face. *Keep your eyes on me*, he was telling her. *Watch me*.

She understood a little better now what it meant to follow an alpha. He was in charge of her survival. And in the werewolf world, he was supposed to be.

He pointed at her, and then at the truck. Mimed pulling a

trigger. She sucked in a breath and nodded. Oh, God, they were doing this. He held up a single finger, then a second. *One, two, three.*

"Go," he whispered, then as she bolted upright and ran, he transformed nearly instantaneously. A fierce growl exploded from powerful lungs as he raced through the grass in the direction of the voices.

Birds shot from the treetops as she ran. She heard shouting, then more howls as she dashed to the truck and yanked open the door. She felt for the gun, found it, and froze. She crouched behind the door and watched through the window, her instinct for self-preservation taking over.

In the short brown grass of the meadow, Mr. Fenner's white wolf form lunged at a black wolf and a tawny-hued one the color of Dom Gaudin's human hair. The black wolf charged Mr. Fenner and knocked him backwards, then sprang at him as the tawny one circled behind. Mr. Fenner raised his head and opened his massive jaws. As the black wolf fell on him, he clamped his jaws around the black wolf's shoulder. Its howl cut through the forest like the cry of a human in pain.

Then, before the tawny wolf could get to the white wolf, Katelyn's alpha wheeled around and hurtled himself at it. The tawny wolf feinted left, then attacked Mr. Fenner's right flank. There was a rolling ball of brown and white. Blood began to spurt. Whose, she couldn't tell.

The gun in her hand, Katelyn ran toward the meadow. Blood was gushing from a large rip in the white wolf's side. The black wolf pushed him over just as the tawny one positioned himself over Mr. Fenner's thick neck. Then the black wolf fell down on top of Mr. Fenner, pinning him. Mr. Fenner flailed and fought, but Katelyn could see that the fight was going out of him. The tawny one threw back his head and howled; he was about to go in for the kill when Katelyn stopped and raised the gun.

"No," she whispered, not wanting to do this as she aimed at the tawny one's head, knowing she had a good chance of making the shot. Her vision telescoped. She could see the hairs on the tawny wolf's face, the intelligence in his eyes. He was going to kill Mr. Fenner.

And what then? Would she be able to draw breath enough to reason with him then before they killed her, too?

Katelyn took a breath and held it in, as she'd been taught to do. Took aim.

Her finger found the trigger. She began to pull. She could almost hear the bullet chamber.

Then at the last minute, she raised the gun into the air. It went off, startling all three wolves. At once, the black one leaped off Mr. Fenner. The tawny one got in a parting nip, then disappeared into the trees with the black one as the report of the weapon echoed against the hills.

The white wolf became a man in rags, writhing in pain.

Katelyn ran to Mr. Fenner and stood over him, aiming her gun in the direction his attackers had fled. All she saw was shadow.

"No," he said in a breathy voice. "Don't waste the bullets."

"Can you get to the truck?" she asked him, glancing down. She saw blood on his hand, and in the grass.

"Keep the silver away from me," he said, pushing himself up on his elbow. "Give me a minute. I'll start to heal."

She kept watching the trees. "I'm sorry," she said. "I shot wide."

"Best thing you could have done." He kept his voice soft. "You could only get one. If the other one figured out what we had, he could report back to the Gaudins."

"But you might have died."

His smile was strained, but it was there. "It's not about me, darlin'," he said. "It's about the pack."

She was amazed. She imagined him as he must have been before he started losing his mind, and she understood a little better why Justin and Cordelia were both so distressed by his condition. They weren't supposed to protect the alpha; if he could no longer protect them, he had to be replaced. But that didn't mean that he had to die, did it?

"Do you want me to help you get up?" she asked him.

"No. Keep covering us."

Us. They were in this together. She nodded and kept the gun aimed at the trees, sweeping slowly left and right in case the two werewolves tried to circle back around. When her grandfather had been teaching her to shoot, her arms would quickly tire. Holding a gun was harder work than they made it look like on TV.

Behind her, the grass rustled. Mr. Fenner was on his feet with his tattered clothes wrapped around his waist.

"Let's go," he said.

⊶ ⊷

They got in the truck and drove back toward the Fenner

house. As soon as he could get phone coverage, Mr. Fenner made a call not to Justin, but to Regan. He told her to put Arial on speakerphone — and to make sure they were alone. He told them about the attack ... but he didn't mention the gun.

"Set up a guard around the house. And I want some scouts in the woods. No mercy, you hear? We catch any of those bastards, we make 'em sorry they were ever born." He hung up. "Not a word about the gun or the mine," he said to Katelyn. "I'm positive this is the general vicinity. *She* probably told the Gaudins where it is. Now we just got to figure out exactly where." He thought for a moment.

"Mr. Fenner," Katelyn began, "she loves you. When I first met her, all she could talk about was you." *Because she was terrified of you*, Katelyn thought silently, but Cordelia's feelings about her father were very complicated. As miserable as he had made her, she still wanted to come home to him.

He shook his head. "Love's not a factor when it comes to pack security. She knew someone had bitten you but she didn't come to me."

"She couldn't believe it was a werewolf," Katelyn said. "She thought it might just be a dog. Because I'm not from here, she thought I might not know the difference between a wolf and a husky. We were going to see what happened when I changed. Or *if* I changed."

He huffed. "That was not a decision she should have made. She should have said *nothing* to you. Come to me."

"But I made her tell me. I threatened her. I said that if she didn't, I'd ask my grandfather about it. That's the only reason she told me anything."

"She still should have come to me," he insisted.

"I was halfway out the door and on my way home to talk to him," Katelyn said. "What was she going to do, kill me?"

He didn't answer, and she nearly choked on sudden fear. "Did — did those other girls know? And that man who died? Is that what happened to them?"

"No," he said. "We don't attack people."

"But you said you'd kill *me*," she blurted. "And . . . Quentin—"

"We live by different rules. Our rules. But we don't punish humans for not following them. That's like blaming a bear for hibernating. So, she really did think a dog might have bitten you?" Katelyn heard a tremor in his voice and she was angry all over again for the whole big mess.

"A dog," she agreed. "Or . . . she thought it might have been the Hellhound." She heard herself lower her voice, and waited for him to make fun of her, the way all the Fenners had scoffed at Cordelia's pathological terror of the supposedly mythical monster.

Silent for a moment, he shrugged, and he looked old and tired. "That night she thought she saw it? I almost thought so, too. Like to scare me to death, the way she started shrieking. We put guards out everywhere. Nothing."

That doesn't mean she didn't see it, Katelyn thought.

"But I've come to a different conclusion." She felt him looking at her and took her eyes off the road to meet his flinty gaze. "I think a Gaudin bit you. She planned it with them.

Picked you out the day you got here, ran you to ground. A Gaudin bites you, you go to her, she turns you into their spy."

"No," Katelyn said, startled. But why couldn't it have been a Gaudin who'd bitten her? "Wouldn't you be able to tell? Wouldn't I smell like a Gaudin?"

He blinked the same way Justin did when her ignorance caught him by surprise. "No. We have individual scents; we don't have pack scents," he said. "But we do have instincts. Loyalty to the pack, for one." He set his jaw. "At least, *most* of us feel loyalty."

"I don't feel any loyalty to the Gaudins," she said. But neither did she feel any loyalty to Mr. Fenner. Not a minute before, she'd considered shooting him. "I could have killed you in the meadow. I didn't."

That gave him pause. Then he nodded. "That doesn't mean you're loyal. It just means you're not stupid."

They reached the house. Mr. Fenner told her to bring the gun and she put it in the pocket of her jacket and followed him back into the yard. His daughters swarmed him, bringing him a robe and fussing over his wound; he was fake-crotchety with them, smiling as they fussed over him, batting their hands away and stomping into the house. Katelyn wasn't sure where she should be in the parade. Arial and Regan had glued themselves to either side of Mr. Fenner. Doug and Al went next, and then Justin. Katelyn stepped in behind him, and the door shut behind her.

They sat at the dining-room table and Mr. Fenner described what had happened. The group was thunderstruck — Justin especially — when she pulled out the gun. She put it down on the table but no one moved to examine it. In fact, Arial excused herself and hurried to the bathroom.

"Gaudins in our territory," Justin said, when Mr. Fenner had finished.

"Don't sound so shocked, boy," Mr. Fenner said. "We're in theirs."

"One thing, Daddy," Regan said. "If she took you near the mine, wouldn't you be able to smell all the silver inside it?"

"Maybe there isn't any," Justin said quickly, and Katelyn stole a glance at him. "Maybe that's just as much of a myth as the Hellhound."

"Oh, Lord, not *that* again," Arial said as she came back into the room. "I thought we'd heard the last of that."

The two sisters tittered. They thought they'd heard the last because Cordelia had been banished, Katelyn translated. She had been the only one in the family who had believed in the Hellhound — the Bogey Man of the werewolf world. *Misbehave and it will come and get you* . . . Except, as it turned out, maybe Lee did as well.

"Perhaps the silver is buried deep," Mr. Fenner said. "But it exists."

That caught the attention of everyone at the table, but no one pressed Mr. Fenner to elaborate. Katelyn spun a fantasy where each new alpha learned various secrets of Wolf Springs. And that if the alpha wasn't in his right mind, he might begin to spill them.

Heads turned toward Katelyn, as if she knew the secrets, too. She just shrugged and picked up the gun.

"Put that down!" Arial cried. "Daddy, you should get rid of that!"

"She's the only one who can use it, and we can't trust her," Regan concurred.

Their husbands remained silent. Mr. Fenner sat very still. Then he glared at each of them in turn.

"Are you questioning my judgment?"

"No, of course not, Daddy," Arial whined, practically batting her lashes at him. "It's just, well, you know, we're still upset about what a lying, cheating *bitch*—"

"Enough!" he thundered, slamming his fist on the table. "Do you take me for an idiot? I *know* what you're trying to do." He rose from his chair. "Don't push me, girl. *Ever.*" Then he winced, and Katelyn saw his hand start to move toward his wound. But he slammed his fist down on the table instead. Concealing his vulnerability. Masking his weakness.

"She was the best of you," he said brokenly. He sighed heavily and lowered his head. Katelyn thought he might be crying. But when he raised it again, his expression was hard. "This is a war council. Let's get down to it. Twenty will go. Ten will stay behind with the kids. We'll leave tomorrow morning, before dawn. It's an eleven-hour drive to the Bayou des Loupes. If we leave early enough, we can prepare before moonrise."

"We should wait until the full moon," Justin said. "Some of us won't be able to change."

"I'm not waiting that long. They're already nosing around up here. Sometimes the first change comes in the heat of battle," Lee Fenner replied. "That's how they used to do it back in the old country. Take the pups out, attack some Vikings." He chuckled as if the image amused him.

"So what should we do if we still can't change?" Katelyn asked. "Should we pack weapons?"

"That's a good question," Mr. Fenner replied. "Ordinary bullets don't kill us." He turned to Justin. "We'll be out in the bayou, away from the humans. What do you think?"

"Swords. Decapitation works," Arial said quickly, before Justin had a chance to respond.

Regan rolled her eyes. "You'll get the Hellhound after us yet, sissy, if humans start finding heads floating in the water."

Cordelia had explained to Katelyn that the Hellhound was thought to keep watch over all werewolves to ensure that they didn't violate the code by which all werewolves lived — to shield their existence from humans, and never to attack humans. To obey pack hierarchy and maintain loyalty. Werewolves who broke these edicts could suffer the worst penalty — death, and not a pleasant one.

Justin turned to Katelyn. "Guns make noise. The most important rule is to keep *all* the packs safe from discovery, not just ours. That's a universal law. Humans can never know of our existence."

"Even when we're slaughtering rival werewolves," Regan said.

Heat rushed across Katelyn's face. That rule had nearly gotten Cordelia killed. Katelyn had had no idea what she'd been asking — demanding — of Cordelia when she had forced Cordelia into telling her what was happening to her. By rights, Cordelia should have gone to her father and told him about the new girl. But Cordelia had been afraid of what Mr. Fenner would do. Because he was the alpha, yes, but also because he was suffering from dementia. Cordelia had risked her life to protect Katelyn — and now they were going to war with the pack that had taken her in.

"That's why we're going to the swamp," Mr. Fenner said. "No humans around. Us against them."

"I like the sound of that," Arial said.

Katelyn studied her, trying to reconcile her bloodthirsty aggression with her runway fashion-model appearance. What it must be like to have spent your entire life in and around the tiny town of Wolf Springs without anyone realizing that a pack of werewolves lurked in their midst. If a werewolf was mauling the victims — and it certainly looked that way to Katelyn — then he — or she — should be put to death for two reasons: taking human life and risking discovery.

It had to be Mr. Fenner. And once that was confirmed?

Except that the wolf that attacked me wasn't Mr. Fenner.

She stirred, realizing the others were looking at her. Al and Doug, the husbands, hadn't said a single word.

"We haven't fought another pack in centuries, but that doesn't mean we aren't ready to fight," Mr. Fenner said. "Justin hasn't had time to bring you up to that level, but the Fenners have been getting ready for this war for a long time." He spoke in the strange, almost happy tone he used on occasion. "And I wish we could wait it out until you and Jus could shift."

"Don't forget that I can shift, Daddy," Regan said, preening.

"How can I forget that, little gal, when you remind me every chance you get?" he asked her, clearly amused.

When Katelyn had been bitten, she'd suspected Regan. But either Regan had been a consummate actress when demanding to know who had bitten Katelyn, or she hadn't been Katelyn's attacker. Katelyn decided she'd been hasty in assuming Regan was innocent.

"Kat, take the rest of the day to look for the mine. If you find more bullets and weapons, this will go a lot faster."

He gave her a strange, almost pleading look. "You do that for me, darlin', I might be disposed to grant you a favor."

Cordelia. She knew that was what he meant. Her heart began to pound, and he gave her another long look.

"I will." She got to her feet. "Starting now. See you." She heard how rude she sounded but she didn't back down.

Mr. Fenner chuckled and nodded at her as if impressed with her forthrightness. "Justin will go with you," he said.

"On it." Justin stood.

He and Katelyn headed for the front door, Katelyn wondering if this was the wisest thing to do. Lucy had agreed to stand down, but what was the point of throwing Justin and her together even more?

"Be careful of the Hellhound," Regan called after them.

"And the Hell*bitch*," Arial added, and the two sisters started laughing.

21

Katelyn and Justin had no luck finding the mine and he barely got her home before her grandfather showed up, telling her that Trick's parents had arrived from wherever they'd been and picked Trick up from the police station.

Katelyn called him immediately, and he picked up.

"Kat," he said. "Mike. I didn't do it."

"I know." She chewed her lower lip so she wouldn't cry. "*They* know that now, too, right?"

"I guess." He didn't sound convincing. "This all started when Haley died. It keeps getting worse. I want to tell you that I wish you hadn't moved here, except I'm such a selfish bastard that I'm glad you did."

A single tear ran down her cheek.

His breath caught. "I'm going to keep you safe."

"I know you are." *You'll keep my heart safe.*

This was love. She loved Trick Sokolov and she always would. No matter what happened in her confusing, complicated life-within-a-life, there would always be an entire world inside her where she loved Trick and he loved her. Beyond dreams of flying on a cloud swing and the realities of running with werewolves, even if she died in the next heartbeat or was forced by Lee Fenner to let Trick go, there would be a secret forever place where she and Trick would be together. And if it had taken all the tragedies and terrors in her life for her to realize that, then she was glad for them.

And now she knew what friendship was, too. Cordelia had risked everything to help her. Katelyn could, and would, do no less. A strange new kind of peace settled over her, the knowledge that she wasn't a powerless victim. Even in this dark place, the darkest place, there was hope.

"Keep the faith, Vladimir," she said to Trick, and then she hung up.

Next, as she had planned, she told her grandfather that she was going over to study at Paulette's in the morning. She figured that she could call him in the afternoon and tell him that she was going to spend the night there so they could work on some school stuff.

Then she took a very deep breath and said, "So, do you want that gun back?"

There was a barely perceptible pause, and then he answered, "Why don't you keep it in your car?"

And another pause as she said, "Okay."

People kept guns in their cars in Wolf Springs. Obviously, he assumed that she didn't know her gun was very special.

⸺ ⸎ ⸺

In the morning she drove to the Fenners', and when she made the call to her grandfather about spending the night at Paulette's, he seemed distracted and told her to have a nice time. His lack of questioning was one of the first lucky breaks she'd had in a while. But it concerned her, too. He was usually so protective of her. And with another death, she had assumed he would have been even more so. Something was up with him. She remembered how he had snuck out and lied about it, and she wondered what secrets her grandfather was keeping from her. For now, those questions would have to wait.

After traveling south all day, switching drivers and gassing the trucks and cars as fast as they could, the Fenner pack had reached the border between Fenner and Gaudin territory: Bayou des Loupes — Bayou of the Wolves, not named as such on any map.

Katelyn held her breath as the sun sank beyond the horizon. The bayou was muddy and dark; ropy vines and trees hung over the water, and strange, knobby wooden growths jutted up beneath the surface. Things skittered and glided and the air felt heavy, wet, and leaden. It wouldn't snow, but it might rain, and the wind made the tree trunks sway.

"Got your gun?" Mr. Fenner asked. She nodded. It was in a holster he had given her, pressed up against her ribcage. "Get it ready." He looked up at the sky. "Sun's coming down. They'll wait for moonrise. It's tradition."

"Then we should attack *now*," Arial said.

She and Regan stood with their husbands while Justin was with some of the other men in the back. And everyone was staying in their clothes. Did they assume they wouldn't need them again? Were any of the Fenner werewolves around her preparing to give their lives for the pack?

Justin came up beside her. He looked down at her gun with a wounded look in his eyes — she hadn't told him — then he slid his hand in hers and gave it a squeeze.

"Stay behind me," he murmured. "I'll protect you."

Studying her face, he chewed the inside of his cheek, then exhaled harshly. He looked at his uncle, then pulled Katelyn away from the group. He glanced left and right, searching for something, then drew her with him into a shadowy den of ferns and vines, turning her toward him. Her senses clicked into place and she could hear his heartbeat, fast. Smelled him, and only him. Every cell in her body hummed, as if tuning itself to his vibration.

Except . . . he wasn't Trick.

He cupped her head between his large hands, licked his lips, and kissed her. Gently at first, and then his hand came around to the back of her head, cradling her as his tongue stole between her lips and he gave into passion. He yanked her against his chest and wrapped his other arm around her back, then moved down to her waist. Her hands found his face, the softness of the curls around his ears, the ropes of muscle across his shoulder blades.

One more kiss, she told herself, *and then never again.*

"I can't stand it that you're here," he whispered. "People are going to die. I don't want you to be one of them."

"I won't die," she promised, but she gently moved out of his embrace. Her blood was singing, but she knew why, knew her wolf part was awake, aware. "I won't die."

He took her hand. "I'm going to get you out of here. We'll run. They'll be so busy they won't be able to catch us."

But she saw despair in his eyes. He didn't believe that.

"If we ran, we'd die for sure, wouldn't we?" she asked him.

He closed his eyes. Nodded. "Sooner or later, they'd come for us," he said. "And they wouldn't make it quick."

She took a breath. "I didn't tell you about the gun because—"

He trailed his fingertips over her lips, silencing her. "It doesn't matter. It was the right thing to do. You don't know me. You don't know *us*. I told you that becoming a werewolf was a fantastic thing for you. But here we are, about to fight a rival pack." He looked pale. "If anything happens to you, I'm going to kill my uncle."

She believed him. Shaking, she laid her hand on his chest and tried to make herself breathe. Closing her eyes, she listened again to his heartbeat. Justin was a good man, but he just wasn't *her* man. She hated what was happening to him and to his world, though. It was as if death kept circling her, them. She thought of her dreams and the voice in the forest;

something had been stalking her every night since she'd arrived in Wolf Springs.

"I'll kill him anyway," he said. "None of this should be happening. He led us to this. They know he's weak and they're trying to take us over. They've been trying ever since I was a kid. That's why we need to be strong."

His heart was picking up speed, beating preternaturally fast. She found herself responding, excited by his ferocity, and she took a fearful step away.

"Kat, Kat," he said, reaching for her. "When this is over . . . if I make it . . ."

"You will make it," she said.

He took a deep breath. "If something happens, I know Lucy will take care of Jesse. Be sure to tell him how much I love him."

Then he took her hand and walked her back to the group. Arial raised her brows at the sight of the two of them and she nudged Regan. Regan's answering smile was poisonous.

Then Justin tightened his grip around Katelyn's fingers so hard that he rubbed the bones together. Katelyn looked up at his face, then followed his line of sight.

Dom Gaudin and Cordelia moved from the trees. Dom was carrying a white flag, and his arm was wrapped around Cordelia's waist. She was thin, and her red hair had grown a few inches.

"Cordelia!" Katelyn cried, and heads whipped in her direction.

She began to run to Cordelia, but Justin jerked her to a

standstill. Arial and Regan flashed her looks of disgust, and Cordelia held out a hand to her.

"Kat!"

Dom murmured something to Cordelia; she lowered her arm and raised her chin. Her expression was strained and miserable, but her head was held high. A bit of the old Cordelia was still alive, then. Katelyn was relieved to see it.

Mr. Fenner gave Katelyn a long look and strode toward the couple. "Justin!" he barked. Justin moved to stand beside him. Cordelia didn't hug — or even acknowledge — her father.

Mr. Fenner, Justin, Dom, and Cordelia disappeared back into the trees. The sky darkened into twilight, everything leeching to gray, then to dark gray. Moonrise would come soon. Katelyn remembered nights at the beach when she and Kimi would wait for the green flash on the water's horizon, holding their breath, squinting, giggling. But this was anything but a game.

"I don't like this," Regan said. "It's another trick."

"They had a white flag," Doug pointed out.

"When have they ever acted honorably?" Regan said. "And as for *her* . . ."

Katelyn's dislike and suspicion of Regan re-emerged. Regan was an ambitious backstabber. Katelyn doubted she had ever put the pack before her own wishes and desires. Her father just had never realized it.

"Get ready," Arial said.

Moments later Justin re-emerged. He glanced over his shoulder and then began striding toward Katelyn. The air reeked with the smell of silver. Justin gagged and clapped his hand over his mouth. In the same moment, the sky exploded with flares going off and fire bombs hurtling through the air toward them and exploding all around. Katelyn screamed and fell to the ground, her hands over her ears. The Gaudins were striking first.

Thoughts and words flew out of her head as she cowered against the earth. She didn't know anything that was happening around her; everything was chaos. Bodies and people and blood —

— and smoke.

Fire!

Justin was crouched over her, his arms around her waist, dragging her somewhere. The silver stench was overpowering. The smoke, paralyzing. She couldn't remember how to move her body. She just screamed and screamed and screamed.

"They're trying to drive us toward the water," Justin said.

He fell backwards and Katelyn landed on top of him. Then a flash of fur hurtled itself at the two of them. Still screaming, without thinking, Katelyn's hand found the gun in her holster and fired off a shot. The wolf howled and plummeted to the ground less than six inches from her feet. Frantically she kicked at it as Justin threw his arms around her, then rolled her sideways and got on top of her.

Trees were going up like roman candles; werewolves were transforming all around Justin and her. She didn't recognize anyone, didn't know who was on her side and who was an enemy. She only had four silver bullets left and she cursed herself for not sneaking more out of the garage.

Luc Gaudin rushed at her, changing as he ran. His clothing burst off his body and he raced toward her on two legs that were rapidly changing into the legs of a wolf. His jaw stretched, his eyes looked mean.

Justin yanked the gun from her hands and aimed it at Luc's half-transformed head. It exploded. Katelyn screamed uncontrollably.

"Kat, stop!" Justin bellowed, handing back the gun and furiously wiping his hand on his pants.

Fire rose around her, caging her, and she whirled in a panicked circle. A gray wolf flashed past, and Katelyn's mind registered that it was Regan. Regan leaped through a hole in the wall of fire, and then the hole closed up.

Heat blazed around her. Through the whoosh of the firestorm she heard shouting, gunfire. She was going to die like her father and her mother. The wind shifted and smoke poured over her, choking her, and Katelyn stumbled forward and ran into something that gave way. She grabbed it, felt it. A vine. Desperately, she gave it a tug. It held.

She jumped and began to hoist herself up the way circus people and gymnasts did: looping the vine around her ankle, propelling herself upward. Coughing, feeling her skin blistered, she kept going. Surrounded by smoke, heat, noise, her eyes closed, she kept on climbing. Then the vine jerked hard and as she caught her breath, she inhaled smoke and began to cough uncontrollably. As she convulsed, the vine jerked again, and she was sure it was going to give way. She thought she was going to say, "Help," but what came out was "Trick."

She tried to scramble up, but was coughing too hard and suddenly her hands slipped and skin tore from her palms. The vine was still wrapped around her ankle so she used it for leverage, pushing up as hard as she could, waving her hand above her head, trying to feel for a more solid section of vine. Leaves brushed against her fingertips and she stretched as hard as she could, finally wrapping her hand around a thick branch, scooting along it onto a weighty limb. She let go of the vine with her other hand and hung for a moment while she fought for control of her body. Then by sheer force of will, she did a slow chin-up, then leaned forward, just like in her dream. The wind blew against her face, wafting away the smoke. And she looked down.

It *was* her dream.

Her nightmare.

Werewolves were burning. Racing in and out of a ring of fire, they were crazed, biting at each other, bleeding, smoking. And in the center, rising from his knees, Justin raised his hands over his head. His shirt had been torn off and he was covered with blood and soot. His hair was slicked back. To his right, past the wall of flame, the bayou was alive with animals fleeing the fire. The smell of silver coated her skin like oil. Someone had dumped silver into the water, just as Luc had said.

Justin threw back his head and saw her. He reached up his hands but she was at least twenty feet above him, and she couldn't go back down the vine. It had caught on fire and flames were traveling like a dynamite fuse toward her perch.

There was a splash like a cannonball in the water. She

craned to see, and her vision telescoped. It was Doug, Regan's husband. Somehow he had fallen into the bayou brimming with toxic silver.

Before she could talk herself out of it, Katelyn swung to the next tree, scrabbling for handholds. As soon as she was sure she was poised above the bayou, she sprang off. She executed a simple swan dive, moving too fast to see where Doug was, then shot into the water. Something bumped against her beneath the surface and she reached out a hand. She touched something slimy and jerked her hands against her chest, kicking hard.

She broke the surface and looked around. The world was glowing. Doug's head was in the water; he was lying face down. His body shimmered with red light and she grabbed him around the neck and tried to flip him over as best she could, but he lay so still. She started swimming to shore, grateful that she was still in shape. There was no fire on that side of the bayou, but the trees danced with the reflections of the inferno behind her. Who could survive that?

Then her feet kicked against sticky, mucky silt and she stepped into what felt like quicksand. Something made her turn around to see a large shape undulating through the water. Alligator? It was coming at them. She felt for her gun. She didn't have it. She had lost it.

"Doug, Doug!" she tried to shout, but she was too hoarse. She tried to drag him but he was too heavy for her. She reached into the water and tried to bend his legs at the knees to get them onto the mud bank. She had no clue if that would do any good.

It was still coming.

Silver is poison, she thought as she bent over Doug.
She put her ear to his mouth and felt at his neck for a
pulse.

No pulse. She immediately began compressions.

The snout of the alligator appeared from the water, black
and glistening against the firelight.

"No, no, no," Katelyn rasped, freezing. Doug stirred
faintly. She shouted, "Alligator!" as she ran around to his head
and grabbed him under the arms. "Doug!"

The alligator's head rose out of the water. Doug's head
flopped forward. He vomited down his front.

"Help!" Katelyn cried, tugging at him. "Justin!"

Doug gasped and tried to scoot up the bank. But he lolled
helplessly, slack and barely able to move, as Katelyn kept hold
of him. She could see the alligator's eyes. There was no
intelligence in them, only intent.

Her instinct for self-preservation told her there was
nothing she could do for Doug. If she wanted to live, she had
to abandon him. But her sense of decency forced her to stay.
She growled, trying to stare down the alligator as her bones
throbbed with pain. She could feel her body shifting.

Now, now, now, she thought. *Change. Kill it.*

But the sensation ebbed. The alligator was glowing; the
bayou glistened with silver and scarlet and Katelyn began
swearing at Doug, begging him to help her, losing her balance
and falling hard into the muck.

The alligator darted forward.

Then it began to writhe. It jerked again. Its jaw opened,

closed, then it fell awkwardly to one side. Someone was shooting at it.

It bolted hard, jaw snapping, almost catching Doug's foot. Then, slowly, it began to slide back into the water. Doug was screaming in terror.

Katelyn looked from the animal to the fiery bank. She saw the silhouette of a man wearing a gas mask over long, shoulder-length hair. He was standing with a rifle against his shoulder pointed directly at her. An icy tremor rattled her bones. It was Dom Gaudin. Obviously he had known about the silver, and now he was going to fire at Doug and her.

Then he lowered the rifle and blew her a kiss.

She gave him a solemn wave. He watched her for a moment, then the smoke closed over him.

"So sick," Doug said, gasping.

"Can you walk? We have to get out of here."

"Go," he ground out. "Go help."

She was afraid that if she left him, Dom would shoot him after all. So she crouched closely beside him, acting as a human shield, wondering if Justin was still alive. Now that imminent danger had passed, she began to shake, and Doug patted her hand.

"It's okay, Kat."

His words were slurred. He was still out of it, so she wiped her eyes and pulled herself together. Flopping his arm over her shoulder, she tried to lift him up — but he was as limp as a ragdoll.

"Can you change?" she asked him.

"No."

She could barely hear him.

"Okay, I'm going to get someone," she said, though where in all the chaos, she had no clue. She wished she had a bottle of water, anything to dilute the effects of the silver in his system. On his skin, in his eyes. He had probably swallowed some, too.

"I'm coming back," she said.

He didn't respond. His eyes were glassy and his mouth was slack. He couldn't be dead. She pulled off her jacket, wadded it up, and placed it beneath his head. Then she took off running, hoping that this side of the bayou would take her to where the Fenners were making their stand.

Katelyn raced through the smoke and gunfire, around burning weeping willows and cypress trees. If either pack had thought to keep this fight off the radar, that wasn't happening. As she rounded a pine, she heard Justin shouting, and put on a burst of speed.

"Justin!" she yelled, nearly colliding with him as he came in sight.

He made as if to touch her, then jerked back. She knew he could smell the silver from the bog on her.

"Come on!" he said.

Fenners in human form flanked them; wolves bounded past toward a line of Fenner trucks and cars. They were doubled over in pain, gasping and vomiting. From the silver in the air, she guessed. They were retreating.

"Get in, get in!" Justin yelled.

Katelyn jumped into the bed of a truck. Lee Fenner lay sprawled beneath her on a tarp, and Arial was crouched beside him with one of his hands pressed between both of hers. She was crying, and Mr. Fenner's face was ashen. He was muttering and Katelyn strained to hear.

"I stopped him then, but I couldn't stop him now. So many dead. So many dead," Mr. Fenner rasped.

She glanced around, wondering if any of the others knew what he was talking about. No one seemed to be paying attention.

"Where have you been?" Arial demanded, staring at her. "If you'd been there, if you'd shot Dominique Gaudin, Daddy would be all right."

Katelyn tried to remember the last time she'd had the gun. Justin had shot Luc with it and she didn't know what had happened to it after that.

"Doug," Katelyn said to Justin as she set her down. "He's on the other side of the bayou. He's hurt."

"Where?" Justin asked.

"I'll show you," Katelyn said.

"No," Arial insisted. "Stay here and protect the alpha. He's more important than some bit-in human."

So that's how she feels about Doug. And me, Katelyn thought. She knew Arial's priorities were misplaced. The pack wasn't supposed to protect the alpha. The alpha was supposed to protect the pack. Someone else needed to stand up and lead. She glanced at Justin, whose face was drawn. His eyes were watering, and he was studying his uncle.

"Arial," he said, "I'm taking over."

"Oh, no, you're not!" she cried, cradling her father's head. "This is a Fenner pack. My father is our alpha. He just needs a few minutes." She looked down anxiously at Mr. Fenner.

"I'm a Fenner," Justin said.

"Don't even start with me." She bared her teeth.

"Arial! Justin! Where's Doug?" Regan yelled hoarsely, coming up behind them. She looked at Katelyn. "Where have you been?"

"Doug's hurt," Katelyn told her. "Come with me."

"We have to get Daddy out of here," Arial insisted. "He's hurt."

"Someone needs to wait for us," Regan said.

"We'll get Doug and leave in my truck," Justin said.

Katelyn scrambled out of the truck. She gestured to Justin and Regan to follow her as she began to retrace her steps. Behind her, the truck carrying Arial and Mr. Fenner roared to life and peeled out. She heard more departing vehicles and doubled her pace. Behind her, Justin and Regan struggled and coughed, their erratic heartbeats pounding in her ears; the silver was doing a job on them.

Through the smoke, she saw a handful of Gaudins in human form wearing gas masks. Their side of the bayou was practically empty. The Gaudins were leaving the scene of the massacre they had brought down on the Fenners.

Doug was lying where she had left him, his face turned the other way. She approached, detecting no heartbeat at all. Alarmed, she reached him first, fell to her knees beside him and peered at his face.

His skin was blackened as if he'd been burned. His blood-shot eyes were open, unseeing. She hesitated, then touched his carotid artery with two fingertips. There was no pulse.

She felt someone standing over her and looked up. It was Justin, grim-faced, pasty, exhausted. He whirled around and caught Regan in his arms.

"He's gone, Regan," he said. "Don't look."

Regan threw back her head and screamed. The scream became a howl. The bayou echoed and more voices raised in unearthly crazed shrieking, howling, weeping. Regan rained fists on Justin's chest, fighting to get free, but Justin held her. She coughed and choked.

"Kat, get up. We have to get out of here," Justin said. "Now. The silver is killing us."

"Let me see him. He's not dead!" Regan cried. "Let me go, Justin!"

Katelyn got up. "Justin, we can't leave him here," she murmured. Where she'd seen Regan only as a cruel, devious bitch, now she was seeing her as a girl with the man she loved — unwilling to leave him, distraught with grief.

"Do you have the strength to carry him?" Justin asked her. She didn't.

"No!" Regan yelled. "I won't leave him! I'm staying!"

"You're not." Justin kept hold of her. "They already have one hostage. Cordelia. We can't let them have another daughter of the alpha, even though you won't be as valuable now that he knows where Uncle Lee stands."

"What are you talking about?" Katelyn asked.

Justin kept a tight hold on Regan. "Dom offered to stand down — stop this fight — if Lee forgave Cordelia."

Katelyn was speechless. "And Lee *didn't*?"

"He didn't." Justin turned to Regan again. "They might

just kill you, Regan. But they sure won't let you go if they capture you."

"I don't care," Regan said, breaking his hold and flailing her arms, trying to kick him, as he attempted to recapture her. "Let me go to my husband, you cheating, lying bastard!"

Justin wrapped himself around Regan, but Katelyn could tell he was tiring. He said, "Regan, I'm sorry." She kept struggling. "Kat, in my pocket," he said. "Gun."

Katelyn wasn't sure she'd heard him right. He looked over at her with a cold, steely gaze. "I have a gun. Get it out."

"And do what with it? Shoot her?"

"No, hit her with it, knock her out. I can't hold onto her much longer."

"Doug!" Regan screamed. "Let me go to Doug!"

"You're not your own person, Regan," Justin bellowed. "You can't just do what you want! You'll hurt the pack. Damn it, Kat, get my gun!"

"No," she shouted at him, backing away. "Let her go to him! He's her husband!"

"Kat, I let you have your way," he said. "In the forest. You know what I mean."

He was talking about Babette. She sucked in another breath, hoping Regan was too upset to pay attention.

"Now we do this *my* way," he said. "We have to leave *now*, and we can't leave her here or she'll die."

Katelyn shook her head. It was too much, all too much. And she wouldn't be a party to it anymore. She whirled on her heel and bolted.

"Kat!" Justin shouted. "Come back here *now*!"

Shaking her head, eyes tearing up, Katelyn ran into the thick bayou. How could he do such a thing? Even *think* of doing it?

She heard the roar of engines and hurried toward them. Steve was limping toward an open door. A werewolf in wolf form shot past her.

"Kat," said a voice. Arial's husband Al stepped into view. "My God, Kat."

"You don't know what's happening back there," she said, panting. "Doug's dead, and Justin's making Regan *leave* him there."

"Doesn't matter right now. We have to get you out of here." With an oily, anxious smile, he reached out a hand. "C'mon."

And then she remembered that she was their secret weapon.

Images of what her life was going to be like crashed around her like the walls of her house. Something to be fought over. Someone's hostage. A Fenner hostage.

She couldn't do this. Wouldn't be a part of this.

"Hold on," she said to Al. "I need to get the gun."

"Kat!" he shouted, as she started walking away. Walking only, so he wouldn't realize she was trying to escape. She glanced at the idling cars loading up with Fenners. She could see into the back of the truck where Arial was crouching over Lee. The alpha was spasming, his whole body flailing, and then it just stopped. And she knew, deep down, that he was gone. Then fresh howls of grief pierced the sky. Lee Fenner was dead.

So many emotions spilled through her — rage, despair, relief — that she wheeled into the trees, pushing at the branches, gasping in the poisonous, smoky night. Stumbling and fleeing. Denying all of it.

This is not my world.

I am no one's secret weapon.

Al shouted her name, and yelled for others to help him find her. As she barreled through the forest, his voice grew fainter and fainter. She kept going with no thought but to keep going.

I'm leaving, she thought giddily. *It's happening. I'm really going.*

She left the Fenners behind, and the moon, as the tree-tops huddled together above her and threw her into darkness. Her vision kicked in and the woods were covered in white light. A fairyland. Safe haven.

She looked over her shoulder. No one seemed to be following her. There had to be a road somewhere. She could hitch a ride. Make a call. Get a plane ticket. Live. Call Trick and ask him to come to her.

Be free.

"Yes," she said under her breath.

Then the forest went dark. She was only mildly disappointed; it had happened before. Often.

And then the darkness unfolded and reared up. It was a massive shape, a *monster*, towering above her. Its head was enormous; its huge, fiery eyes were *smoking*. Teeth — fangs — glistened white and dripping as it opened its mouth. She smelled the stench of its breath, felt the heat as it poised in the air and studied her for a heart-stopping second. The forest went dead silent.

Hellhound. Come for a disobedient werewolf.

Like me.

Katelyn fell to her knees.

And then it attacked.

ACKNOWLEDGEMENTS

First of all, my deepest thanks to Debbie Viguié, my wonderful co-author and dearest friend. My gratitude to our agents, Howard Morhaim, Kate McKean, and Caspian Dennis for all you do for us, and to HMLA assistant Alice Speilburg as well. Becky Stradwick, our editor extraordinaire, thank you so much for all your insight and support. I am grateful. Thanks to my family, especially my daughter, Belle. You make me howl with joy.

— N.H.

To my brilliant co-author Nancy Holder, thank you for keeping it all fun. Thank you to our agents Howard Morhaim, Caspian Dennis, and Kate McKean for their tireless efforts on our behalf. Thank you to our fantastic editor, Becky Stradwick, for all her support. Thank you to Alice Speilburg for helping to keep me sane. Finally, I need to thank Mandy Winn, who has always embodied the spirit of the wolf and is a good friend.

— D.V.